LAURIE HARTMAN

COWGIRL IS A STATE OF MIND

iUniverse

Cowgirl Is a State of Mind

Copyright © 2012 by Laurie Hartman.

All rights reserved. No part of this book may be used or reproduced by any means, graphic, electronic, or mechanical, including photocopying, recording, taping or by any information storage retrieval system without the written permission of the publisher except in the case of brief quotations embodied in critical articles and reviews.

This is a work of fiction. All of the characters, names, incidents, organizations, and dialogue in this novel are either the products of the author's imagination or are used fictitiously.

iUniverse books may be ordered through booksellers or by contacting:

iUniverse
1663 Liberty Drive
Bloomington, IN 47403
www.iuniverse.com
1-800-Authors (1-800-288-4677)

Because of the dynamic nature of the Internet, any web addresses or links contained in this book may have changed since publication and may no longer be valid. The views expressed in this work are solely those of the author and do not necessarily reflect the views of the publisher, and the publisher hereby disclaims any responsibility for them.

Any people depicted in stock imagery provided by Thinkstock are models, and such images are being used for illustrative purposes only.
Certain stock imagery © Thinkstock.

ISBN: 978-1-4759-4253-8 (sc)
ISBN: 978-1-4759-4254-5 (hc)
ISBN: 978-1-4759-4255-2 (e)

Library of Congress Control Number: 2012914324

Print information available on the last page.

iUniverse rev. date: 03/26/2015

Sincere thanks to anyone who contributed in any way to *Cowgirl Is a State of Mind* during my bumpy journey to becoming an author, especially Steve and Amanda.

CHAPTER 1

The rustic iron gate between pastures swung easily, supported by a thick cable and towering post. Riley held the gate for the cattle moving in her direction and the grey gelding at her side watched with interest. After passing through the lead cows that had made the journey in years past began to spread across the gentle rolling Midwest Sandhills of thin grass and wildflowers. The solitary cowboy trailing the herd reached for the gate from atop his horse. While he barred the opening Riley mounted her grey.

The pair rode around the disbanding herd, the sounds of leather squeaking and prairie grass swishing against the horses' legs. The calm was interrupted by Riley's lively gelding when he snorted and jumped at a bird taking flight. Riley laughed and kept the horse in check.

"I guess I should be glad he didn't try to launch me," she said as she searched with her foot to reclaim her stirrup.

"He's probably wondering where the barrels are. I doubt he's used to seeing wide open spaces except from inside the safety of his trailer," teased the cowboy, her older brother Jeff. "You and your barrel racing," he added good-naturedly.

"Aw, there's a nest," she said, ignoring him. She reined Novocain, her gelding, to get a better view. Cradled in the dry grass near Black Eyed Susans were cream-colored eggs speckled with browns, rust and lavender.

"Meadowlark," said Jeff, pointing as the yellow underbelly of the bird disappeared from view. He didn't wait but kept his rangy bay horse moving.

Riley saw only the striking landscape that included red cattle with white faces grazing the expansive hillside. She trotted to catch up.

"I thought black cows were in," she said.

"When I came out here the old fellow who hired me had Herefords. After I bought the place I just stuck with them." Jeff continued to talk as they rode, and she was impressed at how much he had learned about ranching since adopting the lifestyle despite having been raised in the city. "I'm really glad you stopped to visit," he added.

"It's been a while, hasn't it? I know I should stop more often. It's not like I'm never in the area," she said with a pang of guilt. "But now that you have your adorable baby girl..."

"I suppose I won't be able to keep you away," he finished for her.

"Somebody's got to spoil her," she justified.

Jeff smiled and tipped his head to see the position of the sun in the cloudless sky from under the brim of his cowboy hat. "Are you sure you have enough time to help check the rest of the cattle? When were you planning on pulling out?"

She wrinkled her nose. "Three o'clock at the latest, I guess."

He seemed content with her answer in correlation to the present time. They rode on until they reached the crest of the Sandhills dune. Open land stretched as far as Riley could see except for a lazy stream below and a little timber of ancient cottonwoods around a ravine. The horses descended the hill, their back ends jostling from side to side, and as they got closer to the trees pieces of white cottonwood fluff drifted through the air.

"I don't like the looks of this," Jeff remarked when he saw a lone cow standing on the other side of the creek. "Only one is never a good sign."

They entered the trees to see a partly submerged calf, only its muddy white head and red back visible. The calf let out a feeble noise. The cow answered and did not seem to be bothered by the presence of humans. They crossed the creek and Jeff got off his horse. He lifted the reins to Riley and took the rope off his saddle. He headed for the water and slipped at the ruddy edge where cattle had stood earlier to drink. He forged on, his boots sinking in the mud before water filled them, then water came over his knees. Jeff got the loop around the calf's neck and threw the length of rope to the muddy bank, then he reached under the calf to assess the situation.

"Appears the little bugger's caught in a dead limb," he said. "He's plumb worn out." He left the water, using his arms for balance and fought the mud. "Sand everywhere but here," he grumbled. He put a wet hand on the neck of Riley's grey horse and looked up at her. "I want you to hold the rope snug while I work on freeing the calf." She nodded and when he picked up the end of the rope he grinned. "Unless you want to trade places."

She grinned back. "I'm company, remember?"

"You'd better switch horses," he told her. "Mine is more suited for the job, and I wouldn't want you to get muck on your fancy barrel saddle."

"You're just jealous mine's nicer than yours," she replied nonchalantly and dismounted. She tied Novocain to a cottonwood along the cattle path that continued up the short, steep bank. Then she mounted Jeff's bay and dallied the rope around the saddle horn.

"Snug it up, but not too tight," Jeff instructed.

"I don't have much room behind," Riley said with a look over her shoulder.

"The rope's to help keep his head above water," Jeff said dismissively on his way to the water again. "He's not going anywhere."

Riley made sure the rope was tight and the savvy ranch gelding kept a close eye on the rope. The calf remained motionless while Jeff reached under it, toiling with the branch he could not see, but as soon as the calf was freed it floundered to get away. Jeff was knocked off balance and consequently submerged. The gelding was trying to keep the rope tight by backing proficiently, but was running out of ground. Riley released the dally, jumped off and grabbed the rope. The cow bawled, encouraging the calf that was headed right for Riley. The bay, no longer having a job with the release of the rope stood where it was, but wide-eyed Novocain looked like he would take flight if it weren't for the fact he was tied to a tree. Before Jeff made it out of the water he was witness to the unavoidable collision between the calf and Riley. She went down in the mud and then the calf crashed into the bay and bumped into its mother. Not waiting for solace the calf kept going, up the embankment's worn path. The cow trotted behind, its full udder swinging. Jeff reached dry ground as Riley was getting to her feet.

"I think I remember hearing the words *plumb worn out*," she mocked.

Jeff didn't reply but retrieved his wet hat from the edge of the water. He slapped it against his leg, sending water and sand spraying and then put it on his head. He walked to his horse, put a foot in the stirrup and swung a leg over.

"Ready to help fetch my rope?" he asked with a grin.

It was some time later when they rode away from the cow and calf that were now with the herd. Jeff had retrieved his rope and finished coiling it.

"So how far back is this putting you?" he asked.

"I've got time," she replied, but knew she would be cutting it close.

"You want to take a shower before you head out? You managed to get mud up and down one side of you, but looks like your purdy saddle was spared."

"I'm going to a rodeo, not prom. And I'll always smell better than you."

He laughed. "We'd better get moving so you can get on the road," he said, and with that they pushed their horses into a trot.

The altercation with the calf wasn't the only thing not going to plan that day. Three hours after leaving her brother's place Riley encountered road construction that put her on a detour. Not wanting to go thirty miles out of her way she took what she thought would be a shortcut on a gravel road, but it turned out to be a bad idea. She hit another pothole and cringed, feeling bad for Novocain in the trailer. She glanced at her watch, discouraged at the late time, and then the pickup was jerked by the horse trailer.

"Great," she muttered, causing the big black dog on the passenger seat to look at her with his head tipped and an ear raised. Riley took her foot off the gas and let the truck and trailer come to a crawl, allowing the dust to dissipate before braking. She pulled over as far as she could, careful to avoid a cockeyed acreage for sale sign, its red arrow pointing at weeds.

"Want to get out, Wooly?" she asked.

The curious expression of the old Newfoundland-mix changed to confidence and his big tail thumped against the door.

Out of habit Riley looked for traffic as she waited for Wooly to get out, but there was nothing. Probably nothing for miles, she thought. She let him have the smooth track and she walked on the loose gravel to the trailer. There were no problems to be seen on this side but despite the jungle of the weeds on the other, along the edge of the road, she could see there was a blown tire. She took in a deep breath, backtracked and stepped up on the wheel well of the trailer so she could unlatch the drop-down window for Novocain.

"Hi, fella. Looks like we'll be here awhile," she said, accepting her predicament.

The grey stuck his head out and casually looked around. It was hot, typical for mid-June and there hadn't been a cloud in the sky all day, making for miserable conditions inside the motionless trailer within a short amount of time. But before she would unload Novocain she would gather the things to change the tire. She wasn't looking forward to fighting the weeds while changing it and doubted that Novocain would be pleased with the weeds either, but she couldn't tie him on this side, not on the road. Wooly shuffled ahead to the shade provided by the gooseneck of the trailer where the spare was carried, and Riley looked at it with a sinking feeling. She tried to recall the last time she checked it and hit the spare with the heel of her fist. It barely bounced back. She muttered again and Wooly gave her the same curious expression as earlier.

Riley knew the pickup's spare wouldn't fit the trailer because she had failed to put normal size wheels back on after her ex-fiancé changed them as an excuse for her to get better gas mileage. She took in a deep breath again while thinking it was just like Peter to try to improve on things. She headed for the cab of the truck, now focused on the bulky cellular phone that Peter had given her for hauling, about the only thing she still had that he had given her. It was 1995 and technology was knocking on the door as a mere formality before bursting in, and Riley didn't like it. But, she thought with a look of both repugnance and gratitude, today she was glad to have the phone on hand.

She didn't seriously consider calling Jeff because of the distance already traveled, and when she tried to call rodeo friends

Cowgirl Is a State of Mind

she thought might be in the area nobody picked up. She pushed the numbers for information and waited, hoping to find a town nearby where she could get the tire replaced, and let out a sigh of relief when she got an answer. She jotted down the one local name and number she was given called Tapperd's Repair, in Whispering Pines. Looking at her map she determined she must be only a few miles from that small town, also noting it was still over an hour's drive to the rodeo where she was supposed to be running barrels that evening. Although irritated with her negligence she knew that beating herself up over it wouldn't do any good, while at the same time knowing she wouldn't let it happen again.

She dialed the number and listened to it ring. When it stopped, a recording came on. "Tapperd's Repair. Open 7:30 to 5:30 Monday through Saturday. Open Sunday by chance. In case of an emergency you can try 555–1212." The voice was deep and gravely. Reliable, she thought. She hung up and tried the emergency number, but there was no answer and no answering machine.

The trailer swayed gently from Novocain getting restless from the heat, flies or just plain boredom. Riley knew she needed to make up her mind on what to do but put off making a decision, looking at the countryside and then watching Wooly instead. Wooly had moved from the shade of the trailer to inspect the activity of a field mouse and Riley was amused to see the old dog roused by the tiny critter. He trailed it to the weed filled ditch but as the mouse got deep in the vegetation Wooly lost track of it, stopping near the acreage for sale sign. Riley looked at the sign with hope. Perhaps someone lived there who could help. She decided to take a gamble—obviously she couldn't hurt the bad tire any more.

"Let's go, Wooly," she said confidently.

Back on the road she crept along, hearing a chunk of rubber hit the trailer when she turned the direction she believed the red arrow on the realtor sign intended to be pointing. On her left was nothing but a thin grass pasture, few trees and a windmill, its blades stationary with lack of wind. A little timber on her right hid the immediate view, but in the distance was an odd outcropping of hills, *bluffs* she believed they were called. The bluffs looked like they stretched for several miles, and she remembered seeing them when pondering what to do about the tire.

Half a mile further a barn with a partially dead tree resting on it came into view and then a small farm house. The realtor's sign near the drive was overgrown. She turned into the driveway and stopped. It didn't appear that anyone was living there. The one-and-a-half story clapboard farmhouse was badly in need of paint, the faded white cracked and peeling. A window on the main level was boarded over and most of the lattice was missing from under the simple full length front porch. A tall spruce at the far corner of the porch, probably once regal, now needed attention.

The yard looked like the prairie and it was hard to discern exactly where the driveway was between the yard and the barn because of it. Her eyes settled on the pens near the barn where the weeds were as tall as the fence. Weeds or not, if one of the pens were in decent condition she could put Novocain there and stay the night. She had spent plenty of nights in the primitive living area of her horse trailer—it would be just like another night on the road. She made a U-turn between the house and barn and then parked along the lot fence, facing the road. Wooly was standing on the seat with anticipation.

Riley held the door for Wooly and he scrambled out, best he could for his age, and a solitary cricket chirped somewhere in the grass. They entered the barn through the large sliding doors that were already open. Wooly began to investigate and the early evening rays coming through missing strips of wood between planks striped him like a zebra. The barn looked to be structurally sound, other than the missing battens and damage where the tree was leaning on it, and when she opened the door to the first stall it swung easily, as if soliciting to be useful again. She checked to make sure the stall was free of protruding nails or other dangers to her horse and she checked the lot fence. There were papers in the weeds that she picked up.

The trailer wheel well was the temporary resting place for the papers. After turning Novocain in the lot and filling his bucket with water from the trailer she retrieved the trash, which were actually weathered realtor flyers. She pulled one from the rest and, without thinking about what she was doing, worked at the wrinkles while she tried Tapperd's emergency number, again with no luck. Then she dialed the shop number and read the flyer while she waited for the answering machine. At the appropriate time, she began to speak.

"Hello. This is Riley Montgomery, passing through, and I've got a bad trailer tire. I think my spare is okay but, well, it doesn't have enough air in it. I'd appreciate it if I could get it fixed yet tonight or early Sunday morning so I can get back on the road. I'm parked at the acreage for sale on Flat View Road…for the night." She hesitated, thinking *that* was a dumb thing to say on the answering machine of someone she didn't know. She left her number and added a thank you before hanging up. With the next day being Sunday, it was possible that Mr. Tapperd might not even get the message. If she didn't get a response she would unhook and drive to the little town the next morning. She would never make it to tonight's rodeo in time to compete anyway.

She set about to feeding Novocain. He heard the feed sack rattle and trotted to the fence and waited, somewhat impatiently, his only concern supper. He was used to being on the road, used to being stabled at unfamiliar places. After tending to the gelding Riley started the generator and wrapped up the hose to the water storage in her trailer. Wooly came back from exploring in the barn, having heard the generator and knowing it meant relief from the heat. Riley met Wooly at the walk-in door to the trailer, but instead of getting in the old dog fixed on colorful kittens frolicking near the porch. He ambled toward the kittens that continued to play, unaware, and when he was upon them they looked like characters in a black-and-white slapstick movie falling over each other in their attempt to escape. Wooly was dumbfounded as the kittens he considered new friends scattered for cover under the porch, leaving him standing alone. Riley laughed and walked over to the dog.

    After consoling Wooly she made the high step onto the side of the porch, using a column for support. The blue-grey flooring was worn and faded from years of use and seasons of changing weather. The thump of her boots echoed softly as she walked to the opposite end, where the soft needles of the tall spruce were within reach. The landscape offered wide open pastures as far as she could see and the road, getting narrower in the distance, led to a small cluster of lights revealing what must be the town Whispering Pines. A minute passed before she turned to the house and peered in the window nearest the front door, but the fading light just revealed a large room with fallen plaster.

    Wooly was struggling to get to the top step and after reaching it sat on his haunches and panted. Riley sat down beside the Newfoundland and scratched behind his ears. His panting tapered off while she watched the big round moon come up and then it was just the drone of the generator in the background. The stars were making their presence known in the black sky when Riley stood up and descended the stairs, each one groaning from unaccustomed use.

CHAPTER 2

Riley was crawling back into bed after taking care of Novocain the next morning when she heard a vehicle. She had unplugged the noisy generator and Wooly stood at attention at the trailer's screen door. She hopped down from the bed of the gooseneck and reached for the long-sleeved shirt hanging nearby. She used it to cover the boxer shorts and T-shirt she had slept in, then slipped on her tennis shoes and pulled back her hair. In the pale dawn light she watched an older utility work truck come to a stop near her pickup. She opened the door for Wooly and stepped out behind him. The door on the utility truck was swinging open with a reluctant squeak.

"I'm Jay Tapperd," said the man after he got out. "I apologize for coming so early."

She thought his voice sounded like the one she had heard on the answering machine the day before and Wooly, beside her, was unconcerned. The man was broad and tall but he moved easily for his size. The sleeves had been cut from his button-up shirt and revealed large, muscular arms, leathery tan from years of working outside. He looked like he could have been first string on the high school football team—twenty-five years ago, she thought as he came closer.

"Jay Tapperd," he repeated, extending a hand. In person he gave her the same reliable impression as his voice had earlier.

"Riley Montgomery," she heard herself say and accepted his hand, which became lost within his. The gradual approach of the sun was allowing her to see his strong jaw and weathered face, which was clean shaven and as tan as his arms. Brown hair peeking out the back of his ball cap was sun bleached and there were hints of grey at his temples, bringing out the grey flecks in his eyes. She thought the high school cheerleaders had probably considered him first string material as well, and realized she was staring.

"Hope you don't mind me coming so early," he said again. "I already had something planned this morning… I got your message while rounding up things for that," he added and looked like he thought he was talking too much. He looked past her. "Where's your trouble?"

She blushed and turned to the trailer, pointing. "Over there," she said needlessly, feeling foolish.

He was all business as he inspected the tire, and then he looked at the other tires and the spare. "Where you driving to?" he asked, slowing for a moment but still concentrating on his work.

"I'm entered at the Little Creek rodeo this afternoon and then headed home to Owen."

He nodded and looked at his truck. "I didn't have any new tires that will work but I did find some decent used ones. How about I put one of the used ones on your trailer, air up your spare and send another with you just in case? Do you make it out this way much?"

"If I don't start winning money consistently I'll have to stay home," she said to herself more than to him. "But I'm not ready to quit yet. I should be back in a couple of weeks."

He nodded again. "After you get a new tire you can return these and settle up then. Does that work for you?"

She wondered if she had heard him correctly. "You'd do that?" she asked, looking him in the eye.

"No problem," he replied and looked away. He walked past the storage compartments on the side of his utility truck and began pulling tires from the open cargo space in back.

"You brought them with you?" she said, impressed.

He didn't answer but continued to organize what he needed. Riley went to her pickup where she kept her own supply of things. Jay was rolling one of the tires beside him when she rounded the back of the trailer, meeting him.

"I have one of these," she offered, displaying a device made to be driven upon with the good trailer tire, eliminating the need for a jack.

"Good," he said with approval. "Let's do it."

They worked without having to discuss what needed to be done and during that time the sun cleared the horizon, welcoming the new day. When they finished Jay was putting the extra tires in the back of her pickup when a vehicle came down the road, billowing dust. Jay shook his head without bothering to look and the pickup slowed and then stopped at the end of the driveway. The white extended cab Dodge with chrome and black accents including a grill guard was obviously made for working, yet was classy and easy on the eyes.

"He's with me," Jay told her. "That tire shouldn't have gone bad on you," he continued. "And don't count on your spare. You need to get it checked. It didn't lose air for no reason." He carried his tools to his truck, put them away and then walked back to her trailer to get something he had forgotten. "Do you need anything else? Your horse going to load okay?"

"I've got everything I need," she answered, thinking it was nice of him to ask.

The driver of the Dodge evidently changed his mind about waiting. He drove across the tall thin grass in the yard, faster than he should, swung around and came to a stop close to Riley. She stood her ground.

"Jay didn't tell me he had to help somebody cute," he said while tipping back his black cowboy hat with a finger. He had short black hair, light brown skin and the appealing bad boy look of not having shaved a day or two. His dark eyes twinkled and he smelled good, of cologne and tobacco. Riley guessed he was her age, and was sure she had seen him before.

"Miles Deroin," Jay said simply for an introduction from several feet away and went back to what he was doing.

"Good morning," she said indifferently to Miles. "Riley Montgomery."

Jay glanced over his shoulder at the tone of her voice but Miles didn't seem to notice. He was deep in thought.

"I've seen you and that big grey running barrels," he said. "Didn't you win at Gordyville?"

His comment, bordering on flattery, took her by surprise, but she remained neutral. "No. It was a nice run, but not a win. You rodeo?"

"Some," Miles said, adding with a grin, "I get around."

Jay, walking to the door of his truck to leave, again shook his head.

"Nice to meet you," Riley said before stepping back and turning for Jay's truck.

"Likewise," Miles said slow and deliberately. He watched her walk to Jay before letting his truck roll forward, then "Get a move on, old man," he told Jay as he rolled by him. "Don't forget you only have me for a couple of hours."

Jay opened his door and got in. He looked at Riley and started his truck.

She gave him a grateful smile. "Thanks again. Are you sure I can't pay you something now?"

"I'm sure," he said and switched his look to the rearview mirror at Miles, who was waiting at the end of the drive. "I should be the one paying you for giving me something to irritate Miles with," he said, the corners of his eyes wrinkling.

She laughed and when his truck began to move she took a step back. Soon he and Miles were gone. The quiet returned but before the cloud of dust they created drifted away she was headed for the trailer to get dressed.

"C'mon, Wooly," she said. "Let's get Novocain and hit the road."

* * *

Later that morning Riley saddled up and headed to the Little Creek rodeo arena to warm up her horse. As she neared the open gate a friend, Kelly Lynch, rode toward her. Kelly was married to a calf roper named Connor.

"Where were you last night?" Kelly asked.

"Tire trouble," Riley said, letting her aggravation show. "I could have changed it myself, but I experienced a blonde moment before leaving home and didn't have air in the spare."

Kelly, a pretty, outspoken blonde, laughed. "Goes to show there's no hair color preference for negligence. You probably would have won the perf. What a bunch of dinks."

"That's about the way my luck's been going lately. How'd you do?"

"My gelding's still too much a greenhorn, but we're getting there," Kelly replied. She leaned forward and flicked a bug off an ear of her horse. "This ground really sucks."

Riley scoffed. "Most rodeo ground sucks for barrel racers, you know that."

"This is hard on top and slick underneath. I heard that barrel horses went down both Friday night and last night."

"Both nights?"

Kelly nodded and they continued to ride side by side along the fence. Near the entry table outside the arena a group of men and women with beers in their hands broke out with laughter.

"Party time already," Kelly commented.

Riley didn't reply. She was preoccupied with tall and slender Miles Deroin in the group. He was talking to one of the cowboys, unaware of Riley and indifferent to the redhead clinging to his side. Riley remembered why he looked familiar—she had labeled him a cad long ago.

"He's a looker, isn't he?" Kelly teased.

Riley blushed.

"Now that I think of it," said Kelly, "I've never seen you partying. You don't mingle much, do you?"

Riley's short laugh was cynical. "Let's just chalk it up to bad luck. Besides, I get enough of people at work sitting behind the reception desk at the law firm in Owen. 'Prescott, McLane, Briggs and Matthews,'" she mimicked. "'This is Riley, how may I help you?' I wish I had a dollar for every time I've said that."

"I have to admit I'm spoiled working with Connor on the ranch every day," Kelly said. "I assume you have to dress up?"

"Yes, but that's not as bad as being stuck inside for eight hours a day." Riley shrugged. "But I make decent money. I don't come from a ranch background or even the country…I was a city girl." She raised her brows. "I guess I still am. But I don't feel like it."

Kelly chuckled. They had circled the arena and were back near the entry stand. The group was dispersing. Miles and the redhead were walking to an extravagant horse trailer that was hooked to a newer pickup.

"That's the redhead's rig," Kelly informed. "Her name's Miranda. I'd never seen her before last week. When I saw her run barrels, I wasn't impressed. Probably has a rich ex-husband…

but I bet he ain't rich no more!" She laughed enthusiastically. "She has a horse for break-away roping too, but watching that didn't impress me either. Why don't you rope?"

"Because I'm not very good at it. My mare—she's at home in the pasture—is actually better at roping than barrels, but I'd rather stick to barrels. And Novocain's a lot of fun."

"Novocain. What kind of name is that? I gotta admit it is cute though."

Riley smiled. "His registered name is That'll Take Novocain. When I was told his name before buying him, it reminded me of the first time I got stitches as a kid. When the doctor gave me the anesthetic, which I remember hurting like heck, he told me that when he was young he had a horse that rode so rough he was completely numb by the time he was done riding."

"I've had a few like that in my day," Kelly said and laughed again.

"I'd better get serious about warming up."

"Good luck tonight!"

Riley smiled her thanks and trotted away.

* * *

Miles Deroin and Jay Tapperd stood outside the fence at the Little Creek rodeo. Miles, wearing the cowboy hat he was rarely without, was holding a beer but Jay, with a ball cap on his head, was empty handed.

"I thought I was seeing things when you came walkin' up to me after I roped," Miles said in jest. "You never come out to play."

Jay didn't answer. The pickup that delivered the barrels exited the arena and an official was making sure the barrels were properly set on the markers. The announcer rattled off the list of barrel racers entered for that performance, and when Riley's name was broadcast Miles laughed with gusto and slapped Jay on the back.

"Now I get it!" he said. "She must've mentioned she was running here this afternoon."

Jay turned from Miles, preventing him from seeing his expression.

"How about a little friendly competition?" Miles taunted.

Jay kept his back to Miles. "This time I think you'd lose. You know you would or you wouldn't have brought it up." There was humor in his voice.

"You're smarter than you look, ol' boy," complimented Miles.

The first barrel racer came in through the side gate that the pickup had used because there was no center alley.

"You thinkin' about getting back in the game?" Miles asked.

This time Jay threw him a warning look.

"Uncle," said Miles, giving in. He took a drink of beer while he and Jay watched the horse have difficulty with his footing as it rounded the barrels.

When it was Riley's turn, she maneuvered Novocain along the front of the chutes. The gelding burst into a run as soon as she released him and he quickly covered the distance to the first barrel. She checked him and he began his turn only to have the ground underneath give away. He scrambled to keep his balance and Riley fought to stay on without hindering his efforts, but Novocain came down. A commotion followed as the horse and rider fell into the metal fifty-five gallon drum.

Miles chucked his beer at the nearby trash can and nimbly cleared the fence. Jay wasn't far behind. Novocain made it to his feet and trotted away, his head held high. Miles reached for Riley as she was pushing herself off the ground.

"Take it easy," he cautioned as he helped her up.

The announcer started in with encouragement and sympathetic applause rose from the crowd. Her first concern her horse, Riley looked for Novocain. The gelding, appearing to be none the worse off, was playing keep away with Kelly near the gate.

"You okay?" asked Jay.

"Yes," she said, noticing for the first time that he was there.

"You've got blood on your face," Jay told her.

Riley touched her cheek and winced.

"And your sleeve…" he said.

Riley raised her elbow to look at the tear and felt a twinge of pain as she did so.

"I'm okay," she insisted.

Miles put an arm around her and took the initiative to lead her away. Jay picked her hat up off the ground and followed. At the gate Kelly and her husband Conner were waiting with Novocain.

"Quite a show, girl," Kelly said.

Miranda, the next barrel racer to compete, glared at Riley and Miles as she rode past on her way into the arena. Riley kept a wary eye on the redhead before focusing on Novocain. Miles joined her in inspecting the horse.

"He seems to be in better shape than you," offered Kelly. "It doesn't look like there's anything wrong with him."

After not finding anything obvious, she gave a relieved smile to Miles, then to Kelly and Connor and lastly Jay.

"Now what about you?" asked Jay.

"I'm okay," she repeated.

"You hit that barrel pretty hard," said Kelly. "You need to take something for pain. I've got Bute for your horse and drugs for you too, if you don't have any on hand." She let her temper show. "I already told them I'm not running in this crap. We're pulling out. How about I drive your rig as far as our place?"

Riley's mouth opened to object.

"I'll drive her," Miles offered.

Jay guffawed and Kelly laughed.

Miles's eyes twinkled. "Or not."

"C'mon, Connor," Kelly directed, and together she and her husband started to leave, taking Novocain with them.

Riley gave Jay a helpless smile. "Gotta go where my horse goes," she said. Then, seeing the concern on his face, added, "I'm okay, really."

Jay handed her the hat lost in the fall.

"I'm entered in a 4D barrel race in Iowa next weekend," she told him, "but I'll make it back this way in the next few weeks. I'll bring the tires and pay you then."

"Don't worry about it," he said.

"Thanks again, for everything. You too," she added looking at Miles, who winked in reply.

She started to go, and when she looked back all she could see was horses and riders.

* * *

It was dusk when Riley made it to the outskirts of Owen, a large city with half a million residents. She left the interstate with other vehicles, each of them having their own agendas within the bustling city. Fifteen minutes later she signaled her intentions to turn onto a street in a somewhat rural setting and as she slowed those behind her impatiently braked, before once again speeding on their way.

Two horses grazing in a paddock raised their heads and idly watched the pickup and trailer. Beyond the pair of horses was a large new colonial style house. The lawn was well manicured including recently planted trees, replacements for the huge trees that had been removed to make way for the new residence. Countless houses had been going up, crowding out pastures and cropland, each new home larger and grander than the one before it.

Riley again slowed, this time to make her last turn. Her destination did not have a pretty fenced paddock near the road nor did the drive lead to a grand dwelling. The recent addition of a three-rail fence was a feeble attempt to keep up with the new acreages changing the landscape, but it had never been painted. And there wasn't a house at all, only two barns—one old and majestic and the other a small carriage house, both with an apartment in their lofts. The barn loft was where Benjie, a freelance artist and decorator lived, while the carriage house was what Riley called home.

Wooly was happy to get out and he struck off before Riley unloaded Novocain. Being a competitive athlete in training the gelding didn't have the luxury of grazing all day in the pasture but instead had a stall in the barn with an attached dry lot. After being turned free he pawed the ground and then rolled in the dirt. When he got to his feet he shook, creating a small cloud of dust around him. Riley took a minute to check on her other two horses in the pasture.

She gathered the things she wanted to take with her from the truck and trailer. Inside the walk-in door of the garage where her Pinto hatchback was parked, she flipped on the light and climbed the stairs. Her armload of items was deposited on the kitchen table. She kicked off her boots, peeled off her jeans and gingerly removed her shirt. Her shoulder was sore and her elbow swollen around the strawberry, but she appreciated the fact the wreck hadn't been worse. This was nothing that a hot shower and aspirin couldn't cure.

She took folded money from a back pocket of her jeans and laid it on the table near the rodeo newsletter there. Curious, she picked up the newsletter and flipped to the page with the barrel racing standings. Before her recent slump she was in third place with money won, barely ahead of fourth or even fifth for that matter. Average, she surmised. She should be used to being in an average place—there had been few times in her life when she had enjoyed the glory of being number one. But, she considered, there was nothing wrong with being average either. It wasn't as exciting as being famous but it wasn't as bad as never having done anything. She lobbed the newsletter to the table and walked away, headed to the bathroom.

Looking at herself for the first time since the fall she saw the cut and bruising on her cheek that promised to look dreadful by morning, but it would bother her bosses more than it would her. While brushing her teeth she summarized she was just as average as her standings in the rodeo association—average height and weight, average teeth including a few crowded ones on the bottom, eyes much prettier when she put mascara on. Just a few years over thirty the lines near her mouth and eyes were from too much sun and laughing, not worry. She cupped water from the tap with her hand, spit, and then freed her auburn hair from its ponytail.

Turning the knob at the shower she thought about her conversation with Kelly, and was thankful that horses had come into her life. She had grown up within bicycling distance of a stable, ultimately convincing the owner to let her clean stalls in exchange for riding lessons. She had put in long hours, appreciating the chance, and eventually came to realize that working with horses fulfilled something missing in her life as a young adult. Her parents had become wandering free spirits, perpetually reliving the '70s even before she graduated high school, and she had no idea where they had been the last year. Jeff hadn't brought up the subject of their parents during the visit and neither had she. She thought about her tire trouble and smiled at the memory of Jay and Miles, but the smile changed to a frown as she recalled the worthless men she had dated and Peter, her ex-fiancé. It was four years ago that he and Riley had pooled their money to purchase land with plans to eventually build a house. All their friends and casual acquaintances were sure they would be married and, of course, live happily ever after…everyone except Holly Vanderpage, who was now Mrs. Peter Breck. Apparently Holly had had her eye on Peter for quite some time, spinning her web while Riley was amateur rodeoing. Riley did win the barrel racing title that year, but her and Peter's relationship was a casualty because of it. The coveted trophy buckle she worked so hard to obtain remained in its box, tarnished with bittersweet memories.

Riley shrugged off her bad luck with men, thinking that although her relationships didn't last, her obsession with horses had.

CHAPTER 3

Traffic was picking up the next morning while Riley was on the road for work. She dropped the tires off at the repair shop and ten minutes later pulled into an empty space in the parking garage. She checked the back of her skirt and headed for the office building, moving a little slower than usual because of feeling the repercussion of losing to the barrel the day before.

Inside she weaved her way through the crowded lobby to the elevator. She stepped in the elevator with several others and pushed the button for the fifth floor. The elevator leisurely made its way up, lurched and then paused before the doors slid open. To her right, behind a wall of glass, were the offices of the lawyers she worked for.

The large letters spelling out "Prescott, McLane, Briggs and Matthews" graced the front of the circular reception desk. A woman and a young man sat together in the waiting area off to one side and another client, obviously unhappy, was at the desk. Fran, who shared duties with Riley, was patiently dealing with him.

"I realize you have an eight o'clock meeting with Mr. Briggs," Fran was saying politely. "But it isn't quite eight yet. He'll be here shortly."

Riley made her way to her chair behind the circular desk. "I think I saw Mr. Briggs on my way in," she said for Fran's sake. "He'll be here, Mr. Twombly."

"I'm in a hurry," said Mr. Twombly curtly, but with both women present he gave in. He sulked off to find a lone seat in the waiting area, almost bumping into the youngest lawyer of the firm, Mitch Matthews, who had just arrived. Mitch apologized and continued on his way to the hall behind the desk, appearing preoccupied.

Fran looked at Riley with grateful eyes. The slender fifty-something woman's short hair style was sporting new pink highlights. Fran took good care of herself and looked younger than she actually was.

"I'm sorry I'm running late," Riley said. "Your hair looks good," she added.

"Thanks. You're not late—everyone seems to be early," Fran whispered. "Everyone but Briggs." She stared at Riley's face. "What happened to you?"

"Hit a barrel yesterday," she replied. "Literally."

"Ouch!" The phone rang and Fran turned to answer it.

Riley clicked on her computer, one of the items she had added to her love/hate list. From the hall behind her she heard voices and then Bill Briggs's seventeen-year-old daughter appeared. They had come up the back stairs, making Riley assume that Bill didn't want Twombly to think he wasn't already at the office. Cynthia, who had been working at the firm during the summer since she was fifteen, exaggeratedly laid her new glitzy purse on the reception desk. She looked down at Riley and twirled the hair behind her ears to show off her new earrings. Riley could ignore the girl no longer.

"Morning, Cynthia," she said.

Evidently satisfied, Cynthia picked up her purse and went to her own desk. Then Bill Briggs made his appearance.

"Sherman Twombly!" said Bill. "How good to see you. Did the girls offer you coffee? Come on back."

Twombly joined Bill, leaving his coffee that Fran had already provided.

"Fran, would you bring us some morning brew?" Bill asked.

Fran glanced at Riley before getting up. Riley rose too and went to retrieve the abandoned cup. While she was up she went to the waiting woman and young man.

"Is there anything I can get you two?" Riley asked pleasantly.

"We're waiting for Prescott," the woman said crossly. "Is he here?"

"I'll go check," Riley assured.

After obtaining the cup Riley started for the hall. Passing Cynthia's desk she couldn't help but overhear her talking to one of her friends on the phone. When she passed Mitch Matthews's office he looked up from the papers in front of him. She spoke briefly to the other lawyer and then headed back, only to be stopped by Mitch, who was standing at his door.

"Hello," he said. His brow furrowed when he got a close look at her battered face.

"Good morning, Mr. Matthews," she said and wondered what he must be thinking. She had always been intimidated by his cultured attitude and good looks, and he had the most striking blue eyes she had ever seen. *Bedroom eyes*, she thought they must be, and hoped she wasn't blushing. "How are you today?"

"Good. And you?"

"No complaints."

Now his brow went up and he continued to look at her face. "I've got to go...client waiting," she said and took a step.

"Are you helping with the hospital fundraiser this Saturday?"

She grimaced, remembering. "Yes, I'll be there." The law firm had begun the benefit several years before and all the employees were expected to help. "You?"

"Wouldn't miss it," he said frankly.

He was clearly looking forward to it and Riley smiled at his perspective. It wasn't that she didn't want to help, but that she would rather be doing other things.

"Did you need something?" she asked.

"No. Just saying hello."

She started to move while still looking at him. He gave her a warm smile before stepping back into his office. She continued on her way and wondered, not for the first time, why he was single. He had been with the firm about a year, relocating from back east somewhere after a divorce. Maybe he wasn't over his ex-wife she supposed, and left it at that.

The rest of the morning quickly passed as employees and lawyers completed their daily tasks, or pretended to, while clients came and went. Riley picked up her tires during lunch and went through a fast food drive-through. She had eaten by the time she got back to the parking garage and checked her reflection in the rearview mirror. Taking up the space in the mirror—and most of the back of her hatchback—were the tires, but she also saw a man and woman standing near a little red sports car. It was impossible not to notice the woman who was dressed in cream-colored riding breeches and black knee-high boots. Her blonde hair was in a tidy bun.

Riley opened the door and swung her legs out, wishing she hadn't worn a skirt. From the corner of her eye she saw the man coming in her direction. It was Bill Briggs. He was one of those unfortunate men who would always be a little portly, soft and boring, but was lucky enough to have money to make up for it. He looked at her legs and didn't seem to be in any hurry to bring his gaze up to meet hers. She thought about asking what he was doing in the general public parking garage for a conversation opener, but in reality didn't want to know, so she said nothing.

"Did you win a lot of money over the weekend, cowgirl?" he asked while inspecting her bruises. "Did Sherman Twombly call? Make sure you get me on the phone when he does. You know he wants to follow up from our morning meeting."

"Not yet. Fran or I will make sure you get his call."

"What about Cynthia?" he said abruptly. "I expect she's doing a great job."

"She's a very... bright girl," she replied. "You go on without me. I forgot something in my car."

"Don't be late—you wouldn't want your wages docked," he said and chuckled before he strutted off.

The little red sports car backed out of its parking place. Riley fumbled with her car door in attempt to look busy as the woman drove past.

* * *

Riley was cleaning out her truck later that day when Benjie crossed the drive from his loft apartment above the barn. His shoulder-length hair of various shades of grey and bright silver was not in its usual loose ponytail.

"Hello! Your hair's damp—have a hot date?" she teased.

"No, I have a consultation at seven o'clock," he said exaggeratedly. Benjie was a popular decorator, especially with wealthier older women, renowned not only in Owen but other large cities as well. Just under fifty years old he had distinguished good looks and a faint accent, but Riley had never been able to determine its origin. His name was Jameson Benjamin, not giving any hints to heritage, and he seemed reluctant to talk about himself. He had never acted like he was interested in her in any way other than a good friend, and Riley greatly appreciated their association.

"Tell me about the new job," she said.

He waved his hand in lofty dismissal. "The Stonehenge family was thrilled with what I did to their house and now his country club wants a facelift. Maybe I can finally get into that club now."

She laughed, knowing he was making fun and that it was simply *Stone* not *Stonehenge*. "Well, I guess I should be honored that you are bothering to speak to me," she said with a curtsy.

"Yes, yes, you should." They smiled at each other and then he motioned to her face. "What happened?"

She frowned. "Basically a weekend of nothing but trouble."

An evil grin appeared. "Did I miss some action? Man trouble? Or, better yet, a cat fight?" He rubbed his hands together briskly.

"You know better than that."

His expression changed to one of affection.

"About all I have to show for the weekend," she said looking at the tires in the back, "is a new tire and less money than I had before in my checking account. I even missed a perf."

He looked from the tires to her. "Perf?"

"Performance," she clarified. She pulled the realtor flyer from the sack of trash in her hands. "A tire went bad on a detour and I ended up staying at this abandoned place overnight. At least the repair guy came out early Sunday morning and got me back on the road."

"Good old rural hospitality," he said matter-of-factly while accepting the wrinkled paper. There was a faded photo of the house and barn with a brief description. "Eighty acres partially rolling hills, pasture and some farm ground," he read. "One-and-a-half story house with ten-year-old standing seam roof, ten-year-old furnace and central air. Well water." He handed it back to her. "Mm. Cute."

"It isn't that bad," she said slapping him with the flyer. "But it's odd the house is empty. It looked like it had been empty for quite a while actually."

"Somebody probably went berserk and murdered their family there," he said, starting to leave.

"Shame on you."

"I'll help you put that tire on one evening," he said and lifted a hand to wave. "Don't do it yourself. You doing anything Friday night?"

She shook her head.

"Me neither. Want to stay up late, watch movies and get drunk?" he asked jokingly.

She smiled and shook her head again. "A movie, yes. The rest, no. I have the fundraiser for work Saturday morning. I think it would be unwise if I showed up tipsy."

"So true," he said and sighed dramatically. "Ta-ta," he added before walking away.

CHAPTER 4

Traveling the interstate it still took Riley half an hour to get to the other side of Owen Saturday morning. The bruise on her face was fading and the aches all but gone, and the fact she was wearing a T-shirt, jeans and boots instead of dress clothes put the finishing touches on the start of the beautiful day. She pulled into the modest parking lot at the location of the fundraiser and recognized several cars that belonged to fellow employees. The buses and vans had not yet arrived with the honored guests, children with physical handicaps or long-term illnesses. A small admission fee was charged to the general public but the majority of money collected was through sponsorships and donations, and it was turning into one of Owen's most successful fundraisers.

Outside the front doors of the one-story building Cynthia Briggs was excitedly telling her friends about the new horse she had talked her parents into buying. Bill, her father, had been opposed to the idea for as long as Riley could remember and she wondered if the woman she had seen with him in the parking garage had anything to do with him changing his mind. Inside, Fran stood ready at the check-in table, looking attractive in jeans and a pink blouse that matched the highlights in her hair. She was visiting with someone dressed as a clown, complete with face paint and colorful yarn wig.

"Riley!" Fran exclaimed. "Look who traded one suit for another today!"

Past the makeup Riley saw deep blue eyes. Those eyes, she thought, and the clown smiled.

"Mr. Matthews!" she blurted at the same inopportune time that Bill Briggs and his wife Karen walked by.

Bill gave Mitch a scornful look. Mitch appeared to be momentarily embarrassed and was probably red faced, but the makeup made it impossible to tell. Mitch Matthews the clown regained his composure. He dramatically shrugged, made a big clown frown and walked away, his giant clown shoes flopping. Riley watched him go, thinking maybe there was more to him than she had given him credit.

The chatter of excited children filled the building as the youngsters flowed through the doors. Riley passed booths and displays on her way to the outdoor activities, where she had been designated to help. Outside, behind the kiddie carnival and petting zoo were the pony rides, where five ponies were saddled and ready to go. She introduced herself to George, a middle-aged man with a ball cap and grey stubble of a beard, who was in charge.

Children of all ages flocked to the ponies and the morning passed quickly. It wasn't until the temperatures climbed that the children, or more likely their parents, lost interest. The ponies were getting a well-deserved break and George looked like he could use a break as well. After asking Riley if she would handle things he wiped his balding head and headed for the air-conditioning. Riley gathered the water buckets and went to fetch water. Returning, she tipped the bucket to make it easier for a pony to reach the water. She sensed someone nearby, and turned to see only a few feet away was her ex-fiancé, Peter Breck.

"I thought it was you," he said, the sound of his voice stirring memories. He hesitated and then motioned downward. "Did you know your water's spilling?"

She realized one of the legs of her jeans was wet and laughed, nervous and embarrassed. She set the bucket in the puddle, feeling like she was moving in slow motion, and unconsciously snuck a glance at his ring finger. Along the edge of the gold band was pale skin but otherwise he was very tan. His light hair was still cut the same and he was wearing the same designer clothing as when they were together. When she couldn't keep from looking him in the eye any longer, she saw warmth and caring. Not knowing how to handle that, she diverted her attention to the pony.

After a pause, "How have you been?" she asked.

"I've been working a lot."

"Still in Chicago?" she asked, regretting the words as soon as they came out. She didn't want him thinking she had been keeping track of him.

"Yes... I have to make a quick trip back tomorrow. I learned how to fly... I have a little two-seater."

The pony rubbed against her and, thankful for the distraction, she scratched it.

"Um, the land we bought together sold, quite a while ago actually," he told her. "I should have contacted you sooner... I'm sorry."

The way he said it made her wonder if he meant for the apology to go with the explanation of the land or for something else.

"I guess I was waiting for you to ask about it," he said. "It was just easier not to bring it up."

She understood. It was the same reason why she had never asked.

"I couldn't help but invest it for you. I don't think you'll be disappointed," he added with a bashful smile.

When he smiled like that in the past he always reminded her of a little boy sneaking one of his grandmother's cookies, cookies that had been baked especially for him. Cute as it was it no longer melted her heart, and she realized she was in charge of her emotions again. She let herself laugh. It was just like Peter to want to improve something.

He relaxed and smiled, genuinely this time. "I'll have my secretary get you the information next week. I wasn't sure if you were still with Prescott and McLane." There was a moment that nothing was said, then, "Still hauling those horses?" he asked.

She was about to answer but little voices sang out.

"Daddy! Daddy!" Two little girls with blonde wisps of ponytails sticking from either side of their heads scampered toward him. Trailing behind the girls was Holly, pushing a double stroller. Peter looked from his family to Riley.

"It was nice to see you again," she told him.

He reached out with a hand but stopped before touching her. "You too," he said, and then he was gone. When he reached the girls he scooped them in his arms, asking, "Want some ice cream?" to which they chorused their approval.

"Here, you push this thing for a while," Holly dictated.

He put the girls down and they ran, teetering and bobbing, toward the building and he took possession of the stroller. Riley picked up the bucket and before standing up all the way saw that Holly was looking in her direction. She bent down again, busying herself with the pony, wanting to avoid a scene.

"Mommy! Where are you?" one of the small girls called out.

Holly continued looking a little longer, scowling, before turning away.

CHAPTER 5

The DuMont fairgrounds were picturesque and historic and one of Riley's favorite places to run barrels. She drove by the livestock buildings and then the main arena and found a place to park under a tree that would provide shade later in the day. It was still early—she had left home well before dawn. Today's barrel race was a 4D, or Four Divisions, where the top time of the day determined the winners of the remaining three divisions by adding specific fractions of time to the winning run.

Wooly was with her when she walked to the back of the trailer. She had brought all three of her horses, and young Dobbie was impatient to be unloaded. Registered as Double Your Bid, the sorrel was a futurity prospect that couldn't compete for almost a year and a half to remain eligible and Riley knew that he needed more attention than she had been giving him. He gawked around when she tied him. Then she unloaded Novocain and Dually, her mare, also red in color, that preferred roping over barrels. After she filled their water buckets, she saddled Dobbie.

Dobbie, as she expected, was feeling fresh. Riley had purposely allowed extra time to ride the greenhorn and covered the bustling grounds from one end to the other, occasionally stopping to talk with friends. By the time it was Dobbie's turn for exhibitions he worked the pattern well, and when she rode back to the trailer he was much less preoccupied with his surroundings.

After Dobbie she rode Dually while ponying Novocain beside, exercising them both at the same time. Novocain enjoyed his lack of rider and showed his vigor by snorting or shying from time to time.

"Somebody's happy," she heard and recognized Reece Cordhall, a prominent Midwest farrier.

"It's a beautiful day," she granted. "What's not to be happy about?"

"You've got a point there," he agreed.

After their forty-five minute warm up she headed back to the arena on foot, wanting to see if there had been any changes to the pattern or location of the timer since the earlier exhibitions. The competition was already in progress when she entered the building. A petite woman on a big bay horse sprinted down the alley, and as Riley watched the run, and several more, she made note of the ground and other relevant conditions.

Walking back to the trailer she reflected on the pattern and visualized her run. She slipped into automatic pilot as she finished getting ready: leg wraps and bell boots for Novocain, long-sleeved shirt and hat for herself, the competition bridle. There was nothing left to do but the last minute warm-up and mental reminders for them both.

Rock and roll music was playing over the loudspeaker when she got close enough to the arena to hear what was going on. The announcer stated that exhibitor number forty-one was up next. Riley was competitor sixty-three. She rode to a nearby spot to lope circles, careful of the grass that was slick under horseshoes. Because Novocain was a free runner he needed a few maneuvers to reinforce keeping his hind end underneath him and his shoulders up when turning the barrels. He was full of energy, but paying attention.

Riley felt ready when the announcer called her name. She had already positioned Novocain where she wanted him as the competitor before her exited the arena. She was aware of the announcer still speaking but was no longer listening—her complete focus was on her riding and her horse.

Novocain began to hop, almost in place, as they came closer to the mouth of the alley. He was ready to go, coiled like a spring, eleven-hundred pounds of heart and muscle waiting to be let go. She put all her weight in the stirrups as he hopped past the protruding fence until it no longer posed a danger of catching her leg, then her seat and upper body switched to a forward position and she released her hold on the reins. Novocain burst in to a full run.

With her seat and legs she encouraged the gelding to hustle. Both hands were on the reins to help guide and steady him and her eyes fixed on the point just before the first barrel where she wanted to be when she would ask him to start the turn. When she cued him at that point he responded instantly; he checked his momentum and wrapped the barrel so closely her leg skimmed the top all the way around. As he straightened from the turn his powerful hind end pushed away and he covered the ground quickly to the second barrel. She sat deep in her saddle and cued him again. He gathered his body to shorten his stride, wasting no time, and made a pretty arc around the barrel.

As they left the second barrel the crowd was silent, watching the near flawless run unfolding. Riley knew that although Novocain was running hard and fast he was also running carelessly, and she feared he would crowd the last barrel. They were covering ground to it very quickly and she caught herself overanalyzing, debating how much to let him turn it on his own. As they closed in on the barrel she failed to raise her inside hand or sit back to cue him to gather for the turn. Her body reacted by stiffening as she realized she was neglecting to *ride* her horse.

She felt Novocain hesitate, as if he was questioning how she was riding now versus their practice and training sessions. It caused him to falter in his stride, momentarily losing track of his feet. As he pushed away from the misstep a back hoof caught the edge of his front shoe, jerking him and pulling the shoe off. He stumbled but his momentum kept him up and he quickly regained his form, however they had bumped the barrel as they rounded it. Hoping for the best she encouraged him to hustle and they sprinted for home, in silence except the sound of Novocain's hooves pounding the ground. Just before they crossed the timer the crowd moaned, and Riley knew the barrel had gone over.

She sat up in the saddle and began to pull up Novocain. He was blowing air out his nostrils and feeling good, proud of the effort he had given her. As soon as he stopped she turned to look behind her, to the far end of the arena, as if she had to see for herself the barrel lying on its side.

"That would have been top time, but with the tipped barrel it's a no time," said the announcer and then he went on to say who was up next.

Riley moved Novocain out of the way of the other contestants getting ready for their turns, stepped off and loosened the cinch. She stroked Novocain's neck for a job well done and then walked him to help ease his heavy breathing. Someone brought her the shoe that had been left at the third barrel. She checked his front hoof where the shoe had been pulled. He hadn't torn up the hoof, which she was thankful for.

The runs continued and Riley took Novocain outside to walk him. Her irritation for tipping the barrel festered because she blamed herself. She replayed the run in her mind and put the pieces together. As she walked Novocain she encountered a few sympathetic smiles or comments like "nice run regardless." Each time she politely responded by saying thank you or she managed a smile as a way of accepting their gestures of support. Many who were giving casual console had been in the same situation themselves at one time.

"Spot of bad luck, eh?" said Reece Cordhall as their paths crossed.

"It seems to happen at the worst times, doesn't it?"

"Yes, it's not like we're at a twenty-dollar jackpot. There's big money up for grabs today." He motioned at the horseshoe she was carrying. "I'll put that on for you later if you'd like."

"That'd be great!"

"My daughter, Amy, is up pretty soon, but bring your gelding over to our trailer after."

"What number is she?"

"One-hundred-thirteen," he said looking toward the arena.

Knowing Reece wanted to keep moving, she told him, "I'm number one-twenty-one on my second horse, but I'll bring Novocain over as soon as I'm done. I appreciate it very much. Good luck to Amy."

"Thank you. No problem. See you then."

Later, Dually gave Riley a nice, honest run for a respectable time of about two seconds slower than the top times of the day. Dually didn't have speed horse breeding like Novocain did, which hindered her from clocking. Riley knew that with a more serious conditioning regimen the mare could shave off some of her time, but she also knew that would require a change of priorities, and for now her full-time job and Novocain came first.

Amy Cordhall's time was sitting good to win a check in the 2D. Amy was a natural rider and Reece was behind her one hundred percent to see that she became a contender in the barrel racing world. He wouldn't accept any money from Riley for resetting the shoe.

The drive home seemed endless and she knew it was because of the tipped barrel that was her fault. She accepted misfortune much easier when she felt there was nothing she could do about it, but today's bad luck she considered no one's fault but her own. Dually hadn't won any money either, sending her home empty handed. She was encouraged, however, by the fact that Dobbie worked well and had gained confidence from the outing.

She unloaded the horses at home in the dark while thunder rumbled in the distance. In her apartment she turned on the television to hear the weatherman promising rain, sounding like a politician drumming up votes as if it were his doing. It was becoming a very dry summer and the lack of rain was the latest topic. After the cheerful weather report she turned the television off and checked the phone for messages. Nothing, but Fran's number was on caller ID—twice. It was after ten o'clock, so Riley did not call her back.

She was wrapping a towel around her after showering when the phone rang. Because of the late hour it surprised her. She wasn't quick enough to answer and frowned when she saw it was Fran again. She pushed re-dial and said, "Hi, Fran, it's me," when Fran picked up.

"Riley, I'm sorry to be calling this late," said Fran brokenly.

Riley was getting goosebumps from the sound of her voice.

"What is it?" she heard herself say.

"Peter... He was flying from Owen to Chicago this morning."

Memories of Peter the day before flooded back and she remembered him saying he had bought his own plane. She slumped into the nearest chair.

"I'm sorry, Riley. The plane crashed. He was alone..." Fran said and then trailed off. "No one knows yet what happened."

"Oh," was all Riley managed. She thought about his parents and his two little girls she had seen the day before.

"Are you going to be all right? Is Benjie home...or I can come over if you want. We can both go to Benjie's."

"No... Thank you. I'll be okay."
"You want to talk a while?"
"No, I'm all right, really. I appreciate you telling me."
"See you at work in the morning? I'll understand if not."
"I'll be there. If I'm a little late, don't worry...I'll be there."
"Call if you change your mind."
"I will. Thank you, Fran."
"Bye," said Fran.

Riley didn't move until she heard beeping on the other end. In a daze she went to the dresser, pulled out some clothes and dressed, and then picked up the phone. Benjie's lights had been on when she put the horses away and it wasn't unusual for him to be up late.

At Benjie's she filled him in on seeing Peter at the fundraiser and the few details she knew of his death. The discussion evolved and she found herself questioning her routine life as it was. She fell asleep on Benjie's couch, the sting of the tipped barrel completely forgotten, insignificant in comparison to Peter's death.

CHAPTER 6

The day before Peter's funeral, Riley was standing at a filing cabinet behind the reception desk, facing the wall. She heard the front door open, then the office became silent. With the files in her hand she turned to see a distinguished older gentleman and a much younger woman and recognized them as William and Holly Vanderpage. Holly let out a small stifled sob, daubed her eyes with a lacy white handkerchief and leaned heavily on her father, who patted her arm.

"Good morning, Mr. Vanderpage," Fran said respectfully to Peter's father-in-law.

"Good morning," he replied, his voice weary. "May we speak to Robert Prescott? We don't have an appointment." He looked genuinely apologetic.

"Of course, Mr. Vanderpage," she said, focusing on the phone and pushing buttons. After a brief discussion, "He'll be right out," she told him.

There was shuffling and murmuring in the waiting area, the clients not happy with the thought of being upstaged by the intruding couple. Mr. Vanderpage appeared uncomfortable but Holly stood straighter than before, her glossy black heels making her as tall as her father. She scanned the room, and when she saw Riley their eyes locked.

"You!" Holly exclaimed, her emotions erupting.

Mr. Prescott, who had just come from the back hall, hesitated with the outburst.

"What are you doing here?" Holly demanded, her face distorted. "Even now must you be a ghost in my life?"

William Vanderpage gently put an arm around her shoulders, keeping her stationary.

"Just what possible charms could a simpleton rodeo tramp like you possess?" she spat out.

Riley, wide eyed and self-conscious, stood frozen in place. Then Peter's demeanor at the fundraiser came back to her, and anger welled inside. Everyone in the room but Holly was forgotten and before Riley knew it she was standing in front of her, ready to battle. Despite the fact that Holly's heels put her several inches taller, Riley met the hateful glare with her own look of determination. Then she watched Holly's arrogance dissolve to indecision, then doubt, and instead of saying what she wanted Riley heard herself say, "I'm sorry you lost Peter. At least you have his little girls." Then she turned on her heel and disappeared down the back hall, leaving Holly and the gaping crowd behind her.

She hurried down the stairs with the files still in hand, not stopping until she reached the exit. She pushed the doors open to the landscaped courtyard and didn't slow down until she reached a bench. She collapsed on the seat. She didn't notice the sounds of traffic or the sunshine reflecting off the doors when they opened again. It wasn't until Mitch was a few feet away that she saw him, and her unease changed to indifference when she recognized him. She sniffled and looked at the ground. Mitch sat down beside her, took the files and offered a handkerchief.

"Unused, I swear," he said, raising the palm of his hand.

She accepted it, wiped at her eyes and then blew her nose.

"You can keep it," he added with a timid smile.

She choked slightly and looked at him with gratitude. He patted her on the back, his hand lingering.

"You handled that very tactfully," he told her. He brushed away a tear on her cheek.

She looked at her hands and wadded the handkerchief. "That witch," she said, after clearing her throat. "She got what she wanted and it still didn't make her happy. What a waste."

He was silent for a minute. "You can't blame a guy for being stupid once in a while," he offered. "She knew as time went on she couldn't hold a candle to you."

Their eyes met. So he had seen it too, she thought. She had begun to doubt her feeling as to why Holly had lashed out. Her lip trembled and she fought to hold back tears. Mitch put his arms around her and gently pulled her close. His compassion and the physical contact she had been lacking for so long moved her. She relented, no longer trying to contain what was bottled inside. Just as each person mourns for their own reasons, she cried.

When the tears subsided she allowed herself to be held quietly. Then she shook the self-pity and lack of confidence, feeling her resolve coming back. She pulled away and used a corner of the handkerchief to daub her eyes.

"Mascara check," she said, opening her eyes wide.

He smiled and with a thumb wiped a smudge.

She took a deep breath. "I guess this means I won't be going to the funeral, huh?"

Her comment making light of the situation caught him off-guard and his amusement showed. He stood and offered her a hand up. Together they walked back to the building, not touching, but close.

* * *

That Friday after work Riley carried her cooler from her apartment, then she locked the door. She was up in slack early the next morning in the vicinity of Whispering Pines, where Jay Tapperd's shop was, and his tires were in the back of her truck. She was only entered in one rodeo over the Fourth of July weekend, the weekend known in the rodeo world as Cowboy Christmas, because she had overlooked the early deadline for the other holiday rodeos she usually attended. She figured it was for the best. Although she felt she had successfully pushed her frazzled emotions aside all week, she found she was looking forward to the light weekend ahead of her. She was only taking Novocain and she gave the grey gelding two spaces in the horse trailer. Wooly was standing at the back of the trailer, waiting, when she stepped out. She made a quick walk around inspection of the rig and then helped Wooly into the cab.

She was heading down the driveway when Mitch called her apartment. The phone rang several times before it quit.

CHAPTER 7

Red, white and blue pennant banners on the arena fence fluttered in the early morning breeze and the sun made its way over the horizon. The grass was tromped from foot traffic and plastic cups and triangular snow-cone papers littered the rodeo grounds. Novocain, finished with his grain, took a long drink from the bucket at the trailer. Water slobbered from his lips when he lifted his head, splattering the wheel well. He reached for the hay bag and looked around as he ate, as if taunting nearby horses not yet fed because their owners were still sleeping.

Riley relaxed in her camp chair just outside the door of the trailer, dozing occasionally. Wooly lay at her feet. Arriving just before ten o'clock, Novocain had spent the rest of the night tied to the trailer. Riley had fallen asleep shortly after going to bed but partiers woke her, and her sleep after had been fitful. At least her dreams of Peter were becoming less intense, and this one reminded her of the sale of the land. Come Monday, she would look into it. She checked her watch. She would have to get saddled pretty soon and warm up Novocain.

Not far from where she was sitting a trailer's door rattled with commotion. It swung open with a man barely keeping his balance at the threshold. His free hand flailing in the air was holding a boot and his unbuttoned long-sleeved shirt flapped with his movements. As he was losing the battle with gravity a cowboy hat flew over his head from inside the trailer.

"Quiet!" loudly whispered a giggling woman from inside. "You said you'd be quiet!"

He was hopping on the ground, trying to pull the boot on. Tall and slender, his Wranglers fit snug and there was a big belt buckle at his waist.

"There isn't anybody up yet," he retorted, standing and playfully grabbing at the brunette who had emerged at the door. She kept him at arm's length, teasing, and then she saw Riley. She jabbed in the air, causing the cowboy to look at Riley too. He grinned and then did a double-take.

"Whoops," he said, barely loud enough to be heard. He picked up his hat with a smooth motion and started in Riley's direction, putting the hat on as he walked.

"Morning," he said, touching the brim and briefly making eye contact. It was Miles Deroin.

Riley watched him walk away, as did the brunette standing in the trailer door.

* * *

The rodeo grounds were coming to life when Riley rode to the arena. Again she was thankful to be up in slack this morning— the low key setting suited her mood. During Novocain's warm up calves were being herded to pens by the chutes and the rodeo committee attended to things behind the scenes. The arena ground was decent and had been worked earlier that morning. Novocain was feeling good and tried to buck, but by the time the barrels were set on the markers in the arena, she and Novocain were ready.

They had just as nice a run as the weekend before, but this time she didn't lose her concentration and the run went without a hitch. Leaving the arena the announcer gave her time, saying it was the fastest so far. There was a smile on her face as she dismounted and loosened the cinch. She patted Novocain on the neck before walking him, letting him catch his breath, then she stopped him to remove his leg wraps.

"Is that smile for the run itself or the time you posted?" she heard behind her.

She stood with the leg wraps in hand to face Reece Cordhall.

"Well, hello," she said. "Both! At least I rode him right this time." Novocain started to walk around her. "I've got to walk him…" she said, wanting to take care of her horse.

"Mind if I walk with?"

"No, of course not." She maneuvered Novocain beside her.

"Here, let me take those," he said, reaching for the handful of leg wraps.

They walked away from the arena, Novocain still breathing heavily.

"How old is he?" Reece asked.

"Eleven."

"Where're you up next?"

Embarrassed, she said, "I didn't get entered anywhere else this weekend."

His face reflected his surprise.

"It was a bad week," she said, not elaborating. "What about Amy?"

"There's a youth rodeo close to home, but her horse has been off since we got here. I don't know if it's a touch of colic or he's sore or what. We were up late last night with the vet. I happened to be out stretching my legs just now when I heard the announcer say your name, and wanted to see your run."

"I'm sorry to hear about Amy's horse."

They walked in silence for a moment.

"Does she have a backup horse?" Riley asked.

"Her rope horse can run barrels, but, well, that's a waste of time really. The competition is just too tough."

She didn't say anything. She knew what he meant. They continued to walk with Novocain, who was relaxing and his breathing less labored. Riley expected Reece to say he would be heading off, but he didn't.

"Where're you guys from?" she asked.

"We have a ranch about an hour and a half north of here. It's where I grew up... I inherited the place more than bought it. We have a good crew that runs the place now. Between shoeing horses and hauling Amy, there's not much time for me to handle what needs done at home. My wife—she's from New York originally—she got into computers and the stock market, and, well, when they took off, she practically made us millionaires." He said it self-consciously.

"Aren't you lucky," she said laughing.

"Yes, yes, I surely am," he admitted. "I don't know what Anne saw in me all those years ago. We'll also have a boy, Andy. He's sixteen and has Down syndrome. He adores Amy."

They reached her trailer. She slipped Novocain's bridle off and put the halter on. He drank from his bucket and Reece laid the leg wraps on the wheel well. Riley began to unsaddle.

"Would you consider selling him?" Reece asked.

She had just pulled the saddle off and stood with it in her arms, the question taking her by surprise.

"Your gelding?" he said, smiling at her reaction. "Would you consider selling?"

Although the word "no" was forming, her mind was telling her to think about it.

"You going to stand there holding that saddle all morning?" he asked, the smile still on his face.

"What's this?" an attractive woman walking to them asked pleasantly. Despite the muggy morning she looked cool and didn't have a hair out of place. "If my husband's flirting with you, he's not being very gentlemanly about it."

"My wife, Anne," Reece said to Riley. He offered to take the saddle.

"I've got it. You can open the trailer door," she told him, then, "Nice to meet you," she said to Anne.

"Any word on Amy's gelding yet?" Reece asked his wife.

"No," said Anne. "Doc Newmarket called and said he'd be by pretty soon. Amy was all but crying when I left the trailer."

"We'd better head over there." He turned to Riley. "Think about selling, would you? He'd have a good home, and you know he'd be used."

"I will," she promised, more to herself than him.

She untied Novocain and continued to walk him, and half an hour later was still deliberating Reece's inquiry. Giving in to intuition, she made up her mind to let Amy ride Novocain and see what the Cordhalls wanted to do. She had intended to leave for Whispering Pines after her run so she could return the tires before going home, but that could wait. She had no reason to hurry back to Owen.

After tending to Novocain she struck across the fairgrounds in search of Cordhall's trailer, locating it by the veterinary truck that was parked nearby. She overheard the vet giving a dismal recommendation of treatment and turn-out time for the barrel horse due to him having ulcers. Amy did indeed look as though she were holding back tears. Riley didn't know the young girl well enough to know if the tears were for the horse or for herself because she would be without a barrel horse. Amy and her brother, Andy, led the horse away. Reece had a grim look on his face when he saw Riley.

"We've been in worse fixes," he said.

"Not good, huh?" Riley asked, knowing full well it wasn't.

"No. But it could be worse. Doc gave the horse something for pain and he'll get better, but I feel bad for Amy."

"I thought about your asking to buy Novocain," Riley said. "If you're serious I'll price him, but he's going to be high."

Reece's expression went from concern to interest and then he laughed. "I wouldn't expect anything else. When can she try him?"

It wasn't much later when Riley and Amy were working with the big grey. Amy was a good rider and fit Novocain's style. They weren't able to ride in the arena because of other activities going on but Riley felt the horse and girl made a good pair. Reece and Anne apparently thought so too, and the price Riley had quoted, which equaled a year's wages at the reception desk, didn't concern them.

Amy helped put the gelding away after trying him out. Typical for a young girl interested in horses, she had already fallen in love with Novocain. Not only was he a neat horse, but the fact he could make her a winner tugged at Amy's barrel racing dreams. Reece, Anne and Andy were at the trailer when Riley and Amy finished with the gelding.

"Amy, you and Andy let us talk to Riley, okay?" Reece told her.

"Can we get something to eat?" Amy asked.

Reece opened his wallet and handed her a couple of bills. "We'll meet at our trailer in an hour, okay?"

"Sure thing, Dad! Bye, Riley! Bye, Novocain!" she said before they hurried away.

"Nice kids," complimented Riley.

"Thanks. I like to think so," he said. "Amy and Novocain really seemed to hit it off, didn't they?"

"They sure did."

"So, as far as you know, he's sound? No issues?"

"Yes," she said definitively. "I wouldn't lie to you." They had already talked about the maintenance program the gelding was on and the minimal concerns she'd had with him in the past.

"Normally I'd have a vet check done and I did consider asking Doc Newmarket to stick around. But I trust you," he told her, "and this feels right. I do wish we had the chance to let her breeze through the pattern before committing…"

"I don't want you to buy him and then be unhappy, for your sake or his," Riley said. "How about I let Amy make her barrel run on him tonight?"

Reece and Anne exchanged looks, both of them looking like they thought it was a good idea.

"If he wins money and you buy him," Riley went on, "the winnings are yours. If he wins money and you don't buy him, I get fifty percent. If something happens to Amy during the run, I can't be held responsible. If something happens to Novocain while in your care, I expect you to buy him at the price we agreed."

"What do you think?" Reece asked Anne.

"It's up to you," she said.

He looked from Anne to Riley. "If she wins money on him tonight I suspect we'll be buying him."

They shook hands, sealing the deal.

* * *

That evening Riley waited with Amy and Novocain before the run. There was a large crowd present and the bright lights lit up the arena as if it were still day. The announcer and clown were entertaining while the pickup in the arena unloaded barrels.

"Why don't cannibals eat clowns?" the announcer asked the clown.

"Well now, I don't have the slightest idea," replied the clown, raising his arms in mock exasperation. "You'll have to tell me... Why won't cannibals eat clowns?"

"Because they taste *funny*," said the announcer, followed by *ta da da* from the band.

Laughs and moans came from the crowd and Riley smiled. She had heard the joke several times already at earlier rodeos that summer. She was nervous, much more so waiting for Amy's run than if she were the one competing. She had coached Amy during Novocain's warm up and Amy helped put the protective boots on his legs. Amy was riding in her own saddle but Novocain was wearing his usual competition bridle.

Amy was the last to run of the fifteen contestants. The tractor would only make one quick trip around the pattern halfway through the barrel race, and Riley knew the ground would be deep by the time Amy ran. Because rodeos survived in part because of paying spectators it was a priority to keep them entertained—the barrel racers couldn't get catered to with a tractor drag every five runs like the big 4D barrel races.

The timers were set and the barrels in place, and the first of the barrel racers came in. There was no center gate or alley and it took some patience for the riders to position their horses, ready to run, as they entered through the side gate.

"Remember to try to ease him over to where you want him, and then let him go," Riley told her even though they had talked about it earlier. "Don't pick at him—he knows his job."

Amy nodded, looking serious. Riley was excited for the girl but would be glad when the run was over. Novocain had run twice in one day before, and usually his second run was better than his first. But this was a good-sized pen with a big pattern and she hoped Amy could keep his big motor in check. If she let the gelding run too wide open and free he would run past the barrels, or worse, run off with the girl.

The tractor started up and quickly made a couple of passes over the ruts in the ground at the barrels. As soon as it parked the next barrel racer was entering the arena.

"Let him run," Riley continued to coach. "But remember to really check him and say 'whoa' about two strides before the first barrel. I think he'll run hard tonight and I don't want him running off with you."

Amy's eyes got big. Riley didn't intend to scare her but had begun to doubt her idea to let Amy compete tonight. With the noise of the crowd and the horse and rider's adrenalin, the decision could be a wreck just waiting to happen. But, she rationalized, she had confidence in Amy's riding and would have to trust that Novocain was honest enough to do the job he was trained for.

The crowd was cheering as the barrel racer in the arena headed home. Just one more and then it was Amy's turn. Riley looked up at Amy.

"Ready?" Riley asked.

"I think so," Amy said, looking confident but there was a crack in her voice.

"You'll do fine," Riley said with an encouraging smile. "Remember to think about what you're doing all the way through the pattern, not about winning."

Amy nodded. She fidgeted in the saddle and put her minimal weight on her feet in the stirrups. The last contestant before her was rounding the third barrel.

The barrel racer left the arena as the announcer stated her time. "And our last barrel racer of the night is Amy Cordhall. Amy's ranked in the top fifteen this summer. She has to beat Riley Montgomery's time of 18.448 to take over first place."

Riley walked with Amy and Novocain to the gate, and then it was up to Amy. The young rider had both hands on the short reins, and Novocain started hopping when he went through the gate. Amy was looking to the point near the first barrel that she wanted to aim for and was able to hold him as they made their way along the fence in front of the chutes. She wasn't quite ready but Novocain lunged, and she let him go.

Novocain was flying. Riley was afraid they were going to badly overrun the first barrel, but as they closed in Amy shouted "Whoa!" and tugged twice, hard, with both hands. She dropped her outside rein and grabbed for the saddle horn, keeping her inside hand on the rein. Novocain was half a stride past the barrel before he responded, but he snapped back quickly and wasted no time heading to the next one.

Novocain was almost to the second barrel before Amy said "Whoa!" this time but as soon as the word was vocalized he was turning it, so close that Amy lifted her leg to avoid hitting it, a savvy reaction that impressed Riley. They seemed to gather momentum as they raced toward the third. The announcer was talking excitedly and the crowd cheering. She checked him at the third barrel, much like she had at the first two, and Novocain instantly shortened his stride and made a flawless turn. In a blur of big grey horse and small girl in a glittery red shirt and fringe, they sprinted to the finish line.

"Nice run!" said someone from the stands.

Riley exhaled, realizing she had been holding her breath. Amy was pulling at Novocain to stop, which he did just before hitting the gate where Riley was standing. Although Amy's eyes were huge she had a smile from ear to ear.

"She *almost* took the lead!" bragged the announcer. "But Amy Cordhall will have to settle for second with an 18.567. That was beautiful, just beautiful. That big horse didn't even know that little gal was on his back, now did he?"

They were obviously the crowd favorite from the cheers and whistles that were coming from the stands. Riley smiled at the comment of the announcer but knew Novocain had been fully aware of his petite rider—Amy had ridden him just as Riley had coached.

"Good job, Amy," Riley said proudly.

They moved out of the way and Amy dismounted. Riley loosened the cinch so Novocain could get more air and gave him a loving pat. "Good job," she whispered.

Amy threw her arms around Novocain's neck. "Wow," she said. "I've never gone so fast."

Riley gave her a hug. "You did super. You rode him like a champ. I'm proud of you."

"Thank you," Amy said and she hugged Novocain again.

The gelding was beginning to tire of all the attention—this wasn't part of the routine he was used to.

"Let's walk him," Riley said, picking up on the horse's body language.

They didn't have a chance to walk far when Reece and Anne arrived, with Andy right beside them.

"We'd have been over sooner but I had to write a check," Reece said after the hugging and congratulations subsided. "Of course we'll want some coaching now and again."

"I'll be more than happy to," she said. "Amy, would you hold him while I take his boots off?"

"Yes," said Amy, quite happy to take the reins of her horse.

"How about we walk him together?" Riley suggested when she finished her task.

Amy looked at her dad, who gave his okay. "We have stalls," she said. "Dad, can we put him in a stall after?"

"I'll have things ready for you," he told her.

"I'll take those," Andy said to Riley, reaching for the horse boots. He was smiling broadly. "My sister's a winner."

"Yes, Andy, your sister's a winner," she agreed.

CHAPTER 8

Riley swung her legs over the side of the gooseneck bed, dropped to the floor and reached for her long-sleeved shirt the next morning. She slipped her feet into her tennis shoes and put a hand on the trailer door before realizing she didn't have to take care of Novocain. She smiled for Amy because of their awesome run and felt sad at the same time. She would miss her friend and faithful partner. Then she felt Wooly's wet nose against her hand.

"Hold on," she said.

She took a few minutes to get dressed. Instead of just going out to feed Novocain as intended she wanted to say good-bye, and chances were good that she would bump into someone she knew if she went looking like she had just tumbled out of bed.

She was pleased to see that Novocain's bucket had been topped off with fresh water. He had finished his morning grain and was contentedly eating hay. He raised his head to look at her but didn't offer to leave the leafy flake of hay, not even when she spoke to him. Knowing that most horses don't have loyalty to humans like dogs, she didn't take it personally—he had been taken care of and that was all that concerned him for the moment. She turned to leave and saw Anne Cordhall stepping out of the living quarters of their trailer. They waved to each other.

After maneuvering her truck and trailer away from the other rigs, lawn chairs, coolers and even a pair of boots, she made it to the street. She stopped for gas and hot coffee then was on the road to return the tires.

The area of highway previously under repair was finished so there was no longer a detour. The blinker ticked with her intentions to turn off the highway, and she admired the Fourth of July decorations and the tall pines lining either side of the paved road that lead to the heart of Whispering Pines. At the city park women were covering picnic tables with red-and-white material and men unloading grills near a shelter. She drove by a mom-and-pop gas station humming with customers but found the people on the main street downtown were in no hurry.

There were several CLOSED signs on doors. It never occurred to her that Tapperd's might be closed for the day. She passed a small grocery store, Decker's Grocery, as a couple came out. Wanting to satisfy her craving for something sweet and to pick up ice for the cooler, which she had forgotten earlier when getting fuel, she drove around the block and parked in a vacant lot.

"I'll be right back," she told Wooly.

She crossed the street to Decker's and then cased the aisles. Rounding a corner she encountered a man standing in front of the baked goods, looking lost. He was the first African-American she had seen since leaving Owen and currently the only other customer in the store that she was aware of. He was wearing tan carpenter boots and his faded denim coveralls were patched but clean. He was shirtless, revealing well-defined shoulders, and there was sawdust on his shoulders and in his very short hair.

The black man looked up as if she had startled him and she thought how much older his face, complete with beard stubble, looked than what she was expecting. She said hello as she walked by, and guessed he had seen better times in his life.

By the time she finished shopping, except for finding ice, or anything sweet that she wanted for that matter, he was at the checkout. The teenaged checker, popping her chewing gum and looking like she spent her paychecks on hair accessories and makeup, looked at the black man with scorn. On the counter was a loaf of bread, potato salad, lunchmeat and half a gallon of milk and he was digging in his pockets, plunking on the counter what he found.

"Oh, honestly, Ernie, you've got to be kidding me," the girl asserted while eyeing the pile of change, wadded bills and lint in front of her. Grudgingly she counted the money. "Still almost fifty cents short," she said curtly. "What do you want to put back?"

Ernie reached into his pockets again as if maybe he missed something.

"Excuse me, Tiffany," Riley said, reading the checker's name tag. "Here's a dollar."

Tiffany stared defiantly.

"Are you going to take it?" Riley asked, meeting her look.

Tiffany took her eyes away and snatched the dollar then stuffed it in the register. She slammed the change on the counter, chucked Ernie's items in a paper sack and thrust it at him.

Riley slid her basket toward Tiffany, politely said she would also like two bags of ice and asked where she might find them. Tiffany pointed outside as she rang up the items, keeping her eyes on what she was doing.

The large ice chest sat off to one side in front of the store and Riley chided herself for not having seen it earlier. Then she saw Ernie coming her way. Evidently he had been waiting for her.

"Is she always like that?" Riley asked when he got closer, her attention divided between him and the latch on the chest that didn't seem to be working.

He motioned her out of the way, then hit the chest near the handle with the heel of his fist, popping it open.

"No. Usually she's worse," he replied.

She laughed. "I detest rude kids. They just grow up to be rude adults," she said while reaching for the bags.

"Let me carry those for you," he said and took them before she could refuse. "Where you headed?"

She gestured across the street.

Nothing was said while they walked to her trailer. She set the grocery sack inside the primitive living area, got a hold of the cooler and pulled it closer. Ernie handed her the ice.

"Thank you," she said and leaned inside the trailer again.

"I'd better git," he said. "I wanted to say thanks. You're a good person."

"I expect you'd have some argue your opinion," she said with a laugh. "But you're welcome. I'm Riley by the way."

"Nice to meet you. Ernie, Ernie Warden."

"Can I give you a ride, Ernie?" she offered.

He shook his head. "It's not far."

"I need to find Tapperd's Repair Shop. Can you tell me where that is? Is he open today?"

"Jay's open most every day," he said, pointing. "That way. Right by my house. You got troubles?"

"No," she said closing the door. "I've got to settle up with him. I have some of his tires."

"Oh! You're that gal Miles was talking about."

Miles again, she thought. "Get in. Let me give you a ride and you can point the way."

He directed her to the opposite end of town from where she had entered, which in reality was only several blocks. On the corner was a small house with a large metal building beside it that took up most of the remainder of the block. TAPPERD'S

REPAIR in black iron letters adorned the building and the majority of the space in front of the building, and the house as well, was gravel. Riley recognized the utility truck Jay had been driving the day he changed her tires and there was a white flatbed pickup parked near it. Ernie pointed and said that was the place at the same time that Jay Tapperd came out of his house, looking at something he was carrying. He glanced up to see her truck and trailer and his ground-covering stride hesitated, as if he recognized it. Then he moved on, again concentrating on what it was that he was carrying, and disappeared through a large overhead door in the metal building. Riley made the turn and parked on the gravel in the vicinity of the open overhead door. She got out and Wooly stuck his head out the window.

The metal building was larger inside than she expected. Jay was leaning over the front of a Jeep with its hood up. If he was aware of their presence, he didn't show it. Along one wall was a large work bench with machines and tools, jugs of oil and antifreeze. There were a few classic cars covered with dust and lawn mowers and snow blowers parked in neat rows. Three large round fans were spinning, trying to lessen the heat of the summer day.

Ernie carried his groceries to an ancient refrigerator. Riley hung back. Then Ernie walked toward Jay, motioning her to follow. Jay didn't stop what he was doing until they were standing beside the Jeep.

"Hello," he said. He picked up the faded red shop rag from a fender and wiped his callused hands. "You two come in together?" he asked Ernie.

Ernie nodded.

Jay looked at Riley. "How'd you get tangled up with this riff-raff?" he asked.

"She rescued me from the clutches of Tiffany Decker," Ernie told him.

"Ah," said Jay, respecting Ernie's lack of details. He leaned over the engine. "She never gives me any trouble."

"Go figure," Ernie scoffed.

"Guess I'd better get those tires I loaned you," said Jay withdrawing from under the hood.

"I'll get 'em for you, Jay," Ernie said, heading for the door, then he stopped.

"Two sixteen-inch ratty ones," Jay said before Ernie had to ask. "You'll know. Just put them somewhere along the wall."

Ernie continued on his way.

Riley followed Jay to an old wood desk next to the refrigerator. He sat down, rifled through a stack of papers and handed one to her. She wrote the check and Ernie came back, rolling a tire with each hand.

"Your trailer empty?" he asked, raising his voice to carry the distance.

"Yes," she said, and because of the inquisitive look on Ernie's face added, "I got an offer on my barrel horse yesterday at the rodeo, and the rest is history."

Ernie made a grunting noise of approval. Jay didn't say anything and pushed away from the desk to open the door of the refrigerator.

"Got one for me?" Ernie asked expectantly. He left the tires along the wall and crossed the shop floor.

Jay handed Ernie a frosty cold soda and offered one to Riley. She accepted it, told him thank you and then asked if she could let Wooly out. Jay nodded and proceeded to pull out extra chairs. Returning, she sat down and Wooly lay at her feet.

Jay and Ernie bantered local topics and from time to time one would ask Riley what she thought. It finally became quiet except for the hum of the industrial-sized fans and the last of their sodas had turned warm. Then a chain of fireworks went off, prompting Ernie to start in again.

"You going to the picnic an' fireworks tonight?" he asked Jay.

Jay gave Ernie a look as if he should know better than to ask. "I thought they were going to ban them this year because it was so dry."

"Oh, no," Ernie told him. "They decided to have it. Heated discussion, of course. What I heard the committee pushed to get people in town…give the local economy a shot in the arm."

"Politics," said Jay, standing.

Ernie and Riley stood as well. Even Wooly got to his feet.

"What about you, Riley? Going to stick around for the fireworks?" Ernie asked.

"I think I'll head for home," she said.

They walked to the overhead door. A car drove past, crunching gravel that had spilled from the parking area onto the street. It stopped at the T intersection.

"Flat View Road," Riley said, reading the street sign. "Isn't that the road I was on with tire trouble?"

"That's the one," Jay confirmed. "It's about three miles to the Colby place from here. Colby's the name of the folks who owned the place and everyone still calls it that."

"Why is it empty?"

"The well is bad. The place's been empty a few years now."

They watched the car disappear in the distance, then Ernie looked at Jay as if waiting for the conversation to continue. When Jay gave no indication, Ernie began.

"Cap Henderson's been trying to buy it from Chloe—Ms. Colby—but she won't have none of it. She knows he'd doze the house and she doesn't want that."

"That's too bad. It could be a cute place," Riley said.

"Corbin and Chloe kept it real nice in their day," he went on. "The farm used to be a lot bigger, almost a thousand acres, but it got sold off over the years. Corbin farmed and ranched and Ms. Colby taught school to all the local kids, including me an' Jay. Well, she tried to teach us," he said with a grin directed at Jay. "Ms. Colby did some rodeoing too, and she was pretty good. Then after Corbin died of a heart attack, she quit teaching and started rodeoing full time, said life was too short not to do what a person wanted. That was back in the mid-sixties if I remember right." He slapped at a fly buzzing his bare, black shoulder. "Ms. Colby once said there's a spring back there, somewhere behind the house, with enough water for the whole town. But nobody believed her. I think folks just didn't want to mess with her or Cap. When she dies then Cap'll probably get it bought."

"Maybe that's what's keeping her alive," Jay said dryly. "To keep Cap from getting it."

A car pulled up in front of the shop and an elderly man struggled with the door getting out. Jay made his way to the car.

"Who's Cap?" she asked Ernie.

"The no-good that farms the place now," he said, then he was turning. He went to the refrigerator and got his sack of groceries out of it.

"Are you sure I can't give you a ride?" she asked when he came back.

"C'mere." He walked a few yards further and then stopped, looking at her.

She walked to him and he gestured to a large old house across the street from Jay's, gleaming with fresh paint. The wraparound porch was beautiful with ornate molding and railings.

"Yours?" she asked doubtingly.

He nodded. "It's on the historic register. Most the exterior restoration was grant money." He set his groceries on the ground.

"I was a pretty fair carpenter in my day. Then my wife left me an' I started drinking. I was the town drunk for a time...just got sober last year." He forced a smile and swallowed. "After I sobered up, nobody'd hire me. Well, they would for the sh—" He stopped and looked apologetic. "They would for the crappy jobs they didn't want to do themselves, but that was it. I needed something to do to keep occupied, keep my mind off the booze. That's when I applied for the grant money and got it." He was looking down and scuffed the gravel with the toe of his work boot. "I sometimes go out with only spare change, without my wallet, like today—I started doing that when I wanted to quit so I wouldn't have money to buy the stuff. Old habits are hard to break...and besides, the town expects it." He remained looking at the ground.

"And here I was beginning to think you were hustling me," she said lightly, touched by his story and not knowing what was appropriate to say.

"Aw, I'd never do anything like that," he said looking at her as if to make sure she believed him. "I've learned a lot though. Like those years I pissed away. I'll never get those back, but I can't do anything about that now. Just like my wife running off. Well, maybe I could've done something different about that...maybe if I'd have been different she wouldn't have left. But I treated her pretty good, I thought. I guess that's a choice she made." He looked away again. "I think God's got a funny sense of humor. I mean, He lets us make choices, then I think He just sits back to see what happens, how things play out. Guess He just shook His head at me. But I'm trying now."

She smiled affectionately.

"You talking her leg off, Ernie?" Jay said to him, not wasting time as he walked by on his way to the overhead door. "By god you used to be the town Einstein and then always smashed—you gonna go to Bible thumpin' college now and become a preacher or something?"

Ernie, embarrassed with the realization that Jay had overheard, retorted, "If I do I expect to see you in the front pew ever Sunday morning, Brother Jay."

A closemouthed smile showed on Jay's face. "Put those groceries back in the fridge," he directed. "I need you to take me out to Freddie's so I can bring Mae's car back to work on." He reached inside for the button to close the overhead door. "He's got to wait in town on her or he'd give me a ride himself. Lock the walk-in door when you come out." Jay continued to move as he spoke. "Or do you have something better to do? You gotta fill out Bible school applications or something?"

"Nope, nope, I'd be happy to help, you know that," Ernie said while picking up his sack and scurrying to get under the door before it got too low. "Riley, why don't you come with? I'll buy your lunch when we get back—I owe you fifty cents!" The closing door showed only the bottoms of his coveralls.

"You'd be doing me a favor if you came along," Jay told her. "It'd keep him from talking to me."

They grinned at each other.

Ernie popped out the walk-in door a second later. "We'll be going right by the Colby place," he said and pulled the door shut. "I haven't been out there for a coon's age and I'd enjoy having a snoop. This got me thinking. If it doesn't rain pretty soon we might have to tap into all that water Chloe Colby says is there."

"Is that okay if Wooly comes along?" she called out to Jay, who was already headed to his old flatbed.

"Sure," he replied.

At Freddie's, Ernie and Riley waited until Jay got Mae's car started. He headed back to town with it and they followed in Jay's flatbed.

"What did Jay mean when he called you the town Einstein?" Riley asked Ernie as he drove.

"Oh, he just said that 'cause I helped design and fabricate some things for him for a government job once. He actually made quite a bit of money off that when he got the bugs worked out. He thinks I'm a lot smarter than I am. I always seemed to be able to figure my way around things and I have a knack for coming up with oddball stuff. I made a bit years ago for Ms. Colby when her barrel horse quit working. What her and I fashioned together was just the ticket and that ol' gelding went back to taking her to the pay window."

The Colby place came into view, first the barn with the tree on it and then the house. Jay continued on toward to town. The dust he generated drifted over the realtor sign in the yard.

"Damn shame about that tree," Ernie mused before he turned into the driveway. "I think it was lightning… Guess it was pure luck there wasn't a fire." The flatbed rolled to a stop in front of the barn and then Ernie looked at the house. "I don't know why I parked clear over here," he said, talking to himself.

They got out and Wooly headed for the front porch. Riley wondered if the kittens were still there.

"Ms. Colby'd have a fit if she knew the place had gone downhill this bad," said Ernie. "Sad, downright sad. 'Course Ms. Colby isn't a spring chicken herself anymore."

"Where is she?"

"Old folk's home south of town. Been there several years now. Her mind was still sharp last I heard but her body's giving out. No family around to take her in."

Wooly let out a soft "woof". He had found the kittens.

"It's probably not locked," Ernie said.

"What?"

"The house. I bet the back door's not locked."

"Serious?"

"Sure. Oh, I 'spect the front door is, but not the back. What if somebody needed to get to the cellar?"

"For what?"

"Hidey hole, in case of cyclone. Twister. You know, tornado."

She thought maybe he was pulling her leg. Ernie started for the house, leaving her. She jogged to catch up.

Ernie was right. The back door opened with a creak. They brushed cobwebs out of the way and entered the small, outdated kitchen. Battered wainscot covered the bottom half of the walls and there was stucco on top. Ernie pointed to a large trapdoor in the floor.

"Hidey hole," he said. "Watch for snakes."

She threw him a startled look.

"I haven't seen any rattlers for a couple years," he said with a grin at her reaction. "But keep your eyes open. With the house being closed up this long, you never know. And watch it if you go in the well house too."

"That little shed behind the house?" she asked.

Ernie nodded. "That's where the pump is."

She glanced about, her skin crawling, but soon became distracted. The door was open on the dusty oven, the sink had faded material hanging under it and the refrigerator was older than the one in Jay's shop.

"Did Jay say somebody lived here a few years ago... *like this?*" she asked.

Ernie was on his way down the cellar stairs. "Sure. The roof's good, isn't it?" he replied, out of view and his voice echoing.

"How is it?" she asked, moving to the edge and looking down.

"Dirty, but not too bad. I was wondering if I could get an idea of where that spring was."

"From the cellar?"

"Old folks, 'specially old folks like the Colby's, would leave stuff laying around. Like this paperwork on the furnace when it was replaced." He blew dust off the papers in his hand.

She withdrew from looking in the cellar and walked down the hall that led to a bathroom, more outdated than the kitchen, and then a bedroom. She came back, passed through the old kitchen and made the step up into the larger side of the house, an addition when the owner was apparently experiencing good times. She walked across the first room to the second, the fallen plaster crunching under her boots. When she reached the front door she gazed through the glass at the tall spruce tree.

"Shame, just a shame," said Ernie joining her and looking at the ceiling. "But it looks worse than it is. I helped put the new roof on. Too bad my credit's still in the toilet, this place could be a real project." He went around a corner and disappeared. Riley heard him on the stairs and then overhead. A minute later he returned. "I remember a wood burning stove in here," he recollected. "By that wall."

"What about the furnace? Plumbing? Wiring?" she asked, not listening.

He shrugged his bare shoulders. "The furnace looked okay," he said deliberately as if he was thinking about too many things at one time. "Plumbing probably needs work from being shut down so long, dry seals and such. Wiring...it'd best be replaced. And new insulation too. The foundation looked okay, but then I didn't really look at it." He stopped. "Why?"

She didn't answer. She wasn't sure herself.

"You interested in the place?"

"I don't know. I hadn't considered it before now." She chewed her lip. "I've got some money but, as stupid as it sounds, I don't know how much."

His face went blank. "How can a person not know?"

"It's a long story. Plus, what would I do for a job out here?"

He took in a deep breath and his shoulders went up again. "The way I see it, computers are really going to change things. You could work from home. Are you educated?"

She laughed. "I get by."

"No offense a' course!"

"None taken. Let's go see about that spring out back," she suggested.

They left the way they came and walked past the well house. Several yards further, along the fence line and off to one side of a small, overgrown orchard, Ernie looked for signs of where he thought the spring might be, but with no luck.

"Let's get a bite to eat then go visit Ms. Colby," he proposed.

She agreed. She found herself interested in the possibilities the little farm, and change, had to offer.

When Riley asked Jay if she could leave her trailer parked for a while, not only did he say yes but he strung one of his extension cords from the shop to her trailer. She started the air conditioner and saw to it that Wooly was comfortable before using her portable phone. Dialing Benjie's number with intentions of leaving a message asking if he would check on her horses, she was surprised to hear him answer.

"I didn't suppose you'd be in," she told him.

"I'm bored to death," he said. "I passed up the chance to go away for the weekend because of the Stones and their country club venture, but they postponed. I'm about to crawl up the wall. When're you going to be home? Want to do something?"

"That's why I called," she said, knowing he would be disappointed. "I'm not coming back today. Remember that farm where I stayed overnight when I had tire trouble?"

"I remember the realtor flyer."

"That's the place. A carpenter and I just came from there... My common sense is arguing with my want to."

"Whaaaat?"

She laughed at his reply and because of the giddy way she was feeling. "I've met some really good people here. Ernie, he's the carpenter I mentioned, and I are going to talk to the woman who owns the farm. I don't have any reason to hurry home, and besides," she added to give Benjie the opportunity to reply with his brand of amused sarcasm, "there are fireworks tonight."

"Fireworks?" was all he said.

"It's fireworks or driving home in the dark."

"How far is the drive?"

"I don't know…three or four hours I guess. That's with a trailer."

"Would one more be welcome? A road trip sounds awesome, even by myself…" he paused as if thinking. "I don't relish the thought of staying home all day on Independence Day."

"You bet! I don't know if there is a motel or something not already full, but I have room in the trailer." She tried to recall if she had seen a motel in Whispering Pines—she didn't think so. Benjie was talking again but Riley was distracted by a white Saturn pulling onto the gravel.

"…shower, check on your horses and head out," he said.

She watched Jay came from the shop. He rested a hand on the door of the Saturn. The dark-haired woman inside laughed delightedly at what he said to her.

"…but you've got to tell me where you are," said Benjie.

She told him, they told each other good-bye and she put the phone in its bag. The woman backed away and was gone, but the sound of her laughter lingered in Riley's ears.

When Riley and Ernie went to lunch at Wanda's, the small cafe on main street, Jay went with them. The establishment was full with the Fourth of July crowd and the sounds of cutlery and chatter filled the room. Riley felt their stares while she waited with Jay and Ernie. After a short wait a middle-aged woman ushered them to a table. Her name tag said "Marie" and she had a haircut that any rebellious youth in Owen would be proud to have, Riley thought, with longer hair framing her face and short hair on the back of her head. Her nose was long and narrow and the haircut only seemed to draw attention to it. Marie was rather inquisitive but pleasant and seemed to be hitting on Ernie. Riley teased him about it after Marie took their order and left.

"No way," Ernie argued.

"Told you," Jay insisted. "He wouldn't believe me."

Mortified, probably more from Jay having said it than the fact itself, Ernie covered his face with his hands and moaned.

CHAPTER 9

Whispering Pines Retirement Home was appropriately nestled in a grove of pines on the outskirts of town. The receptionist at the desk viewed Riley curiously and made small talk with Ernie before divulging Chloe's room number.

"I feel like a celebrity hanging out with you," Riley said in jest when they were alone. They moved to the side of the wide hall to make room for an aide pushing a cart with medications and paper cups.

"Where do you come up with this stuff?" Ernie objected but looked flattered. "I used to work here, years ago," he confided, and nodded to confirm. "Odd jobs and such. It used to get me a lot of carpenter business from the residents' families when they'd stumble across me doing work here. I still do things here from time to time when they need it. That's me—Odd Job Ernie." He switched from talking to mouthing the names of occupants on the doors and then said prolifically, "Chloe Colby."

Chloe was napping in an overstuffed chair. There was a wheelchair next to it. The small woman's face was full of wrinkles from years of being outdoors and her thick long braid laying over one shoulder was completely white. Ernie motioned to the well-used saddle displayed in a corner, the imprint "All Around Cowgirl 1967" barely visible.

Chloe stirred and opened her eyes, fighting to come awake when she realized someone was in the room.

"Hello, Mrs. Colby," Ernie said, raising his voice and kneeling in front of her. "Do you remember me? Ernie Warden?"

"Ernie," she said warmly. "Of course I remember you. Why, you're all grown up now."

"I brought someone to see you. This is Riley Montgomery," he told her.

Chloe took note of the ponytail, blue jeans and boots. "What do you want?" she asked.

Riley and Ernie exchanged looks.

"We've been out to your place, the Colby place," Ernie explained. "We were wondering about the spring you once said was out back."

A wistful look came over Chloe's face and she leaned back in the chair.

"Riley here might be interested in buying if there's water," Ernie said.

"You're not from around here, are you?" Chloe interrogated.

"No...I live outside of Owen," Riley replied.

"What do you do for a living?"

"I work as a receptionist for a law firm in Owen to pay the bills, but to live I ride horses and do some barrel racing."

"Any good at it?"

Riley smiled at the practical question. "Sometimes."

Chloe looked satisfied with the answer. "Know how to rope?"

"Yes, but I'm not very good at it."

"Single?"

"Excuse me?"

"A man in your life?" Chloe prodded.

Riley smiled and shook her head. "No, no man.

Chloe, softening, chuckled. "They can be a lot of trouble, can't they? No offense, Ernie. I admit I was pretty lucky with my Corbin... Men like that don't come along every day. Miss Montgomery, please forgive my belligerence. I shouldn't be so suspicious, but I'm not going to have Cap Henderson sending someone in here to buy the place so he can get his hands on it. He farms that bit of tillable ground and wants to plow the whole place under. Damn farmers." With a gnarled hand she reached for the tiny paper cup on the nearby over-the-bed table. She took a sip, rested her arm in her lap, leaned back again and closed her eyes. The cup tipped, threatening to spill. Ernie took it and set it on the table. "Did Cap mow?" she asked, her eyes still closed. "He's supposed to mow and keep an eye on things."

Riley thought about the sorry condition of the yard.

"Yes, he did," Ernie lied.

Chloe cleared her throat and opened her eyes. "There's water there," she confirmed. "Corbin found it one summer it was so dry, much like this year has been. It's over by the fence line, by that catalpa tree. There are...were raspberries there too. Muley Jones would remember."

Ernie and Riley exchanged looks again. She had seen the tree with large heart-shaped leaves.

"Muley?" said Ernie. "I haven't seen him since I don't know when."

"Get Muley. He'll find it for you. I'll pay for it." Chloe looked at Riley through tired eyes. "That house needs someone in it, someone who cares."

Riley placed her hand over Chloe's. "We'll talk later, okay?"

Chloe's reply was a silent nod.

They called Muley from Jay's shop. Muley wasn't home, but his wife said she would have him call when he got in. Ernie continued with small talk on the phone but Riley wasn't listening. She was hoping that Muley would be available to look for and, with a bit of luck, locate the spring.

CHAPTER 10

Wooly cocked his head, recognizing the sound of Benjie's Mazda as it rolled to a stop outside. Riley watched the big dog's tail swing back and forth lazily as he made his way across the shop. She heard Benjie greet the dog, then she heard another familiar voice.

"Fran!" Riley exclaimed and went to meet them. "What a great idea, Benjie."

"I thought so," he replied.

"You look nice," Riley told Fran, who was wearing shorts and once again the color of her top brought out the highlights in her short hair.

"I have to keep up with Benjie," Fran justified. "Isn't that red shirt perfect with his silver hair? And to think it's *natural*...that just makes me mad."

Riley laughed at Fran. "I gotta warn you, Benjie, ponytails are frowned on out here unless you're a girl."

"I'll watch my back," he replied indifferently, distracted with the sight of old metal advertisements mounted on a wall, forgotten over time by their owner.

Jay continued to work on Freddie's car, evidently used to others being in the shop while he worked. Benjie headed for him.

"The stuff you have collecting dust on your walls would go over big in Owen," Benjie said to Jay when he got closer.

Jay looked up from what he was doing, then from Benjie to the walls. He reached for a shop rag and wiped his hands.

"Oh?" he said.

"Yeah. Old is new again."

"You're practically drooling," Riley told him.

Benjie chuckled but made no apologies. He extended a hand to Jay. "Jameson Benjamin—everyone calls me Benjie."

"I don't think you'd appreciate that," Jay said still wiping his hands.

"I expect you are right," Benjie said, noticing.

"Nice to meet you anyway. Tapperd, Jay."

"Mind if I get a closer look?"

"Knock yourself out. There's more in the corner"—he pointed—"behind those mowers needing work."

Benjie's eyes revealed his excitement.

"You sure keep some things to yourself," Fran told Riley, referring to Jay.

Riley introduced Fran and explained to Jay that they worked together.

"Is this yours?" Fran asked, indicating the shop with a sweep of her hand.

"Yes, ma'am," he said before there was a clatter coming from Benjie's direction. "Excuse me."

"Handy man, I like that. And polite too," said Fran after he left. Then she saw Ernie coming through the open overhead door. He had shaved and put on a white sleeveless T-shirt under the coveralls.

"Had to take a bit of a nap," Ernie confessed as he came closer.

"You know this guy too?" accused Fran. "You *have* been holding out on me."

Riley again made introductions, adding, "Fran appears to be wound up today."

"It's Benjie," Fran validated. "He's so charming. And that hint of accent! Do you live here?" she asked Ernie.

"In Whispering Pines? Yes."

"Quaint town. I must admit it's gorgeous out this way."

"It's nice, I guess. Small, simple," Ernie admitted. "You know how it is when you live the same place your whole life."

Fran nodded, although she didn't know. "Is there a motel close by?"

"There's one. It's a dive, but even so the town's pretty full of people for the fireworks so it's most likely full," he said and then hesitated. "My...my house is set up to be a bed and breakfast. Nobody's ever stayed there...but there's no reason why you can't if you want."

Fran was interested, willing him to continue.

"They can bunk with me," Riley said, not sure if Ernie really meant it. "There's enough room in the trailer and I have a spare cot."

"No, it's okay," he said firmly. "If they want to stay at my house, they're welcome."

"And just where might that be?" asked Fran.

Ernie went back out the door he had just entered and pointed. "Right there."

Fran walked smartly across the shop. She looked where he pointed, doubt all over her face. She followed through with raised brows. "Where?"

"That one."

"That one?"

He nodded and a self-conscious smile appeared.

"Holy smokes. Wait 'til Benjie gets a load of this! Breakfast too?"

Ernie blushed, the color obvious despite his dark skin.

"Give the guy a break, Fran," said Riley, laughing. "He's a humble bachelor not used to having people in his house, let alone making breakfast too."

Fran clearly made note of the fact he wasn't married. "So true. My apologies, Ernie. I'm getting too old to be patient. Where're the fireworks going to be?"

"City park," Ernie told her. "You probably saw it on your way into town."

"You coming with?" she asked him.

"I…I think so," he stammered.

"Of course he is," Riley said hooking an arm in his. "Wouldn't have it any other way. Ernie and I are becoming quite good pals. Rumors are probably circulating already. And I've got to give him credit for giving me the idea to buy the Colby place… Remember I told you about having to stay overnight at that abandoned place when I had tire trouble?"

Fran gaped. "Riley! What would I do without you at the office? You wouldn't leave me alone with Cynthia!"

Riley laughed again. Then there was a racket from across the room as one of the metal advertisements fell from Jay's grasp, high on a ladder. Benjie retrieved it as if it were an architectural find.

"It's okay," he assured. "I have just the place in mind for this one," he said to himself.

Benjie carefully leaned his new acquisition against the others. Jay descended the ladder while looking at Benjie like he was a little boy on Christmas morning.

"Ernie, I've got a couple of things to take care of," Jay told him. "Would you see that everybody gets to the park when they're ready? I'll be over later."

"Yes, sir," said Ernie. He turned to Fran. "How about I show you my place now?"

Benjie, joining them, had a puzzled look on his face.

"You're going to love this!" Fran said.

It was just a minute's walk to Ernie's house, with Benjie asking questions about the restoration the entire time.

"Do you think about decorating constantly?" Riley teased. She, Fran and Ernie went up the stairs to the wraparound porch but Benjie hung back, admiring.

"This lacks only wicker furniture, hanging plants and wind chimes to make it worthy of a movie set," he commented.

The solid oak door opened to a foyer and a classic ornate staircase. Ernie started up the steps. Fran slid her hand across the smooth rail as they went up, Benjie's eyes took in every detail and Riley admired the living room below. Upstairs was three large bedrooms, each with its own up-to-date bathroom. The rooms were free of clutter, each bed was made and the dressers had runners and few knick-knacks. Benjie, of course, appreciated the woodwork and architecture while Fran was smitten by Ernie's tidiness and obvious organizational skills. Ernie told them his room was downstairs and they could have their pick of these.

After making their choices they walked the several blocks to the holiday festivities that were already in full swing. They skirted the caterers and Ernie led the way to the end of the line. The receptionist from the nursing home and Marie, the waitress from the café, were not far in front of them. The pair of women and others looked at the outsiders joining the line. Ernie and Benjie were deep in conversation about Ernie's house and Fran rolled her eyes, wanting to have some time of her own to talk to Ernie.

Their chit-chat slowed when they reached the choices of plump hot dogs, burgers, baked beans, chips, coleslaw and every desert imaginable. After filling their plates they found an empty picnic table. The waxy surface of the checkered tablecloth in the muggy evening air held their paper plates like a magnet and water rings accumulated under the plastic cups. Occasional firecrackers went off and talk recommenced after people ate their fill. Riley had gone back for dessert when Jay arrived. She smiled when she saw him and offered him a plate.

As darkness fell the focus switched to the fireworks display. Families had spread out blankets or set up chairs while others remained seated at the picnic tables. The night became filled with color and loud booms, periods of suspenseful waiting and approval from the crowd.

After the exhibition the onlookers dispersed, some walking while others jockeyed their vehicles from parking spaces. Riley and her friends made their way toward Jay's shop, taking their time. Away from the well-lit streets they watched flickering lightning bugs give their own simple show. A rumbling train could be heard in the distance and the air smelled of spent fireworks.

Riley let Wooly out of her air-conditioned trailer and then she joined the others standing outside Jay's shop. Jay informed them that Muley had called and said he would meet them the next morning at the Colby place. Riley was surprised that Jay didn't offer beer to anyone, thinking perhaps he didn't out of respect for Ernie. A straggling series of firecrackers went off. Ernie dug in his pockets. Riley smiled as she reminisced how their friendship had begun. Ernie happened to look at her, and smiled back.

"Look what I bought," he said holding up lottery tickets. "I figured my day was going so well I should try my luck."

"You do know your chances of getting struck by lightning are better than winning the lottery?" Jay said.

"Doesn't matter. Besides, you don't have to win the lottery to be a winner," Ernie said matter-of-factly.

* * *

Ernie sat in his recliner, listening to the sound of Fran and Benjie in their bedrooms overhead. It was odd having others in the house again, but he liked it. It was dark except for the lamp near his chair and he was tired, but his mind wasn't ready for sleep. His thoughts went to a previous July 4th when he had arrived home to discover his wife had left town with another man—a much younger white man. He wondered how he had ever made it through those years. He should have left the town with its cruel comments behind his back, but he didn't have even the ambition for that. Now he was thankful, and a little proud, that he had gotten back on track to have beaten the bottle. It was difficult, some days much harder than others.

He thought of Riley smiling at him like he was somebody. She had welcomed him as being included as one of her friends, and they had accepted him too, without giving it a second thought. He thought of Marie and Shirley, the receptionist at the nursing home. They had actually *looked* at him today, and he thought about Fran. He was experiencing something he hadn't in a long time, something he had forgotten even existed. He couldn't put his finger on it, but he felt like he was ready to live again.

Jay flipped off the light in his living room, walked to the bedroom and undressed in the dark. He got in bed and watched the ceiling fan slowly circulating above, illuminated only by the street light intruding through the top half of the window. He was usually able to ignore his feelings, but in the darkness and silence they would sometimes come back. Every day he tried to keep busy working in the shop, dealing with other people's problems, tiring himself to the point that when the day came to an end he would quickly fall asleep.

He reflected on the satisfying day, mostly seeing Riley's face. She had many of the same facial expressions Molly did, especially her quirky smile when something amused her. He found himself avoiding looking at her because he was afraid she would see him looking. He was thankful her laugh did not have the same ring Molly's did, if he was remembering right.

It was a lifetime ago, and he knew he should be over it by now. They were typical carefree young adults who thought the rules didn't apply to them. Their entire summer had been full of rodeoing and partying, every free moment spent together. Molly wanted to get married and he finally gave in. They had a simple outdoor wedding. Both were doing well in their respective rodeo events, his steer wrestling, hers barrel racing and break-away roping, and both were contenders for top spots going into the finals. She began to plan the honeymoon she wanted and they would leave the week after the finals.

Life was good. Then she began to get moody and sick, especially in the mornings. He felt naive but happy when she returned from the doctor's office and told him she was pregnant. The doctor said it was okay for her to compete at the finals, after all she was only six weeks along. Jay had already bought the house and the shop was being built. Molly's center of attention turned from her barrel horse to redecorating the house, especially a room for the nursery.

The weekend before the finals they attended a friend's wedding. The reception was typically rowdy and boisterous and Jay, as usual, drank too much. Molly had quit drinking because of the baby and was the one driving her Mustang on the way home that rainy night. Cattle were out on the highway; the little car hit one of them on Molly's side and rolled the car into the ditch. It was several hours before the accident was discovered. Jay's big drunken body with minor injuries had been pinned in the car. He was unable to move but was conscious much of the time.

Laurie Hartman

They all said Molly had died instantly, but he knew better. He had heard her curse before hitting the cow, the screeching of the tires, the thump. He remembered the sound of crunching metal as the car rolled, and her whimpering after the car came to a stop. He could not reach her, could not even touch her. He blamed himself, and he never drank another drop of alcohol after that.

CHAPTER 11

The morning quiet was broken by Benjie's laughter echoing in Jay's shop. He vigorously scrubbed one of the metal signs in a large tub, sloshing water on the coveralls he had borrowed from Ernie that were too big. Jay had paperwork spread across his desk but was making no progress with Benjie around, and didn't seem to mind.

"It's about time you got up!" Benjie exclaimed when Riley came in.

"Nice duds," she replied.

"I brought extra clothes along, but not for this!"

She wasn't ready to deal with her zealous friend so early in the day. Her eyes went to Jay and the chipped white mug with vapor rising from it that he was holding. He motioned to the pot a few feet away. She smiled gratefully.

Wooly lay on the concrete beside her chair. She sipped her coffee, appreciating the pungent aroma and easy silence. She rubbed Wooly with her foot. Benjie started to whistle a tune.

"Did I detect an accent?" Jay asked Riley.

"Yes, but I don't know where he's from. He's never told me much about his personal life, and I've never asked."

They watched Benjie and after another lapse of unspoken rapport, Riley inquired about Fran and Ernie.

"Benjie said they were talking about making omelets when he left," Jay said.

Riley choked on her coffee. Their eyes met and they smiled. Jay got up to turn on the big fans. On his way back the phone on the desk rang. It was Ernie, inviting them over for breakfast.

* * *

A breeze kicked up by the time they arrived at the Colby place and puffy white clouds crept across the blue sky. Benjie was in full-blown decorator mode, making exterior recommendations before he got out of the car. He made a beeline to the front yard, wanting to get a better look at the front of the house. After seeing whatever it was that he wanted, he sidled up to Riley and whispered, "I can see you living here," and then he was gone, hurrying to catch up to Ernie who was at the back door.

Inside the smell of plaster and abandon was stronger than Riley remembered. Benjie quickly scrutinized the small kitchen, bathroom and bedroom, but slowed his pace after making the step into the first of the two large rooms, having found inspiring potential. He made noises and took notes and Riley shadowed him, up the enclosed stairs and then back down. Benjie was heading for the front door when Fran, like a curious kid, flipped a light switch and squealed when it popped.

"The power's on?" said Benjie incredulously.

"I'd better check," Ernie said, troubled.

Benjie progressed to the door and fresh air wafted in after he finally got the door open.

"I'd completely take out this room's ceiling," he said enthusiastically, stepping over fallen plaster and motioning to the damage above. "Make it cathedral, remove that ghastly wall hiding the stairs and make a loft of that half the upstairs. Part of this wall would come out and the kitchen put there—under the loft, the old kitchen made into a laundry and mud room, the bathroom remodeled and updated, the downstairs bedroom left as a spare or an office. This all needs to be torn out anyway, right?" He looked for Ernie. "Where's Ernie?"

"Yes," Ernie confirmed, returning. "Everything needs to be gutted. I'd recommend new wiring and the insulation will have to be replaced. I'd have to see the plumbing to say what it needs." Then to Riley, "I shut the power off to the house but the yard light'll still come on at night."

Benjie put his hand on the wall between the two large rooms. "This, I take it, is a load bearing wall?"

Ernie nodded.

"But it could be partially knocked out to open up this space, right?"

Ernie nodded again.

"I can see the kitchen sink there… You know, instead of having a window to look out Riley will look into this room," Benjie told them. "Let's check out the foundation and cellar," he proposed to Ernie, and started that way.

"You know, he's right," said Fran. "This could be beautiful. Very spacious yet cozy."

Riley was inspired with Benjie's enthusiasm and ideas but held back. "What about a job? I can't just move out here without some kind of income."

"I don't know," said Fran. "Train horses, give riding lessons… Don't they walk crops to cut weeds?" She grinned.

Riley smiled feebly, feeling apprehensive. "Let's find Ernie and Benjie."

They found them in the cellar, the door in the floor of the dated kitchen leaning against the wall. Riley descended the steps, but Fran preferred to stay where she was.

"The furnace and foundation look okay," Ernie was saying. "The plumbing obviously needs work but with the remodeling, what needs to be replaced could get swapped then."

"Don't forget we've got to find out about the water situation first," Riley reminded.

Benjie frowned. "When's that guy supposed to be here to look at the well?" he asked.

Benjie grew tired of waiting for Muley, and he and Fran headed back to Owen. Riley took Ernie's car to town to pick up lunch. When she returned Muley's truck was parked behind the house and the men near the tree that Chloe had described.

"Looks good, Riley!" Ernie shouted and gave her a thumbs up. "Muley says there's water here, and he can get it to the house."

Riley was not all that surprised, thinking from the beginning that Chloe knew what she was talking about.

Muley was a big, tanned man about the same age as Ernie and Jay, with a ball cap on his head and a wad of tobacco in his mouth.

"So, if I can swing this place," Riley asked him, "what exactly needs to be done with the water?"

"Would 'ave to dig a new well an' install new pipe to the house is all, barrin' no problems," he said. "Me an' the boys, we don't have anything goin' on right now. We could 'ave a new well dug in a week an' water to the house. Barrin' no problems, of course." He spit.

"You don't think there would be any complications?" Riley pressed, watching him.

His mouth puckered in a funny shape and he shook his head. "Looks purdy routine. No trees 'tween here an' the house to deal with."

She believed him. She looked at Ernie, who had a satisfied smile on his face. She gave him a quick hug, which embarrassed him. "Thank you, Ernie," she told him. "We need to go visit Mrs. Colby."

Chloe was sitting outside with other residents who had visitors. Her face lit up when she recognized Ernie and Riley.

"Hello!" she said and motioned to the bench beside her. "Did you get Muley out to the farm?"

"Yes, we just came from there," Riley said, sitting down. "Muley did find water, just where you said it was."

Chloe gave Ernie a "told you so" look and then asked Riley, "So what do you think of the place?"

"I find I'm falling in love with it, to tell you the truth."

"Good," said Chloe, delighted. "Let's talk."

And they did. Chloe and Riley talked so long about so many things that Ernie left and came back later, because Riley needed the ride. And when Riley left the nursing home that day, she no longer thought of Chloe as an old woman who owned a farm that she wanted to buy, but as the grandmother she never knew.

CHAPTER 12

Due to a heavy workload that Monday, Riley wasn't able to get away from the law firm to talk to the bank about a loan. She was frustrated and found herself frowning at the sound of the door opening at fifteen minutes before closing. There were no more appointments scheduled and all the lawyers were gone except Mitch Matthews. She pasted a smile on her face and was surprised when she looked up to see Mr. Vanderpage, Peter's father-in-law. She expected Holly too, but he was alone.

"Hello, Mr. Vanderpage," she said standing to greet him. "I'm afraid Mr. Prescott has already left for the day."

"I'm here to see you, actually," he said and laid his briefcase on the tall reception desk.

"Me?"

"Yes. But first, I must apologize for Holly's outburst. She had no right."

Although Riley agreed she said, "I'm sure she was under a lot of stress."

He looked at her gratefully. "I must say this visit will be much more pleasant than the one previous." He clicked open the briefcase and took out a white envelope. "I personally wanted to give you this. It's a check for your share of the money from the land that you and Peter bought together. The land in fact sold a few years ago, about the time the twins were born. It was a difficult pregnancy and they were premature. The only things Peter accomplished during that time was taking care of Holly and the girls and working just enough to satisfy his clients. Holly was...quite needy during that time."

"She doesn't know about the money," he continued. "Peter asked me to handle it in the beginning. The market was excellent at the time of the sale and it sold for several times what you two paid for it. It generated marginal interest when I managed it, but when Peter got his hands on it... You hadn't asked about it so I guess he felt he could take some liberties. Nothing risky, mind you, but you know Peter." His eyes glistened and he went from addressing Riley to staring at the envelope.

Riley rounded the large desk and was still comforting him when Fran and Mitch came from the back hall. Fran walked to her desk but Mitch hung back. Mr. Vanderpage pulled away and held Riley at arm's length, looking like he wanted to say something, but he didn't. Instead, he closed the briefcase and handed her the envelope.

"I think you will be very pleased," he said.

"Thank you," Riley said.

He looked back with a sad smile and she watched him leave.

"What was that all about?" asked Fran.

She shook off the gloom and lifted the envelope. "I have money. Remember all those years ago when Peter and I bought some land?"

Fran's brow furrowed with concentration. "Oh yes. That's part of the exclusive high-class Merritt subdivision now, isn't it?"

Riley shrugged. She hadn't kept track. It wasn't that she had forgotten about the land or the money, she just hadn't done anything about it. She vaguely remembered the day she signed the papers when the land had sold; a courier had brought the paperwork to her to the office.

"I must not have told you," Riley said. "That day at the fundraiser, when I talked to Peter…" she paused in memory and respect, "he mentioned the land selling and said he would see that I got my half of the money. Mr. Vanderpage stopped to give me the check. He said Holly didn't know anything about it." She opened the envelope.

"You're lucky there," said Fran.

But Riley wasn't listening. Her mouth gaped as she stared at the check. Fran and Mitch came closer.

"What is it?" asked Fran.

Riley turned her head toward Fran, who impatiently peered over Riley's shoulder.

"Oh my God!" she exclaimed. She grabbed Riley's arm. "Oh, my, God!" She looked at Mitch, her eyes big. "It's almost two hundred fifty thousand dollars!"

* * *

Riley took that Friday off work. It was noon before she made it to Whispering Pines and she drove directly to the retirement home. She had talked to Chloe earlier in the week, telling her that she was going to buy the Colby place. Residents were playing bingo but she found Chloe in her room reading a book.

Chloe's lawyer had the simple papers ready to be signed. Riley spent several hours with Chloe, not just about details of the sale but merely visiting, and barely had enough time to open an account at the local bank before it closed. Then she stopped at the local insurance agent, who promised to have something worked up for her when she stopped the next weekend.

Ernie wasn't home but she found him at Jay's shop, along with several other men. She thought it must be farmers' and ranchers' happy hour because of the beer and gossip, gossip that dwindled when she walked in. She headed for Ernie.

Riley asked if he would do the work that was needed at the Colby house and if so, how soon could he start? He stammered and said he would be proud to work for her and, of course, he would be available right away. She told him she was going to the farm but would be back the next morning and for him to have an idea of what he wanted to be paid for the job. She waved at Jay, who was the only one doing any work.

When she arrived at the farm it took two trips to transfer the cot she usually kept in the trailer, a fan and her cooler from her hatchback to the house. Both times the kittens watched curiously from under the broken lattice on the porch. Wooly had been left at home under Benjie's care because her car was too small for the big dog and it didn't have air conditioning.

She did a walk-through of the house and wondered what she had gotten herself into, then she walked the perimeter of the eighty acres. The small section of crops was at the far end of the property, evidently adjacent to Cap's land because he had farmed the ground between the fields, joining the two. The pasture had good fencing but the pens at the barn needed work, other than the one she had left Novocain in earlier. And the barn…it *was* a shame about the tree falling on it, as Ernie had said. Her eyes sparkled when she considered having the barn torn down and a metal building put up instead, one large enough for an indoor arena. But for now she would make do with the barn as it was and ask Cap or some other farmer to work up the large, flat area behind it for a makeshift arena.

That night she lay on the cot inside the house looking into darkness, wishing Wooly was there. The soft drone of the fan was comforting, but she thought the house seemed to groan and creak an awful lot. "Hello…" she said and listened to her voice drift into emptiness. She remembered Ernie's comment about snakes and considered moving the cot to where light from the yard pole filtered in through a dirty window, but didn't. She wasn't squeamish by any means, but lying in the strange house alone was much different than her familiar bed in the gooseneck of the horse trailer.

* * *

Saturday morning Riley again found Ernie at Jay's shop. Today there was no one else there, just Ernie and Jay.

"You're giving Ernie quite the reputation," Jay told her. "Those guys were wagging their tongues a mile a minute after you left."

Riley laughed. "Sorry, Ernie."

"Don't be," he responded and hooked a thumb in his coveralls.

Jay, grinning, went back to work.

Ernie suggested they go to Conrad's, the local lumberyard.

"That'll be a start," he told her. "Then you should check in Owen for what they have to offer and compare price. Paul Conrad has high overhead, but he'll know you can buy in the big city so I bet he'll work with you."

They walked to Conrad Lumber, passing Murphy's Pub on the way which had a rustic overhang and wooden plank sidewalk. Inside Conrad's the aroma of lumber greeted them. Behind the counter was a sandy haired high-school-aged girl wearing a ball cap and smock, both with the lumber yard logo.

"Hello, Ernie," she said agreeably.

"Hi, Cathy. Your dad around?"

Before she could answer a man with a smock that matched hers entered from a side door. A customer with a cigarette in his mouth followed him in.

"Hello, Ernie," said the man in the smock. "Ma'am," he added nodding to Riley.

"Morning, Paul," said Ernie.

Paul joined his daughter behind the counter and started to fill out a form. "That gate will be here the middle of the week, Cap," he said to the man who had come in with him.

"Who's this you got with ya Ern?" drawled Cap looking Riley over.

Cap Henderson? she thought. He was nothing like she expected. She guessed he wasn't much older than her and between his attitude and the fact his shirt was unbuttoned to show off his lean, tan torso, it was easy to see that he was full of himself. She suspected her eyes were showing her dislike, and didn't care.

He looked at her looking at him, lifted his ball cap and scratched an ear under sandy colored hair.

"Cat got your tongue, Ern?" Cap asked. He took a drag from the cigarette.

"This is Riley Montgomery," Ernie disclosed. "She's buying the Colby place."

Cap's eyes narrowed. Paul slid the paperwork across the counter and Cap continued to look at Riley while he reached for the pen and scribbled his name. A woman came from the office behind the counter and scowled, furrowing the lines already present on her late thirty-something face.

"Paul, you let him smoke out there?" she said crossly.

"See you 'round," said Cap, still looking at Riley.

No one said anything until the door banged shut behind him.

"I'd say his plugs were a little frosted when he heard you bought the Colby place," said Cathy.

The reference to the Colby place caused the woman to look at Riley much the same way that Cap had when Ernie divulged her name.

"Leave him alone," she snapped.

"Oh, Mom, you know Uncle Cap thinks he's the bad ass, er, the baddest bull on the range," Cathy told her. She started to leave and the woman was on her heels, reprimanding her for her language.

"What can I help you with, Ernie?" Paul asked, trying to salvage the store's ambiance.

"I'm sure you know by now this is Riley and she bought the Colby place," replied Ernie.

"I'd heard rumors that someone was talking to Chloe about buying. Nice to meet you, Riley."

"You too," she told him. "We're going do some serious remodeling and Ernie recommended I come here first."

"Why, thank you, Ernie," Paul said, flattered. "Let's go back to my office."

An hour later, Ernie concluded the conversation by asking Paul to come up with a package deal. "Plumbing, drywall, insulation, appliances including washer and dryer, new windows, the works," he said.

"I'll sharpen my pencil," Paul promised. "I appreciate you considering us."

On the walk back to Jay's shop, Ernie said, "I think Paul really wants your business. You realize this remodel is going to cost a good chunk of change, don't you? I mean, you'd have a long way to go before you'd be broke, but this'll eat a lot of your budget."

Riley assured him that she had crunched numbers. She refrained from asking about the relationship between the Conrad's and Cap because of Cathy's reference to him as her uncle, but Ernie volunteered the information.

"Patty, the crabby woman, is Paul's wife. You probably gathered that. Cathy's their kid, you probably gathered that too, their only one. Cap is married to Peggy, Patty's sister." He looked at Riley as if seeing if she was interested in what he was saying. "Cap 'n Peggy don't have any kids, that's the one thing going for her in that marriage that I can see. They say opposites attract, but I've always wondered why she settled for Cap."

CHAPTER 13

Riley drove back to Owen that evening. Sunday afternoon she was in the shade of a large tree near the barn, holding Dually for the farrier while he replaced the mare's shoes. Several women boarders were riding in the arena, their jovial voices carrying. It was usually only on weekends that the women came out, but they always had a good time with their horses. The women's children were riding too, or playing in the sandbox and yet another testing his skills on a bicycle with training wheels. Dually stomped at a fly and Riley flicked the lead rope at the mare's legs to shoo the pest away. The farrier, Ed, was an older man who didn't talk much.

A jogger on the road caught Riley's eye. His white running shoes flashed with each stride and his aviator sunglasses reflected the sun. Then he turned, heading up the drive. Riley smiled when she recognized him as being Mitch. A minute later Mitch stopped in front of her, bent over to catch his breath and took the sunglasses off. The farrier glanced up, wiped his sweaty brow, then went back to work.

"What in the world are you doing out here?" Riley asked.

Mitch remained with his hands on his knees and lifted his head.

"I used to marathon when I was younger. Today I parked at Happy Acres."

"That park is five miles from here," she said, impressed.

"Five and a quarter," he corrected, standing. "Is there water close by?"

She motioned to the hose near the barn. She watched him go to it and then realized the farrier was talking to her.

"Ready for the next one," Ed repeated. "That one's just a trim, right?"

She nodded and looked at the mare's feet. "They look good, as usual," she told him. "I'll be right back."

She led Dually away. Mitch finished drinking from the end of the hose and met up with her at the pasture gate, where all the horses had gathered. She took the halter off Dually and put it on Dobbie.

"How many horses do you have?" Mitch asked.

"Just these two are mine," she enlightened.

He fell in step beside her but kept a safe distance from the horse.

"I did have three, but I sold one."

"You sold one?" he said with disbelief. "I thought girls were too attached to their horses to sell them."

She smiled and positioned Dobbie to accommodate the farrier.

"Horse people are about as varied as snowflakes," she told him.

Ed chortled, making her laugh at his rare expression. Mitch looked like he thought he was missing something.

"You know," said Ed. "Like no two women are alike."

Mitch lifted his chin and a smile appeared. "Okay, I get it."

"You asked about farriers when you move," Ed said to Riley. "I have some other guys' business cards in my truck. I'd sure enough accommodate you but I'm pretty busy right here in Owen."

Mitch again looked like he was feeling left out.

"I'll miss using you," she said to Ed, and could no longer avoid looking at Mitch. "I bought a place about three hours from here. I'm quitting the law firm."

His disappointment was obvious on his face but not in his voice when he said, "I'm happy for you, but I hate to see you go."

If she didn't know him better, she would have believed his tone. "I haven't told Prescott or Briggs yet," she said.

He shook his head. "I won't say anything."

The sound of scattering gravel was accompanied by a child's wail. The boy with the small bicycle had managed to take off the training wheels, with unfortunate results. Mitch went to the boy and helped him to his feet.

"Are you all right, big guy?" Mitch asked.

The mother arrived, first coddling the boy and then bragging about his attempt when he stopped crying.

"Do you have any big Band-Aids?" he asked Riley. "It looks like we need a little first aid here."

The youngster was clutching his knee with a large strawberry scrape. Riley smiled at Mitch's control of the situation and his easy way with the child.

"There's a kit on the seat of my pickup," Ed offered. "Under some junk."

Riley continued to hold Dobbie for Ed while Mitch tended to the boy and his mother. Mitch sent them on their way about the same time Ed finished, and after Riley put Dobbie away, they watched Ed leave.

"Doing anything later?" Mitch asked.

"No, no plans," she replied, thinking she wouldn't get in a much needed nap after all.

"Would you like to go to dinner? I've been wanting to go someplace nice, but I don't want to go alone. There would be no work conflicts, since you're leaving," he added with a comical frown.

She laughed, reminded of his clown costume at the fundraiser.

"About five?" he asked, taking a step back.

She hesitated.

"All rightee then, it's settled," he said, taking charge and another step back. "I'll be here at five sharp. Jeans are fine and have an appetite. I'll treat you right."

She smiled and he looked pleased.

"Gotta run," he said donning the sunglasses, and then he was gone.

Mitch did pick her up promptly at five. They ate at a rustic steak house where the food was good and the atmosphere even better, and she was pleasantly surprised to find she enjoyed his company. Then they went up to her apartment to watch the movie he had brought along. She fell asleep leaning against him. When she woke, she was aware of him next to her. She didn't sit up or pull away, instead finding that she liked him being there. It was he who moved after a minute, twisting to look at her. His eyes pulled her in, and now she knew why they were called bedroom eyes. He touched her face, and only then was she able to quit looking at him, because she had closed her eyes. She felt the warmth of his breath before he kissed her.

* * *

Mitch left very early the next morning. Riley saw him to the door and then went back to the bedroom where she sat on the edge of the bed. She didn't notice the sun was coming up until the alarm went off. In the waning light she looked at the pillow where Mitch had been laying, the indention of his head still there. She let her smile show and pushed away the guilt.

At work Fran was full of questions about the Colby place. After Riley answered she commented there was something different, a "happy glow" she called it. Riley blushed and turned away, leaving out information about the time spent with Mitch.

"When are you quitting?" Fran asked at length, her voice low.

"I don't know...I've got to talk to Mr. Prescott. I'll do that this morning."

The talk with the senior partners went well. They said all the right things including being disappointed to see her go.

"So… When will your last day be?" Mr. Prescott asked.

"I guess at the end of this month," she said with hesitation. "Can I let you know a definite date in a few days?"

"Yes, yes, that's fine," Mr. Prescott assured. "Can you see about getting an ad for your replacement in the paper?"

"Of course. I'll get something worked up for you before lunch."

As word of Riley's leaving circulated through the office Cynthia appeared resentful for not being the center of attention and Bill Briggs was aloof, perturbed that Mitch Matthews knew before he did.

* * *

Later that week Riley called Ernie. She had received a copy of Conrad Lumber's bid via fax and had decided to go with them to provide the bulk of remodeling supplies, if Ernie agreed. He had seen the bid as well and said yes, he thought that would be the way to go. He told her he would get Paul to the Colby house for measuring before the weekend, and if they needed anything he would call.

That night she couldn't sleep. With the purchase of the Colby place and what was going on between her and Mitch, she had too many things on her mind. She finally got up, figuring she may as well put the time to good use. She went to the closet and pulled the chain dangling from the bare bulb overhead. She doubted she would ever wear the majority of clothes in front of her again, so she took most of the outfits from hangers and put them in boxes. Shoes with heels, handbags and scarves, too were transferred. For the time being she was only concerned with giveaway items, not packing for the move, and there was still room in a box. She pulled open a dresser drawer where she found forgettable T-shirts and an awful sweater received from someone at work in a Christmas gift exchange. She recalled wearing the sweater, once, because the giver kept asking about it.

There was still something at the back of the drawer. It looked like a gift box, thin and square, and she recognized what it was before she picked it up. She lifted the top of the box and gazed at the trophy buckle she had won about the same time she and Peter broke up. The large, silver oval with gold braid around the edge and barrel racer symbol was prettier than she remembered. She touched the inscription and thought back to those days.

* * *

The next morning, Riley stifled a yawn at her desk.

"Late night? Been stepping out on me?" Mitch whispered with a smile, but Riley detected a hint of investigation.

She put a finger to her lips and said, "I don't kiss and tell."

He moaned softly and put his hands over his heart.

She laughed, not so much for his antics as for the fact it made her feel good to know he had been thinking about her. He had respected her space all week, and she was impressed.

"I'm going to ride horses as soon as I get home from work," she told him. "But would you like to come by later? Maybe we can grab a bite to eat."

He looked very happy.

Fran, coming from the hall, curiously asked, "What am I missing?"

"Just work," Mitch said innocently.

Riley smiled but didn't answer. She swiveled in her chair, evading the woman with pink highlights and suspicious look on her face.

CHAPTER 14

Saturday morning after arriving at Whispering Pines, Riley parked in front of Ernie's house. They walked the few blocks to Conrad Lumber, where details were ironed out and a hefty down payment check written.

"The cabinets and appliances should be here within two weeks," Paul said. "I'll see that the whirlpool tub and other bathroom fixtures get here right away, since Ernie said he wanted to get the bathroom livable for you first. Windows will be about three weeks out. I'll store whatever comes in if you aren't ready for it at no charge." He extended a hand to Riley and then he shook Ernie's hand too, his gratitude to the black man obvious.

Leaving, Ernie commented on the weather. It was another dry and sunny day. Riley agreed it had been a dry summer and then offered to buy breakfast, saying she felt like celebrating.

"You bet. I have to drop this off at Jay's first," he said lifting a roll of duct tape and bundle of welding rods.

Jay was the only one working of the half dozen men present in his shop. The loitering men's arguing of cattle prices and lack of rain ceased when they came in.

"I'll wait here," Riley told Ernie.

While she waited, she read the flyers taped to the wall near the door. One was a large poster advertising the upcoming county fair. The list of events included an open barrel race.

"Ready?" asked Ernie.

Riley turned to him and saw Jay in the background acknowledge her. She waved in response.

At Wanda's it was quiet except for more farm related talk by men gathered in a corner and clinks of cutlery.

"Morning," Marie said as she arrived at the table, pencil and pad in hand. She was letting her hair grow out. "Know what you want or would you like menus?"

"Good morning, Marie," said Riley. "I'd like bacon and eggs, over easy, with wheat toast, please. Coffee, black."

Marie scribbled and looked at Ernie expectantly.

"Yeah, me too," he said not looking at her.

Riley was surprised at Ernie's coolness toward Marie, who left looking a little let down. Ernie, his eyes still on the table, took his silverware out of the napkin wrapped around it and wiped off the fork. The seconds ticked by before he raised his eyes.

"I do have some dignity, you know," he said. "Well, let's say I found it again. Those gabby old hens acting all chummy now that I've sobered up an' met you were the same ones talking behind my back when my wife left."

Riley put a hand on Ernie's arm. It was still there when Marie arrived with their water glasses. Water sloshed when she set the glasses on the table.

"Oh, my!" said a flustered Marie. With jerking movements she mopped the mess with a white rag she pulled from a pocket.

Riley was trying hard to keep from giggling before Marie finished. "Maybe she'll back off a little now," she said after the woman walked away.

Ernie slapped the table and laughed, his moment of misery having passed.

After breakfast Ernie drove them to the Colby place in his old sea foam green pickup. As they unloaded tools from the back Riley asked where the huge undertaking would begin.

"Muley said he'd be here first thing Monday morning," he told her. "While he's working on the well I have a high school kid coming to help inside. Tommy's a good kid...not what you'll expect, but a good kid. I'll get Tommy working then when Muley's ready, I'll help him tackle the water situation and plumbing." He picked up a crowbar, anxious to get started. "I got other help lined up, too. You won't even recognize the place next weekend," he promised.

They spent the rest of the day tearing out plaster and lath, a dusty, tedious job, not quitting until it was early evening. The result of their labor was several inches deep on the floor. Riley's arms and neck were aching and she proposed they stop for the day.

Ernie's bare shoulders sagged. "Thank God," he said. "I was ready to quit a long time ago."

She laughed at him. "Will this stuff clear out pretty fast?" she asked waving her hand through the air, stirring the fine plaster dust hanging in the air.

His expression didn't look encouraging. "You're not thinking about staying here tonight?"

"That was my plan," she said and refashioned her ponytail. "But this stuff is awful. My hair feels like straw."

Ernie rubbed the short hair on his head, sending up white dust. "I wouldn't know about that," he said with a grin. "Why don't you spend the night at my place? The thought of sleeping in this just ain't right. And, if I might say so, you could use a shower."

She laughed again and conceded.

When Ernie rounded the corner by Jay's shop, Jay was walking from his house to his flatbed truck. Ernie honked. He parked behind Riley's car on the street in front of his house, then carried her cooler into the house while she took her overnight duffle bag.

"You'll have to ignore the bachelor mess," he told her. "I've been meaning to get rid of some things but just haven't done it." He set the cooler down and motioned to the stairs. "Take your pick of rooms and take your time cleaning up. I'm going to run to Decker's Grocery before they close. I'll be right back."

She put her bag on the bed in the first room she came to and then walked to one of the tall, narrow windows. Ernie was on the sidewalk headed to Decker's. Jay's flatbed was gone from his house across the street. The street lights flickered on. She let the curtain fall, ready for that shower.

When she made it back downstairs, Ernie called to her from the kitchen. He was at the counter, skinning potatoes. He looked out of place, still dusty and dirty except his hands and forearms, in the kitchen that was spacious, up-to-date and sparkling clean.

"My cupboards were almost bare," he said. "Hungry?"

"It seems like I'm always hungry lately. Hungry and tired," she replied. "What can I do to help?"

He motioned to a bowl of strawberries and said, "You can get those ready." Then he pointed to a drawer and the pantry, both made of wood that gleamed from repeated polishing. "Knives are there, and anything else you should need is over there. I have shortcake too." His brows went up and down.

"You've done a lot of work in this house, haven't you?"

"Hope you like it. It's an example of what you'll be getting from me at the Colby place."

"I love it. It's beautiful." She opened the drawer.

"My wife loved it too, 'til she got bored." He threw the potato peelings into the trash can under the sink. "The house wasn't always like this. She wanted me to turn it into a bed and breakfast for a long time, said if she was going to be stuck here she wanted the chance to talk to civilized people now and again. So I went to all that trouble and expense, then she up and leaves before one guest set foot in the place. Well, I doubt that's entirely true," he said bitterly. He dumped the potatoes into a pot of boiling water on the stove. "Didn't mean to subject you to my jabber-jawin'," he said with his back to her. He turned around with a closemouthed smile, but it was forced. "You don't mind keeping an eye on things while I shower, do you?"

She shook her head.

"Add your touch to things as you see fit. I've learned to cook but it might not be to your liking."

After supper they washed the dishes and then said good night. She went upstairs to her room and wondered what his wife had been like. She walked to the window and looked out. Jay's house was dark and his flatbed still gone.

* * *

Early Sunday morning they went back to work on the house. It wasn't until the sun was high overhead that they called it quits. Riley made lunch from things in her cooler and they sat on the tail gate of Ernie's old pickup to eat.

"I really appreciate you giving me this job," Ernie confided. "I'll do a good job for you."

"I know you will, Ernie. It seems like fate that we met, doesn't it?"

"That it does," he said, and they exchanged the same look they had the night after fireworks when he talked about lottery tickets in front of Jay's shop.

She hopped down. "I've got to head for home. Same place, same time next weekend?"

"You know where to find me."

She left one friend to find another working in his flower bed near the big barn in Owen. Benjie was wearing his weathered off-white hat that always made her think of the *Minnow's* bumbling first mate Gilligan. Wooly was stretched out in the shade nearby. The old dog didn't get up when Benjie did but instead thumped his tail against the ground. Benjie removed his gloves and laid them near his gardening tools.

"How are things going out there?" he asked when she approached.

"Good. We started the tear out. The new well is scheduled to get underway tomorrow."

"How soon do you want me?" he asked eagerly.

"Not for a while. I'm realizing this project is going to be a lot of work and will take longer than I thought."

"They always do. How long before you move?"

"I don't know. The days are flying by. I think I'll pay the rent through next month, that way I can leave some of my furniture here until the house is ready for it."

"Whoa! Brakes on that kind of talk!" he said holding up the palm of his hand like a cop directing traffic. "No way! I'm not going to let you take that junk you call furniture to your new home brimming with the Benjie touch. That would be a crime, just a crime." He cupped an ear with his palm. "What's that I hear? Ah, yes, just as suspected, it's the remodel police! No, we're going to go furniture shopping before you move in."

He was right, she should buy new furniture. She could afford it after all.

"You're right, again," she said.

"Of course I am. That's why you're paying me the big bucks!"

She laughed.

"Um, by the way, whose fancy black Mitsubishi is that I see parked out here sometimes?" he asked. "It's odd that it's only here *overnight*."

She smiled, embarrassed.

"Aha! I knew it! Fill me in!"

She briefly told him about Mitch, blushing when adding, "It's nothing really."

"Nothing, huh? You've been looking pretty happy lately."

Riley couldn't argue, but she didn't think that Mitch was the main source of her recent state of mind.

CHAPTER 15

The week passed quickly for Riley. She accepted Mitch's offer to help her pack, although she didn't need it. Friday before she left work he told her that he would miss her while she was gone and to call him, if she wanted, when she got home Sunday.

When she arrived at the Colby place a few hours later Muley was just leaving. The new well and piping was almost finished. The back yard was torn up with piles of dirt and trenches scarred the ground.

Ernie and his helpers had completely gutted the old kitchen and the bathroom. There were no fixtures, only holes in the floor and open plumbing. Moving through the rest of the house required navigating a maze of new fixtures, sheets of drywall and cables of wire.

In the room that would be the new kitchen, Ernie said, "We'll gut this room next and the floor'll be pulled up. The floor has to come out because of the new plumbing, plus that'll make it easier to transform it into a kitchen. And since the wall between the two rooms is going to be holding cabinets, I want to reinforce it."

"I want to help," she said ambitiously.

"Are you sure?"

She nodded. "Show me what you want me to do. I'll work until I can't anymore, then I'm going to crash here tonight. You've already put in a full day but I'm too excited to not do something."

He looked disappointed at the prospect of spending the evening alone, and Riley noticed.

"I'll stay at your place tomorrow night, if that's okay," she said. "By then I'll really be looking forward to a shower, not to mention good company."

"Of course it is," he replied contentedly. "You know you're a glutton for punishment," he added, then started to round up the appropriate tools she would need.

"You haven't seen any snakes have you?" she asked, looking around.

He smiled an ornery smile and because of his silence she looked at him.

"No. Nothing," he told her. "You're safe here."

"Shame on you," she scolded.

He headed for the door. "Don't work too late. I'll be back in the morning. Call if you need anything in the meantime. I have a phone by the bed."

She worked for several hours. When she lay down on the cot that night she fell asleep within a matter of minutes, this time barely noticing the noises the house made.

* * *

Riley and Ernie continued gutting the interior, confirming that the side of the house with the old kitchen had been the original building and the two larger rooms and upper level added later. The wall between the two halves was thick with stucco and brick and a door between the small bedroom and addition had been covered up.

"Benjie will have a heyday with this," she predicted. "Let's use it. I like it."

The day passed with the majority of the walls getting knocked out and the ceiling demolition started in what would be the great room. From time to time Muley would come in to discuss something with Ernie or ask for his help. Before Muley left he said he would be back on Monday to make sure the well pump was working and to finish the dirt work. He added that he was going to run a new line to the barn which Riley appreciated, and she thanked him for thinking ahead—no doubt the old line would be rusted and worthless.

Ernie was thrilled with their progress. He talked nonstop while they put things away late in the day. When they walked to his sea foam green pickup, he wiped his brow with a sweat-stained handkerchief.

"It'll be nice when we can get the air conditioner up and running," he said. "I've never been known to sweat much but I'm thinking I need to start wearing a shirt under these coveralls to sop up the moisture."

Riley couldn't help but laugh at him.

At Ernie's, he was at the kitchen counter starting supper when she came downstairs after showering. He had already cleaned up.

"Your hair's still wet. This might not be pretty," he said with a jab of a thumb to his head, "but it sure is easy." The hardboiled egg in his hand threatened to pop out but he managed to keep hold of it.

"I'll finish drying it before going to bed. I was hungry," she warranted.

"I thought we'd grill steaks tonight. I've also got garlic bread and salad with the works. Won't take long at all."

"Sounds perfect."

"I took the liberty of asking Jay to join us, but he said he had to go to Northboro. Was going to see Marta I guess, or maybe his dad. Now there's a character for you!"

"Marta?" she asked, thinking back to the stunning dark-headed woman in the white Saturn she had seen at Jay's on the Fourth of July.

"The things us boys got into when we were kids!" he said with a laugh, reminiscing. "And here'd come Oliver, threatening to use his belt on us." This time the hardboiled egg did get away, squirting to the counter like a bar of soap. Ernie scrambled after it, scattering salad greens and croutons, but the elusive egg went to the floor. He cursed under his breath and picked it up at the same time the phone rang.

"Go ahead," she told him with a smile. "I'll take care of this."

"It's probably a wrong number," he surmised as he tossed the egg in the trash under the sink. "But I am tickled to say I've gotten several offers for work since starting on your place."

* * *

The next morning she suggested that Ernie take the day off, saying she needed him for the long haul. She didn't have to talk much to convince him. Before going to the Colby place she stopped at the mom-and-pop station for gas, ice for her cooler and aspirin for her sore muscles.

Instead of tearing out she cleaned up the existing mess, which was significant. She made trip after trip from the house to the dumpster, adding her white powdered footprints to those of Tommy's tennis shoes and Ernie's work boots on the flattened grass. Before leaving the Colby house she gazed at what had been accomplished, and was happy with the drastic changes.

At home in Owen she took more aspirin before soaking in the tub, where she fell asleep. It was after six o'clock when she woke. She called Mitch, feeling he was expecting it.

"Good to hear from you," Mitch said, sounding sincere. "How was your weekend?"

"Wonderful. The house is torn up and a disaster, but it's beautiful. I helped tear out walls. Most of my muscles are reminding me that I'm a wimp."

He laughed sympathetically. "How about a massage? I'd love to give you one, no strings. Have you eaten yet?"

At the mention of food she realized she hadn't eaten, and had no doubts that he would give a more than satisfying massage.

"Pizza? Chinese? Italian? You name it, I'll deliver," he said, taking advantage of her hesitation. "This is your last week in Owen and I don't know when you'll have time for me again."

"I was going to say okay, but if you want to grovel some more..."

"It must've been the lawyer in me sneaking out! I'll attempt to watch that. What do you want me to bring?"

"You don't have to. I'm sure I have something here I can put together."

"It's no problem, really. I'll call it in and pick it up on the way. Okay?"

"All right. That sounds nice."

"Any requests?"

"Surprise me," she said.

"I'll be right over!"

* * *

Riley's last week working as a receptionist was a pleasant one. The workload was lighter than usual and the office relaxed and low key. Even Cynthia and Bill Briggs were polite, suspiciously so, Riley thought. She joked to Fran that they were probably glad to see her go.

Thursday evening Ernie called to say the bathroom was ready for fixtures and he planned on installing them the next day. He also told her that Muley and his sons had stayed to help after the well was finished, resulting in the majority of new plumbing and wiring getting installed.

Friday evening Mitch arrived early for their date and surprised her with a gift of pearl earrings. They were going to a new restaurant and she was feeling pretty special on the way there. He walked her in with chivalry and the hostess ushered them to the back, to a large party room where Riley was again surprised with streamers, balloons and people she knew. Fran was in front.

"Happy going away party!" they chorused.

Riley looked at Mitch accusingly. He pulled her close and they were surrounded by co-workers.

After a speech by Mr. Prescott on her behalf, a token gift and dinner the majority of party goers graduated to the bar. Riley and Fran excused themselves to go to the powder room.

"Work isn't going to be the same," Fran moaned. "I'm really going to miss you."

"I'll miss you too. A lot. I'd never believed anyone if they'd told me a year ago that I'd be doing what I'm doing. I'm excited and nervous at the same time."

"Maybe it's as simple as your subconscious telling you that settling for what you have would be the safe thing to do."

Riley smiled. That thought had crossed her mind already. "For the past few years I honestly thought I was happy, but when I'm out there, I feel...*alive*."

"You're a country girl at heart. You belong out there," Fran summarized before giving her a supportive hug.

CHAPTER 16

Mitch kept his distance while Riley loaded Dually and Dobbie into the trailer Saturday morning. She latched the door and during their walk to her pickup he put his arm around her. He gave her a lingering kiss and they said their good-byes. She helped Wooly in the cab, then Mitch stepped back and watched her go.

About noon she pulled into the Colby place. My place, she thought. The realtor sign had been removed from the road and was propped against the barn. Ernie's old pickup was the only vehicle around. She unloaded the horses and put them in a lot. Young and curious Dobbie inspected every inch of his new accommodations, blowing air through his nostrils and looking comical. Dually, a veteran like Novocain was more interested in finding something to eat than worrying about boogeymen. Wooly went to meet Ernie, who was coming from the house.

"It's good to see horses out here again," he said.

"It's good to have them here."

He helped her fill buckets with water for the horses and one for Wooly, using the new hydrant near the barn. After the horses were settled in, she was anxious to see the house.

"Oh, it's still tore up and we've a long way to go, but there's been good progress," Ernie told her.

Eagerly she opened the back door. New subfloor lay in front of her, ready for linoleum, and Ernie had replaced the door to the cellar. The new door was much lighter so it would be easier for her to handle and it fit in the opening in the floor better. The gutted walls had new wiring along the studs but they were barely visible because of the fluffy pink insulation. She could easily envision what the new laundry and mud room would look like when it was finished.

Not much imagination was needed in the bathroom. The new whirlpool tub, stool and sink were in place, ready to be used. The walls were covered with tile on the bottom and the water-resistant drywall on top was ready for paint. The tile on the floor matched that on the lower walls.

"There's new plumbing under these floors," Ernie said tapping a scuffed toe of his work boot. "Same as the new kitchen."

"It's just beautiful," she told him.

He smiled with her approval. "The little bedroom," he said heading that way, "doesn't look much different than before, just bare."

He was right, the little room was in much the same condition as the mud room. But when Riley went through the opening where the original door had been between the two parts of the house, she was astounded at how large the room was with the changes. The ceiling was gone, revealing the rafters, and the wall concealing the stairs torn out. The modifications were backing Benjie's inspirational ideas.

"Go on up," Ernie encouraged.

She began the ascent to her new loft bedroom. At the top on her left was the framed-in closet, tucked under the slope of the roof and big enough for clothes and storage. There was one window in the shell of a room and she crossed the floor to it. Looking out she could see the barn and the horses. Then she crossed the floor again, to the unfinished wall that was waist high. She looked down at Ernie in the great space below.

"I don't know what to say," she told him. "It really is beautiful. I hope it's what Benjie had in mind, because I just love it."

"And you haven't seen the kitchen yet," he said.

Her eyes sparkled and she quickly but carefully made her way down the open sided stairs. A sharp left and a dozen strides later she was in the new kitchen, where the walls were gutted and there was no floor, only sheets of plywood laying on framing members with new plumbing lines visible below.

"I've still got to frame in the cabinets," he said somewhat apologetically. "And there might be minor changes when the appliances get put in…can't be helped." He walked on the islands of plywood to a window that also provided a view of the barn and horses. "I thought this'd be a good place for the table, and I want to get the new windows in before we put the drywall up around them. I made an exception in the bathroom."

Impressed beyond words, she continued to look around.

"I think you need to show Ms. Colby one of these days," Ernie said.

Her face lit up with the prospect, but then she reconsidered. "You don't think she'll be disappointed at the changes we've made, do you?"

"Maybe. But I think she'll understand. And I'd rather have her see it this way than what it was before. We're lucky the new roof was put on when it was."

They remained in their own thoughts for a minute.

"You don't mind if I take the afternoon off, do you?" he asked sheepishly.

"Of course not! I don't expect you to work every day, which you've obviously been doing," she said looking around to back up her comment.

Ernie harrumphed, then, "I suppose you're going to spend the night here."

Riley knew the expression on her face showed her answer. Ernie shook his head and walked to the door, once again telling her to call if she needed anything.

Riley worked in the barn instead of the house that afternoon. The tack room, about ten by ten feet, had been used for storing grain in the past, obvious by the remains of oats in the dust. After sweeping and removing cobwebs in the corners she built saddle racks on a wall, using Ernie's tools. She refrained from moving her things from the trailer to the tack room, wanting to monitor for mice first, and since she was used to living out of her trailer on weekends the tack was fine where it was. Other than the tack room that was situated just inside the big barn doors and the stalls lining the other side there was nothing in the barn except loose hay, a project for another day. There was a little loft, accessible by a wood ladder on a wall, and it only contained a few old bales of straw.

By dusk Dually and Dobbie had devoured everything but the weeds in their lots. Riley sparingly gave them some hay she had brought and knew she would have to get to work on the pasture fence before the hay ran out. She took a box that included toiletries from her truck and carried it to the new bathroom. While she soaked in the bubbling water of the whirlpool tub, Wooly lay on the floor with his big head resting on his paws and the wicks of the candles flickered in the slight breeze from the window.

* * *

Steam rose from the cup of coffee sitting on the little table in the trailer. Riley, standing at the open door with a notepad, alternated from gazing at the Colby house to adding items to the growing list of things needing to be done. Painting the house would have to wait, but she could trim the limbs of the spruce touching the porch, replace the broken lattice and mow, if she had a mower. She scribbled some more.

Wooly ambled around a corner of the house. The kittens eyed him suspiciously and darted to safety under the porch. Then the sun was clearing the horizon, throwing its golden rays on the house. The sight evoked a smile. Ernie had been right—a person never could guess what God had up His sleeve.

* * *

Wanting to beat the heat of the day Riley spent the morning patching the pasture fence. Some of it would have to be replaced eventually, but for now patching would do. She watched the horses play when she turned them out and then she worked on repairing the lot fence that was damaged by the tree that fell on the barn. She tried her best to ignore the tree, something that she couldn't handle on her own. She got the fence repaired and then began to tackle weeds, most of which were varieties she had never seen before. She worked until she couldn't take it anymore. Heading for the house she walked around the back of the barn, skirting the overgrown grass and more weeds and realized that cleaning up the place was going to take a lot more work than she anticipated, including transforming this area into an arena.

After lunch she saddled Dually. She rode the eighty acres of the Colby place, which didn't take but twenty minutes, and longingly looked at the odd bluffs that started at the edge of her property. She would have to find out who owned the land and ask their permission to ride there. She rode along the crops and fence that divided her land from Cap's and then ended up on the same road where she had had the flat tire. She stuck to the road going home.

When she was almost home she heard a vehicle behind her so she moved Dually to the ditch. The vehicle slowed and then it rolled to a stop. It was Jay in his flatbed. She dismounted, tucked a wisp of loose hair under her cowboy hat and led the mare to the truck. Jay was wiping his neck with a rag and he repositioned his ball cap. His shirt with the sleeves cut out was wet with sweat.

"Hello," she said. "You look like you've been working."

"I've been doing things for Freddie. You remember Freddie?"

She nodded, thinking back to that day he stopped at Jay's shop. "How's he doing?"

"Good," he said and scratched the back of his neck where a leafy stem protruded from under his shirt. Without thinking she reached to get it. He looked surprised and completely at ease at the same time.

"Fruits of your labor?" she asked.

He smiled a little. "Have you lined up anyone to take care of that tree?"

"The one on the barn? Not yet."

"Want me to take a look?"

"I'm sure you have better things to do," she told him dismissively.

"I've still got some life left in me today. I drive this road quite a bit and that tree has irritated me since the first day I saw it on the barn." He took a deep breath that sounded like a sigh. "If I go home I'll end up working in the shop or somebody'll show up wanting something anyway."

"Are you sure?"

"Yep."

"All right. I'll put my mare away."

He used the flatbed as his work area to sharpen the chain on a saw while she unsaddled. After she put Dually away he was adding oil and gas.

"Ernie mentioned you'll probably have a wood burning stove," he said glancing at her and then back to what he was doing.

"We've talked about so many things. I do remember him saying something about a wood stove," she said, feeling her reply was pathetic.

"You'll be glad to have one this winter, especially if the power goes out."

She considered what he said while she watched what he was doing.

"Do you want me to show you how to use a saw? Or do you already know?" he quickly added as if he might be wrong with his assumption.

She laughed. "No, I don't know how. I'm not very good with mechanics. I can handle a drill but that's about it."

He smiled his little smile again and went back to working on the saws. "Part of your tree is still green…that means you'll only want to burn the dead part of it this winter. The green would cause problems in the chimney and it wouldn't burn well to begin with."

"Interesting."

"I'm going to drive back there. Do you have gloves?"

She nodded. "Watch for junk. I don't think there's anything back there but it's pretty overgrown."

"I'll take a quick look."

Jay left to check behind the barn and she went to her pickup to get her leather gloves and to swap her cowboy hat for a ball cap. Then she walked behind his flatbed when he drove around the barn. She stood out of the way while he efficiently maneuvered the truck and backed it where he wanted it.

"I'm going to get the tree off the barn first," he said when he got out. "After it's down I'll show you how to use the small saw and we'll get started. How does that sound?"

"What more could a girl want?" she said and made a face.

He grinned and with one pull started the bigger saw. Within minutes the tree teetered, but did not fall from its resting place on the barn. He returned to the truck for a heavy strap. He wrapped one end of the strap around the tree trunk and hooked the other end over the ball on the bumper of his truck.

"I want you over there," he said motioning.

Obediently she moved to the place he indicated and then she watched him pull the tree off the barn. He freed the strap, tossed it on the flatbed and picked up the little saw.

"Don't be afraid of it, but be respectful," he told her. "Stick to the little limbs and I'll get the big ones. I have a splitter that I'll bring out one day and we'll take care of the big pieces then. I'd suggest stacking the dead away from the green… Do you know the difference?" He asked it diplomatically.

She took a look before nodding.

"Pile or stack the green somewhere out of the way until next season," he said. "It should be ready to burn next year."

He demonstrated how to start the saw and then he showed her how to make the cut. He shut it off and handed it to her. It wasn't as heavy as she thought it would be. Then Jay was behind her, reaching around her to show how to position her hands on the saw. She was momentarily distracted as she thought how much bigger he was than her.

"Don't overdo it, and don't do anything dumb," he said, his face close to her cheek. "Make your cuts about fourteen, sixteen inches apart. Go ahead and start it up."

She pulled the line twice before it started, and then it died. The third time she pulled he adjusted the choke to keep it running, and then he moved away. She leaned over a limb and made the cut, thinking it wasn't as hard as she anticipated. She grinned but didn't look away from what she was doing.

Jay worked in another location of the tree while she concentrated on what she was doing. When she became weary of the weight of the saw she shut it off. She tossed pieces of wood to a pile and Jay continued cutting. After some time she went back to the saw. She held it like he had shown her and pulled the cord. It just sputtered, but on the second try she started it, and kept it running. She smiled broadly and looked at Jay some distance away. He smiled back.

Jay didn't stop until the sun was going down, and even then he didn't dawdle but set about loading his oil, gas and sharpening equipment on the back of his truck.

"It doesn't look like there's serious damage to the barn," he told her as he hoisted the big saw to the flatbed.

Riley walked past the smaller saw that had been sitting idle the last forty-five minutes on her way to get a closer look. She thought there were an awful lot of splintered and missing boards but she trusted Jay's judgment and what he said made her feel good.

"Some of the smaller wood'll be good for kindling," said Jay. "How much kindling you need depends on how good you get at starting a fire."

She redirected her thoughts from barn repairs back to the wood. She looked at the scattered cut pieces on the ground, the pile she had made and the big chunks that needed to be split. There was a lot of wood there, a lot of work, and all of it would have to be moved closer to the house before winter. Jay went to retrieve the saw she had used. He had an amused look on his face and Riley realized her bewilderment must be showing. She also felt bad for not picking up the saw herself.

"What do I owe you?" she asked

He tucked the saw between the big one and the gas can on the flatbed. "Nothing."

"I don't expect you to have done all this for nothing," she asserted.

"Don't worry about it. We're practically neighbors," he said as if that explained things.

For some reason she expected this from him. "At least let me offer you a beer or something… I have a few things in a cooler in the house."

"A Coke sounds pretty good—if you've got one," he said over his shoulder while situating the tow strap behind the seat.

"Can I show you the house? Ernie's been doing great work."

"Yeah, I'd like that," he said. "Want a ride while I move my truck?"

Inside the house he inspected the work in progress with a satisfied look. "Son of a gun he's doing a bang-up job, isn't he," he commented. "This will be very nice for you." He took a drink. "You must still be staying in the trailer?"

"Yes. Only the bathroom is livable."

He looked around a little more before saying he needed to go. Riley walked with him to his flatbed.

"Do you have a phone out here?" he asked.

"Just the portable in the truck."

"Make sure you keep it charged," he said. "It'll probably be a couple of weeks before I have a free weekend to work on the tree again. Let me know if it's in the way before I get to it."

She scoffed. "I'm just glad it's not on the barn anymore. Thank you," she told him with sincerity.

He opened his door, got in and said, "You're welcome." He turned the key and the engine came to life.

Riley stepped back and raised a hand to wave. Then she watched until his red tail lights could no longer be seen because of rolling dust.

Inside her trailer she added to her list to contact the phone company, and scratched off *tree leaning on the barn.*

CHAPTER 17

The next morning Riley was having a hard time waiting for Ernie. He pulled in at a quarter to seven and she met him when he was getting out of his pickup. Wooly, as if knowing she was going somewhere, was at her side. After saying hello she asked where she should buy horse tanks and a lawn mower.

"Conrad's got 'em but I'd buy the mower from Jay Tapperd," he told her and pushed the door shut. "He has new and rebuilt ones."

"I remember seeing them! I thought I'd have to drive to Northboro. I guess I'll wait until Jay opens and run into town."

"Oh, sometimes Jay's open first light," he said as if everyone knew that. "You might've already missed him if he had to be someplace."

Her brows went up. "I'd better get going. I've got errands to run too, so it might be a while before I get back."

But Jay's work truck was gone and the shop locked. Disappointed, she headed back to her pickup, with Wooly at her side. She was pulling her to-do list from her pocket when a late model four-door Chevy flatbed drove up. The driver, one of two men in the front, both of Mexican or Spanish origin and both wearing cowboy hats, asked if Jay was around. Riley told them no. The boy in the back seat rolled down his window and spoke to Wooly. The big dog was attentive to the lad.

"Do you know when he'll be back?" the man asked. Because of his enunciation and manner he gave Riley the impression he was well-educated. His teeth were near perfect but his wire-rimmed glasses, dark from the bright sun, hid his eyes. She shook her head again.

"Good morning," said the man from the passenger side. He was an aged version of the younger cowboy but his words thick with Spanish accent. He had flyers in his hand.

"Morning," she replied.

"Is that your dog?" the boy asked.

She nodded and folded her list.

"Let's leave the stuff with a note," the younger man told the older one. "We can call later."

They all got out and while the men walked to the back of the truck the boy pet Wooly. The older man laid the flyers on the flatbed and the breeze promptly threatened to relocate them. Riley went to the rescue. The flyers advertised dirt work and custom haying. The men placed their load near the door and when they came back the older man thanked Riley.

"Where are you from?" she asked.

"Over near Spencer," the younger man said. "It's about twenty miles southeast of here. How about you?"

"I just moved here, up the road," she said and motioned. "I'm Riley Montgomery."

"Very nice to meet you," he told her. "Trace del Oro. This is my dad, Chigger, and my son, Shortbread."

Chigger nodded again but Shortbread hardly noticed, engrossed with Wooly. Shortbread's hair was light, perhaps his namesake, Riley thought, but otherwise he did look like Trace and Chigger. She guessed he was about eight years old.

"Which of you is looking for work?" she asked.

"That would be me," said Chigger deliberately as if searching for the right words. "I'm usually busy with hay but there's no much rain. I think I need to try another trade for now."

"Would you be interested in clearing a spot for me and working up the ground for an arena?"

"Si." He was attentive. "How soon?"

"Whatever works for you. I'm not in a hurry, but..."

"Do you have time for me to come look right now?" Chigger asked. "I could do the work this week. If you hire me I give you discount if I can use you as reference."

She laughed. "I don't know how much good that would do you. Yes, we can look right now. You can follow me there if you want."

Trace was already walking to the driver's side of the flatbed.

"We be right behind you," confirmed Chigger.

Riley headed for her truck. Wooly reluctantly left Shortbread to join her, and Shortbread watched the big dog go.

"C'mon, Short," said Trace.

Like his feet were heavy with lead, Shortbread started to go.

"He can ride with me and Wooly if he wants," Riley said.

"Can I?" he begged his father.

Trace looked at Riley as if to make sure it was okay, then he told the boy yes. Shortbread ran across the gravel.

There were two beat-up muscle cars parked near Ernie's pickup when Riley drove up the driveway. She assumed they must belong to Tommy and the other high school kids Ernie hired to help. After she came to a stop, Shortbread got out and then held the door for Wooly. It was hard to decipher which of the two had become more attached to the other. Trace pulled in beside her.

"Back here," she directed, leading the way. "Next year I might have the barn taken down and a metal building put up. Do you see anything that suggests I wouldn't be able to do that?"

Chigger assessed the area with his eyes. "I don't see why not." He left Riley, Trace, Shortbread and Wooly at the edge of the grass and began poking around in the weeds.

While they watched Chigger, sounds of Ernie and Tommy working in the house resounded in the yard. Trace turned to look.

"There are kittens under the front porch," Riley told Shortbread. "But they're not tame."

"Can I go look?" Shortbread pleaded to his dad.

"Yes, but be careful," Trace instructed.

Wooly tried to stay beside Shortbread but in the boy's haste the old dog couldn't keep up. Shortbread slowed down.

"He's adorable," Riley told Trace.

"Thanks. He's a good kid." He looked from Shortbread to her. "You said you just moved here?"

She nodded. "Ernie's been working in the house for a few weeks but I just started staying here Saturday. In the trailer," she added.

Chigger left the grass and weeds. "I can start in couple of days," he said.

"That would be great!"

"Come show me what you want, and where," he told her.

They walked the area with Riley telling him what she had in mind. Chigger priced his work and they shook hands in agreement.

"Time to go, Shortbread," Trace said loud enough to be heard when they were ready to leave.

Shortbread crawled from under the porch, cradling a kitten he had managed to capture.

"No..." said Trace.

Looking disappointed but not surprised, Shortbread gently set the kitten on the ground. It scurried back to safety. Then together he and Wooly crossed the yard.

"Can we come back again?" Shortbread asked.

"Anytime you want," Riley said. "Maybe next time the house will be decent and I'll have cookies."

He smiled broadly at the thought.

"We have to go," said Chigger.

"Bye!" said Shortbread.

When they were going down the driveway Riley returned Shortbread's wave, his smiling face visible through the back window.

This time when Jay's shop was in view, she saw his work truck there. The things that Trace and Chigger had placed outside had already been picked up. Her footsteps were the only sound in the shop except for the hum of the fans until she heard Jay say hello behind her.

She turned and watched him finish the walk. "I came to buy a lawn mower," she said almost absentmindedly.

"What'd you have in mind?" he asked, wiping at his hands with a shop rag. He went around her on his way to the mowers.

"I don't know. Something reliable," she said, joining him. "If it has an engine I'll probably have trouble with it."

"You handled that chain saw pretty good yesterday."

"That's because you were right there in case I had trouble."

His reserved smile appeared. He proceeded to point out the good and bad of each of the mowers.

She took in a deep breath. "I think I'll take a push mower. The place isn't that big and I could use the exercise."

He stepped behind one and pushed it out of the row. "Then I would suggest this one. It'll get the job done and hasn't been used hard."

"Okay," she said. "What else do I need?"

He gave her a funny look.

"I haven't had to mow for years. It was one of the things taken care of with the rent."

"Life of luxury, eh?"

"Yeah, I guess you could say it was."

"Didn't have to worry about snow either?"

"Nope."

He grinned and pushed the mower across the shop floor. "Good choice of mowers with this one," he said. "That'll leave you money for a snow blower."

Now it was she who looked at him oddly. He left the mower to get a gas can.

"Winter can be pretty nasty out here," he said on his way back. "I can clear your drive with my tractor when the snow's deep if you want, that is if you don't have someone else already lined up."

It was hard for her to think of snow in the middle of summer with the fans going and a lawn mower in front of her, but she had no doubts that he knew what he was talking about.

He checked the oil and gas levels, showed her how to start it and gave a quick lesson on things to check if she had problems. Then he picked up the gas can, pushed the mower out of the shop and lifted it to the back of her truck. Riley went to the cab to get her purse.

At his desk she watched him write out the receipt. She filled in the appropriate numbers on her check and handed it to him.

"Thank you, Jay," she said.

"You're welcome," he told her and put the check with others in the desk.

She started to leave. "I'll try not to be a bother, but can I call if I have trouble with it?"

"You know you can," he replied.

She told him thank you once more and left.

Before leaving Whispering Pines she also purchased water tanks and a garden hose from Conrad's. She smiled when water spilled into the tanks from the hose attached to the new hydrant, and again when the lawn mower started the first time she pulled the cord. She mowed the rest of the day, first the yard that hadn't been mowed since God only knew and then between the road and lot fences until it got too dark to see. When she finally made it to bed, she was tired and achy and happy.

CHAPTER 18

Cap Henderson stepped out of the shower. He had tangled with a cow that morning and didn't want to go around smelling like one all day. Before showering he told Peggy she should join him, but she said she was leaving for some stupid thing in Northboro, he didn't remember what. He grunted. He had been meaning to talk to that gal who bought the Colby place and figured now would be as good a time as any. It would give him the chance to do a little prospecting, see what kind of woman she was, and maybe he'd get lucky after all.

As Cap pulled up to the Colby place, Ernie and Tommy were working in the new kitchen and great room. Tommy was a skinny computer geek with skin problems and dark framed glasses but he was a good kid and a good worker, just as Ernie said. Tommy had been saving money to buy accessories for his new computer and was telling Ernie how they were going to change the world. Riley, alone in the laundry and mud room scraping excessive sealant off the floor, listened to their conversation.

Cap popped a mint in his mouth before he reached for the knob on the back door. He opened the door and stepped in, his hand still on the knob. Lazily he took in the changes and when he saw Riley kneeling on the floor looking at him, a smug smile formed. The faint morning breeze slipped in through the open door behind him, carrying the fresh scent of soap and a wisp of cigarette.

Riley got to her feet. "Don't you have the decency to knock?" she asked sharply.

"It's not like you've set up housekeepin' yet," he replied. His eyes looked her up and down and settled on her breasts.

"Eyes up here," she said firmly.

He brought his look to hers, still smiling. Ernie and Tommy, out of sight, had gone silent.

"Just what is it you want, Cap?" she asked impatiently.

"Why, I wanted to talk about taking care of the place, of course. You know, the farming, or anything else you might need," he said suggestively.

Ernie appeared in the doorway of the new kitchen, the opening wider than before with Chloe's wheelchair in mind. Cap switched his attention to Ernie and then past him, trying to see. Ernie sidestepped to block his view.

"Whatever it is you're peddling, I'm not interested," Riley told him.

Cap looked at her again, pursed his lips and wet them with his tongue. Then Tommy was slipping around Ernie in the wide doorway. Cap watched him go down the hall and they heard the bathroom door close.

"Where'd you come up with him?" Cap asked. "With all the beefy farm kids to pick from why'd you come up with this one?" He didn't wait for an answer. "Give me a tour?"

"No," Riley said defensively and stepped in front of him.

He could easily see over the top of her head. "I like a saucy woman," he told her. "And here the bar talk is that you're quiet."

"Get out of here," she said, angered. "We've got things to do."

Tommy came from the hall. Cap watched him go back the way he came.

"Just trying to be helpful," said Cap. "Thought you might appreciate having a real man around."

Riley leaned exaggeratedly to look past him, outside.

"And who might that be?" she asked. "Did you bring someone with you?"

His eyes narrowed. He reached for the cigarettes in his shirt pocket and put one in his mouth. "What're you looking at?" he snapped at Ernie, the cigarette moving with his words.

Ernie shrugged. "First Chloe gets the best of you, and now Riley."

Riley went back to work and tried to hide her smile. Cap glared at Ernie and then stormed out. Riley couldn't help but giggle. Tommy poked his head over Ernie's shoulder.

"Ker-pow," Tommy said. "Ern, you'd better watch your back. He's gonna be gunning for you."

Riley frowned, not having considered that before.

Ernie shook his head. "He's all smoke. He'll tell a big story at the bar and milk it as long as anyone'll listen."

"Are you sure?" asked Riley.

"Oh yeah. I oughta know. I heard him enough in my drunken days." Ernie gave her a reassuring smile before turning back to the kitchen.

* * *

Riley stood at the kitchen counter, waiting for the workers to finish installing the phones, one downstairs and another in the loft. With a contented look she gazed into the great room, envisioning, and tapped the end of a carpenter's pencil on her bottom lip. False timber beams that were to be installed along the roof line over the great room were to be delivered in the next ten days and they would complement the rustic, southwestern look of wood and stucco she had decided on, and wood handrail would be put along the open side of the staircase to the loft. She would drive to Owen to pick out wall coverings and shop for furniture as soon as the house was nearing completion.

"We're done, ma'am," said one of the men. He placed the receiver on the new phone hanging on the wall just outside the kitchen in the great room.

"Already?" she said putting the pencil down.

"It's easy in new construction like this," he replied. He picked his tool bag off the floor and the other worker came from the loft.

"Upstairs is ready to go," he said.

Riley saw them out. Then she went to the new phone and pushed the numbers of the law firm where she had worked for so many years.

Mitch returned to his office, having just been at the reception desk. He still couldn't get used to seeing the new woman sitting where Riley should be. His phone buzzed.

"Yes?"

"You have a call on line three," said Cynthia sweetly, and the image of her batting her eyes formed in his mind. "A Miss Montgomery."

That got his attention. He had begun to wonder if she would ever call. Without saying thank you before disconnecting he pushed the blinking button.

"Mitch Matthews," he said professionally, not taking any chances.

"You're the first one I'm calling from the phone in the house," Riley told him.

He refrained from saying it was about time or how much he missed her. Instead, "It's so good to hear from you! How have you been? How is it going out there?" he asked.

"It's great. We've come so far with the house," she began, and he listened as she talked for a minute. "I was really expecting to make it back this weekend, but I've got to be here when they deliver beams for the ceiling and we're not sure yet when that will be."

He turned the pages of the appointment calendar on his desk. "Can I come out? I've got to be in the office Saturday morning but I could drive out after, spend the night."

"Really? You want to do that? But this place is a wreck."

"If you're there, that's all I need."

"You're such a romantic. Oh! Would you mind meeting me at the county fair? There's a barrel race that afternoon…and a dance after. Want to go to the dance?"

"Whatever you want," he said as positively as he could. The idea of dust and livestock wasn't appealing but he would deal with it. "Tell me how to get there."

CHAPTER 19

Riley was relaxing in a folding camp chair, staying with Wooly and her horses at the trailer during the commotion of the county fair parade. Dobbie resembled a statue watching the goings-on in the distance, and Riley alternated from keeping an eye on Dobbie to browsing the magazine in her lap. The late afternoon barrel race had been uneventful with only locals attending and Dually had won her some money.

She was reading when the round toes of Roper cowboy boots appeared before her in the grass. She lifted the publication to shade her eyes, first seeing jeans that were fairly new and then the tails of a short-sleeved, button-up shirt. It was Jay. She had never seen him wearing cowboy boots—he was always in work boots. Wooly was wagging his tail with recognition.

"Hello," she said. "You know you're missing all the excitement of the parade, don't you?" She got up and went to the trailer where she reached in for another chair, then she almost bumped into Jay when she turned around with it. He was standing right behind her.

"Oops," she said.

"Sorry," he replied, and took the chair from her.

She watched him walk away, thinking his shirt-tail hung just right. Then she took two beverages from the melting ice in the cooler and picked up another chair in case there was more company. Jay, waiting for her by his chair, adjusted his ball cap. She offered him one of the sodas.

"Thanks," he said. He popped the tab and sat down. "Nice buckle."

She thought back to that morning when she had put the buckle on her belt, the buckle she had won before she and Peter broke up. She told him thank you and sat down.

"What about you? Do you ride?" she asked out of politeness.

"Some. But I don't compete anymore. Haven't for years."

It surprised her. "I guess I never thought of you riding," she confessed.

"I only ride colts now." He looked across the fairgrounds. "And I don't get that done as often as I should. And they need to be broke first," he admitted with a bashful smile. "I won't… *can't* ride them anymore until the buck is out of them." He leaned back. "I get to thinking I'll ride more from time to time, but never do. I have a handful of broodmares and raise a few foals."

"Really?" she asked, interested.

They talked about bloodlines. He said he had been dabbling with barrel and race horse lines to add speed. He asked about Novocain and then Dobbie and Dually. Only with her prompting did he keep talking, telling her about horses he had raised over the years and some of their accomplishments. She was impressed, both with what he was telling her as well as the fact that she had gotten him to talk about himself. When they eventually turned quiet, Riley felt the silence between them was one of the most natural things in the world.

They watched the parade wrap up and then Kelly Lynch and her husband Conner were coming in their direction.

"Hi ya," Kelly called out. "Your mare had a nice run today."

"Thanks," Riley replied and stood.

"We can't stay," said Kelly. "I saw you and wanted to say hello. I've missed seeing you at the rodeos. Do you miss hauling?"

"I've been too busy to think about it."

"Amy Cordhall and Novocain have been doing great. Miranda...the redhead... Remember her?"

Riley bit her lip and tried to put a face with the name.

"The night at Little Creek when you went down at the first barrel?" Kelly prodded.

"Oh, yeah, I remember now."

"Miranda was winning at Chaney until Amy and Novocain came in and cleaned her clock," Kelly said, clearly tickled.

Riley laughed.

Kelly looked at Jay and then back to Riley. "You guys hungry? Want to get some delicious and nutritious carnival food?"

After tying Wooly in the shade of the gooseneck of the trailer they walked to the midway, where the aroma of fair food was in the air and ancient carnival rides in full swing. The dinosaur rides sounded as old as they looked, but any question of reliability was disregarded by the participants who shrieked with joy. They threaded their way through crowds including those in front of games attempting to win a prize.

They picked the food vendor of their choice and joined the end of the line. Kelly and Connor looked over the menu posted at the serving window, but Riley saw Cap Henderson. He was with a petite woman wearing jeans and boots and her blonde hair was in a ponytail.

"Have you had the pleasure of meeting Cap?" Jay asked.

"Yes and no," replied Riley. "I've met him but wouldn't say it was a pleasure."

Jay grinned. "That's his wife Peggy."

Riley looked at Jay, speechless.

"Did you know that she and Paul Conrad's wife are sisters?" She nodded. "Ernie told me."

"I know Peggy. She's nice," Kelly interjected. "She helps out at brandings."

"What would you like?" Jay asked Riley. They had reached the order window. "I'll buy."

"I feel like I'm always getting the good end of this friendship," she said with a little laugh.

He diverted his bashful but twinkling eyes.

After eating Kelly and Connor left, saying they had fair business to attend to. Jay gathered up the trash, deposited it in a barrel and they began the walk back to Riley's trailer, which was some distance away. The band was setting up in the arena, not far from where her trailer was parked, and she wondered just how much of that would Dobbie take calmly.

"Are you staying for the dance?" Jay asked.

"Yes, actually I'm waiting for—"

She was interrupted by a shouted greeting from Miles Deroin who burst from a crowd. Beside him was a tall, flawless looking woman with long dark hair, and Riley realized it was the woman she had seen in the white Saturn at Jay's. She had brown skin like Miles and Riley assumed they were brother and sister from their striking resemblance to each other.

"You old dog," Miles accused Jay while looking at Riley. He grabbed Jay's hand and pumped it vigorously. "Moving in on my girl?"

"I think you have that backward," Jay told him.

The woman with Miles leaped at Jay and gave him a big hug that he reciprocated. She slid down the side of him, he released his bear hug embrace and she stood with her arms wrapped around one of his.

"You remember Miles, don't you?" Jay asked Riley.

Miles and Riley grinned at each other. She was thinking about his early morning trailer break at the Fourth of July rodeo.

"Of course," Riley said. "How's the brunette?"

Miles laughed, put an arm around her and started to lead her away, leaving Jay and the woman behind.

"You know she doesn't mean anything to me," he said persuasively, but Riley was listening instead to the woman telling Jay she thought she and Miles made a cute couple.

Miles walked Riley to her trailer, talking all the while.

"Let me untie my dog," Riley said, escaping. "You sure have a way with the ladies, don't you?" she said over her shoulder.

"It's a curse, I'm afraid," Miles said plunking into one of the chairs. "I used to think it was a blessing," he sighed dramatically, "but have come to realize it's a curse."

She laughed. He wasn't arrogant, but full of life and high spirits.

"I suppose you're going to tell me that was your sister back there," she said, and as the words came out knew she was soliciting information concerning the woman she assumed was Jay's girlfriend.

"Oh, yes, it was, er, it is," he confirmed. He swiped a sleeve across his forehead and then repositioned the black felt cowboy hat on his head. "I guess I don't think of you as a stranger in these parts who doesn't know anyone. That's Marta, my twin sister. We get along great, but now her and Jay…" His voice trailed off as Mitch's sporty black Mitsubishi came into view. It rolled to a stop a few yards away and Miles let out a long, low whistle.

The car was a head turner to begin with and it was one of the few vehicles on the fairgrounds not farm related or covered with dust. The door opened and a white Adidas partly covered by denim appeared. Mitch stepped out and stood behind the open door, smiling broadly at Riley. She thought he looked like he was posing for a photo shoot, but had to admit he did look good.

"Found you," Mitch declared before shutting the door.

"Nice ride," Miles complimented and left his chair, entranced with the car.

Mitch looked at Miles like he hadn't seen him before.

"Did you have any trouble finding the place?" Riley asked as she made her way to him.

Mitch quit looking at Miles and met Riley with an affectionate hug. He managed to get in the beginnings of a passionate kiss before she politely pulled away. Miles turned from the car, his mouth open with a question that never came out.

"Apparently you two aren't related," he said instead.

Riley blushed. "Miles, this is Mitch Matthews. Mitch, Miles Deroin."

Dobbie's water bucket rattled against the wheel well of the trailer and Riley excused herself to check on him.

"Duh-roy-in?" Mitch asked, incorrectly pronouncing the name.

"Dee Ruin," Miles replied as if used to clarifying. "French Canadian, on my mom's side." He went back to looking at the car and Mitch scrutinized Miles. "I'm a truck man myself, but for a car this is pretty nice. It must've cost as much as my Dodge. What do you do?"

"I'm a lawyer," Mitch said and waited for the reaction he expected was coming.

Miles let out another low whistle just as Riley returned.

"Riley," he said. "Did you know this scallywag you're hooked up with is a *lawyer*?"

"He can't be perfect you know," she said with a little laugh.

Mitch laughed too, looking quite pleased. He sat in a chair and pulled Riley to his lap.

"Well, I'll be," Miles continued with the sham of an impressed look on his face. "Educated folk in our little backwoods county."

Miles sat down too. The band was beginning to play and he tapped a foot with the music. A few minutes later Jay and Marta arrived. Marta, still clutching Jay's arm and talking, ceased her chatter when they walked around Mitch's car.

"Nice!" said Marta, but Jay was looking at Riley sitting on Mitch's lap.

"This is Mitch," Riley said and then she nodded at the new arrivals, saying, "Jay and Marta."

Jay looked from Riley to Miles with surprise. "So you were civilized for once and made introductions?" he asked with disbelief.

"What do you take me for?" Miles said offensively and stood up. "I'm not a total clod." He hooked an arm in Marta's and gave her a twirl. "Who's up for dancing?"

Marta laughed delightedly, and then they were gone. Because of the noise of the band Riley wanted to put Wooly in the trailer. She said as much and left with the dog.

Jay, looking uncomfortable, watched her go.

"You go on," Mitch told Jay. "We'll be along in a minute."

Jay glanced at Mitch before leaving, going the same direction Miles and Marta had gone.

Before Riley stepped out of her trailer, Mitch was there. He put his arms around her and started kissing her neck. He worked his way to her lips.

"I've missed you so much," he said. "Have you missed me?"

"I haven't had time," she said breathlessly.

He pulled away, insulted. She regretted her remark, although it was true. She hadn't intended to hurt his feelings and drew him back against her.

"Not until I saw you again," she said honestly, trying to make up.

He hugged her then pulled back.

"You smell like...a horse," he told her.

"Of course I do. I've been here since ten o'clock this morning."

His hands slipped to her hips. "Is that new whirlpool tub of yours two-people friendly?" he asked, caressing.

"Did you want to skip the dance?" she proposed, her face close to his. "Go home now?"

His willing expression changed to one of deep thought. "No, I want to show you off a little first."

When they reached the dancers, Mitch parted the way to a spot that suited him. There they danced to several upbeat tempos.

"Don't they believe in good old-fashioned slow dances?" he remarked. "I'm ready to go. Is there a decent bathroom close?"

As soon as they were off the dirt of the makeshift dance floor the band began to play a romantic melody. Mitch threw his arms up in disgusted resignation and struck off by himself. Riley had barely caught her breath when she saw Miles.

"Come with me," he said eagerly and took her by the hand.

She looked in the direction that Mitch had gone but didn't see him, and soon they were lost amongst the bodies in motion. When they reached Jay and Marta, Miles grinned at Jay mischievously, but just a few dance steps later a Barbie doll clone stepped in.

"Excuse me," the knockout blonde said to Riley, "but I saw him first."

Miles hesitated and then allowed her to take him away. At the same time an older gentleman tapped Marta on the shoulder, and then she too was whisked away.

"You might as well dance with 'er, Tapperd," the gentleman called out to Jay. "I've got your Marta."

Jay grinned, first at the old man and then at Riley, this time with submission. She put her hand in his that he offered and felt his other, warm and comforting, on the small of her back. His shirt was damp beneath her touch and once again she was reminded of how small she felt this close to him. The crowd became non-existent during the next few minutes, and just as periods of silence between them seemed so natural, so were their steps as they moved together.

It was Miles who brought an end to the mood, swinging by with his flavor-of-the-month partner. Riley heard Marta's joyful laugh and picked out the dark-headed beauty and old gentleman. Then she saw Mitch searching at the edge of the crowd. Her feet stopped moving.

"I've got to go," she told Jay, almost pleading.

Slowly he loosened his hold, but he didn't let her go. His eyes probed hers as if trying to determine the source of her regretful tone, something she wasn't sure of herself.

"Thank you...for the dance," she said.

Respectfully Jay took a step back, and then the drummer was striking up a beat. "Conga!" chorused the dancers and Jay and Riley were jostled as the lively line started to form.

"C'mon, big brother!" Marta was saying and then, as part of the conga line, she was dragging Miles and reaching for Jay.

Jay allowed her to snatch him, and Riley watched until he was swallowed by the dancers. When he was out of sight she attempted to leave but had to wait until she had the chance.

"I was kidnapped," she offered when she reached Mitch. She tried to read his face but couldn't because of the shadows of the night.

"I can't say I blame him," said Mitch. He put his arm around her and headed to the trailer.

* * *

"This will be very nice," Mitch commented. "Your contactor has been doing good work."

"I think so," she said.

After spending the night in the horse trailer, they had come to the house to make coffee. Riley suspected Mitch needed some semblance of normalcy, even if the aroma of brewing coffee competed with that of the new construction. She wiped a drop of spilled water off the granite countertop with the shirt-tail of her oversized shirt and exposed her panties in the process.

"Sweet," Mitch said. "But I don't suppose there are any tanning booths in Hooterville."

"Whispering Pines," she corrected. "Probably not. Maybe that's my calling—maybe I should open a tanning salon out here."

"Yeah. That'd look awesome on your resume."

"Let me show you around."

She had no doubts that he was impressed. When they were in the loft bedroom he grabbed her and drew her close.

"I can't wait to see this room when it's finished," he told her.

She laughed and pulled away.

"What about this view?" she asked at the rail overlooking the open space.

He gave her a lustful look, then joined her.

"It *is* nice," he said. "I'm happy for you, but I wish you were still in Owen, still working in the office."

"I know," she said softly. They stood at the rail, each lost in their own thoughts. "Would you like to go to town and get some breakfast?" she eventually asked.

"No, let's go to Northboro, check out real civilization."

"Really? I've never been there. I'd love to see it."

It was only a forty-minute drive in Mitch's sporty car. First they came upon a fairly new hospital on the edge of town and then a residential area. Mitch insisted on finding a car wash before they went anywhere so he could rid his Mitsubishi of the county fair dust. After breakfast they stumbled upon a farmer's market and quaint shops. They did a lot of browsing but the only things purchased were a sketch of the two of them by a sidewalk artist and a frame for the drawing.

CHAPTER 20

The false ceiling beams and the workers to install them arrived early in the week. Ernie had put a hold on the kitchen, instead focusing on prepping the ceiling in the great room so it would be ready. Riley was amazed at the changes the rustic, prominent timbers made and knew that once the walls were textured the timbers would complement the stucco beautifully. She thought the long abandoned house was beginning to exude warmth and personality as if it had been holding out, waiting for her to prove she was staying.

Saturday morning she drove to town for groceries. Jay saw her at the corner near his shop and flagged her down.

"Are you going to be home this afternoon…early evening?" he asked as if expecting her to say no.

"Yes, I don't have any plans."

"I can come out and finish that tree if you'd like."

"Don't you have something better to do on your Saturday night?"

"Nope," he replied. "I started that tree and told you I'd finish it. I'm busy tomorrow but later today works for me."

"I'm on my way to Decker's. How about I pick up extra and feed you supper after?"

He hesitated but looked like he thought that might be nice. "Okay," he relented. "But don't be doing anything fancy."

"I don't even have a kitchen yet," she said with a laugh. "But I'll promise more than skinny meat sandwiches."

He smiled faintly as if he couldn't help it.

At Decker's she bought several ribeyes because she had no idea what Jay liked but figured she couldn't go wrong with having plenty of steaks to offer. She also bought garlic bread in foil, baked beans in a big tin can and mixed nuts plus beer, soda and iced tea, and the last seven packages of Zingers on the shelf. The little chocolate cakes would have to suffice for dessert because Decker's didn't have a bakery. Then she stopped at Conrad Lumber to purchase a propane grill and picnic table—she had been meaning to buy both anyway.

She was in the barn pitchforking old loose hay into the box of Goliath when Jay arrived. She saw that Trace del Oro was with him and then they were out of sight from her view, the log splitter bouncing behind.

Trace had the splitter unhooked and Jay was situating the flatbed where he wanted it when she and Wooly made it to the back of the barn.

"Hope you don't mind me tagging along," said Trace.

"Not at all! How's Shortbread?"

"Good. He'd be mad if he knew I was here without him. My mom is taking him and Megan—I have a four-year-old daughter too," he said with a sideways glance at her, "to a movie this afternoon."

"That's nice of her," she replied. She smiled as she pictured little Megan and she wondered if she was as engaging as Shortbread, but nothing more was said.

Jay showed her how to operate the splitter. He and Trace divided their duties between running the saws and helping get the big pieces to the splitter, and it wasn't long before the remainder of the tree was cut up. Riley picked up limbs too small to be of any use and tossed them to the substantial pile while Jay and Trace put tools away. Trace proposed the pile be used for a bonfire one day and Riley thought that was a wonderful idea.

"You're staying to eat, aren't you?" she asked him when Jay was pulling away with the flatbed and splitter. They and Wooly fell in behind, following the tire tracks in the black dirt along the edge of the arena.

"That's the reason I'm here," he said with a grin. "I was stopping for the things that Dad and I left at Jay's earlier—the day we met you—and asked if he wanted to get a beer. That's when he told me he was coming here."

"Thanks for helping. I owe you. I owe Jay, too," she said looking ahead at the entourage that turned the corner of the barn and then disappeared.

"No you don't."

Jay had parked on the drive in front of the barn and by the time he got out Riley and Trace were within hearing range. Jay motioned to her pickup in the yard, specifically the grill and picnic table still in the back of it.

"I thought you weren't going to any trouble," he said.

"I needed them anyway. Honest."

Jay didn't reply but headed that way. Trace got to her pickup first and hopped up in the box. He slid the picnic table to the tailgate where Jay and Riley took over, then they did the same with the grill.

She asked Jay if he would be in charge of the steaks. They started inside, Jay seasoning the meat on the granite counter that had no cabinet doors above or below and Riley using a primitive can opener on the beans. Trace handed out requested drinks from the cooler, got paper plates and plastic utensils ready, made conversation and cruised the house.

The productive late summer day continued to unwind while they waited on the steaks. Jay manned the grill, Riley sat at the picnic table and Trace propped himself on the top, swinging a leg and snacking on mixed nuts. After they ate steaks grilled to perfection they talked and laughed until the sun went down.

Neither Jay nor Trace seemed to be in a hurry to leave and Riley didn't want to see them go. Ultimately the guys contributed to the black plastic trash sack that Riley held open and it was Jay who said it was time to be heading home. Almost as soon as the words were spoken he struck off, and was in the shadows beyond the range of the yard light before Trace reluctantly went too. Riley started for the dumpster behind the house and heard Jay laugh. She knew it was Jay, although she had never heard him laugh like that before.

Jay was rounding the back of the splitter when Trace jogged across the driveway. He didn't need to see Trace's long face to know what was on his mind. It was then that he laughed, the guttural sound more bitter than amusing. He caught himself and in a lighter tone said to Trace, "Give it up, del Oro. She's got a boyfriend." He reached for the door handle and spoke over the roof. "Some lawyer dude from the big city, about your age."

Trace was taking in the information when Jay ducked to get in the truck. His words of advice were more for himself than they were for Trace. It was just as well there were boundaries—life was easier with low expectations.

* * *

Trace opened the back door of his parents' one-story farmhouse and stepped in. Shortbread and Megan were singing a nursery rhyme and he could hear a country song playing on the radio in the background. Then his mother, Emelee, was talking to the kids, telling them not to slip on the wet bathroom linoleum. A minute later they emerged from the bathroom in pajamas and with damp hair.

"Dad!" Shortbread exclaimed. He broke into a run and Megan tried her best to keep up.

Trace knelt and gave them a hug. Then he kept an arm around Shortbread while Megan scrambled onto her father's knee, her short little legs dangling like a kitten hanging from a tree limb. She was petite with green eyes and a peppering of freckles.

"Shortbread said I was ugly," she said, pouting.

"Did not," Shortbread said defensively. "I said you looked like a goat the way your hair was sticking out. I like goats."

"How was the movie?" Trace asked.

"Good! We ate popcorn."

Megan nodded in agreement. Trace looked at his mother and smiled.

"We had a wonderful time," said Emelee. "Didn't we, *niños?*"

"Yes," they chimed.

Megan stretched to give Trace a kiss on the cheek. He kissed the top of her head and then he leaned to kiss Shortbread, who made a face and pulled back.

"All right, get to bed then," Trace said. He released the group embrace and they wiggled away.

"Night, Dad," they chorused, their earlier disagreement forgotten.

"Good night," he replied. He stood up and watched until they disappeared through the doorway of their shared bedroom.

On his way to the humble kitchen he pulled out his checkbook and wallet, then he plunked them down on the table beside the centerpiece of a napkin holder containing bills. He went through the bills, separating his from the rest. He took quick inventory of what was in front of him compared to how much money was in his checking account. He barely had enough, but enough was good. He hadn't been working very long as a ranch hand at Focus Ranch ten miles away and was happy for the work. Bruce Focustacia, owner of the ranch, seemed to be an honest and good man. As much as Trace wanted to be on his own he knew he could never manage working full time, especially on a ranch, and taking care of Shortbread and Megan too. He sighed, his disappointment mixed with resignation. He was almost thirty years old with two children and living with his folks, but deep down knew he was doing the best he could.

He heard Shortbread and Megan giggling and then they were quiet again. He smiled. They were good kids and he loved them. He knew Megan was not his and sometimes found himself doubting that Shortbread was too. He had met Savannah when he was attending college in Albuquerque. She was a pretty fair-haired thing, down on her luck, and he was a country boy in the big city. He happened to be walking past a bar on his way back from a part-time job interview and she was on the sidewalk arguing with her boyfriend. The guy hit her and Trace intervened. It cost him a front tooth, and a whole lot more before she was through with him.

He thought he was in love and maybe she loved him too, at least for a little while. They lived together for a while before she got pregnant and Trace asked her to marry him. He thought she was happy, he thought he was happy. He quit school, got a full-time job at a factory and Savannah worked as a waitress at a small cafe not far from the modest little house they rented. Shortbread arrived and was an adorable, good baby. His birth name was Samuel, named after Savannah's father, but earned the nicknamed Shortbread because of his small stature and clump of sandy hair that never darkened.

Shortbread was about ready to start pre-school when Trace found out Savannah was pregnant again. He found the home pregnancy results in the bathroom trash. They hadn't been close for weeks—intimately or otherwise. He waited for her to tell him, but she didn't until she began to show and could hide it no longer, and by then he had quit hoping she loved him, quit hoping the baby might be his. He was accepting the fact the life he was living was not what he let himself believe it was, but kept his thoughts and emotions to himself. He concentrated on Shortbread and did what so many people do in similar situations—nothing.

It was a miserable rainy day when he got the call at work that Savannah was in the hospital with labor pains. On the way in to the hospital he met a man coming out. Trace not only noticed the man because of his sandy colored hair and light build but also because he seemed to be avoiding him.

Megan was born several hours later but Savannah was not interested in her new daughter. Then she became too depressed to take care of either Megan or Shortbread properly and Trace began missing work. Emelee happened to call one day when Trace was running an errand. After talking to Savannah she had a good idea of what Trace was going through, thanks to common sense and mother's instinct, and soon she and Chigger were on the road to Albuquerque. When they arrived Savannah warmly told them how much she appreciated them coming, then shortly after said she was going out for a walk. She never came back, and Trace didn't go looking for her.

Trace, Shortbread and Megan moved in with Emelee and Chigger. Their small ranch outside Albuquerque was on the edge of a new housing development and Chigger was offered a price he couldn't refuse. It was shortly after that they relocated to where they lived now, twenty miles southeast of Whispering Pines.

A shadow on the table caused him to look up to see his mother. She sadly smiled and he smiled back. He didn't like to worry her.

"Let it go, *mijo*," she said. "Who are we to question the direction our lives take sometimes?" She put her hand on his shoulder and he reached to put a hand on hers. "I don't know what I'd do without these little *niños* in my life."

Chigger sensed the subject matter when he entered the kitchen by the back door and purposely laid his wrenches noisily on the table. "Aw hell, who says that Trace is mine?" he said with twinkling eyes.

Emelee slapped his arm. "Chelmsford Ray del Oro! You know better than that," she scolded.

Chigger was grinning when he opened the door to the freezer for a carton of ice cream. "Who wants some?" he asked, then made his way to the counter.

Emelee began to obtain the bowls and Trace smiled, thankful for them both.

CHAPTER 21

Riley put the last of her dirty clothes in the washing machine and measured out detergent. The splash of water filling the machine masked the drone of the central air turning on. She went to the kitchen to get her ball cap and leather gloves that she'd left on the granite counter. The kitchen was almost finished, almost ready for Benjie's touch. Although she loved the great room's earthy, natural tones she wanted some color in the kitchen and as a result picked hunter green. The cabinets were maple and so was the front of the refrigerator, the oven gleamed with chrome and glass and the big squares of floor tile had been laid shortly after the ceiling timbers had been installed. It was Sunday, Ernie's day off, and Riley had plans to work outside. As much as she loved the progress being made in the house there were other things that needed her attention.

She headed across the driveway with Wooly tagging along. Dobbie and Dually were grazing in the pasture and she resisted the urge to go riding. She got the machete from her recently acquired assortment of yard tools and set to work clearing weeds along the lot fences and barn. Over time the weeds in the lots had been flattened by the horses and she was tired of looking at those that remained.

The weeds were dead and brown and as a result they scattered seeds and leftover pollen with each strike of the blade, making Riley wish she had worn a long-sleeved shirt instead of a tank top. The irritating pollen was sticking to her and after pulling an unknown ivy off the barn she was really itching.

It was close to noon when she went to the house for lunch. She took time to rinse off her arms, face and neck but didn't remove the ball cap with her ponytail sticking out the hole in the back. After a quick sandwich and iced tea she was heading out again but Wooly, lying on the cool floor of the mud room, was apparently comfortable where he was.

"Enjoying the good life?" she asked. The big dog left his head on his paws but kept his expressive gentle eyes fixed on her. "I'll see you later then, bum," she told him affectionately.

Eventually all the weeds were down. She held her gloves in one hand and used the bottom of the tank top to wipe her sweaty face. She scratched the back of her neck and stretched, the action welcome and relaxing, and saw a vehicle on the road in the distance. She went through the stall door of the lot where she finished, chucked her gloves down before she came out the main door of the barn and lifted the handle on the hydrant. She picked up the hose and pulled the end of it to the tank, not paying attention to what she was doing but instead watched Jay's work truck slow and turn into the driveway.

"Hello!" she called out and walked around the front of his truck before he came to a stop. "What brings you out here?"

Jay turned the key but didn't get out. He looked at her—oddly, she thought—before speaking through the open window.

"I've been meaning to ask if you'd want to ride my young horses before the weather turns," he told her.

"Really?" she said attentively and scratched her arm.

He didn't speak right away but did continue staring at her. "They could stand to have more miles on them, and I'd appreciate it if you would. Miles has put some time on them this spring. I thought maybe you'd like to go see them…if you're interested." He paused. "Maybe now isn't a good time."

She put a hand on the truck and eyed him, building courage to ask what his problem was. She scratched the back of her hand and Jay looked where she was scratching, causing her to look too. Her hand was covered with blotchy red as were her wrists and arms, even on the soft inside crook of her elbow she saw as she rotated her arms. The rash was everywhere, *everywhere*, she realized. She lifted her eyes to his and knew he was trying to keep from smiling. She felt her face go red and he let his smile show.

"What's so funny?" she demanded.

"If you keep that blush happening it hides the rash from the poison ivy."

She hit him on the chest with the back of her hand, almost whacking her arm on the frame of the door in the process.

"Quit!" she begged, looking for a sign from him that it wasn't as bad as she thought, but was not reassured. "I must look like…"

"Like hell," he finished for her.

"What do I do about it?" she moaned, accepting her fate.

"Do you have baking soda on hand?" he asked.

She nodded and scratched, knowing she had an open box of the stuff in the refrigerator. He leaned across the seat of his truck to the passenger side and dug in a tote on the floor. She watched him, trying to avoid looking at the rash and wondering how bad her face was. She touched her cheeks and groaned silently. Her fingers were still on her face when he sat up and turned to her with a small bottle of pink liquid.

"Take a long soak in the tub with baking soda and then put this on. Shake it up first. That ought to stop the itch," he said.

"And if it doesn't?"

He smiled sympathetically. "There's a hospital and doctor clinic in Northboro. You look pretty bad," he paused and looked apologetic, "but unless you're allergic it's not serious."

She shook her head at the probability and continued to look at him, feeling misery, embarrassment and gratitude all at the same time.

"I 'spect you'll pull through," he said. "If you do, you think you'd want to start riding my colts pretty soon?"

A glimmer of amusement struck her with his making light and she nodded, momentarily forgetting the rash.

"I'll talk to you later about it. You're going to be pretty miserable for a while," he said and started the truck. "I'm glad you said yes."

"I'm looking forward to it," she replied and scratched behind an ear, tipping her ball cap in the process.

"Don't forget your water tank is filling. And stop scratching," he reminded before he backed away.

* * *

Although Riley had been making sporadic overnight trips to spend time with Mitch she cancelled the upcoming one, knowing he would be appalled to see her with the rash let alone want to touch her. She was walking across the driveway after riding that Sunday morning when Jay stopped. Again he stayed in his truck. He said he had come from Freddie's and was headed to check on his horses.

"You'd think you were related to Freddie as much as you help him out," she told him while feeling self-conscious about the rash and expecting him to make some comment.

"He's my uncle, actually," Jay said. "Haven't you figured out by now that just about everybody is related out here? Why, the town's population would be cut in half if it weren't for close ties."

She laughed, appreciating not only that he didn't mention the poison ivy episode but didn't appear to notice the remaining rash either.

"Do you have time to go see the colts? Talk horses?" he asked.

At the original homestead place of Jay's father were several good-looking broodmares with foals. They grazed contentedly and ignored the two-legged intruders. A sorrel colt playfully kicked at a butterfly, stirring up another sorrel and the two dashed away together.

"They're both by a roping stud that Miles had at his place for a while," Jay said.

A petite dark grey foal peered from behind her mother and watched the frisky colts at play.

"What about that one?" Riley asked, pointing to the grey.

"She's out of my oldest mare, an own daughter of Essential Webster. I bred her to a thoroughbred and that filly is the result."

"She's nice, I like her," Riley said.

"Come on, I'll show you the others."

He drove to another pasture, about a mile further, and parked in front of the gate just off the road. In the distance, at the base of the bluffs, stood a small band of horses under the meager shade of a few cottonwoods. The horses watched them attentively and swished their tails at insects. Jay whistled, just like Miles had done at the county fair, and the horses began heading their direction, first at a walk and then trotting. A bay and a sorrel led the way while a palomino and a grey seemed content to bring up the rear. Then a pair of bays on the edge of the group frolicked, scattering the others.

The horses, confident and majestic, continued their forward momentum until they were several yards away. One of the bays proudly flared his nostrils but a smaller horse came closer before stopping an arm's length from Jay. It stretched its neck to reach him.

"This is Bubbles," Jay said as he touched the nose of the yearling. "Marta named her. She's practically a pet. She would put her nose in the water tank and blow bubbles when she was a baby."

Riley laughed as she pictured it and Bubbles came nearer for more attention. Soon the others were coming closer too, inquisitive but wary.

"That grey gelding is a full brother to the grey baby you like," he said. "He's one of the two-year-olds I want you to ride." Bubbles nibbled on the lower leg of his jeans and he gently pushed the horse away. "I usually have most of them sold by now and I really don't have the time to put into them. Well, I guess I could make the time but the horses are supposed to be a hobby. I can't justify not being at the shop for them. Miles—he's got a gift with horses, way better than me—he's spent about thirty days on each of the three two-year-olds. There's no guarantees they won't buck at all but at least they've been started." The young horses were beginning to lose interest and slowly wandered off, eating grass as they went. "I could bring them to your place, supply their hay, help you get started on them if you want." He looked at her as if to see if he had to keep selling the idea, but apparently understood that she was undeniably interested. "Actually I'd prefer if you'd let me help with the first ride. I don't want you getting hurt. There isn't much time left this fall but it would sure help me out, and if it works you can ride for me next year too, after Miles. I'll pay cash or you can pick one in trade, or both."

"I'd love to ride them," she confirmed without hesitation.

"Good," he said, satisfied. "Since you don't have an arena fence yet I'll take some ten-foot fence panels to your place and set up a round pen."

They started the walk back to the gate. A cloud of dust from Cap's candy apple red pickup on the road made them turn their backs to him to avoid the dust and gravel being thrown, but not before Riley saw him gawking.

"It's real pretty up there," said Jay. "On the bluff I mean."

Riley focused on the horses and the hills behind.

"There are the beginnings of a corral from logs of trees up there but it was never finished," he went on. "There's a well too… Who'd think there would be water that high up? When I was younger I thought it would be a nice place to build a house."

Because of a change in the tone of his voice she switched her look from the bluffs to him, and caught his shoulder flinch when he was aware of her looking.

Jay cleared his throat and pointed. "The pasture connects to Raney's and then it's the Colby place, just about where the bluff stops. There are gates along the way. A person can ride most all day and never ride the same place twice if they didn't want to." He continued to keep his back to her, even when he turned to face the road. He gazed across the vast flat land, his truck in the foreground. "You can see for miles from the bluff."

She wondered what he was missing in his life. He certainly seemed happy enough when he saw Marta at the county fair.

"Well," she began optimistically, "we'll have to go riding there one day after we get those colts going good enough."

He looked at her and she watched the emptiness in his eyes fade.

"Yes, we sure will," he agreed.

CHAPTER 22

Riley hooked up the trailer, removed the dividers and checked all the tires with plans to pull out for Owen the next morning. She was confident that everything she wanted from the garage apartment would fit in one load—all she wanted was her bed and dresser for the spare room and the rest of her boxed items. She and Benjie were going shopping and she would spend time with Mitch as well. Dobbie and Dually were turned out to pasture and Jay had agreed to check on them via drive-by.

There was already a vacant atmosphere in the apartment and she was glad to have a minute to herself before Benjie got there. Then they loaded her bedroom set and were toting boxes when the Goodwill truck arrived. They helped with the pieces of furniture she was giving away and while they worked Wooly watched from his favorite resting spot near Benjie's flower garden. When they were finished they ordered a pizza to be delivered to Benjie's and spent the evening going over paint swatches and discussing the decorating to be done.

The next morning they took her pickup to downtown Owen, Benjie looking forward to the buying expedition as much as Riley was.

"First we're stopping at my favorite place with American made as well as imports," Benjie said with exuberance. "You won't believe what they have."

Knowing his quirky side she said with a smile, "As long as they have *normal* things we'll be okay." But her doubts vanished when she saw the floor displays, specifically the rustic wood furniture with black iron accents. There was an endless selection of large rugs for the hardwood floor in the great room, many with a southwestern flare, and varieties of ready-made curtains and drapes, lamps, wall coverings and decor.

"Normal enough for ya?" Benjie teased. "What about this?" he prodded, pointing to a big screen television.

She bobbed her head.

In the end not only did she buy the television but a couch, recliner and overstuffed chair, a coffee table, shelving units, a traditional dining room table and roll-top desk plus a unique wood-burning stove, all for the great room. She also chose a kitchen table and chairs of smooth polished pine that was classy enough for the oak in the kitchen yet had simplicity all over it. The delivery date was scheduled and they ventured on. After going to several more shops she found the perfect bedroom set of roughhewn logs. Then it was back to Benjie's where she dropped him off before heading to Mitch's. She left Wooly with Benjie because Mitch's apartment complex didn't allow pets.

It was turning dusk when she reached the modern steel structure that was one of four buildings. There were separate garages and not as many cars in the parking lot as she expected. She parked near the foyer, got out and while dragging her duffle bag across the seat noticed the obtrusive sounds of the city. She tugged at her damp cropped cotton shirt and wished she had taken time to shower at Benjie's. Her well-worn boots were dusty and she was sure that Mitch would think he was dating a hillbilly.

She wondered if he really had any idea what she was like when he asked her out, thinking he probably had preconceived ideas. She had always dressed up for work and she had never seen him other than perfectly dressed, except when he was naked, she thought with a grin.

She pushed the security button, let herself in and took the stairs. Mitch was on the phone when he opened the door for her and he gave her a kiss on the cheek. He picked up his mail that was in the shallow basket on the catch-all table there and motioned to the hall leading to the bedroom, or more specifically, she knew, the bathroom. She watched him shuffle the mail, ultimately organizing the envelopes by size, then he laid them on an end table beside the leather couch and went to the window that took up most of the wall. With his free hand he pulled the shade back and looked out, all the while with the phone to his ear. Riley walked the short hall to the bedroom. Like always, it was as pristine as the rest of his apartment.

Ten minutes later Mitch, still on the phone, came into the bedroom and heard the spray of water in the shower. "Is there anything else, Aubrey?" he asked the new lawyer at the firm. When Aubrey brought up another subject, Mitch let his exasperation show by making a face and holding the phone away from his head while mimicking his associate's continual talk. His eyes went longingly to the closed door to the bathroom, but he left the room.

Riley was dressed and combing her wet hair in front of the mirror when he came back.

"Sorry about that. Work," he said. He kissed her on the neck and then sat on the bed. "How long can you stay?"

She turned to face him. "Just overnight… I'll have to leave by three or four tomorrow afternoon." Her eyes sparkled. "The house is coming together so well! I can't wait for you to see it again. I bought furniture and everything today! Everything! I don't even want to know how much money I spent." Her hands moved with animation and her cheeks were rosy with enthusiasm.

Mitch patted the bed. She sat beside him and he breathed in her fresh scent from the shower. She kept talking and he watched her intently but listened vaguely. He thought how pretty she was and he loved it when she talked like this. Physically she was just the type of woman he liked, and she was a good person. The idea of starting his own practice had been in the back of his mind and Riley would be a great asset with her knowledge of his line of work. And he wanted to buy a house with a yard, not live in an apartment where the walls were shared with others. Things had been rough for him financially the last few years but he was back on his feet and Riley was well off—he had seen the check with his own eyes. He hadn't decided yet if they would have kids, but he was definitely ready to settle down.

He interrupted her talk by leaning her back on the bed and kissing her, wishing he knew what to do about her infatuation with those horses and that farm.

CHAPTER 23

Chigger and Trace delivered pipe panels for the arena and set them up, complete with stationary posts sunk into the ground. Jay's round pen remained intact, inside the arena near one end. Chigger promised to keep a look out for a used tractor for Riley and something to work the dirt in the arena.

Jay dropped off the two-year-olds, but said it would be a day or two before he would have the chance to be there when she rode them for the first time. She respected his request that she wait and used the time to get to know the young horses. They quickly accepted their new surroundings and new routine, including being worked in the round pen on the lunge line. The grey gelding, registered as Awesome Possum, she nicknamed Potsy. She discovered he was very sensitive and suspicious and he intrigued her. She suspected he could intimidate her but reminded herself that Miles had ridden them for thirty days earlier that summer. The sorrel filly she nicknamed Prissy because of her dainty attitude and the bay gelding she dubbed Forbes, despite ribbing from Jay, because of his noble look.

It was a beautiful September day when Jay was there to help her get started. The horses stood in a row tied to the fence. Potsy was the first one brought to the round pen and Jay watched as

Riley worked him on the lunge line. Potsy had been gelded as a weanling for practical purposes but he was still all colt in his way of thinking. Riley worked him in a circle both directions before telling him "whoa." He responded after playfully kicking out at her. The grey stood quietly while she held him, standing just off to one side in case he leapt forward or struck out, but his eyes were fixed on Jay. Jay slowly walked toward the colt with the saddle and pad but Potsy didn't offer to move, not even when Jay settled both on his back. Jay reached for the cinch and threaded the leather through the ring, then tightened it just a little. Potsy flicked his ears and Jay waited a minute, stroking the horse on the neck, then he tightened the cinch a little more. Then Jay left the confines of the round pen and Riley lunged Potsy again. Most of the time the colt trotted or loped without a fuss but occasionally he would buck, and Riley smiled because of it when she saw Jay watching the antics.

"Heads or tails?" she called to him as Potsy continued to circle her.

"Heads or tails what?"

"To see who swings a leg over."

"Miles said this one could buck. Work him some more," he said, which made her laugh.

She worked him almost twenty minutes longer on the lunge line, concentrating on Potsy while Jay spent a good deal of the time watching her. When the gelding finally settled down she asked him to stop and then walked to him. Potsy stuck the end of his tongue out his mouth a time or two and extended his neck to touch her with his nose. Jay, who had left his position outside the round pen, shook his head with mild surprise at the gelding's submissive reaction. He ran his hand down the colt's neck and shoulder before easing his hand to the cinch, and then gently snugged it tight. He turned to Riley.

"You haven't been on him already, have you?" he asked, not allowing her to avoid him.

She looked him in the eye and shook her head. Satisfied, whether it was from the fact he believed she was being honest or that she had heeded his wishes, Jay took the lead rope and put a hand on Potsy's halter, indicating with his expression and actions that what happened next would be her call. Her apprehension that Jay was going to insist he be the one getting on didn't go away but instead deepened. It had been a long time since she had been on a green broke horse, and it was too late to back out now. She pushed the fear from her mind and stepped close to the saddle. She spoke softly to Potsy, collected the reins in one hand and used the other hand to help situate her foot in the stirrup, being observant to Potsy's body language all the while. She reached for the saddle horn, committed her weight in the stirrup and hopped a little to get off the ground. Potsy flicked his ears but stood still, so she swung her leg over his back and settled gently into the saddle. Now Potsy's ears flicked from her to Jay and back again, but she knew Jay would let her know if he read something in the gelding to be concerned about. Without taking her eyes off the colt she slid her other foot in the stirrup and then nodded. Jay released his hold.

At first Potsy didn't move at all, then he took a hesitant step, and then another. It was like he was wondering as much about Riley as she was about him. After half a dozen steps and no signs of Potsy humping his back or dropping his head, or both, she began to relax, and then Potsy did too.

Jay moved to the fence. He wound the lead rope without thinking about what he was doing and watched Riley ride. Potsy worked well for her and she worked him for half an hour, including venturing out of the round pen to the arena, asking for maneuvers and gaits to see just what the gelding knew. Potsy lacked finesse and had a long way to go, but Jay was impressed by what Miles had accomplished with the gelding in thirty days' time.

When it was time for Forbes's lesson it was Jay who got on, and that was only after innocent goading from Riley. The ride went smoothly until something startled the gelding, making him shy and come off the ground snorting and snaking. After the first jump that pitched Jay forward on the swells of the saddle he hunkered down to ride it out if need be, but Forbes reduced his bucking efforts to a stiff-legged crow-hop that didn't last long, which Jay was thankful for.

Prissy was the best behaved of the three and didn't give Riley a bit of trouble, and while they led the trio back to the barn Jay said in jest the money he paid Miles to start them was evidently well spent. Riley tried to talk him into staying, offering to make supper and let him soak in the whirlpool to ease any soreness because of Forbes's bucking, but Jay dismissed the episode like it was nothing and said he had things to do at the shop. Riley was in the barn when he headed for his flatbed, and it wasn't until he knew he was out of her sights before he rubbed his groin and let his pain show.

* * *

The house was coming together beautifully and the renovation almost finished. The spare bedroom was chock full of her old furniture and boxed items plus things for the walls—paint cans, stencils, borders, décor and framed prints, all that would wait until Benjie made it out. One of the last things that Ernie helped Riley with was assemble her new bedroom set in the loft and arranging the furniture in the great room. With humor Ernie complained that she was working him harder rearranging things until they suited her than he ever had during the remodel.

CHAPTER 24

Riley pulled up to Jay's shop and watched him and Marta coming out. Their discussion seemed burdened but before Riley got out of her truck they hugged, then Marta was getting in her car. Jay waited for Riley as she approached but she didn't have the chance to speak before an unfamiliar truck swung in. It was Trace.

"What are you up to?" Jay asked him.

"I'm on the clock running errands for the ranch," Trace answered. "I stopped to tell you we're going to be moving cattle the end of the week. Not a big move by any means and there will be plenty of cowboys on hand, and I thought you might want to bring your colts and ride. Both of you," he said to Riley. "There's a chance of rain but with the dry summer we've had I don't think anybody would mind."

Jay looked like he was deliberating and his eyes went the direction Marta's car had gone.

"How about it, Tapp?" Trace prodded.

Jay switched his look to Riley. She didn't say anything but gave him an inspiring smile. He shook his head and the corners of his mouth went up with his surrender.

* * *

The morning of moving cattle Riley waited in the barn. It was raining and thunder rumbled when Jay pulled in, his headlights cutting through the murk. He made the loop and she was making a dash for the back of the trailer with Prissy and Forbes before he came to a stop. She loaded the horses while Jay got her tack and they jumped into the cab from opposite sides at the same time. Riley took her wet hat off and set it on the seat while eyeing the pair of to-go coffees on the dash. She was reaching for one with anticipation and intended to tell Jay thanks but instead stared at him. She had been in such a hurry she hadn't noticed before now that he was wearing a black felt cowboy hat. Water was dripping from the brim, and he sure looked good.

Jay, acting like he did not notice, turned off the radio, stepped on the clutch and shifted.

"Thanks for the coffee," she said. It came out just above a whisper.

"Yes, ma'am," he replied. He started down the wet driveway, mud and sand accumulating noisily on the flatbed and the wipers flicking across the windshield. He turned on to the road.

"No rain for months, and now this," she said, regaining her normal voice.

"You don't want to stay home, do you?" he asked with a grin.

Her eyes got big and she shook her head.

The rest of the trip was silent with only the sounds of water spray off the highway and the hum of the tires. When they reached their destination the ranch hands were already saddled. The rain had reduced to a drizzle and the majority of riders were wearing dark brown dusters or yellow slickers. Trace found them while they were saddling their horses.

Riley wasn't about to let the light rain dampen her spirits. She and Jay rode side by side toward the gathering of cowboys that were ready to get started. From nowhere a clean-shaven Miles Deroin appeared on a big, stout grey and he squeezed between them. He leaned and put a hand behind Riley on the cantle of her saddle.

"Hi, girlfriend," he told her with a smile, his face inches from hers. Then he looked at Jay and his smile turned mischievous. "Hi, bro. Nice to see you two here."

"Miles," Jay said and slightly nodded.

"So, you happy with how the young'uns are riding?" Miles asked. He straightened in his saddle and focused on Prissy and Forbes.

Jay tipped his chin with approval. "Riley has put a few weeks on them recently."

Miles's brows went up. "Oh? Did I get the buck out of 'em?"

"So far," Jay replied.

"For the most part," Riley added, thinking of Forbes's first ride.

"That's too bad," Miles grinned. "A little buck now and again never hurt anybody—lets you know you're alive." He winked at Riley and then touched his horse with a spur and loped away.

"Is he harmless, or what?" she asked Jay.

Jay continued to watch Miles while he shrugged but looked skeptical. "Depends," was all he said.

They joined the others milling around Bruce Focustacia, the owner of Focus Ranch.

"Sorry about the rain," Bruce addressed the crowd while mounted on a big buckskin, "but I can't control everything."

The crowd laughed and Riley assumed he was good humored and joking.

"At least it'll keep the wannabees from showing up today," Bruce added and the riders laughed again. Without saying anything else he and the ranch hands began to herd the cattle.

The old cows initiated the move and the others followed. The drizzle let up as the last of the cattle formed a long, wide line but it remained grey and overcast. Riley saw Trace and Shortbread riding near the middle of the line of the herd. Trace was a true cowboy and Shortbread looked like he was following in his dad's steps.

Riley hung back with Prissy, not feeling at all useful but appreciative of being there. Jay, riding on the other side of the cattle, seemed preoccupied with keeping a snorting Forbes in check. She watched as Miles rode up beside Jay and began to talk. Jay's expression went from guarded to a frown, but Miles continued to talk and Jay smiled before Miles rode away.

The lead cows knew where they were going and plodded along. From Riley's position near the back she guessed the line stretched half a mile long. They crossed sparsely wooded creek bottoms and a few high ridges with sweeping, spectacular views. The trees hadn't started the change to fall yet but there was a wide variety of late season green, tan and browns, and the yellow slickers made for a pretty contrast.

Shortbread trotted alongside her and then slowed his horse to a walk. He reached into his saddlebag and his dutiful horse continued on without supervision. He fished for a camera and took a few photos, including one of Riley before he stuffed the camera back into the stiff leather bag. Then he brought out an apple and asked about Wooly before taking a bite. After replying she asked him about school, but he only stuck out his tongue. They rode together until he saw the opportunity to swing his rope at a wayward calf and off he went, tossing the apple core aside. Prissy was much better behaved than Riley was hoping for and she saw that Forbes had settled down for Jay, who looked like he was enjoying the ride.

The drive took only a few hours. After the cattle were herded through the gate of their destination the riders gathered to discuss a number of things including who would haul with who to get back to the starting point. Jay and Riley loaded their horses with Trace's in his stock trailer.

As they unloaded and loaded their horses again the skies were promising to clear. Shortbread took more pictures and gave Riley a hug before running to his dad's truck. Jay said he had to get gas as they pulled away and fifteen minutes later he stopped at an out of the way station that he was familiar with.

"Here's some gas money," Riley said, offering some bills before Jay got out.

"Get outta here," he said with a frown.

He began pumping gas and she walked into the little store. There was a selection of items handmade by the locals near the large front window. Jay's truck and trailer were visible outside. She was looking at some bandanas fashioned to be worn like necklaces when Jay walked around the back of his trailer. His long-sleeved shirt was tucked in, his jeans fit just right and he carried himself with a no-nonsense, ground covering walk, much the same way Miles did. She had noticed his walk before but now found that she was noticing a lot more. He was still wearing his cowboy hat and she thought it was a good thing he didn't wear it around her more often. She reprimanded herself but didn't look away before he opened the door and saw her looking at him. He smiled and she smiled back, somewhat embarrassed. He walked over to see what was in the display in front of her.

"Want one?" he asked.

She pulled her eyes away from him and looked at the bandanas, but didn't really see them. He reached around her and picked up a white bandana with a small sunflower and chunk of turquoise near the knot.

"Good enough?" he asked.

She nodded and with that he turned on his heel. She followed him, feeling like a little kid and thinking Marta was lucky to have him.

CHAPTER 25

It was a mild morning that late October day when Riley started riding, but before she finished the wind came up and the temperature dropped. She decided when she got back to the house she would attempt to make a fire in the wood burning stove.

Her stove had never been used except after Ernie had installed it. He had built a small fire to ensure the chimney, pipe and stove were working properly at the time, and she tried to recall how he had gone about it. She put in a log and kindling and paper to get it started, lit a match and watched the little flame grow. Well, that was easy enough, she thought as the fire began to crackle and show promise.

The indication of Riley's fledgling fire was visible to Cap Henderson sitting behind the wheel of his combine lumbering down the road. When he reached her driveway he maneuvered the turn with the huge machine and let it roll to a stop between the barn and the house. He switched gears and the whining sound of the engine reduced in decibel.

Wooly headed for the back door at the same time Riley heard the clamor of the combine. She followed Wooly to the kitchen, feeling smug about the fire. She looked out the small window in the back door and her expression changed to a grimace when she saw Cap, who was just setting foot on the ground from descending the ladder of the cab. She let the curtain fall and begrudgingly opened the door.

Cap adjusted the wadded hood of his loose fitting sweatshirt behind his neck. Wooly didn't seem to want to move from the doorway so Riley left the door ajar and made her way toward Cap. He put his hands in the pocket of his sweatshirt and they came to a stop facing each other. She was wishing she had grabbed a coat.

"Just letting you know I'll be harvesting your crops today. Common courtesy and all to let you know," he said. "Course it'll only take forty five minutes or so, more trouble than it's worth, truth be told."

She crossed her arms, partially from the cold but also because of his leering.

"You know," he continued, "we don't actually have a contract between us. I'm just assuming you want me to finish what I started. You impress me as being that kind of gal." He produced the pack of cigarettes from his sweatshirt pocket and pulled one out. "We ought to sit down sometime together so we can…talk about it. I could free up an evening." He lit the cigarette and looked past her.

She didn't know why he was bringing this up now. They had discussed this year's crops when she bought the property.

"You have much experience with wood stoves?" he asked.

She frowned. Now what he was getting at? Then a pompous smile came over his face and he looked past her again. She could smell smoke, but it wasn't from his cigarette. Intuition caused her to turn and she saw smoke coming out the open door, the wind stirring it. Wooly had moved to avoid it.

Cap was laughing behind her as she briskly made her way to the house. The further she got inside the thicker the smoke was and she flailed her hands. She had managed to make a fire but had forgotten to open the damper to let the smoke go out the pipe to the chimney. She had also neglected to completely latch the stove door and when the glowing fire had been snuffed out it continued to smolder, building smoke which was billowing through the gap.

After correcting her mistakes she opened every window in the house. She got the fans from the spare bedroom and situated them to push the smoke out. The house felt colder inside than it was outside before she was all through. She felt foolish and the nagging assumption that she would be the humiliating topic at the next gossip session at the bar, thanks to Cap, didn't improve her mood.

* * *

Benjie made it out not long after the wood stove fiasco. "Why is there smoke on the walls?" he asked while brandishing a rag on the stucco in the great room.

"I dunno," Riley said innocently, causing Benjie to look at her. "All right, so I had a little trouble the first time I made a fire in the stove," she confessed. Her eyes met his and they shared a laugh over it.

It took almost a week for the two of them to paint, stencil and border, and both were more than satisfied with the results. The days following were windy more often than not, sometimes rattling the glass in the new windows, and every night was chilly. Jay came and got his horses. By the end of the month the once colorful leaves had turned brown and were completely gone from the trees. They crunched underfoot or made little tapping noises as the wind skipped them across the ground, leaving them forgotten in piles out of the wind's grasp.

CHAPTER 26

The day before Thanksgiving Fran and Benjie arrived early in the afternoon.

"We would have been here sooner but I had to pick up a few things," Benjie told her as he brought in the first load of decorations.

Riley laughed and held the back door open for them.

"I swear," Fran said to Riley as she passed through, her arms full. "Besides us, every inch of space in that car was filled with something Christmas related."

Benjie made a point to ignore them, muttering about their lack of artistic appreciation, and went right to work after he brought everything in. Riley called Ernie who was more than happy to loan his extension ladder and assistance. After Ernie got there the two men squabbled as they worked. Benjie, the high-strung artist, wanted things just so, while Ernie, the grounded one, thought decorating for the holidays was a lot of nonsense because it would all be taken down again in a few weeks. Fran and Riley, baking in the kitchen, laughed as they overheard.

Mitch called to say he wasn't going to make it because of his mother. He said he suspected she was feigning health issues to get him to come home for the holiday and that he would, indeed, feel bad if she got worse and he did not go. Riley told him she understood, which she did, and that she wished she could go with him, which she didn't.

Thanksgiving morning Benjie wrapped up his holiday decorating and told Riley she should have already purchased a Christmas tree. He matter-of-factly stated things would be different next year, adding he would decorate the exterior as well. Then he joined them in the kitchen. He and Fran were at odds concerning how firm the potatoes should be before mashing when they heard Ernie arrive in the nursing home van. Benjie hurried to help and a few minutes later Riley was opening the door for them, letting in the fresh autumn air that mixed with the tantalizing aroma of the turkey in the oven. Ernie showed Riley how to fold the wheelchair and then he and Benjie lifted Chloe, Riley quickly folded the chair, rolled it over the threshold and readied it again. The old woman's wrinkled face was already full of reminiscence and now that she was inside the house it appeared she was back in time in her one-time humble kitchen, not the new laundry and mud room. This went on for a minute and Riley was starting to become a little concerned, but Chloe left her little world when Ernie tugged at the sleeve of her coat.

"My goodness Ernie, I wasn't paying attention," she told him. She allowed Ernie to take her coat and tried to hide her emotion.

"Your scarf too?" he asked.

She worked the knot under her chin and he took the silk scarf, then Benjie helped Ernie lift the wheelchair up the step to the kitchen.

"I'll give you the tour," said Ernie.

Riley thought it was appropriate that Ernie be the one showing Chloe the changes, but she did ask Chloe what she thought so far.

"I think I might have been a decent cook if I'da had a kitchen this," Chloe remarked.

There was good-natured laughter. Ernie wheeled Chloe to the great room, where her mouth made a little 'o' as she lifted her head, with some difficulty, to take it all in.

"This is pretty fancy," said Chloe. "A good waste of space, but I like it. You do good work, Ernie."

"Thank you, Mrs. Colby," replied Ernie, looking pleased.

There was a knock on the back door and Riley left them to answer it. She opened it to Jay and a tall, slender elderly man.

"You never have to wait for me to answer the door," she told Jay.

There was a bit of a smile but he mostly looked self-conscious.

"Riley, this is my dad, Oliver. Dad, this is Riley," he said.

The older man had started to take his coat off during the exchange of words and was facing the wall. He became tangled in his coat and cursed under his breath. Jay helped him and then hung the coat on the wall with the others.

"Apologies, ma'am," Oliver said and tipped his ball cap to her. "Nice to meet you. And I thank you for having me today."

"You're welcome." His face was a roadmap of wrinkles but he had a certain charm and she thought he had probably been quite good looking in his day. There was some resemblance between father and son but she suspected Jay must have taken more after his mother's side of the family.

There was a knock again. Jay and Oliver stepped into the kitchen and she opened the door to the del Oro family. Emelee was the first one in. She smiled shyly at Riley as if she were uncomfortable being a guest instead of the one doing the cooking. Riley liked her instantly. She took the covered dish that Emelee was carrying and Chigger assisted with her coat. Trace helped his daughter and prompted Shortbread, the last one in, to shut the door.

"How is the tractor working?" Chigger asked, referring to the used one he had found for her.

"I haven't had the chance to use it much but it's started for me every time," Riley boasted.

Chigger nodded his satisfaction, took the dish from Riley and ushered Emelee to the kitchen. Shortbread asked about Wooly but before she could answer the dog stuck his head around the corner as if having sensed the boy's presence. Shortbread grinned, dropped his coat to the floor and made a beeline to the dog. Trace refrained from getting after Shortbread and instead focused on his daughter.

"This is Megan," he told Riley.

A bashful Megan, hanging onto Trace's leg, looked up.

"Very nice to meet you," Riley said while bending to the little girl's height.

Megan shrank back.

"I almost forgot," Trace said, moving to his hanging coat with Megan still clinging to his leg. He reached into a pocket and then handed Riley a snapshot of her and Jay that had been taken the day of the cattle drive, their cowboy hats and slickers wet. She was smiling happily in the photo and Jay was sporting his typical reserved smile. She held it as if it were priceless.

"I love it!" she told Trace.

"You can thank Shortbread. He's the one who took it."

Before she had the chance Jay was standing in the doorway of the kitchen. She handed him the photo.

"Only one?" Jay asked Trace after he got a look.

"Sorry, buddy," Trace shrugged, but it was obvious he was up to something.

Jay looked at the picture again. "What's this?" he growled.

A grin spread across Trace's face. Oliver stepped beside Jay to get a look and then he started laughing. Jay handed it to Riley, pointing, and she began to laugh as well—a few yards behind them was Miles, smiling and waving.

"You knew he was there all along, didn't you," Jay accused.

Riley didn't care, she thought it was cute. She took the photo to the freestanding cabinet with shelves along the wall just past the kitchen in the great room. Jay watched her lean it against the framed sketch of her and Mitch, where the bandana necklace that he had bought her was hanging.

It wasn't much later that Riley's brother Jeff, his wife Kim and baby girl arrived.

"I'm so glad you decided to come!" Riley said.

Jeff presented her the baby.

"Little Karrie looks like you, Kim," Riley told her.

Fran came to the mud room oohing and awing over the baby. Riley surrendered the little girl and Fran and Kim left with the child to join the others.

"I bet you're a great dad," Riley complimented Jeff who was still standing at the door. "She'll grow up to be a terrific little cowgirl."

"I dunno," he chuckled. "Look how far we fell from the tree of our hippy nomad parents."

Riley giggled. "Yeah, I guess how you're brought up doesn't always mean anything in the grand scheme of things."

"Um, not to change the subject but I brought you a housewarming…gift, I guess you could call it."

"It's not something *alive* is it?" she asked suspiciously.

Jeff motioned outside, and parked so it was the first thing she saw when she looked out the door was the old one ton, four door dually truck they had shared years before in high school. Its black cab was original with the dents and rust acquired over the years, the windshield was cracked and he had replaced the box, which was now a faded white. It wasn't pretty but Jeff had kept it running over the years.

"Goliath!" she exclaimed.

"I thought you might be able to use the old beast on your new place," he offered. "It only seemed right."

Riley grabbed her coat and called for Jay, Trace and Ernie to come too.

She laughed delightedly as she opened the driver's door. There were scattered pieces of hay on the seat and dried mud on the foot pedals, and she remembered it had a manual transmission.

"I forgot it was a stick shift," she moaned. "I'm doomed!"

"At least you have enough room out here to learn how to drive it again," said Ernie.

They joked and laughed on their way back to the house, and the jovial mood continued. Last-minute preparations for the Thanksgiving feast were completed and then laid out buffet style on the kitchen counter. With the extra leaves in the dining room table and chairs from the kitchen there was enough room for everyone. They ate too much, played cards and board games, and good-naturedly argued during football games. Baby Karrie was popular with everyone, especially timid Megan.

Jeff and Kim were the first to say good-bye, then it was the del Oro family.

"Great day, loved every minute of it," Trace praised before giving Riley a hug. "Thanks for asking us."

"Thanks for coming. It was great meeting Megan and your mom."

Emelee said they would be happy to have Riley over any time. Jay and Trace exchanged parting shots before the del Oro family walked out the door.

Chloe remarked she would rather stay at the farm house than to go back to the nursing home, which tugged at Riley's heart. They embraced before repeating the earlier process to get her and the wheelchair through the back door. Fran announced she was going with Ernie to help with Chloe, and from the pleased look on Ernie's face Riley gathered it had already been discussed.

As Jay and Oliver prepared to leave Oliver again struggled with his coat and spewed profanities under his breath. Jay ignored him, used to the old man's impatience. Jay was not like his father in Riley's opinion. Oliver was high-spirited and liked to talk and flirt, whereas Jay was reserved and respectful and didn't talk unless he had something to say. When his coat was finally on, Oliver addressed Riley.

"Make sure your things outside get picked up. It'll snow enough within a week to cover them up," he told her.

"I'll do that," she replied. She handed Jay leftovers as she had done with the others.

"Come on, Dad, I've got to get you back to Northboro," said Jay.

"You're welcome to come back after you take your dad home," Riley told Jay. "I don't know about Ernie and Fran but Benjie and I will be here all evening."

"Thanks. I just might do that," Jay said, his attention on the door, and they both knew he wouldn't.

Cold enveloped Jay and Oliver as they went out into the dim evening light. Before they got to Jay's flatbed Oliver hunched his back against the blustery wind, pulled a cigarette from a pack and stopped to light it. When Jay saw that he was having trouble he came back to help. He took the cigarette from his father and put it in his own mouth. He stood to block the wind, lit the end and took a long drag before handing it back.

"I like her. She's got spunk," Oliver said as he accepted the cigarette.

"You like any pretty girl," Jay retorted. "Those things'll kill you." He didn't release the smoke until he was walking around the front of the truck.

Oliver chuckled over the irony of how he might die in his old age as well as Jay's statement regarding his weakness for women. "She reminds me of Miles' and Marta's mother, bless her soul," he said softly, low enough that Jay couldn't hear.

* * *

Oliver had been right. It was just a few days later when it began to snow, and then it snowed more often than not for a week and a half. Benjie got tied up with a big holiday project which prevented him from helping Riley select a Christmas tree or decorating it as he planned. When she went to Owen to see Mitch they went to a Christmas tree farm where she picked out a tall spruce that reminded her of the one growing at the corner of the house. It was cut down and loaded on her pickup while they watched. Sprigs of the tree touched the top of the windshield and it reached all the way past the tailgate where a big red flag that she thought resembled a Christmas bow was tied.

"Are you sure you can't find a tree closer to home?" Mitch asked skeptically.

She ignored him. She loved her choice and didn't care what anyone thought.

CHAPTER 27

Two days before Christmas it began to snow again, big fluffy flakes that at first were in no hurry to reach the ground. By nightfall snow covered everything, including the twinkling lights in the garland decking the posts and overhang outside Murphy's Pub. A piece of mistletoe hung above the door, as if the patrons needed an excuse.

Jay sat at a table inside the bar, having dropped off a set of specialized hinges for Murphy. He thought the delivery would be a good excuse to stay a spell and pass the time, but it didn't take long for him to remember why he didn't hang out there anymore. A few tables away Cap babbled drunkenly, his voice carrying. When Cap and the men with him got up to leave, Cap stumbled over to Jay while the others settled the bill.

"Not at yer g'rlfriend's tonight?" Cap slurred.

Jay ignored him and knocked back the last of his coffee.

"Mebee I'll jus' take a stop and lookie see at her place when I go by," Cap said, leaning within inches of Jay's face, his breath reeking of beer and cigarettes.

"Come on, lover boy," said one of the men with Cap, hooking his arm. "Sorry, Tapperd."

Jay threw him a glance and nodded and the men left with Cap in tow. Jay pushed his chair from the table and reached for change in his pocket.

Outside the bar, Riley stepped to the side to make way for cowboys coming from the other direction. One cowboy tugged at the hood of his heavy coat in attempt to ward off the wind that had come up and another touched the brim of his hat to her with a leather gloved hand. Cap and the men aiding him came out the door. When Cap saw Riley he pulled away and fell into her.

"You okay ma'am?" a cowboy asked, reaching for her.

"Yes," she said irritably while glaring at Cap.

"Hello, Rhyyleee," he drawled. "Sorry I 'aven't made it out to see you lately. Bet you've missed me."

She managed to push him off and her scowl switched to the men he was with. One of them was keeping him vertical but they were otherwise pretty much useless in her opinion. Then she saw Jay standing in the door.

"Awww, doan be that way," Cap said and reached for her with uncoordinated arms.

Jay moved so he was standing beside Cap.

"Tapp!" Cap exclaimed, weaving. "Doan you worry none, I'll take care of 'er."

Jay raised an arm and drove his elbow back at Cap's face, sending him and the man with him sprawling against the building. The cowboys and Riley looked with surprise at the subtle but effective move.

"Sorry, Angus," Jay said to the unfortunate man with Cap and extended a hand to help him up.

Everyone was looking at Cap, knocked out and lying in a heap with his nose bleeding. Someone chuckled. His friends lifted him to his feet and situated his limp body between them.

"It wasn't my intention to cause you extra work," Jay added.

Angus grinned. "Quite all right. He's not talking anymore."

There was laughter.

"Apologies, ma'am," Angus said to Riley respectfully, then he and his friend walked away with Cap between them. The cowboys walked into the bar, leaving Jay and Riley alone. They hadn't talked or seen each other since Thanksgiving.

"What have you been up to?" she asked.

"Just working. And feeding horses," he said. "You?"

"Nothing... Boring, but that's okay by me."

They both made an attempt to smile.

"You headed home?" He glanced at the street where the snow was being moved by the wind.

"Yes. I was visiting Chloe and stopped at Decker's, but they're already closed. I didn't realize it was this late."

"I better let you go. I think this one's going to be rough."

"Nice to see you," she said.

"You too," he replied.

At the crosswalk she stopped and looked over her shoulder. Jay was hunkered against the blustering snow and never looked back that she was aware of.

Jay wasn't in sight when she drove by his house and shop. At the stop sign the Christmas greetings sign overhead swayed in the wind. She made the turn and after leaving the town's protection against the wind she concentrated on staying on the road in the near whiteout conditions.

* * *

After bundling up to do chores the next morning Riley picked up the snow shovel and opened the door, ready to tackle the white stuff. She was greeted by bitter cold and a wicked wind that threatened to tear the shovel from her hands. Her eyes were big with surprise, and consequently the shovel left leaning against the wall in the mud room.

Later that day she took chicken and store-bought noodles from the freezer and started a big pot of soup, snacking on carrots and celery as she worked. While the soup simmered she picked a book from her collection and made herself cozy in the easy chair.

She was putting wood in the stove when Wooly left her and went to the back door. Before she made it to the door Jay was stepping inside. He was accompanied by blowing snow and cold.

"I knocked, but I don't think you heard with the wind," he apologized and shut the door.

She smiled, happy to see him, and started to brush the snow off his coat.

"I can't stay," he told her.

She stopped what she was doing and took a step back.

"Freddie left a prescription at the shop that I had to run out to his place, and thought I'd check on you on the way home."

"That was thoughtful of you, for looking out for Freddie and me too."

He didn't reply but looked past her. He studied the fair-sized stack of wood along the wall near her muck boots and there was a gallon of lamp oil beside the snow shovel. Another gallon of oil and the lamp were on the washing machine.

"You'll be snowed in by morning," he warned.

She scoffed. "With my driving talents I'm snowed in already. I have plenty of things on hand. I'll be okay." She headed for the kitchen. "The soup is ready. Do you want some? There's more than enough."

He peered into the kitchen. Steam was coming off the pot of chicken noodle soup on the stove and he could smell garlic bread in the oven.

"I left my truck running," he lamely reasoned.

"You may as well eat," she said looking from the pot to him. "At the least let me send some home with you."

Surprising himself, he pulled off his coat.

"Don't bother with your boots," she told him.

"They've got mud on them," he replied, hanging the coat on a hook.

"There are old newspapers there." She reached into the cupboard for bowls. "You know the drill."

He checked to see how bad the mud was and then picked up a newspaper, pulled it apart and placed it on the tile floor in the kitchen, all the while focusing on the sounds of her setting the table instead of the blustery wind outside. He got another newspaper but instead of finishing the trail to the table he made one to the inviting great room. He remembered it being decorated at Thanksgiving but at the time had been more interested in the people there that day than the decorations. There were wreaths of all sizes, an assortment of snowmen, traditional tinsel and twinkling lights and garland everywhere. There was even garland on the wood stair rail, complete with holly, and it continued across the rail of the loft. The tall Christmas tree, something that hadn't been there at Thanksgiving, was simply decorated in comparison to the rest. It was situated near the woodstove but a safe distance away and a little pyramid of firewood was cleverly stacked on one side of the red skirt under the lowest limbs. He started to turn for the kitchen and the bandana necklace he had bought her the day of the cattle drive caught his eye. It was still draped on the framed sketch of her and Mitch and there was the snapshot of the two of them with Miles in the background.

"What do you think of my tree?" she asked from the kitchen.

"I like it," he said, and took care to stay on the newspapers on his way to the table.

"I bought it in Owen. It was quite the sight strapped to my pickup."

He smiled as he visualized it, as well as Mitch's probable reaction.

"I had to ask Ernie to come help me set it up," she continued. "He had to make a stand for it." She set the garlic bread on the table.

Jay already knew about the stand because Ernie had asked him to do some spot welding on it. The welding was nothing that Ernie couldn't have done himself, and he wasn't quite sure why Ernie had asked him to do it.

"Want anything besides soup and garlic bread?" she asked.

Jay shook his head.

They spoke briefly while they ate, and then they got up from the table at the same time. He was dreading the drive, even if it were only a few miles. It was miserable cold and the drifting snow made the road and ditches look the same. Thoughts of staying, knowing he would be snowed in, he pushed from his mind as soon as he recognized them forming. Then Riley left the kitchen. Jay was putting on his coat when she returned with a buffalo plaid muffler. She told him "Merry Christmas" and stood on tip-toe to wrap it around his upturned collar. Then she stepped back, looking pleased.

"I picked that up a couple of months ago in Owen," she said. "I thought of you the minute I saw it. Oh! Wait." She headed for the kitchen.

He fingered the soft edge of the muffler. He wasn't a scarf man but her thoughtfulness touched him.

"This was right nice of you," he told her when she returned. "But I didn't get you anything."

She gave him a warm plastic container that was full of soup. "Sure you did. You do nice things for me all the time, like stopping today."

He didn't say anything and opened the door. He held it open a few inches, permitting the snow and cold to invade.

"Call me if you need anything, all right?" he told her.

She nodded.

"I'll be out after the storm has passed to clear your drive," he said, not bothering to ask if she had anyone else lined up to do it. "But that might not be for a day or two." He watched her smile with gratitude.

Riley remained at the open door while his burly form struggled through the snow to get to his truck. After a minute the truck began to move, and after the flatbed built up speed there was a burst of white when it broke through a grill-high drift. She closed the door to the cold.

Forty-five minutes later she went to the phone and dialed his number.

"Just calling to check on you," she said when he answered. "Making sure you made it home."

"That's right neighborly of you."

"Well, Merry Christmas, I guess."

There was hesitation. "You too."

CHAPTER 28

It was Christmas morning. Riley woke to the relentless blizzard and for the first time thought it was cold in the house. She looked at the thermostat and found it on sixty-eight degrees, right where she'd left it. She got the fire going in the woodstove and then bundled up to check on the horses. The wind tried to suck her breath away and the cold hurt her lungs. Dually and Dobbie, protected by the barn and blanketed with snow, were fine with their big round bale of hay and they had plenty of water. She gave each of them a bright red apple and a flake of leafy green alfalfa for Christmas.

She didn't stay outside very long. In the house, which was turning cozy, she put a festive bandana around Wooly's neck and lit up the Christmas tree and decorations in the great room. She whistled along with holiday music and baked an apple pie, and the sweet smell of cinnamon and pastry lingered long after. Then Mitch called. The conversation started good but deteriorated and Riley found herself promising to visit for almost a week over New Year's, wondering what she would do with the horses as she spoke. The conversation kept nagging at her long after they hung up, and making Christmas dinner for one and the dismal weather report that predicted the storm would last one more night didn't help matters.

She restocked the stove, lit the lamps and candles and shut off the lights with hopes the ambience might rekindle her mood, but the glow from the twinkling Christmas tree and garland weren't enough. She resorted to the pie. With a plate in one hand and a glass of milk in the other she went to the couch. Wooly lay at her feet and she was watching *White Christmas* when the television flickered and then went out completely. By candlelight Riley made her way to a frosty window that faced Whispering Pines. There was nothing but darkness and swirling snow and she assumed the power outage was widespread. The only sounds were the howling wind and a burning log that fell inside the stove with a thud.

* * *

That night Riley slept in the recliner. She woke to Wooly's head on her lap, his big eyes looking into hers, and the irritating persistence of the wind.

There wasn't much heat coming from the woodstove but it was still warm. She prodded the ashes and added the last pieces of wood stacked on the red skirt around the Christmas tree. As cold as it was the power must still be off. She flipped the light switch in the kitchen. Nothing.

She opened the back door for Wooly, only to find snow piled against it. The brunt of the blizzard had passed but it was still snowing. There was snow everywhere. The driveway was full, the trees misshapen from the load, the roof of the barn blanketed in white, her horse trailer and even Dobbie and Dually were covered. Their backs and rumps were host to several inches of the white stuff and icicles hung from their manes. Their heads were mostly free of snow because of the holes they had created in their big round bale of hay while eating from select locations. She scooped the snow away from the door and then called Wooly, who looked at her doubtfully.

"Go on," she insisted.

The big dog reluctantly went out. The attentive horses moved to the lot fence near the gate and Riley had no doubts they were thirsty. She dressed, layering clothes and ending with her pink coveralls, then it was her muck boots, heavy coat with a hood, stocking hat, muffler and gloves. When she opened the door snow covered Wooly was there. He slipped past her and then stood back as if waiting for her to take her turn. She brushed the snow off him and then used a towel on his paws before stepping out alone.

Riley floundered her way to the horses and they waited for her in the drift that encircled the water tank. She knew with the power off there would be ice, but didn't expect it to be as thick as what she found. She made her way to the barn where she got two plastic five-gallon buckets, and passed the hydrant on her way out. With no electric to power the pump the hydrant was useless. Back across the drive she went, to the well house behind the house where she manually pumped water into the buckets. She only filled them half full because of having to fight the deep snow. Going to the barn again she rested the buckets on drifts, making slow progress. The horses quickly drank what she offered and she went back for more, making three trips before they were satisfied.

At noon she went out again. It had stopped snowing and the wind did not seem to be blowing as hard as earlier. After going through all the trouble to get two partly full buckets of water to the horses, they weren't interested. In the house things weren't going much better. She dusted and then brought out the vacuum for the large rugs in the great room, feeling stupid when it wouldn't start. Instead of putting the vacuum away she left it and tripped over the cord, causing her to stumble into the shelves. There was breaking glass and she cursed. She removed the broken glass from the framed sketch of her and Mitch and put the sketch on the kitchen counter for the time being.

It was late afternoon when she went out again. At the well house she began pumping, and with hopes of making fewer trips filled the plastic buckets fuller than before. With the awkward burden she didn't get very far before one of the buckets caught the ridge of a drift, and between fighting to keep her balance in the deep snow and the momentum of the sloshing water she was knocked on her butt where she sat like a stubborn mule, then the water doused her front. Stunned, she gagged and blinked. Then she flopped back and bawled with frustration.

She heard something and quit her wailing. She looked into the vast, depressing grey sky where clouds of a darker shade of grey trundled. She attempted to wipe her teary face with a bundled sleeve but the water on the sleeve had frozen. She tried to get up but her hands were of no help because the bucket's metal handles were frozen to her gloves and she only wallowed in the snow. Her temper flared.

"Arrrrgh!" she yelled and fought to get to her feet, determined this time to make it. Once she was up she smacked the buckets against each other and in their icy state they shattered. She yanked at her gloves—one shot directly into the snow but the other went airborne. The metal handle went with the glove, spinning up and up before starting its descent. The glove was forgotten when Riley saw Jay standing by a snowmobile in front of the barn. She blinked as if she was hallucinating, thinking maybe this was what snow blindness meant, or maybe she was going crazy from being alone too long during the storm. But Jay was still there, and he was *smiling*. She wanted to ask just how long he'd been there, but evidently it was long enough. She glared and turned for the house, retreating as best she could in the snow and falling more than once in her stubborn haste.

Her frosty hands were useless on the door knob and then Jay was reaching around her to open the door, and if she wasn't humiliated enough she heard the whirring of the vacuum cleaner. The power was back on. She tried to ignore the sound while she toiled with the zipper on her stiff coveralls. Without the least bit of trouble Jay took off his coat and boots and then he disappeared through the door into the kitchen.

The annoying sound of the vacuum stopped. Jay returned and helped with her coveralls. She did her best to avoid looking at him. When the coveralls were off Riley found that her other layers of clothing were wet too.

"Having a patch of difficulty?" He asked it with a straight face but she recognized his smile by the wrinkles near his eyes.

She stormed to the dryer and jerked clothes out. After grabbing what would suffice she went to the bathroom, and slammed the door behind her.

When she came out Jay wasn't in sight. The clothes she had left in front of the dryer were folded and in a basket and the dryer was going, presumably with her wet things in it. Her first thought was that he had left, disgruntled over her obvious lack of appreciation, but she found him in the kitchen, making toasted cheese sandwiches and leftover chicken noodle soup was warming in a pan.

"I hope you don't mind," Jay said with uncertainty, then he went back to the sandwiches. He lifted them with a spatula and put them on a plate.

She pulled a chair from the table but didn't sit down. She went to the window and looked out at the snowmobile near the barn.

"On your way to check on Freddie?" she asked.

"Uh…yeah" he replied. He randomly opened cupboards. "Making my rounds."

She went to the cupboard and reached to open the door that revealed the bowls.

"I thought you were making snow angels out there or something," he said offhandedly.

She threw a dirty look his way. His eyes were twinkling. She choked back tears and laughter and then reached over the damaged sketch of her and Mitch for a tissue. Jay spooned soup into bowls and placed the food on the table. He sat down and waited for Riley.

"Would you like a hand outside?" he asked. "I've been out in this taking care of my horses since noon. What a passel of trouble. I'll be out tomorrow to clear your drive as soon as the maintainer gets the road open. Or sooner...if I need something to cheer me up."

She was starting to sit down but stopped. "Jerk," she told him. Then she sat down and blew her nose although she didn't have to—she was using the tissue to hide her smile.

After they ate Jay took his dishes to the sink. He walked to the window.

"Looks like the wind finally quit," he said. "We have a little daylight yet. How about I help tend to your horses before it gets dark and then would you like to ride with me to check on Freddie?"

Her face lit up.

"I have an extra helmet. You'll be glad to have it because of the cold," he said.

"Let me get my old coveralls and before we go my good ones should be dry... Thank you."

He walked past her on his way to the mud room. "Do you have extra buckets in the barn?" he asked with a little grin.

She didn't answer right away. She was still humiliated.

"Yes, in the tack room," she said lifelessly.

"Your tank should be thawed by morning. I'll start getting the horses watered for now." He went out the door and Wooly went with him.

After they got the horses watered they scooped snow from the sidewalk, some drifts almost four feet high, and brought in wood that was stored in the well house. While they worked the setting sun could be seen through clouds that were moving out.

At the snowmobile Jay helped her with the helmet. When she settled down behind him she put her arms around his waist. He pulled out the driveway and then stayed on the snow filled roads in the world of white. He pointed out Cap and Peggy Henderson's place.

Freddie and Mae seemed surprised to see Jay but Riley thought it was because of the fact that she was with him. She saw Freddie watching from a window when they got back on the snowmobile.

"Mind if I take a little detour? Are you warm enough?" Jay asked over his shoulder.

"I'm having a blast," she said over the noise of the engine.

He headed down the snowy road again. The clouds were gone and the skies revealed the full moon beginning its climb. Jay drove past places she had never seen before and it was completely dark by the time they reached a small, one-horse town. Although the houses were lit up only the tavern on the main street of few buildings radiated the warm yellow glow. Jay came to a stop in front of it.

"Ready for a break?" he asked.

She nodded and he shut off the engine.

The few patrons at a table playing cards looked up when they entered. Jay headed for the bar and kept her beside him.

"Tapperd, is that you?" queried an old man. "What're you doing out on a night like this?"

"Well hello, Quincy," Jay said and stopped to shake the old man's hand. "I don't know… What are you doing out on a night like this?"

Riley felt the men's eyes on her as she waited. After the short conversation Jay steered her to the bar where they drank coffee to warm up and made small talk with the bartender.

"Ready?" Jay eventually asked.

She hopped down from the stool. Jay plunked money on the smooth wood and told the bartender thanks. She intended to follow him out but he waited for her to get beside him before he started to walk away.

They left the town behind and the full moon cast long, dark shadows in the snow covered pastures and fields. There was even a shadow of the two of them and the snowmobile on the snowy road. Occasionally snow would spray from the runners and at one point Jay slowed and pointed out a deer crossing the road ahead of them.

The Colby place looked warm and inviting with smoke rising lazily from the chimney and the lights on. Jay pulled up within yards of the back door and he remained on the idling machine after Riley got off. She removed her helmet.

"Aren't you coming in?" she asked with disappointment.

He shook his head. "I'll be out sometime tomorrow to clear your drive. Call in the meantime if you need anything, all right?"

"Thanks, for everything," she told him gratefully.

"My pleasure," he replied.

He cut across the front yard and was slightly airborne before landing on the road. It didn't take long for him to be gone from sight and after he was she realized she was still holding his helmet.

CHAPTER 29

The grader opened the road the next morning and Jay made it out some time later. While he pushed snow from her driveway she scooped to free her pickup and made paths from the barn to the lots and tank.

"I'd stay to help you finish but I'm headed to Freddie's," Jay told her when he got out of the tractor. "And I still have to dig out the place where my horses are."

"You cleared your shop before coming here?"

He nodded. "And repaired two snow blowers and a blade on a pickup."

She frowned. "Not yours I take it."

He shook his head.

"Have time for coffee?" she asked with the scoop shovel propped in snow beside her. She thought he looked undecided. "To go?"

"Sure."

They hung up their coats but left their coveralls and boots on and stepped on newspapers Riley laid out.

"I want you to know you were a lifesaver yesterday when you showed up," she told him. "Thank you. I apologize for the temper tantrum."

He shrugged his broad shoulders, which appeared even bulkier with his coveralls on. "I feel the same way myself sometimes."

The detached way he said it made her stop what she was doing. She looked at him but he didn't look back. Then the phone rang. She considered not answering it.

"Aren't you going to get that?" Jay finally asked with the insistent ringing.

It was Mitch. She tried to keep the conversation brief. Jay was getting cups when she came back.

"I forgot...I told Mitch I'd visit for New Year's—appeasing the gods," she said. "Seems he's a bit put off I was snowed in over Christmas."

Jay poured coffee and offered her a cup.

"Would you mind checking on my horses a couple of times while I'm gone?" She pulled out a chair and sat down. "I'll be gone almost a week. I hate to go, but, well, sometimes I say things I shouldn't because I want to make others happy."

He looked at her briefly and walked from the counter with a cup in his hands. He sat across from her and focused on his coffee.

"I'd feel better if someone who knew horses would check on them," she said while watching him stare at his coffee. She intended to add that the weather looked like it would be decent and she would have things as simple as possible, but the words didn't come. It didn't matter. He wasn't paying attention anyway.

Jay finally nodded as if noticing the silence. "I can do that," he said. He took a drink.

His face was void of expression except for frown lines Riley had never noticed before. She wanted to ask what was wrong but assumed at least part of it was because she was being a nuisance. Everyone asked Jay for favors and she was regretting having made the request. Before she looked away he brought his eyes up to hers, then he took in a deep breath.

"I'll be gone a while, probably have to leave before you get back," he said then looked at his coffee again. "I have to take Marta to a clinic." He did not look up. "She has breast cancer."

Riley felt awful for Marta and was taken aback by what she considered something very personal in his life that he was sharing. He rarely mentioned Marta and never his private life.

"I'm so sorry," she said. She reached across the table and placed one of her hands on his that was cradling the cup. She watched his eyes turn misty.

"They caught it early, but Rene, Marta's mom, well, she had breast cancer too," he said and paused. "Marta wants to go to that clinic out of state to get the best treatment possible." He paused again. "She's scared."

Riley searched for the right words but could think of nothing. "I don't know what to say. I'm so sorry," she managed.

The sound of the clock ticking was the only thing she heard as they sat at the table with one of her hands on his. He sniffled and then got up and walked to the counter. She watched him reach for the box of tissues and cursed herself for not being considerate enough to have thought of it first. He blew his nose with his back to her and then stuffed the tissue in his pocket. He turned around and leaned against the counter.

"Miles is in Arizona. He goes every year at this time, and there is no one else to take her," he said, looking at nothing.

She crossed the kitchen to where he was standing, put her arms around him and nestled the side of her face against his chest. He rested his chin on the top of her head and wrapped his arms around her. They stood that way until she heard him sniffling. She reached for the box of tissues and then held it up, not moving from the embrace. He let go of her with one arm to pull a tissue from the box and blew his nose with it, still holding her with his other arm.

"I feel like an ass for blowing my nose over your head," he said.

She pulled away and smiled sadly, not only seeing his hurt but feeling it too. He turned away, fumbled in his pocket for the first tissue and tossed them in the trash can.

"I'd better get going," he said, then reached for his coffee on the table and took a drink.

She opened a cupboard to get an insulated cup. She filled it with steaming coffee and snapped on the lid. She handed it to him, receiving a fragile smile before he brusquely left to get his coat.

They stood near his tractor that was beside a mound of snow higher than the blade. He had left it running and exhaust escaped in wispy white plumes. A crow cawed somewhere in the distance. The sun was shining, but there was no warmth. He finally looked at her and then walked the few steps to the tractor.

"Tell Marta I said hello," she told him.

"I will," he said before he stepped up and then inside.

Amid the vast winter white she watched the tractor trundle down the driveway. This time Jay turned the opposite way he usually did, headed for Freddie's, and she continued to watch him go.

CHAPTER 30

Riley had become lax about getting up at any specific time and sunshine was flooding her loft bedroom. She stretched, then became aware of an obstinate dripping. It was coming from a window. She left the bed and discovered an icicle was melting, dripping against the sill, and it made her smile. She looked out to see Dobbie playing in the snow and Dually ignoring him. She wondered if Jay still wanted her to ride his young horses that summer. The only time they had spoken since he had told her about Marta's illness was when she got back from Mitch's after New Year's, and that was only because she called to thank him for checking on her horses. She decided to stop at his shop when she went to town that day.

Jay's flatbed and work truck and several other trucks were at the shop. When she opened the door the first thing she saw was the group of men clustered around Jay's desk. Then she saw Jay. He was alone, working on a car some distance from them. She felt butterflies that she attributed to the men looking in her direction.

She was within a few yards of Jay when he looked up. He grinned and set his tools on the car. When she reached him he put his arms around her and lifted her off the floor. Surprised, she laughed and hugged him back, and when he set her down she thought he looked like he even surprised himself. His frown lines were more pronounced and there were bags under his eyes.

"How the hell have you been?" he asked.

She rolled her eyes. "Winter out here sucks."

He laughed, and she realized how much she missed him.

"How is Marta?" she finally asked.

His mouth opened but the unspoken words hung in the air, and he failed at hiding his concern. He looked down, picked up the shop rag from the car he was working on and wiped his calloused hands. She had come to realize it was an edgy habit he had, the only habit she had noticed.

"What are you going to do with your young horses this year?" she asked, changing the subject for him.

Relief showed on his face, but only momentarily. "Miles is riding Prissy and Forbes." He looked at his hands. "He's taking them to the sale in Junction City this weekend," he divulged before bringing his eyes back to hers, then his expression lightened. "I'm keeping Potsy. Will you ride him and the young ones for me this summer? I can bring you half a dozen if you have time for them."

"I'd love to. Want to leave them all summer?"

His brows went up. "If you want to ride them that long, sure. I already talked to Miles about getting them started. I'll see how soon he can take them." There was silence and he went back to wiping his hands with the rag.

"I'd better let you get back to work," she said. "Let me know what you find out from Miles. I want to get the house painted this summer but I'll have lots of time to ride." She took a step back. "Good to see you again, you big lug. Quit being such a stranger." She smiled before turning, not expecting him to reply. When she reached the door she looked back. He had been watching her and she smiled at him again. Then she stepped out and wavered as she pulled the door closed, mindful of the cold knob in her hand.

Jay went back to work and heard the men resume their talking. They were respectful toward him and he knew they would not bring up her visit, at least not to him. Soon he quit thinking about the men, but could not rid his thoughts of her.

* * *

Riley stopped at Junction City to see Prissy and Forbes sell that Friday evening. It wasn't far out of her way to Owen where she was headed to attend a function at Mitch's side the next day. The auctioneer chanted as Miles rode the horses proficiently in the ring to show their abilities, and they fetched good prices. Before leaving she took a minute to walk down the aisles between stalls, looking at the sale horses, and was on her way out when she had to wait for a group of men bantering in front of the exit. An older man wearing insulated coveralls and a ball cap saw her first.

"Pardon us, ma'am," he apologized. He elbowed the man next to him who looked at her and then moved, getting the attention of the man next to him. Most of the group shuffled out of the way while those wrapped up in the conversation turned to see what was going on.

"Thank you," she said and began to walk through them.

"Excuse me, boys, I see my date has arrived," Miles announced as he materialized from the group carrying his saddle. He did not look back as he took Riley by the arm with his free hand. "How ya been, girlfriend?"

"Hello, Miles. Did you buy anything?" she inquired.

He lifted the saddle. "You really think I'd be packin' this if I had a horse? Nope, not me. I got too many the way it is."

"Jay said you were going to start his colts before I took them this summer."

His face clouded at the mention of Jay, knowing he was the one getting the brunt of taking care of Marta. He set the saddle down and fiddled with something, and when he stood up again was flashing an ornery smile.

"Of course I'll start 'em. I'll do like I did last year and'll manage a couple of rides on each of 'em."

She laughed.

"I'm starving," he declared. "Would you do me the pleasure of letting me buy you supper? I'd appreciate the company."

She glanced at her watch.

"C'mon," he implored. "Give Perry Mason a call and tell him you'll be late."

She smiled and unconvincingly shook her head.

"Please? I hate to eat alone," he said turning on the charm.

"I'd have to find a phone," she said lamely.

"You don't have a cell phone yet?" he asked with disbelief.

She shrugged.

"I swear you'd be driving a car like Fred Flintstone if they made them." He dug in a pocket with his free hand. "Most the girls I'm attracted to have their heads in the clouds but not you. Yours is under a rock." He gave her a flirty smile and his eyes sparkled. "But that's probably one of the reasons I'm so attached to you."

She smiled politely. He offered his phone but she tried to refuse it. "I can't," she said. "He has caller ID. I don't think it would be a good idea for him to have your number."

He flipped the phone open and pushed some buttons with one hand while holding the saddle with the other. "Here. The number is blocked. He won't think anything about it if you tell him you're calling from someplace along the road, which is true since you don't have a cell." He gave her a look of disapproval.

She paid no attention to his opinion as she took the phone and entered the number as they walked. When they arrived at his trailer he put the saddle in the storage area over the gooseneck then stood by the trailer while she concluded the call. She handed the phone back to him.

Miles spit tobacco to the side. "You want to ride with or follow?"

"I'll follow," she said giving him a look from the corner of her eye.

He grinned mischievously. "Wise woman. Where you parked?"

She motioned. "Behind those trees."

"Hop in and I'll give you a ride," he told her.

When she pointed out her pickup Miles said, "Don't you have a car?"

"Yes, but it needs work. I don't trust it and haven't bothered Jay to ask him to work on it."

Miles turned quiet. Riley hopped out. Then she followed him to an outdated log-sided building with a tin roof that was much nicer inside than what she expected. The waitress was cute and flirted with Miles, but other than his initial comeback he was respectful toward Riley. His trademark cologne was barely discernible because of the fact he had been at the sale barn all day but she detected the tobacco, and a shadow was forming on his jaw. He moaned seductively when a thick steak, its juices running into the hash browns, was placed in front of him and he continued the spectacle as he made the first cut and put the piece in his mouth.

He was a gifted talker but did not talk about himself, instead recounting experiences he had seen or been involved with over the years rodeoing. Riley sensed he was avoiding any conversation that might involve Marta or Jay, and summarized that he planned to go through life as carefree as he could manage.

When she realized they were the only customers in the restaurant she glanced at her watch, astonished to see it was two o'clock in the morning.

"I have to go," she said.

"But it's still early," Miles protested.

"I don't think so," she maintained.

He sighed dramatically.

She tried to pay for her meal but he insisted it was his treat, and he left a generous tip as well.

They walked across the parking lot that was empty except for his rig and her pickup under a light. It was chilly and their breath was visible as little clouds of vapors. He stood behind her as she unlocked her truck and while she reached in to start it to let it warm up before getting in. She turned around to find only inches separating them. She took note that he was about the same height as Jay, but otherwise there was no size comparison.

"You haven't told me how you've been," he said watching her attentively. "Any chance of ditching that boyfriend of yours?"

"I haven't really thought about it."

His eyes got big and his shoulders went back. "Why, that's a plumb foolish thing to say."

She looked at him, thinking about what he said. It was an astute comment.

"Why don't you give it some thought," he said straightforwardly. "Life's too short not to grab what you want when you can along the way."

She didn't know what to say, thinking maybe she was wrong with her conclusion about him.

He took a step back, then another. "Get yourself a cell phone. You shouldn't be on the road these days without one." He raised his arms above his cowboy hat and wiggled his fingers as he continued to back up, adding, "You never know what kind of *weirdo* you might run into." He grinned before turning.

He didn't look back during the walk to his truck. Then exhaust came out the tailpipe and the amber lights on his truck and trailer came on, but he didn't pull away. Riley took a deep breath and got in her pickup. She changed the country radio station because she didn't want to hear how miserable the subject of the song was, or why. Miles was still parked. He was certainly full of surprises. Thoughts of Jay entered her mind but she pushed them away when she also thought of Marta. She considered what Miles had said, wondering if she had let her life become safe and routine again, just as she had in Owen before buying the Colby place.

She put the truck in gear and pulled away, waving as she drove past Miles. Under the light above she could only make out his figure in the truck. He pulled in behind her and sat idling as she checked for traffic. She drove onto the street, headed east, and watched in her rearview mirror as he pulled out and went the opposite direction.

CHAPTER 31

Before the long winter was over it became routine for Riley to drive to Owen for the weekend. She would leave Friday afternoon and head back right after Mitch left for work Monday morning. The arrangement suited Mitch more than it did her and she reasoned she had more time than he did. But now spring was right around the corner and she found herself wanting to spend more time with the horses, and consequently less with Mitch. How she was going to break that to him she wasn't sure, and gladly stopped dwelling over it when she saw Jay's flatbed coming down the road behind her and Dually. She dismounted and led the mare to his side of the truck, the two of them looking at each other all the way. Jay rested an elbow on the open window and she put a hand on the truck near his arm. Neither spoke for a time.

"I know we don't need words between us, Jay, but this is ridiculous," she said affectionately, and thought he looked pleased with the comment.

"You been riding quite a bit?" he asked.

"Some. I'm anxious to ride your colts."

"Good. But I have a favor to ask before then," he said, looking like he wished he didn't have to ask.

"Name it."

"Would you check on my broodmares while I'm gone with Marta to the clinic next week?"

"You know you don't have to ask. I'll be happy to do it for you."

"Or I can bring them out here if you'd rather not drive back and forth. I'll make it right with you."

"How soon are they due to foal?"

"Not for at least a week, maybe two," he said and then hesitated. "To be perfectly honest, with everything that's been going on I'm not sure. I'd appreciate it if you would just foal them out this spring. I don't have the time or want-to this year." He looked at her like he thought he was being inadequate.

She cleared her throat and felt a wrenching inside for the pain she could see on his face. "You know I will," she said.

He drew in a deep breath. "Miles is riding the two-year-olds and giving Potsy a tune-up right now. I think he has Bubbles sold. I'd ask Miles to foal the mares out, but, well, I don't know if I can count on him."

"It's no problem, honest."

He nodded. "How about I go ahead and bring them here? I can in a few days…uh, I mean after the weekend," he said, knowing she was usually gone to Mitch's.

"That will work."

"I appreciate it." His upper body moved as he put the truck in gear.

She moved Dually away from his truck and thought he was going to say something else, but he didn't. He nodded good-bye and the truck rolled away. She walked down the road with Dually, watching the flatbed get smaller and smaller.

* * *

The next day Riley set up a foaling stall in the barn. She just got back to the house after working on the stall when the phone started to ring.

"Hello?" she asked, not recognizing the number.

"Riley, its Jay."

She could hear a radio in the background and other noises she recognized but couldn't distinguish.

"The clinic was able to fit Marta in earlier so we're on the road," he said and then stopped. She heard Marta talking. "Are you there?" he asked.

"Yes, I'm here."

"I'm not going to be able to bring the mares to your place."

"I'll get them. Where are they?"

He was quiet and then they began to speak at the same time. They ceased talking and there was silence.

"Serious," she finally said. "I'll go get them and handle it." She was insistent, knowing he didn't want to have to ask for help in the first place. "Are they at your dad's place?"

"I didn't mean for you to have to go to so much trouble."

"I owe you. You know I'll be happy to do it for you."

"Yes, they're at Dad's. There's still some snow piled but it's out of the way. You can hook up to my trailer if you want. Do you have caller ID?"

"Yes."

"Then you have Marta's cell number if you need anything. I'm using her phone right now. Be careful. Ask Ernie to help if you need. I don't want you getting hurt." She heard Marta again, or perhaps it was the radio. "The sorrel mare with a blaze is due first, I am sure of that. I'll get you more accurate dates when we get back. None of the mares are nasty, but keep in mind they don't know you."

"Quit worrying. I'll take care of them and things will be fine," she said while wondering what she was getting into. She had never been around foals let alone a mare in foal. "It'll be fun," she added positively.

"You're breaking up," he said and then she also heard the breaks in the connection. "Marta says hello."

Riley felt bad for not thinking to ask how Marta was, and after she did there was nothing but static. She held the phone to her ear until she heard the dial tone.

She drove to the farm where Jay kept the broodmares. All the horses were there for the winter; the broodmares in well-organized pens with big round bales of hay and full water tanks and the young horses had access to the stalk field. The mares were suspicious of her but she was able to catch and load them in the trailer without trouble. The sorrel looked like she might be closer to foaling than Jay thought, at least that's what she was thinking from her research since she told him she would help. She didn't want to let him down.

She checked the mares closely when she did chores the next morning and took notes. The sorrel mare had wax forming at her teats and her belly looked like it had shifted from the day before. Riley rode Dually and Dobbie and when she checked on the mares before going to the house for lunch she saw milk dripping from the mare's teat.

At the house she went to the telephone, nervous at the thought of Marta answering. It wasn't that she didn't like Marta. She thought Marta was a very pleasant person, even though they didn't know each other very well. She stopped thinking about it and dialed the number. She listened to it ring, and then there was a clatter.

"Damn puny phone," she heard Jay say.

"Having a patch of difficulty?" she asked, mimicking him from the day she had trouble in the snow.

There was momentary silence. "How are things?" he asked and by his tone she could tell he was smiling. "You haven't had trouble with the mares, have you?" he asked apprehensively.

"No, not at all. It's been smooth sailing. I got things situated here at home and have your mares. They seem content enough."

"Good."

"I called to say I think the sorrel mare is getting close to foaling."

"Is she waxing?"

"Yes, and she was dripping milk before I came in for lunch."

He sighed. "She can foal pretty quick. But she's never had trouble, none of those mares have. I guess we have that going in our favor."

He told her to do her best and to be careful. She asked about Marta and he briefly told her she was having a procedure done as they spoke and the doctors thought things were looking up. He asked about things at home, twice, and there were periods of relaxed silence between them. Her call was a welcome one and he didn't want her to go. Not long before she had called he thought he must be feeling like Miles did in times like this—he wanted to be just about anywhere but where he was.

The cell phone beeped occasionally before he realized it meant the battery was dying. It was during one of their pauses when he heard the click before the phone went dead. He slowly closed it.

Jay didn't know how long the doctor had been standing in front of him. He stood up and searched the face of the young doctor.

"I think we are heading in the right direction," the doctor said with a comforting smile. "We have a crucial corner to get around, but I'm pleased to say that your sister is doing great."

CHAPTER 32

Riley set her alarm to check Jay's mare at midnight, and then she checked every two hours after that. But there was no new foal, not even when she wearily went out to do the morning chores. She was beginning to doubt that she knew anything about this foaling business.

She looked in on the mare before going to bed and again set her alarm for midnight. Entering the barn at twelve o'clock, she saw the mare looking at her in the dim light, but when she got closer to the stall was disappointed to see the mare had not foaled. She sighed, went back to bed and burrowed under the covers.

The night turned out to be a repeat of the previous one. After doing morning chores she went to town, first visiting Chloe and then stopping at Decker's. She found herself looking for Jay out of habit as she passed his shop on the way home.

She took the groceries to the house and after putting things away exchanged her heavy coat for a lighter one. The light spring breeze made her happy and she whistled a tune as she walked across the driveway. In the barn she picked up a halter on her way to the stall, thinking she would turn the mare out in the lot while she rode, but she stopped abruptly and stared at the spindly-legged foal standing in front of its mother. The baby was already dry.

Riley entered the stall and the mare did not seem to mind her presence. When she reached to touch the baby it darted behind its mother, but it wasn't long before the baby's curiosity got the better of it. When it peeked around the mare Riley slowly reached out her hand and the baby touched her fingers with its nose. She was in awe of the new life and lost track of time.

She eventually started back to the house, walking faster the closer she got. She dialed Marta's cell number and felt disappointed and then foolish when Marta answered instead of Jay.

"Hello, Marta. This is Riley."

"We're on our way home," Marta said. "Is everything okay?"

"Yes, everything is fine. How are things with you?"

"Good! I got an excellent report!"

"That's wonderful news!" Riley was happy for her but before thinking what else would be appropriate to say Marta was asking why she called. "I wanted to tell Jay the sorrel mare foaled," she told her.

"Aw! Hold on."

"So mother and baby are doing good?" Jay asked.

"Yes," said Riley. "The baby is so cute! I lost all that sleep checking during the night and the mare waits till I go to town to foal."

He chuckled. "Colt or filly?"

"Oops. I didn't think to look." She laughed. "Some helper I am, huh?"

"We'll be home sometime tonight. Will you be home tomorrow?"

"Sure," she said and glanced at the calendar, thinking she wouldn't leave for Mitch's until after Jay and Marta were there. Maybe she would postpone until the day after that, or even altogether. "I'll see you then."

"Sounds good."

Riley called Ernie and then made arrangements with the nursing home so Chloe could come see the new baby. Ernie brought Chloe in the van and the three of them spent the rest of the day together, including Riley fixing supper before Ernie took Chloe back. Riley was just dozing off in the easy chair when the phone rang. She hurried to get to it, thinking it would be Jay.

"Hello!" she said.

There was silence.

"Hello?" she inquired.

"Riley?" Mitch asked.

"Oh, hi, Mitch."

"What are you doing?" he interrogated.

"Ohmygosh!" she exclaimed. "It's Friday, isn't it? I'm so sorry." She told him about the foal and how her days were mixed up and he didn't sound quite so irritated after. He said he would drive out, and would leave as soon as he hung up.

* * *

Mitch and Riley were in the barn when Jay and Marta pulled up in Marta's white Saturn. Wooly shuffled to the door ahead of Riley to greet them.

"Hello! How good to see you," she told Marta and they hugged politely.

"You too," Marta said. She was pale and looked tired.

Jay took Marta by the arm. He didn't speak to Riley but they did smile at each other before they walked into the barn. Mitch extended a hand to Jay who hesitated before accepting it.

"You remember Mitch, don't you?" Jay asked Marta and then he headed for the foal.

"Of course I do."

Mitch beamed at her reply. "You're looking good," he said convincingly.

Marta blushed. "How kind of you to say so."

Riley joined Jay in the stall. Mitch's attention went from Marta to Riley and Jay.

"You did good," Jay said, giving her a reserved grin. "She's a nice one. Help me corner her."

They spread their arms and used the mare's body to help situate the foal. After Jay caught the baby he maneuvered it toward the gate. Riley was ahead of him and opened it for Marta.

Marta stroked the foal. "She's *so* soft. Have you ever felt a baby foal?" she asked Mitch.

Mitch looked doubtful, but his expression changed when his fingers touched the downy soft hair.

"It is soft," he admitted.

"Just like a human baby's bottom," Marta said and laughed softly.

There was small talk while they continued to admire the foal. After a time Riley heard Marta sigh and saw that Jay heard it too. He appeared troubled and again took Marta by the arm. She seemed very appreciative.

"I wish I felt well enough that we could all go out for dinner," Marta said wistfully.

A pained look appeared on Jay's face as the words were spoken.

"But one of these days we will," she added confidently.

Jay began to escort her away. Marta stopped at the barn door and looked at Riley and Mitch, who had put an arm around Riley.

"Give me a couple of months," Marta promised, "and we'll all go out to dinner. My treat. I'll see that Miles is there too."

Jay bristled.

"Maybe I'll give Miles a call this afternoon," Marta added longingly. "I don't know what it is about Miles... He has a way of making a person forget their troubles."

"Yeah, like a gunshot to the head," Jay said under his breath and started to move again, gently pulling at her.

Riley and Mitch followed behind. They watched Jay help Marta into the car and then Jay went to the driver's side. He didn't look up as got in and soon he was backing down the drive. Marta waved and Riley waved back. Mitch guided Riley into the barn, and she realized it was probably the only time she hadn't watched Jay leave until he was out of sight.

CHAPTER 33

Cap drove his truck and trailer over the downed barbwire gate and then stopped, cursing Freddie for being too cheap to have a cattle guard installed. He didn't usually turn cows out this early but was tired of feeding hay and feeling restless, so he was pasturing his cattle ahead of schedule. Freddie's was just one of the pastures he leased and because of the heavy winter snow and recent sunshine the grass looked good, good enough for Cap anyway. The candy apple door of the Chevy hung open while Cap walked back to the gate, lifted the post and positioned the bottom of it into the wire loop. He strained to pull the top to close it, the pipe bar pull hanging useless because of his stubbornness.

After getting it closed he took the last drag on the cigarette on his way to the truck, slid in and threw the butt to the ground. He reached over the stack of ledgers and loose papers for a beer in his cooler and toppled the paperwork, cascading it to the floor. He cursed and yanked the beer from the cooler, bringing chunks of ice with it. He flipped the tab, slurped the contents that bubbled out and then guzzled a cold drink.

He eyed the mess he'd made. Maybe he could get Peggy to straighten it. She would do nice things like that for him. Maybe it was *love*, he thought with an arrogant tweak of his mouth, but more likely it was because she felt guilty for not giving him any kids. They'd been trying, or at least *he* had—and the grin appeared again—but with no success. He knew he wasn't the one with a problem, after all Cathy Conrad was his kid, but he just couldn't go around telling that to everyone now could he? He was rather amused that he had that over Patty, but on the other hand he suspected the town talked about him behind his back because they thought his goods were defective, and his eyes turned cold with the thought. Nobody knew that Cathy was his 'cept him and Patty, and he probably would have done the right thing and married her, but she'd zeroed in on Paul Conrad instead. When Paul inherited the lumberyard when he was just a senior in high school Patty thought he would be the better catch, so she let Paul believe the kid was his, even though they hadn't been sleeping together at the time. Cap knew it put Patty's panties in a wad to this day that he started dating Peggy, her sister, and he grinned again. Patty had always been jealous of Peggy, even back when she would leave Peggy in their shared bedroom with her nose in a book while she snuck off to meet Cap somewhere.

He downed the rest of the beer and threw the empty can out the back slider window to the box with the others. He had to stop at the Colby place to talk to that little Riley gal about the farming, but right after that was going home to see what Peggy was doing.

It was after noon when Riley saw Miles's pretty white Dodge and aluminum gooseneck trailer coming down the road from the direction of Whispering Pines. He and Jay were bringing Jay's young horses that she would ride for the summer. Miles pulled in the driveway and made the loop before coming to a stop.

"Oh, you old fussbudget," Miles was saying as he got out. "I don't know what you see in this guy," he told Riley. "How's my girl?" he asked, barely hesitating in his stride to kiss the top of her head as he walked past her.

Riley looked at Jay as if he would give an indication as to what Miles was talking about, but he just shook his head and walked to the back of the trailer as well.

"Aw, hell, when we were kids we'd just go out there and there'd be a new colt, remember?" Miles continued and unlatched the big door. "We didn't need any of that artificial insemination or gestation tables or worrying about when the mare was cycling. You gotta loosen up and let nature take its course."

"Seems Miles thinks I'm making too much work out of getting the mares bred back this year," Jay enlightened.

Miles swung the door open and held it. Jay stepped inside, untied two of the horses and handed the lead ropes to Riley. She led them to the side of the trailer and tied them.

Miles spit. "Granted, you get nice babies every year but I think you just need to turn them out with a stud this season and let it go at that."

Jay reached the back of the trailer with two more and gave Miles a dirty look at the same time that Riley took the lead ropes from him. "Well, now, don't we both know I'd have more time on my hands if I had a little help with Marta," he told him, then went back for Potsy, the last horse.

Miles apparently didn't have anything to say to that. When Riley came back from tying the horses Miles was making a face at Jay, obviously for her benefit. He stopped when Jay saw him and Riley giggled.

"Not you too," Jay said flatly. He offered the lead rope to Riley and then he and Miles were on their way to the barn.

Riley tied Potsy before hustling to help. They were catching the mares so she stood ready at the gate. When they came through the skittish babies stayed close to their mothers. Riley hurried around them to get to the trailer first and held the big door open. Jay led them in and Miles herded the babies. Riley waited for Jay to come out before pushing the door tight and latching it.

Miles began to untie horses from the trailer. "You want these in the lots by the barn?" he asked Riley.

"Yes," she answered. "What's your hurry?"

"Seems crybaby Jay thinks I ain't been carrying my weight and we've got to get too many things done today and not enough time to do them all," he said, talking faster and louder as he spoke. "So I guess we won't be going out to dinner tonight like I planned, girlfriend," he added with a glance at Jay. "I was hoping we could repeat that lovely night we had after the horse sale in Junction City."

Jay looked at Riley and then at Miles, who didn't say any more.

They were turning the horses loose in the lots when Cap pulled up the driveway. The sight irritated Riley, most specifically because she hadn't taken the time to find a replacement to handle her little bit of farm ground. Miles frowned when he recognized it was Cap.

"You should've specified invitation only to this party," he said sourly.

They met Cap just outside the barn.

"How's the nose?" Jay asked.

Riley's eyes got big and Cap looked like he wished he hadn't stopped.

"What'd I miss?" asked Miles.

Jay didn't answer. The three men resembled a Mexican standoff. Cap's hands were in the pocket of his sweatshirt, nervously fingering his cigarettes no doubt Riley thought.

Finally, "What're you doing here, Henderson?" quizzed Miles.

"I was wondering about the farming," replied Cap.

"Do you want to talk to him about the farming today?" Miles asked Riley. He sounded like a butler addressing the lady of the house and she stifled a laugh because of it. Then Miles started in again. "Just what is it you need to know about the farming?"

Cap produced a cigarette from the pocket. "I guess just if she wanted me to handle it again this year," he said and lit the cigarette while keeping an eye on Miles.

"Don't talk like she isn't even here," Miles reprimanded.

Cap took a step back and said he'd come back another day, something he obviously wanted to do from the minute he got there.

"No," Riley said shortly. "Just do it. Get it done when you do your adjoining piece." Cap's attention went from Miles to her. "Don't ever stop here again," she told him firmly. "If you have something to discuss, call me. I have an answering machine."

For the first time since meeting Cap she thought there was a hint of respect in his eyes. He was still looking at her like that when Miles said, "Anything else?"

Cap shook his head, then he began to walk backward, hesitantly at first, as if waiting for Miles to address him again, then he turned and went.

Jay snickered. "I'll give Marta credit for being right when she said you have a way of making a person forget his troubles...at least for a little while."

"How's the nose?" Miles resounded. "We *do* have some catching up to do, don't we?" He slapped Jay on the back. "Come on, Tapperd, let's get this show on the road. We ain't got all day, regardless of what you might think."

Jay looked at Riley and went to the passenger side of the truck. Miles's charade temporarily forgotten, she smiled back fondly and they continued to look at each other until he got in.

Miles hadn't gone very far down the drive before he had the truck in reverse and was proficiently backing the rig. When he stopped she put a hand on Miles's open window and Jay leaned across the seat.

"I almost forgot," he said and extended a hand with some bills. "This is for keeping the mares and babies."

Miles took the money and passed it to her. Riley crumpled the money and tossed it back at Jay.

"You overpaid me last year for riding Potsy, Prissy and Forbes," she said.

Jay was about to argue but Miles started talking. "I almost forgot something too. Trace said I should tell you about the branding we're going to up this way next week. Want to come? Bring your horse, help out, just get away. Whatta ya say?"

She looked at Jay who was wriggling to situate his body to put the bills in his pocket. He shook his head.

"I've got to take Marta. Maybe we're about done though," he added optimistically.

"Good. It's settled then," said Miles. "I'll have Trace give you a call. He already told me he could pick you up on the way." He patted Riley's hand resting on his truck and shot a look at Jay. "Gotta go. Much as I'd like to I can't get friendly right now—I'm within arm's reach." And with a wink he was leaving again.

CHAPTER 34

The day of the branding promised to be a beautiful one, despite snow drifts remaining in isolated areas of the secluded valley where over a hundred cows and their calves milled quietly, preoccupied with hay scattered on the ground. Cowboys riding guard kept the herds' wandering to a minimum. Trace parked with the half dozen or so trucks and trailers already there.

Riley, Trace and Shortbread walked to the hub of activity where pens of solid wood planks, worn smooth from years of cattle being pushed against them, comprised a maze around a bigger pen. A portable black steel box with a fire inside, waiting for the branding to begin, sat inside the big pen and a beat-up pickup with things strewn across its flatbed was parked near it. Volunteers, from cowboys to those wearing tennis shoes and ball caps, stood ready.

"Trace!" someone hollered.

"Hello!" Trace called back. Then, "Riley, this is Wade Green, foreman of the ranch," he introduced as Wade got closer.

Wade looked like the traditional cowboy, complete with stained leather chinks, a frayed peach colored wild rag around his neck and ancient black hat that had seen better days. His waist-length coat to ward off the late spring chill was faded from the sun and the leather gloves he took from between his belt and jeans were soft as butter from use. Something new, intruding on tradition, was the cell phone clipped to his belt.

"Nice to meet you," Riley told him, and he shook her hand.

"Trace, I need you to ride," Wade said, "but I also need someone to help with vaccinations. Think you'd be interested?" he asked Riley.

She would much rather ride but if there was something specific she could do to help, she would. She told him she was willing if someone showed her what to do. He led her to the back of the old flatbed and picked up one of the long syringes there, which she assumed was industrial size. It wasn't much smaller than a caulking gun.

"This is set to dose appropriately with each squeeze," he explained. "All you have to do is stick the needle in the hip and squeeze—basically pull the trigger. Each calf that's being branded gets one shot." He handed the instrument to her.

Riley bit her lower lip. "And when it's empty?

"There are two more right here," he said, indicating, "ready to go," and then he pointed to an middle-aged woman wearing jeans with the hems rolled up. "Mattie will keep them filled for you."

Riley looked at the items on the flatbed. "There are no other syringes I can get mixed up with...pick up the wrong one?"

He shook his head. "You can ask Mattie for anything you need."

She nodded, beginning to feel confident. She had given her own horses vaccinations for years, so plunging a needle into a calf's butt didn't seem too daunting.

"Don't get run over or accidentally vaccinate one of the workers," Wade told her with a grin and left.

The cattle bellowed as the riders started moving them, pushing the first group of cow and calf pairs to the working area. Cowboys took turns roping a calf and dragging it to the fire, where men on the ground wrestled the calf and then designated workers branded, ear-tagged and vaccinated, and male calves were castrated. Smoke and stench rolled each time the branding iron was applied and the calves bawled with protest.

Most of the cows had been through several years of the branding procedure already and knew their calves would be returned. Occasionally a rank cow would attempt to break the line, only to be met by a cowboy on horseback or a well-trained Australian shepherd dog that would turn the cow back.

At noon the clang of an old-fashioned dinner bell lifted the heads of the workhands ready for the well-deserved break. Cowboys put away their ropes and tended to their horses while those on foot placed their instruments on the flatbed on their way to the lunch wagon. Riley made a quick trip to Trace's trailer to check on Dually. When she came back, Trace motioned for her to join him and Shortbread in the crowd. Peggy Henderson was with them.

"Did you see that dog working?" an excited Shortbread asked her.

"I sure did," Riley said. "Maybe I should teach Wooly how to do that."

His eyes got big. "I bet he could."

"We had a stray dog show up at our place," Peggy said suggestively, getting both Shortbread's and Trace's attention.

"No," Trace said and shook his head for emphasis.

Peggy laughed. "Can't get anything past you, can I," she told him, then to Riley said, "We've never met—I'm Peggy Henderson. You must be Riley."

"Yes. It's good to finally meet you."

Shortbread asked Peggy about the dog and while they were talking Miles walked past, winking at Riley as he went.

They filled their plates with sandwiches of thick slabs of beef, baked beans and potato salad and then found a place to sit on the ground with the others. There was a mild breeze and the sunshine warmed everyone, causing many to shed their coats. A colony of prairie dogs within throwing distance stood watch from the safety of their holes in the ground, stock-still and then disappearing in a blink of an eye. The Australian shepherd came to investigate, much to Shortbread's delight, and Peggy pointed out the extent of the colony that went for quite a distance. Then Peggy offered to exchange places with Riley. She had done the job before for Wade, and Riley was glad for the chance to ride.

Riley's new job was to help keep the cows and calves contained on the prairie not far from the branding. She enjoyed riding the perimeter of the herd, watching over the foraging cattle and the cowboys as they cut the ones they wanted from the rest. It was a relatively simple job until two territorial bulls came upon each other. Miles was headed for them, swinging his rope in hopes of keeping them apart, but the big black brutes paid him no mind. Soon their heads were together and dirt was flying. Riley knew better than to get involved but she didn't anticipate them coming her way when one bull broke free from the other. Things happened fast and Dually panicked, wanting to flee the bulls bearing down on her. She managed to get a running start before Riley got her stopped, and still fearful of danger the mare spun to face the bulls. Dually was on the edge of the prairie dog colony, the ground sandy and soft, and she lost her footing. It was when she was struggling with the unstable ground that she stepped in a hole. Riley heard the *snap* before Dually went down and then she herself was tumbling in a cloud of sandy dust. She scrambled to her feet and looked to see where the bulls were, but Miles had been able to push them away. They were still fighting, oblivious to everything around them. Riley's heart was in her throat when she looked at Dually—the mare was standing on three legs. The leg without any weight on it looked odd, jiggly like Jell-O, and the sight of it churned Riley's stomach.

"You okay?" Miles asked with a grim face.

They looked at each other while he dismounted. She was too stunned to answer. Apparently convinced that she was alright he no longer looked back but at Dually, and the look on his face confirmed what Riley suspected. The leg was broken. She walked to the mare and the few cowboys that had seen the accident, including Trace, were riding their way. Miles led his horse to meet them. They were within hearing range but Riley didn't listen. Dually's head was in her arms and she consoled the mare, and herself, the best she could. When the cowboys finished talking they rode away and Miles came back.

"What do you want to do?" he asked after having waited to give her the opportunity to speak first.

"I don't have much choice, do I?" she said, hoping to see a sign in his eyes that she was wrong.

Miles slowly shook his head. "Wade can put her down for you if you'd like. It'd be easier on you than having her shot."

The words cut like a knife. Riley trembled, buried her face in Dually's mane and tried to compose herself. Then she wiped the back of her hand across her face, streaking dirt. Miles was behind her, his hand on her shoulder, and she was thankful for him being there. Tenderly she put her hand on Dually's soft muzzle.

"I can see that she gets back to your place, if you want, to...to bury her there," he said hesitantly.

She was quiet, knowing she had to get on with it. She took in a jagged breath.

"That would be good," she told him.

"I'll get Wade. I told Trace you'd ride with me, um, going home. I told him to get Shortbread out of here." He waited for a minute and then got on his horse and rode away.

Riley said her good-bye before Wade injected the liquid that put Dually to sleep. She shed a few tears and wished she wasn't there when Dually went down, but felt it was her responsibility to the mare. She did leave after they situated the pulleys to avoid seeing them hoist the mare's body into the back of Miles's trailer. With a heavy heart she leaned on the front bumper of his truck and felt someone's presence. It was Peggy, who stayed with her while they listened to the sounds of the men working.

The trip home with Miles was silent. He had put a saddle blanket under Dually's head which Riley considered nice of him—the thought of the mare lying in the trailer troubled her. Miles came to a stop in front of the barn. Neither were in a hurry to get out.

"I'll see if Jay's home yet," Miles finally said. "One of us will bring his backhoe. Do you know…where?"

She sighed. "I'll pick something."

Wooly was waiting for her when she got out and she scratched the top of his head without thinking about what she was doing. She walked to Miles on his side of the truck. He tried to give her an encouraging look but the gesture failed, so he opened his arms to her instead. She stepped close and put her arms around his neck, having to stand on the tips of her toes. His familiar scent of tobacco and aftershave was comforting and the corduroy of his coat's collar soft against her cheek.

Jay pulled out of Freddie's driveway. He hadn't even had the chance to get to his shop after returning from the clinic with Marta when Freddie called, saying the kitchen sink was backed up. Marta was in the last stages of recovery and Jay was appreciative of her progress, but lately had been feeling like nothing more than a nursemaid. Marta's boyfriend, Ken, wouldn't be back from service overseas for at least six months, preventing him from helping out, and Jay's irritation with Miles for keeping himself scarce was getting under his skin. He shook his head, knowing Miles was worthless when it came to serious things, and scornfully thought maybe he should have taken a few lessons from his half-brother when they were growing up. Miles had always been just like their dad, carefree with a no strings attached attitude, unable to cope with real issues or emotions.

Jay remembered his mother vividly. She was short and stocky and loved to bake. More often than not he would come home from grade school to the aroma of something ready to come out of the oven. There would be a plate of goodies and a glass of cold milk waiting for him and he would sit and listen to her talk as he ate. At least he had not been the one to have found her lying dead on the kitchen floor from a heart attack.

He was almost eleven years old when his dad showed up with Rene and her kids, Marta and Miles. Rene was the opposite of his mother in many ways and he remembered her temper directed at his dad a time or two, but she was kind and loving and good to the kids, including him. He eventually came to realize that Marta and Miles were his half brother and sister. He didn't ask questions and it wasn't until he was a young adult that he put the pieces together.

He and Miles developed a friendly rivalry horseback, and Jay knew he never would have become a capable horseman if it hadn't been for Miles. Jay learned to be good but Miles was a natural, evidently inheriting the gift from Rene. Jay's eyes smiled when he thought of the scraps they got into as kids, evolving into brawls when they got older. At least when it came to that he always got the better of Miles.

Unlike Miles, Marta was timid and never comfortable on a horse. But she and Jay had some kind of bond from the beginning, and she had been there for him after Molly died. Jay sometimes felt that Marta had hurt for him almost as much as he did during that time. He conceded that Marta needed him, and she deserved it.

Miles stood helpless with Riley against him. Her hair was dirty and her ponytail crooked from the fall, but he couldn't believe how good she felt. Of all the women he had been with, only one surpassed how he felt about Riley. He almost wished he didn't have so much respect for Jay—he was only human after all.

He recalled the day his mother said they were going to move in with their dad. He wasn't quite sure what she was talking about at the time, but he did come to think it was cool having an older brother. He looked up to Jay almost as much as Marta did when they were little, and then after he started school he found out how popular Jay was. Miles didn't know for the longest time if the girls were interested in him when he became a teenager or if it was because he was Jay's kid brother.

Miles never forgot the hurt when his and Marta's mom died, and when he saw how bad it tore up Jay when Molly died it soured him on wanting to get serious with anyone. He could never quite understand how things so bad could happen to people so good and just figured that not getting too attached in the first place would be the best route to take. And then they met Riley. He didn't know if Jay saw it as soon as he did but to his way of thinking, she and Jay seemed to be about as perfect for each other as he could imagine. He remembered watching them the morning they met—he saw the funny way Jay and Riley tried to act like they weren't looking at each other when they were. Of course he liked her too, right off, but thought that Jay deserved a little happiness, and, at that point in Miles's life he thought Riley was too good a woman for him anyway. As fate would have it things could have worked out for Jay and Riley, but Jay was too damn respectful to go after her when he found out she had a boyfriend, or too afraid to take a chance. Miles wasn't quite sure what was holding Riley back. A blind man could see that she was in love with Jay. Maybe she was just as naive as Jay, or scared, or maybe their age difference was holding her back. All he knew was that they were both about to drive him crazy and her being this close to him wasn't helping any.

Riley's barn came into Jay's view. As he got closer he saw Miles's truck and trailer, and knew the rig hadn't been there before. He turned and started up the drive and then saw them standing by the truck, hugging. Damn him, he thought. Damn him.

He parked and continued to look while getting out of the truck. Riley saw him and without hesitation left Miles's hold. Jay walked around the front of his truck while looking at Miles, who was reaching for his can of chew. Jay switched his look to Riley, whose face was dirty and her hair a mess. She flung her arms around him and hid her face against his chest. Although that was the last thing he expected, he returned the embrace.

Riley was thankful the worst was over and calm cradled her now that Jay was there. A few tears ran down her cheek, dampening his short-sleeved shirt. Jay wasn't wearing a coat and she could feel his chest rise and fall. She took in a deep, purging breath, ignoring the perfume that was of course Marta's. Her feelings for him washed over her and she knew that not only was she in love with him, but that she had felt that way for quite some time.

Jay gently pulled her away but kept hold of her. He looked at her with concern and the look on her face only confused him more. At first he recognized fear in her eyes, but there was something else too, something he couldn't put his finger on. Something about the way she was looking at him reminded him of Molly. No one else had looked at him like that. He leaned back and tipped his head, coming to understand that he did know what it was.

Riley backed away and he slowly let go of her. She didn't pull her eyes from him until she began to move toward the house, and he watched until she slammed the door shut behind her. He wanted to question if what he saw was real, *but he knew.* He turned to Miles, who looked back with no expression.

"We were helping at the branding," Miles said. "Things went bad and her mare broke a leg." He motioned toward the trailer with his head. "She's back there."

Jay took a step toward the trailer and then realized what Miles meant.

"Tell me what happened," he said.

Riley looked out the window, seeing Miles doing the talking. She went to the refrigerator, took a can from the twelve pack of beer that she kept on hand and gulped down part of it. She paced the house. When she looked out again Jay's flatbed was gone. She composed herself and went outside.

Miles, leaning on his pickup, looked up as she left the house and stood on his own while waiting for her.

"Jay went to get the backhoe," he said when she got near.

She hesitated in her stride but didn't stop.

"I have a place in mind," she told him. "Would you tell me if it's a practical one?"

He nodded and followed her across the arena to the edge of the big pasture.

"How about somewhere here?" she gestured. "I'd rather closer to the house, by the orchard, but that's probably not a good idea with the spring there."

"This would be good," he supported.

They moved downed limbs and opened the pasture gate. They drank the wine coolers that Miles had in his truck while they waited for Jay, which seemed like a long time, and they drank the beer Miles had while Jay unloaded the backhoe. Jay was digging the hole when Riley went to the house for the beer in her refrigerator.

After Dually's body was put in the ground Miles parked his truck and trailer in the driveway and Jay went about filling the hole. The sun sunk closer to the horizon as he worked. When the job was done he loaded the backhoe and then he secured it to the flatbed trailer. While he worked the only sound was the clinking of metal as the ends of the straps made contact with the trailer.

Jay hopped off the trailer. Riley was staring at the ground. Miles and Jay exchanged looks, each waiting for the other to say something as if to see who would take charge. Jay shook his head, thinking it would be a cold day in hell before Miles would expect anything less than for him to handle things.

"How many beers have you had?" Jay asked.

"Probably too many to be driving."

Just as he thought, but at least Miles admitted it. He looked at Riley, pale and lethargic, and then gave Miles an accusing look.

"How many has she had?"

Miles smiled wryly. "Probably as many as me."

Jay shook his head once more. "Open the door," he directed. He put an arm around Riley and began to steer her to the house.

Inside he told Miles to get a bath ready and he helped Riley to the kitchen. After sitting her in a chair at the table he began to search the cupboards for where she kept the coffee.

"Water's running," Miles announced. "Even found bubble bath. Boy howdy it's nice in there." He looked around. "It's nice in here." Jay impatiently looked from the cupboards to him. "I'm gonna check out the rest of the house," he announced and was gone again.

Jay was handing Riley a cup of coffee and encouraging her to take a drink when Miles came back. She was looking at him with tears in her eyes and he would have held her if it hadn't been for Miles.

"Check the bath water," Jay told him irritably, thinking it was as if Miles reverted to them being kids when they were together.

"Who's gonna undress her?" Miles asked with a broad smile.

"Get the hell away," Jay said crossly, his attention on Riley. He helped her stand up. "Are you with me?" he asked her.

She nodded groggily.

He assisted her to the bathroom and asked if she was going to be all right. She nodded again and he backed out the door, closed it and then waited, listening. Miles, looking like his feelings had been hurt, came from the kitchen and leaned on the wall across the hall from Jay.

"I'd call Marta, but she's worn out from the treatment," Jay said to him.

"How's it going?" Miles asked reluctantly.

"Much better. The doctor claims she's beating it, almost there."

"Good," Miles said, looking like he was bracing for a scolding.

Jay didn't say anything else. He heard Riley rustling in the bathroom and then the sloshing of water. He leaned against the wall, bent his knees and slid down, coming to rest on his heels.

Wooly sat near him and put his head on Jay. Miles rested the back of his head against the wall and looked down at Jay and Wooly.

Jay woke twenty minutes later with a leg cramp. He moaned and stood in agony. He hobbled in attempt to ease his muscles, cursing the pain and the fact he was getting older. He found Miles asleep on the couch. He returned to the bathroom door and listened, not hearing anything but the drone of the whirlpool jets. He opened the door a crack. Riley's clothes were in a heap on the floor and there were bubbles on top of the water, moving gently. She was asleep, her head tilted to the side. Then he felt Miles behind him, trying to look.

"Jack ass," Jay said, and pushed Miles hard enough that he hit the opposite wall. He pulled the door closed. "She's sleeping. What're we going to do?"

"We?" Miles asked innocently. "I'm starving. Think she would mind if we ransacked the fridge?"

Jay followed him to the kitchen. "Help yourself," he said. He went to the phone and dialed his house. When Marta answered he explained what was going on. She offered to come help but Jay told her to stay where she was. He had decided to leave Riley in the tub unless things changed. After all, he surmised, she was only a little tipsy, she should be fine right where she was.

Wooly brushed against his leg. Jay reached to pet the dog, noting how much the Newfoundland had seemed to age in the past year. He sighed, thinking he felt the same way. He headed for the door and Wooly followed.

Jay went to his truck and reached for the pack of cigarettes he kept in the glove compartment. Although he had quit drinking long ago he did like to have a smoke now and again, and justified giving in to the weakness now under the circumstances. In the crisp night air he stared at the quarter moon and stars and tried to think of nothing. He was partly successful. About the same time the cigarette was finished Wooly lumbered back and together they walked to the house.

"I got a couple frozen pizzas in the oven," Miles told him looking from the cupboards. "Just seeing what she has to munch on in the meantime."

Jay wanted to sit at the kitchen table but didn't feel like listening to Miles, so he went to the great room. He turned on the big screen television, flipped through the channels and stood there, somewhat watching, waiting for the pizza to be done. He didn't trust himself to sit down knowing he would fall asleep if he did.

He returned to the kitchen where Miles was opening each drawer, looking for utensils.

"By god you're helpless, Miles," he said and opened the appropriate drawer for him. "You'd think of all the strange womens' kitchens you've been in over the years you'd be able to recognize where to find things."

Miles grinned. "You seemed pretty familiar around this kitchen," he shot back.

Concede appeared on Jay's face and then he saw Riley standing in the doorway. She was barefoot, wearing an oversized long-sleeved shirt and had a towel around the length of her hair.

"How are you feeling?" he asked.

She managed a smile. "I'd get drunk more often if I knew it would keep you two around," she replied.

Both Jay and Miles grinned.

She put her hands to her temple and sat down at the table.

"Hungry?" Miles questioned going to the oven.

"Yes, I am," she said as if she hadn't been sure until he asked.

"What can I get you to drink?" asked Jay.

Riley tilted her head and looked him in the eye. She appreciated him too much to discard their friendship because of her feelings. She would have to work around them. Jay mustered a smile and she fought the tears threatening to come when she smiled back. She cleared her throat.

"Water would be good," she said.

He went to the counter. Miles elbowed him and Jay pushed him away. While she watched their horseplay Riley continued to smile, but it was a sad one.

CHAPTER 35

Riley spent the summer riding Jay's young horses, hauling Dobbie, painting the exterior of the house, and avoiding Jay as much as possible. She perceived that he was keeping his distance as well and the only time she saw him these days was when he would drive by the house. He evidently trusted her with his horses and on the first of every month there was a check in the mail from him with *horse training* written in the memo. She refrained from riding along the road where she might bump into him, like today.

She and Potsy followed the trail through the rugged bluff pasture of Raney's that was between her place and Jay's pasture where he kept some of his horses. Up here, near the top, there was nothing but trees. It was mid-September, too early for the colors of autumn but the leaves had begun to fall anyway, like the big brown one up ahead that floated down. It joined the rustling vegetation underfoot that was also lifeless because of the drought. A critter path veered off the trail, going under the barbwire fence and disappearing into the trees. After a hundred yards or so they began the gradual descent and the closer they got to the bottom the fewer trees there were. She could see the dry pastures and crops of tans and gold, soon to be harvested, and farmhouses in the distance including Cap Henderson's, the closest, and Freddie's which was much further. Riley felt she and Peggy could become close friends if it weren't for Cap trying to keep Peggy to himself as much as possible.

The trail was wider and free of leaves on the flat and Potsy unquestioningly stayed on it. It left the curve of the bluff and headed toward the Colby place. The tall sparse grass was more a soft tan color than green and along the edge of a big sandy blowout were yucca, their olive colored appendages and stems with empty pods pointing to the sky. When she reached the fence line she followed it until she came to the gate, then after entering her land stayed along the fence to avoid the tall stalks of corn. There wasn't much room due to Cap's quest to farm every available inch. Then there was another fence and gate between the cornfield and pasture, then it was across her pasture, through the tiny timber and past Dually's grave, which was only a bare patch of ground these days, before coming to the pasture gate and the arena. Dobbie and Jay's other horses were tied in the arena and they turned their heads in unison to watch she and Potsy emerge through the trees. Some of the horses were still saddled and the ones that weren't sported sweat marks from being ridden earlier. The arena was the same as it was a year ago except for Jay's round pen that had been removed from one end, allowing room for three barrels. She had put off making a decision about having a new building put up—she had put off making a lot of decisions. Her hatchback had quit running altogether and was parked between the arena fence and the barn and sunflowers had grown up around it. She rounded the mouth of the arena and rode past Goliath and her horse trailer parked near the hydrant. She had used the old truck to move the trailer so she could give it a good scrubbing and that's when the hitch on the trailer stopped working. She would have to ask Jay to fix it or find someone else to do it, but that would be awkward, too, if Jay knew. She resigned to ask him. He would have to be getting his horses before long anyway.

She dismounted at the barn and unsaddled. Wooly was nowhere in sight. The hot summer had been hard on the old dog and what little time he spent outside was usually under the spruce at the corner of the house. The mother cat hadn't come back so there were no kittens to amuse him. Riley took Potsy to his lot and then put the rest of the horses away. When she walked to the front yard she saw Wooly laying under the tree as she expected. She crouched and stroked his soft black hair.

She spoke to the dog and then continued to pet him while looking at the progress she had made with painting the house. The upper level was done, even the shutters and trim that matched the green standing seam roof, with the help of a ladder she had propped in the back of Goliath. Also done were the white porch columns and the floor which was as close a match to the original blue-grey that she could find. All that was left to be done was the very front protected by the porch overhang and there was new white lattice for underneath it in the back of her pickup.

CHAPTER 36

Riley dropped the wet paint brush in the near-empty can, done painting the house. She put her white splattered hands on the small of her back and stretched. There was only one more thing to do, which was replace the lattice under the porch.

While Riley attached the lattice Wooly watched from his spot in the shade of the spruce tree. He had been there all morning, sometimes sleeping but most of the time watching Riley. His eyes tracked her while she put the old, broken lattice in the back of her pickup and while she added the paint can, brushes and tools to the back as well. She drove the truck to the barn to unload it, then she walked to the house, the dry grass crunching underfoot. When she came back carrying her camera the big dog got up and ambled to where she was in the yard.

"You should be in the picture too," she asserted and with that led the way to the back door, avoiding the front steps for the sake of the dog. Wooly trailed her through the house and out the front door, then he laid on the porch at the top of the steps at her request. "Stay," she told him before bounding down the stairs and into the front yard, almost to the road.

Wooly went with Riley when she visited Chloe, only because he wouldn't leave her side. She got permission to bring the big dog in and Chloe was delighted to see him. After getting home, Wooly followed her through the kitchen, to the big screen television and then to the couch where he laid on the rug at her feet. All the while she ate supper he looked at her with his big, gentle eyes, so after eating she sat on the floor beside him and put his head in her lap, and that was how they were when Wooly died.

Before the sun was up the next morning Riley was at the screen door, looking at the very place where Wooly had been when she took pictures of the house. She went out, let the screen close softly behind her and sat on the top step. She was still there when the sun came up and even an hour later when she heard a vehicle on the road. It was Jay in his flatbed. He honked and waved and she managed to wave back.

Riley decided to bury Wooly under the spruce. It took her most of the day to accomplish and when she was finished she put a cluster of large artificial sunflowers on the grave, pushing the stems deep into the dirt. She went back to the porch steps and sat down.

Jay headed home after running his errands. Out of habit he turned on the gravel road that went past Riley's instead of staying on the highway. When her house came in view he thought it unusual to see Riley at the front porch twice in one day, and took his foot off the gas. Besides, it would be a good excuse to talk to her.

He knew Riley was aware of him walking across the yard but she did not look at him, she only stared at nothing. Because of his focus on her unusual behavior he smelled the upturned dirt before he noticed it, and when he saw the mound and sunflowers his heart ached for her loss. He stopped at the bottom of the steps.

"Wooly?" he asked.

She nodded with misty eyes but still did not look at him.

He climbed the steps and sat his big burly form beside her. "You should have called me," he told her. She didn't answer, maybe *couldn't* answer, he considered, and then he looked away as well. He thought it was way past ironic that after all these years someone had penetrated his wall, without any intentions to, while at the same time staying out of his reach, and he didn't know why. But he did know what it was like to have something dragging a person down, and maybe she had her reasons. He didn't think it was an appropriate time to start asking, she was vulnerable enough right now. He took in a deep breath. Riley wiped her tears with her hands and turned her head to him. Jay felt her gaze and let his eyes meet hers, but willed himself to remain expressionless.

"I'm going to get some coffee," she said. "Want some?"

He intended to say no but instead heard himself accepting. He followed her across the porch and into the house. She went to the kitchen but he stopped at the shelves where the bandana necklace and photos were.

Riley spent the few minutes alone in the kitchen gathering her bearings, knowing it would take everything she had not to break down in front of him. She hadn't seen him for months and he shows up *now*. He was wearing one of his shirts with the sleeves cut out and every line on his weathered face with the strong jaw was exactly as she remembered.

"I see you have your old truck hooked to the trailer," he said from the great room. "I haven't seen you on the road lately. Been hauling much?"

"No," she said from the kitchen. She wiped her eyes again and picked up the cups. "No, I haven't been hauling much," she said on her way to him. "Goliath is hooked to the trailer because there's something wrong with the jack or crank on the trailer. I don't know what it is, just that it won't work." She said it like she was reading a grocery list but was glad for the opportunity to tell him.

"Let's check it out," Jay offered. "We have some daylight left."

At the trailer he set his cup on the wheel well and tried to get the jack to operate but had no success. "I'll probably have to get a new part for it," he said. "I won't know until I take it apart. Want to bring it in tomorrow?"

"I guess," Riley said listlessly and picked up his coffee cup. "I don't need Goliath or the trailer right away—I haven't been competing on Dobbie, just exhibitions to keep him eligible for futurities," she found herself justifying, then tried to lighten her tone because he looked like he sensed something more than Wooly dying bothering her. "There's no hurry to get it done. Fit it in when you can."

"Okay, if that's what you want," he resigned. He gathered the tools he used then walked to his truck with her following a few feet behind. He tossed his tools on the seat and got in. "I'm sorry about Wooly," he told her.

She could see the hurt in his eyes for her benefit without even directly looking into them. "Thank you," she replied with as little emotion as she could.

"The house looks good by the way," he said.

"Thank you," she repeated.

Nothing more was said so he started to back down the driveway. He waved hesitantly as if doubting she would wave back. She did, but this time she couldn't bear to watch him leave. She looked at Wooly's grave instead and knew it was a mistake as soon as she did. Her guilt for being rude to Jay compounded the way she was feeling and her throat turned hot and tight. She made it to the top of the porch stairs before crumpling into a crying heap.

CHAPTER 37

From inside their shabby little farm house Peggy watched Cap place heavy blocks of salt in the back of his candy apple red pickup. He was bending over to pick them up off the ground, wearing snug fitting Wranglers and his cowboy hat instead of the usual ball cap. She had always been physically attracted to him and he rarely disappointed in that department, even if he didn't have a clue what romance was. She sighed, and saw the stray black-and-white dog that had been showing up since spring come from some junk by barn. Cap was setting the last salt block in the box when he saw the dog. He reached for a rock and threw it.

"Git!" he shouted, loud enough that Peggy could hear. The dog zipped away with its tail between its legs. Cap muttered crossly, stormed to the door of the pickup and got in while ducking his head to make room for the cowboy hat.

Peggy had been waiting for him to leave so she could load her horse and leave to help move cattle for a rancher in the next county. Cap was mad because he didn't want her going and they had exchanged words because of it. His excuse was that she would be on the road late at night but she knew it was just an excuse. Then she remembered she hadn't taken her birth control pill.

She went back to the bedroom and dug the hidden pack out from under clothes in the dresser. It wasn't that she was opposed to kids, she just didn't want to have any with Cap. She popped a pill in her mouth and went back to the kitchen where she picked up her purse and meat scraps off the counter for the dog.

When she came out of the house the dog was sitting where Cap's pickup had been minutes before. She tried to whistle but it was a failed attempt. The dog came regardless, but hesitantly.

"Hi," she said. She set the scraps on the ground but the dog stopped and sat, looked at her and tipped its head. "Go ahead. They're for you."

The dog didn't move to the scraps until Peggy walked away. She thought the dog had potential but Cap kept trying to run it off, and knew she wasn't doing it any favors by being nice to it.

On her way to catch her horse she checked on the cow in the lot and was thankful it hadn't calved yet. The old cow should have been sold the year before but came up pregnant after all. The last time the cow had calved she had trouble so problems were expected this time. Peggy was surprised Cap had even bothered to bring the cow to the corral but had overheard him saying he didn't want to start coyote problems by offering them a dead cow and calf to feast on.

Ten minutes later she was leaving, choosing to take the gravel road along the cornfield with its dry, yellowing stalks instead of the short route to the highway so she would be less likely to meet her husband.

It wasn't much later that Cap returned home. He ignored the ratting cattle guard that was in need of repairs at the end of the drive and, like always, didn't see the big round bales and junk along the lot fences and barn, but that the new Ford and trailer were gone. He slammed the pickup into park and reached for his can of chew but changed his mind—he wasn't going to let the dry conditions keep him from smoking when he wanted to. He pushed the door all the way open with his foot and pulled a cigarette from its pack. A crow left its perch in a nearby tree, cawing as if mocking him, and flew over the pickup. It let loose a purple and black glob that hit, *splat!,* right on the windshield. Cap jumped out, swearing, and threw his lighter at the bird. He stormed back to the pickup, trying to ignore the disgusting windshield, and ransacked for a book of matches. He lit the cigarette and hotly kicked the door shut. He took a drag and let the cigarette go to work, and then saw the stray dog by the fence of old cow's enclosure. When the black-and-white dog knew that Cap had seen it, it darted around the corner of the pen, out of sight, and between the boards of the fence Cap watched the cow track the movements of the dog. He crossed the gravel and took a look over the fence. There was the newborn calf, still wet. His anger flared again at the thought of having more work to do.

Before entering the barn Cap threw down the cigarette, barely spent. He rounded up the ear tag items stored in a bucket until normal calving season and a six-foot fence panel. He cut the strings off a bale of hay and threw the majority of the bale out the top of the Dutch door near the cow, hoping it would keep her occupied while he tagged the calf. Leaving the barn he heard the crow again and his head snapped up, but he forgot about the bird when he saw the black thunderclouds in the distance. The wind was picking up too. Maybe those know-it-all college graduate weathergoons were right this time, he thought, maybe it *would* rain.

Cap opened the lot gate alongside the barn and set the bucket down, keeping an eye on the cow. She raised her head from the pile of hay but did not offer to move. He situated the six-foot panel under one arm and sidestepped through the gate with it. He left the gate open, knowing the old cow would not go far without her calf. Moving slowly to avoid aggravating her, he leaned the panel against the lot fence with plans to use the panel as a makeshift barrier to keep the cow at bay. He walked back to the gate and picked up the bucket, but before he could get to work on the calf the cow turned her focus—a confrontational one—to him. Cap set the pail down and sat back on his heels against the barn to wait for the old cow to go back to the hay. He reached into his shirt pocket for his pack of cigarettes, ripped a match from the book and struck it against the flap. While holding the book he cupped his hands to protect the flame and lifted the match to the end of the cigarette. He inhaled and thought about Peggy, knowing he shouldn't be so hard on her. Truth be known he was afraid she would leave him some day for someone else, someone she might meet on an outing just like today, and, deep in thought, he didn't know what hit him when the cow lunged. Her massive skull broke his ribs and crushed his heart, and he came off the ground like a rag doll.

The dog raced into the pen, barking and working the cow to get its attention. The old cow quickly tired and stopped, her head hanging low and snot trailing from her nose. The calf, on shaky legs, bawled and when the cow moved from the dog to her calf she swung her head in defiance. The dog stood for a moment and then warily walked to Cap. It sniffed the broken body in the dirt, and the cowboy hat several feet away, and then trotted away through the open gate.

In the pile of hay thrown out the barn for the cow lay the book of matches. During the scuffle the single match ignited the rest, all the little heads of sulfur coming to life. The little flame was stirred by the wind of the oncoming storm and grew. It didn't take long before the fire was licking at the bone dry boards of the barn, traveling to the junk against the wood fence, the dry grass and beyond.

* * *

Riley was working Dobbie on the barrel pattern at a walk when his head came up and he stopped abruptly. About thirty yards away, in the small timber in the pasture, was a deer looking back at them. It was late afternoon, an odd time for deer to be moving, Riley considered. It darted off, flagging danger with the white underside of its tail.

She cued Dobbie to move on, wanting to get finished. Mitch was coming for the weekend and she still had last-minute housecleaning to do. The constant thought of Jay replaced those of Mitch and she was thankful he hadn't been at his shop when she left Goliath and her trailer that morning. She had already made arrangements with Ernie for a ride home and the fact he wasn't there freed her from explaining.

"Whoa," she said, and dismounted. When she loosened the cinch Dobbie was looking off in the distance again and seemed edgy. She led him to the fence and tied him next to Posty who was on the end of the row of horses. There was a low rumble of thunder in the distance and a sharp clap followed. Dobbie jumped, as did the others, then lightning cracked again, close, and the jittery horses pulled back and panicked. Dobbie unintentionally struck Riley, slamming her into the steel pipe fence.

The fire spread quickly, fueled by the dry crops and grasses. It skipped over little barriers where there was nothing to devour and drove wildlife from their sanctuaries. Cattle and horses fled to safer areas of their ranch pastures, some forced to go over or through fences. The potential rainstorm contributed to the fire's destruction by supplying the wind that helped drive the flames, leaving nothing behind but smoldering remains of homesteads and trees that had withstood one hundred years of weather.

Still several miles from the Colby place, sounds of fire trucks and shouting were barely heard in the tumult as attempts were made to quench the wall of flames. Smoke was as much an issue as the threat of the fire, sometimes hiding everything including the location of the blaze. The less experienced firefighters were on the verge of panic and even the veterans questioned their efforts to stop the fire.

"We need to get near town! Move everyone to the Colby and Peterson places and start dousing things," the fire chief yelled to his men. "We've got to try and stop this thing before it reaches town."

Soon the convoy of fire trucks and volunteers' pickups were driving south, temporarily beaten by the fire that was swallowing everything in its path.

Riley opened her eyes but everything was blurry, and her head hurt. As her vision got better she could make out the bottom rail of the pipe fence. Her head was full of noise and she could smell something besides the dirt right under her nose. The last thing she remembered was tying Dobbie. She didn't feel any pain, other than her throbbing head…at least not any searing pain.

"Whoa," she said, barely loud enough that she heard it. Her throat was scratchy and sore and she realized she was having trouble breathing. "Whoa," she said again, louder this time. She heard movement and assumed it was the gelding behind her. She could taste blood…and smoke. *Smoke! What she could smell was smoke!* Immediately her wits came back and she grasped how hot it was. The horses were moving, their hooves right near her. Instinct kicked in and she was on the move, scrambling up the fence.

Riley clutched the top rail and let her head settle from dizziness. Then she strained to see through the dark fog-like conditions, and came to understand the darkness was not from nightfall as she thought, but from smoke. She climbed down, captivated by the glow in the distance, and her legs nearly gave out when she reached the ground. Her heart was in her throat.

She set across the arena, quickly advancing from staggering to running, her target the barbwire gate in the fence where the well had been dug. She knew she couldn't open the gate and hold horses at the same time, and if she let them free where they were they would end up running through wire somewhere. If she could get them through the gate they would have some room to run before coming to their senses. Smoke and embers swirled around her when she reached the gate and then wind whipped them away. She wrestled the gate open and flung it out of the way. She hurried back in the darkness, untied Dobbie and Potsy and fought to hold them while going to the gate. The heat and smoke was getting worse. She couldn't, *wouldn't* let herself think about the fire getting dangerously close. She barely made it through the opening when she let loose of the geldings.

Back she ran for two more. The fire was devouring the pasture and getting near the little timber. The horses were crowding each other and she struggled to untie two more while wondering how she would ever get all them free in time. It took all her strength to handle the barely controllable pair getting to the gate and once there they knocked her down. The rope burned through her hand and the horses were gone. She tried to get up, the smoke and wind and her dizziness making it next to impossible. There was a flash of light, then it was dark again. This time when the wind swirled the smoke she saw it was headlights, headlights from Jay's flatbed. He was getting out. A sound of relief escaped her.

"The last two are tied to the other end of the arena," she shouted when he was closer.

He helped her to her feet. "Get to the truck!" he commanded and then ran for the horses.

She wanted to help but was bent over, suffering vertigo and having trouble breathing. She fought to stay on her feet and strained to look for Jay. The fire was in the timber—only yards from the arena! It was the sight of Jay and the horses materializing from the smoke that kept her from going to pieces. She frantically wondered where Wooly was but just as quickly remembered she had buried him the day before. Then, before reconsidering, she was foolishly rushing to the house.

Inside she snatched up a clothes basket and grabbed her purse off the kitchen counter before using the basket to catch things she swept off the shelves along the wall in the great room, then she dashed to the dining room table.

"What the hell're you doing?" Jay shouted.

She was pulling her laptop off the table when he picked her up at the waist, lifting her off the floor. She looked at the interior of her house as he packed her out. When they passed through the door between the great room and kitchen the lights flickered, and then went out completely.

Strong, hot winds drove the swirling red embers like a blizzard. Jay opened the passenger door of the truck and thrust her inside. He was running around the front of it to his side when fat drops of rain began to hit the windshield.

Jay drove across the yard and through the same gate they had freed the horses. Through the rolling smoke she could see the eerie flashing lights of the fire trucks, some staying on the road but many coming toward them, blocking their escape and then surrounding them. Jay had no choice but to stop amid the chaos of firefighters scrambling to action. Riley got out and jumped up on the back of Jay's truck. The rain was coming down steadily now, aiding the firefighters, but it was too late for the Colby place. The fire was consuming the little timber and had reached the barn. Her little car, pickup and tractor made explosions, small in comparison to the fire, as the fluids in them erupted. And then the flames reached the house.

The steady rain only seemed to drag out the misery of the house once it began to burn. The fire was hindered as it tried to devour the wet exterior and the metal roof attempted to hold, but inside it was ablaze. Glass broke and flames shot out the windows and as the intensity grew inside the roof began to collapse. Thunder rumbled at the same time framing members groaned and gave way. Half the roof fell first, crashing down and sending sparks shooting while the remainder of the house continued its slow burn. The top of the spruce tree gave a dazzling display of color as dry needles and sap popped and burned.

The firemen had quit trying to save the house, instead directing their efforts to soaking the ground to stop the flames from reaching further. About the time the fire approached the fence line and licked at the last bit of dry grass near the road, it was snuffed out. Riley's throat was hot and tight as she looked at the devastation.

Whoops and cheers rose from the firemen. Like worker ants they spread across the Colby place, continuing to applaud their accomplishment and poking at little fires still smoldering. Riley could barely stand to watch.

"Come down from there," Jay directed with a hand out to her. He was blinking against the rain and water was running off the bill of his cap.

"You okay over here?" someone shouted. "I'm a medic." The man stopped and held an umbrella over them as Riley reached the ground. He and Jay knew each other and Jay called him Hank.

"Wha...what happened?" she asked, coughing. "The fire… How did it start?"

"We're not sure yet," Hank the medic replied. "We have one casualty we know of. It appears the fire started at Henderson's."

The vision of Cap with a cigarette in his mouth came to her. "Peggy?" she asked, her voice unsteady.

"We don't think so," said Hank. "Freddie said he saw her on the road with the trailer earlier in the day."

She let out a sigh of relief, grateful she was safe.

"Do you know you have a nasty cut on your face?" Hank asked while handing her a soft white cloth. "Do you remember just how that happened?" She filled them in while Hank watched her attentively like he wanted to learn more than how she got hurt. "Sounds like you were pretty lucky. You need to get that cut stitched up. Let me get an ambulance for you and we'll transport you to Northboro. You could have a concussion, you know, or damage from smoke inhalation."

"No, no ambulance," she said.

"If you were knocked out, you should get checked. Regardless, you need that wound cleaned and stitched," he insisted.

"I'll take her," Jay said.

"Are you sure?" Hank said doubtfully. "What if she goes into a seizure or something?"

"I'll be okay," Riley insisted. "Are you sure you wouldn't mind?" she asked Jay. Rain pattered on the umbrella while she contemplated the concern in his eyes.

He nodded.

"Okay," Hank said with a sigh. "But let me tend to that cut first. I can't send you to the hospital looking like that." He looked at Jay. "And it wouldn't hurt for you to get checked out as well. You got a lot of smoke too, you know."

Jay looked back skeptically.

"All right, Tapperd," Hank said, giving in. "Both of you come with me to the ambulance. No sense standing in the rain."

Inside the ambulance Hank first used antiseptic on the wound. "I'm going to put a couple of butterflies on the cut at your cheek. It will help keep it from bleeding more."

She flinched as he applied slight pressure to her face. He checked her eyes with his penlight and shook his head.

"Having trouble with your sight?" he asked.

She blinked, failing to eliminate the fuzziness she hadn't noticed before.

"I'll let them deal with that at the hospital," continued Hank the medic. "I'll give you some pills for the pain. As the shock lessens your face and head are going to hurt, and I bet you're banged up other places too. Can I take a peek?"

She wondered just how extensive a look he intended to take and he interpreted her look.

"Let me look at your back, okay?" he asked. She gave in and turned. He raised the back of her shirt and made a satisfied sound. "Front?"

Riley turned again and lifted her shirt to her bra for him to see. Jay cringed. The medic prodded her ribs and watched her reactions.

"You're fortunate you didn't crack some ribs. You have some pretty nasty bruises. It looks like you hit a pipe in the fence straight on." He turned to the bag behind him and rummaged in it. "Where's my..? Excuse me..."

"How bad am I?" she asked Jay while Hank was sidetracked.

"You look like... You're black and blue," he told her. "I 'spect you'll need at least half a dozen stitches on your cheek, and you're going to have quite a shiner."

"What's that awful smell?" she asked and watched his eyes go to her hair. She moaned when she felt a mass of long hair missing on one side and the ends were coarse where the damage had been done. She grimaced but knew it could have been worse, much worse, and she thought about the horses. She coughed and cleared her throat, wanting to talk to Jay, but he was leaning to look out the back of the ambulance. Fire trucks were leaving, some having trouble in the wet, sandy ground. She felt woozy and her head throbbed. Maybe the medic knew what he was talking about after all.

The medic was there again and offered her two red-and-white pills and a bottle of water. "Here. These are pretty strong," he said. As he watched her swallow them he continued, his words directed to Jay. "She might act silly and they might knock her out, so don't be alarmed if she goes to sleep. I think if there was any sign of trauma we'd see something by now. But she still needs to be checked out."

Jay nodded.

"I'll radio Northboro hospital and they'll be expecting you," Hank continued. "They'll probably want to keep her overnight." He looked at the soggy condition of them both. "You can stop for a change of clothes before you go, but I'd recommend not letting her shower because she might pass out. She can clean up at the hospital."

Jay nodded again and then he helped Riley out of the ambulance.

"Call me if you need anything," Hank told Jay. "Good luck."

"Thanks, Hank," Jay said, and then he walked Riley to his truck.

CHAPTER 38

It was still raining when they got to Jay's. The front door opened to a small living room with the couch facing away from the door. They walked the length of the back of the couch on the way to his bedroom, also at the front of the house.

"Did you hear the medic's instructions about not showering?" he asked.

Riley nodded groggily and sat on the unmade bed.

"The bathroom's over there," he said, pointing. "You need to get out of those wet clothes." He walked past her and pulled open a dresser drawer. "There are some of Marta's things in the closet. Take what you want." He pulled out sweats and a folded T-shirt. "Are you going to be okay while you change?" he asked while laying the clothes on the bed.

"Yes," she said, but she wondered. She was having trouble seeing clearly, her head and cheek were throbbing and her stomach hurt.

"Okay. Don't go passing out on me or anything before we even get out of town."

"Get out," she said but with fondness.

He backed out the door while keeping his eye on her.

She peeled off her wet clothes, hurting all the while, and wondered what she was going to do. The house and just about everything she owned was gone, and she thought of Dobbie and Jay's horses running God knows where. She pulled on the large, soft sweatpants Jay had left on the bed and then struggled to get the big white T-shirt over her head. She had no intentions of going to the closet to look at Marta's things. She sat on the bed again, sniffled and looked down. The bed had obviously only been slept in by one recently. She looked at the nightstand by the bed, nothing girly there. Then she looked at the dresser, where a stack of familiar small thin boxes at the back caught her eye. She went to the dresser in disbelief and picked up the box on top of the stack, knowing what would be inside. It was a large trophy buckle, dated 1973 with a steer wrestler symbol and inscription. It was in pristine condition, probably never having been on a belt. There was a small photo tucked under the buckle and she took it out to see it better. A young, smiling Jay wearing a cowboy hat was holding the buckle for display and there was a cute dark-haired girl in jeans at his side. Riley looked to see that the second and third buckles were similar to the first, but there were no more photos, and she looked no further through the stack. She put the photo and buckle away and stared at the collection, not aware that many were Molly's. She swallowed hard and felt weak, and when she supported herself against the dresser saw her ugly reflection in the mirror. Her hair that had been singed by the fire stuck out, resembling a cluster of frayed electrical wires. One eye, in shades of black and blue, was almost swollen shut. There was a small cut on her brow plus a gash about two inches long over her cheekbone, held together by the butterflies the medic had placed there. The cut was deep and she reached to touch it despite knowing it would hurt. Oh yeah, that'll take stitches for sure. She thought about Novocain and the story she had been told by the doctor when she was a little girl, making her giggle. She lifted the huge T-shirt. Not only did she have two wide bruises across her ribs, there was another higher up, across her collar bone. Still holding the shirt up, her breasts exposed, she turned away and looked over her shoulder in the mirror at her back. Then the door was opening and she looked across the room at Jay.

He stared but then turned his head. "I'm sorry. I heard you laugh. I thought that was odd, under the circumstances and all." He was blushing as if he had done something wrong.

She pulled the shirt down, wondering what he thought of her. She assumed she knew without having to hear him say it—she looked like hell. She walked to where he was, feeling dizzy on the way there.

"I'm sorry," she told him. "I think the drugs are getting to me." He let himself look at her, cautiously, as if wanting to make sure it was okay, and his actions struck her as funny. She giggled again. "I've got bruises *all* over," she said and started to lift the shirt. "Wanna see?"

He grabbed her wrist to stop her. She reached up with her free hand, put it on the back of his neck and pulled his face to hers. Her actions surprised him but he eagerly bent to meet her lips. He released his hand from her wrist and pulled her close, bringing her to his height. She felt her body being lifted and drawn against his, feeling unbridled emotions of her heart and the desires of her body for him as they kissed. Powerful feelings surged through her, feelings she had never experienced.

Jay was already aroused but was stunned at how alive he felt while kissing her. He had wanted this to happen for so long… He had forgotten when he had given up hope thinking it ever would. His feelings now scared him almost as much as what he felt when he drove to her place earlier, seeing the fire so close and not knowing where she was. He felt like their souls were finally merging and wished the moment could continue.

She was the first to end the kiss with a little "ouch" and what he thought was a sob, and he remembered the gash on her face and bruised ribs. He loosened his tight hold but didn't let her go. Her face remained buried against his neck and she began to cry. He could smell the smoke in her hair, some of which was matted with dry blood. He whispered that everything would be all right, trying to comfort her, not knowing what else to say.

Riley cried for several minutes and he held her the entire time. He could feel her warm tears against his neck.

"I'd better get you to Northboro," he finally said just above a whisper. "The hospital will think we had an accident on the way."

He felt her nod and then she murmured, "I'm sorry. I'm so sorry."

"You don't have anything to be sorry about," he said, feeling doubts rise because of the way she said it, and he felt her softly shake her head. When she did not offer to move he repositioned her in his arms and carried her from the house.

Riley fell asleep shortly after they left Whispering Pines, leaning on him in the truck. The wipers of the flatbed occasionally swiped across the windshield. He tried to concentrate on the drive but found too many questions battling with his emotions. Why can't things ever be simple? he wondered.

He carried her into the hospital. Riley asked him to stay with her while they cleaned her face and then put nine stitches in the wound on her cheek and two at the cut near her brow. They took an x-ray of her chest and did a CAT scan but did not find anything unusual, although she remained dizzy and had blurred vision.

"I want to keep you overnight," said Dr. Lisand, an elderly man close to retirement age. "My intuition says you will be fine but the facts are you still have vision issues and lightheadedness. I want to keep you here, just in case." He watched her frown but was not swayed. "You have your whole life in front of you, what's one lousy night in the hospital?" he said closing the discussion but gave her an encouraging smile.

They settled her in a room and she showered before receiving more medication. Jay refused treatment, saying he was all right, and a nurse gave him access to an empty room with a shower so he could clean up as well. Trays of food were supplied for them but Riley had difficulty eating, her face numb and stomach queasy.

The two of them sat in the dimly lit hospital room, listening to rain fall against the window that overlooked the shadowed parking lot below, and neither said anything. Jay fell asleep in the chair by the bed and Riley watched him sleep before dozing off herself, thinking she would deal with tomorrow when it came.

* * *

Jay was not in the chair when Riley woke at daybreak and it made her uneasy. She left the bed and felt the pain of her battered body as she did. Her vision was good when she looked out the window, but the source of her relief was Jay's flatbed in the parking lot. The skies were still overcast and there were puddles on the cement, but it was not raining for the time being.

She brushed her teeth, not thinking about what she was doing but about Jay. She was anxious for him to come back to the room. She was ready to talk, or at least apologize for the kiss, even though it seemed he had enjoyed it as much as she did. Her stomach was in knots and she knew it was from butterflies and the fear of unanswered questions. She spit and looked at her black-and-blue swollen face in the mirror. She looked awful, and wondered what Mitch would think. She froze. The toothbrush clattered into the sink and she was rushing to the phone. She punched at numbers, becoming more flustered when she had to go through the operator to get an outside line. She got Mitch's answering machine and left a message, stumbling over words.

Jay entered the room expecting to see Riley still in bed, but she was standing by the phone. She had just hung up. He resisted the urge to walk over and put his arms around her. It seemed like the natural thing to do but he wasn't about to go on the assumption that their kiss the night before, no matter how strong, changed anything. She had been pretty emotional after the fire, and with good reason. He would follow her lead. Riley turned with a look of anguish, holding a hand to her mouth.

"I forgot about Mitch," she blurted and moved her hands to her temple. "He was going to come out last night, and I completely forgot."

Well, if he'd made it to Whispering Pines last night, Jay thought, evidently he knew by now the house was gone. So where was he? "Does he have a cell phone?" he offered, thinking the guy had everything else.

She shook her head. "Not that I know of."

He was silent, not knowing what to say.

"When can I leave?" she asked.

He paused, still standing where he had been when she voiced her concern over Mitch. "I don't know. How are you feeling?"

"Good, I guess." She sat on the edge of the bed. "What am I going to do?" she asked pitifully while looking up at him.

He looked back blankly, wondering just what it was she was referring to—them, him, the house, the horses, Mitch?

"Good morning," Dr. Lisand quipped as he entered the room. He looked from his clipboard and the look on his face changed with the uneasy ambiance. "How's my patient this morning?" he asked, continuing to sound cheerful.

Jay stood there, detached, while the doctor looked Riley over and tested her eyes.

"No more stomach pains or queasiness?" the doctor inquired.

She thought about the turmoil she was feeling and shook her head no.

"Very good." He instructed her to walk a straight line, asked several questions and took notes. "You will probably have a nasty scar there but things certainly could have been worse." He gave her a piece of paper for prescriptions. "One of the nurses will be in shortly. After, you are free to go but don't forget to stop at the check-out desk." He glanced at Jay who was not paying attention, said good-bye to Riley and then walked out the door, studying his clipboard as he left.

Riley and Jay looked at each other. This time the silence frustrated her. Jay's unflappable quietness, something she so respected about him, was now driving her crazy. She wanted him to take charge, tell her everything would be all right, hold her.

"I need a smoke," he said, and then he was leaving.

A smoke? She thought she must have misunderstood and, feeling lost, watched the back of him disappear around the corner. She wiped at tears that formed, wincing from the pain and thinking her life was as disastrous as her face. Maybe she could see him outside, she thought, that would help. She could see that it was still cloudy and dismal on her way to the window and when she reached it she searched for Jay. There he was, standing off to one side, but he wasn't alone. Mitch was with him.

Jay had just lit the cigarette, considering it a shame to pollute the fresh air after the rain when he saw the familiar black

Mitsubishi turn into the hospital parking lot. He scoffed—at least Mitch's arrival would keep him from thinking—and then drew in a long breath of nicotine. He saw Mitch look at him while picking a place to park and after getting out of the sports car he headed straight for Jay. He was wearing spotless white Adidas, jeans and his polo shirt with a logo Jay didn't recognize was tucked in.

"No one called me," Mitch told him, his voice strained. "I stopped for gas in town and heard she was here."

"Took you long enough," Jay said not refraining from saying the first thing that came to mind.

"I worked late and fell asleep on the couch," Mitch snapped, offended. Then, "Why am I explaining this to you?"

"How do you think she got here?" Jay shot back. He exhaled and watched the smoke dissipate before following the comment with a got-one-up-on-you look. Mitch's mouth hung open. He looked like he had so many questions he didn't know where to begin. Then he looked fighting mad as if cornered with nowhere to go, but didn't act on it. During all this Jay stood where he was, acting like Mitch wasn't even there. He figured if Mitch wanted to learn anything from him he would ask, and eventually he did. The ash on the cigarette grew while Jay told him what happened, sticking to details and saying no more than necessary, and he longed for another cigarette as he salvaged the last drag. He located the butt disposal with his eyes.

Mitch stood as straight as he could and dramatically took in a deep breath. "Well, I guess I owe you a debt of gratitude then," he said and extended a hand. "Thank you very much for everything you did. I'm anxious to see her. I'll handle it from here," he said in such a way he could have been giving closing arguments at a trial.

Jay's eyes narrowed. He looked at the offered hand inches from his own and angrily flicked the cigarette butt to the ground. He fixed on Mitch and leaned forward.

"Take good care of her," he warned.

Riley's heart sank as she watched Jay walk away. Then the white Saturn was zipping into the parking lot and abruptly came to a stop, not bothering to find a parking place. Marta jumped out and ran to Jay. He opened his arms to her and held her briefly before she pulled back and talked, animatedly. Jay nodded a few times, put an arm around her and walked her to the open car door.

Mitch walked to the room the receptionist had directed but the person he saw looking out the window couldn't possibly be Riley. There must be a mistake, he thought. He went back to the reception desk but the woman assured him it was Riley's room. She saw Mitch's dismay.

"The beautician will be here this morning for the nursing home residents in the adjoining building, if you are interested," the woman suggested. "She is young and just out of school but I hear she went to Blakely's in Owen. She knows all the latest cuts."

Mitch nodded his thanks and once again went to Riley's room, preparing to enter as positively as he could.

"I apologize for not getting here sooner," he said from behind her.

She turned from the window and he faltered when he saw her face.

"I'm sorry..." she said, her eyes searching his.

He looked past her, put his arms around her and held her for a minute. He wondered why she wasn't crying. He composed himself before he pulled back and held her at arm's length.

"Are you okay?" he asked while successfully looking at her straight faced and concerned. "Sounds like you had a pretty bad ordeal. You're lucky you came out of everything all right." He touched her hair. "The receptionist at the desk said a stylist is here. How about a cut? I always thought you'd look good with short hair." He couldn't read her vacant expression. "Did you lose everything in the fire?"

"Yes," she whispered with misty eyes.

"Hey, everything's going to be all right," he said holding her again. He hoped she had full insurance on the place. She sniffled but when she did not cry he released her. He turned his attention to the clothes on the bed. He lifted the sweatpants and frowned. "Is this it?' he asked.

She stared, in a daze, then managed "Yes" again.

"Where are your shoes?" He looked around and then at her. "How about I see how soon they can work you in with the stylist? We'll get you pretty again, get out of here and I'll buy new shoes for you before we go home." He headed for the door. "I'll be right back."

When he was out of sight Riley turned and walked to the window, not wanting to. It had started to rain again and the big drops were leaving wet trails as they ran down the glass. And, as she feared, when she looked out the window, Jay's truck was gone.

CHAPTER 39

Riley fingered her hair, thinking she had been five years old the last time it was that short. Mitch went on about how cute it was, but all she had seen in the stylist's mirror was her swollen black-and-blue face and stitches. He had persuaded her to go into a store with him but because of the stares she was getting they were in and out quickly. Now, back in the car, he was looking pretty pleased about how things were going until she insisted she had to check on Dobbie.

"But Tapperd said he would take care of her," Mitch protested.

Riley didn't bother to correct him by saying Dobbie was a gelding. "He's my horse, my responsibility," she asserted. "What if there's something seriously wrong with him? Please, let's just do it and get it over with."

Northboro disappeared behind them with uncomfortable silence in the car. Riley stared at her clasped hands, trapped in her thoughts. Half an hour later she smelled smoke and her head came up. It had stopped raining and the dismal grey clouds were breaking up, showing the blackened, stark remains of the jutting hills and plains in the distance. Mitch's eyes got big when he saw the extensive damage.

"How about making a detour past your place?" he suggested.

"No," she said curtly. "I don't want to see it."

He looked at her and then back to the road.

"I need to say good-bye to Chloe and Ernie," she said. "You can drive out to look if you want but I'm not going."

He hesitated as if considering it. "No, no, that's okay. Maybe some other time, when you're ready."

Riley said nothing.

Ernie was wheeling Chloe to a bench outside the nursing home when they arrived. Only Riley got out of the car. While Ernie wiped rain off the bench Chloe made the effort to tuck white hair that had escaped from the braid under her scarf and that's when she saw Riley. From the look on her face Riley had no doubt they already knew what happened. She hugged Ernie and then bent to hug Chloe. Ernie situated the wheelchair at the end of the bench where Riley sat down. Chloe took Riley's hands in her own and looked into Riley's pained face. Drops of rain fell from needles of the pines while the old woman searched for the right words.

"I don't know why bad things have to happen," Chloe finally began. "I think God sometimes lets tough things happen so we'll grow and change…for the better. I guess it's like with our horses. Those of us who love our animals don't push them past their limits and I'm sure they wonder about some of the things we ask them to do…like doctoring their wounds, vaccinations, time in the practice pen, trips in the scary trailer. But there're reasons for all those things. We know that, but they don't. You came out of the fire all right, and your horse, and your memories… No one can ever take your memories, or your feelings. The house and things that were in it are replaceable." Riley didn't say anything and Chloe looked like she was beginning to wonder if she was even listening. "I've had my share of heartbreaks and tried my best to accept them as part of God's plan, and some things I still don't understand to this day. Maybe I'll never understand. But we do learn to appreciate things—not material things but the things that really matter—so much more after we've suffered hard times...or lost something, someone dear to us." She paused and then concluded with "I love you," something that had never been said between them.

Riley fell into Chloe's arms, let the tears come and blubbered that she loved her too.

After a minute Riley raised her head and pulled away. Ernie was still standing, trying to stay strong for the women. She got up and gave him another hug. Not trusting herself to speak, she managed a smile for the two of them and started to walk away.

"Got fifty cents I can borrow?" Ernie asked softly.

Tears filled her eyes again, but this time it was more than just sorrow that stirred her emotions. She hugged them both once more.

"Stay out of trouble," she scolded, trying to lighten her broken voice. She didn't allow herself to look back until she was at the car, opening the door.

Then Mitch drove to Jay's shop, but the flatbed wasn't there and the door was locked. Riley directed him to Jay's dad's farm, thinking that's where he would take the horses.

She saw the horses tied in a lot before Mitch pulled in. Jay was with them. Marta was sitting on the top board of the rustic wood fence where tall sunflowers reached. Marta called out "Over here!" and despite Riley's state of mind—or perhaps because of it—she thought the scene looked like something on a big, beautiful billboard. She acknowledged Marta but made her way to the horses and Jay, stepping over puddles with her new shoes as she went. Marta came down from the fence and started to talk to Mitch. The stray black-and-white dog that had been at Cap's when the fire started was there, watching from a safe distance.

"How are they?" Riley asked looking at the horses and keeping them between her and Jay. Potsy's tail was full of cockleburs and all the horses were splashed with mud.

"I didn't find anything significant," Jay said from the other side of Potsy. "A few small cuts, but they all look okay."

She stepped close to Dobbie, who didn't seem to have suffered from the ordeal. She checked his legs and ran a hand under his belly. Potsy, beside Dobbie, turned his head and reached for her with his nose. She distractedly pet him. Jay rested a hand on top of Potsy's neck and looked at Riley.

"Would you keep Dobbie for a while?" she asked, not looking back at him. "Maybe I can board him where I used to live, I don't know, I... I haven't thought about it."

"You're welcome to leave him here until you're ready to ride again, or start over. You know that."

"No..."

He held a business card over Potsy's neck, close to the mane. "Here," he told her after glancing to make sure that Mitch was still talking to Marta. He turned the card. On the back was a phone number scrawled in his handwriting. "I got a cell phone yesterday. Call me if you need anything. Anything."

She reached for it and their fingers touched. Then he was pulling his hand away and leaned down to lift Potsy's leg. She heard Marta's bubbly laughter not far behind her.

"Riley, Mitch is almost as sweet a fellow as Jay," Marta said.

Riley closed her hand around the business card just before Marta gave her a hug.

"How are you? Really?" Marta asked.

"I'm alright," said Riley and managed to turn up the corners of her mouth.

Marta smiled a heartening smile. "I love your hair!"

"Come along, honey," Mitch said, smiling at the compliment and reaching for Riley. "We'd better get going."

She took a few steps with him but then stopped and turned back to Jay.

"I'll call you about Dobbie," she told him. "And my truck and trailer, if you're sure you don't mind keeping them."

"You know better than that."

Mitch was tugging her elbow. Jay couldn't help but watch her let him lead her away.

After the black sports car drove away Marta crossed the pen to where Jay was. He tried to evade her.

"You should go after her, you know that, don't you?" Marta told him.

He shook his head. "I'm too old for her. What do I have to offer?"

"You are not," she protested. "She's crazy about you. I can see it plain as day."

He had thought so too, but she sure hadn't followed through on anything to convince him.

"No, she must want something I can't give her."

Marta didn't say anything as if she knew he had made up his mind.

"I'm gonna saddle up," he finally said.

Marta stood in front of him, looking hopeless. Jay wanted to hug her but was afraid to do so for his own sake, so he walked around her, headed to the barn.

CHAPTER 40

Riley began to adapt to life with Mitch in his city apartment. He discouraged her from getting a job, instead prompting her to enroll in classes to further her education, recommending she concentrate on law. It was the first week of December and she was sitting in front of the computer, looking into schools, when Mitch came home from the office bursting with enthusiasm. He was talking even before he placed his keys in the basket on the table by the door.

"Bill Briggs and one of his clients are planning a winter vacation. Bill wants to know if we'd like to come along," Mitch announced. "I know he's only asking to help with expenses. His investments have been dwindling since Karen, his wife, realized that Alen, Cynthia's riding instructor, was a major contributor to the divorce."

Riley turned the computer off and wondered why he always spoke of people at the office like she didn't know them. He was walking to where she was sitting with an expectant look on his face and then the phone rang. He detoured to answer it but continued to look at her.

"What do you think?" he asked.

She doubted that he really wanted to know what she thought about spending any time with Bill and Alen.

The discussion continued at the lawyers' Christmas party, where they were seated at the same table in the restaurant as the snooty couple.

"We'll spend a few days at my condo in Manhattan," Bill was saying.

"The view is to die for," Alen interrupted while fingering the string of pearls around her neck.

"After New York then we're going to Florida," Bill continued, wanting to cement the deal. "Maybe try snorkeling or a mini cruise. And then fly to the dude ranch of my client's in Arizona to wrap it up. It usually snows in New York, making for a beautiful Christmas, and then we'll start the New Year in warm climates." He looked at Riley. She had noticed he always made a point of fixing on her scarred cheek whenever he looked at her. "Brad—my client with the Arizona dude ranch—his wife Gabrielle does some of that rodeo stuff like you used to do. You two would get along famously. I hear Brad complain about those nags of hers all the time."

* * *

Riley and Gabrielle did hit it off. They were both country girls who happened to be with men who wore a suit and tie for a living. As they flew low over Manhattan after dark both of them were awestruck by the brilliance of the night lights reflecting off the water on either side of the New York City borough. After landing and getting off the plane they skirted piles of snow to a shining black limousine.

Bill Briggs's condominium was on the fourteenth floor. While the others chose their bedrooms Riley walked to the balcony. She slid the doors open and stepped out, again amazed at the urban beauty. Then Mitch was behind her, putting his arms around her and kissing her on the neck.

"Maybe we should relocate here," he said. "Have you ever seen so many lights? What a view."

Riley smiled at his high spirits. He had been very happy lately.

"I'm going to make sure no one took our room," he said. He kissed her neck again and was gone.

She took a deep breath, surrendering that she was glad to be there.

* * *

It was snowing on New Year's Eve. The black of night was held at bay by street lights and holiday decorations. They had just had dinner and were chatting and laughing while leaving the restaurant.

"That was a damn good steak," said Brad. "I would guess it came from the Midwest."

Bill nodded in agreement. "And the lobster from Maine, I'm sure of it."

They strolled the festive crowded sidewalk, in no hurry and taking in the decorations and department stores' luxurious window displays.

"When we were little my parents would bring us to Manhattan for Christmas shopping," Alen said, momentarily looking wistful, then she stopped at Bloomingdale's. "Look at this one," she directed.

Gabrielle and Riley exchanged glances. Although Alen had not worn her snug-fitting breeches nor put her hair in a tidy bun during the trip she had failed to leave behind her instructor attitude.

Bill dutifully joined Alen to look at the display of an angel suspended over a glittering staircase. In the background were pastel colored fabrics and shining stars.

"That flight of steps looks like a person could actually walk on it," he said.

"What does an angel need stairs for?" said Brad cynically. Gabrielle slapped his arm. "What?" he asked innocently, then his eyes went past her, to Mitch who was kneeling in front of Riley.

Alen gasped and a crowd was already gathering. Some even went so far to take a peek at the diamond in the little black box in his outstretched hand.

"Will you marry me?" Mitch asked.

Riley was speechless. He had taken her completely by surprise—it was the last thing she expected. She saw the hope in his eyes and knew that he, as well as everyone else, was waiting for her answer. She heard herself say yes. There was applause and cheers and Mitch was getting to his feet. He kissed her passionately and then slipped the ring on her finger.

* * *

Two days later, on a lazy Sunday afternoon, they were off the coast of Florida enjoying warm and sunny weather. Riley managed to steal some time alone and was relaxing in a chair with a book on the deck of the ship. She lifted her hand to look at the diamond. It reflected the sun and highlights bounced off the scar on her face. She sighed, got up and set her paperback by her bag. She walked to the rail and looked across the water. On the beach clusters of tall grasses moved in the breeze and a couple was flying a kite.

Riley went back to her bag, dug out the cell phone Mitch had bought her and made her weekly call to Chloe. She had not seen Chloe since the fire—she simply could not bring herself to go back. Not yet. Their visit was short because of poor reception and Riley didn't mention the engagement ring, blaming it on not having the chance because of the bad connection. After their visit she did not put the phone away but instead pushed numbers by memory and listened as it rang on the other end. Then, "Tapperd's Repair. Open 7:30 to 5:30 Monday through Saturday. Open Sunday by chance. In case of an emergency you can try 555-1212," she heard. The recording gave her butterflies. She was about to disconnect when someone picked up.

"Hello," said Marta on the other end. "Hello?"

Riley did not close the phone although that was her intention. Her first thought was resentment toward Marta, but she could not be bitter toward someone who had done nothing to her deliberately.

"Marta? Is that you?"

"Riley?" Marta said with surprise.

"Yes. I just called on a whim."

"Where are you? You're not in Whispering Pines, are you?"

Riley looked across the water at the couple on the beach. "No. How are you?"

"Fine, just fine, everyone is. Ernie has a girlfriend! She's here visiting for a few days—a lively gal from the big city." Marta said more but the phone was cutting out.

Riley smiled at the thought of Ernie having a girlfriend and made a mental note to call Fran with hopes it was her. She had not kept in contact with Fran, or anyone else, for that matter. "I suppose I need to be making arrangements with Jay to get my horse. Tell him I'm sorry if I've been a bother."

"Oh, no," assured Marta. "As a matter of fact at Christmas, Jay, Ernie and Miles were talking about some of the times you all shared. They miss you."

"More likely they miss my bumbling misadventures," said Riley.

Marta laughed, and Riley joined in. "Jay is helping move snow or I'd bring him to the phone. Ernie is helping too," Marta said and then there was nothing but static before the connection was picked up again. "I just happened to be in the shop doing paperwork for Jay."

Riley felt relief when Marta said that Jay was not there, and then she became apprehensive that Mitch might come looking for her.

"I better go," she said calmly, although she didn't feel that way. "But please tell everyone hello for me."

"You're breaking up…reception isn't…" There was a longer pause and Riley thought she heard Marta say that Jay would be looking forward to hearing from her before the connection was lost altogether.

Riley closed the phone, thinking Marta sounded happy. Apparently everyone in Whispering Pines was happy.

* * *

Arizona was hot but dry and Riley liked it immediately. A new dark-green Ford Explorer driven by a ranch employee picked them up at the airport. During the drive Gabrielle told them of the ranch's history and how it had turned into a resort while remaining a working ranch. Riley listened as she looked at the landscape of sand and tall cactus.

"I could be a rancher if I had a place like this," Bill remarked as they pulled up to the front of the enormous ranch house type building. The others seemed to be equally impressed.

Three boys dressed as vaqueros met them at the Explorer to get their luggage and Gabrielle and Brad led them inside. The main room that was decorated with southwest colors and designs had vaulted beamed ceilings, stucco walls and built-in wood cabinets. Off to one side several heavy wooden tables were set for dining in front of a massive fireplace.

"Reminds me of where we went on our first date," Mitch whispered to Riley.

She smiled politely, thinking it reminded her of the Colby house after the remodeling. Gabrielle walked to the glass patio doors and they followed. She slid open the door to present an elaborate bubbling fountain striped with shadows and sunlight from strategically placed beams overhead.

"This is our Ramada," Gabrielle said. "We host quite a few weddings and receptions here."

Mitch pulled Riley close and said to everyone that the Ramada would be just perfect for *their* wedding, then told Gabrielle to let them know what upcoming dates were available. Riley again smiled politely and tried to hide her panic attack.

* * *

From the Ramada Riley watched riders on a trail, silhouettes against the setting sun. Gabrielle and the others had tried to persuade her to ride several times but she had refrained from doing so, mostly to keep peace with Mitch. She thought about Dobbie, and knew that a good part of the reason why she was putting off making a decision was because it meant having to contact Jay.

"Why aren't you riding?" asked Gabrielle coming out the sliding glass doors.

Riley just shook her head, too foggy from being deep in thought to respond.

Gabrielle stood beside her and they watched the silhouetted riders. "How did you and Mitch meet?" she asked.

The question seemed to come from nowhere and took Riley by surprise. She was not thinking back to their beginnings—in fact Mitch was not in her train of thought at all—but that Gabrielle had seen she wasn't the person she had been pretending to be.

Gabrielle sensed her unease and looked apologetic. "It's probably hard to believe but Brad used to rodeo. That's how we met," she said and nodded with validation. "We dated a long time but he kept saying he wasn't ready for a commitment." They smiled at each other. "Then some playboy cowboy from the Midwest started chasing me. He was awful cute and harmless but it sure made Brad jealous." Gabrielle laughed. "Miles—that's the playboy—he still comes through here every January."

Riley smiled at the mention of the name and Gabrielle's description, but the odds were too great that it could possibly be the Miles she knew. Gabrielle started talking before Riley was paying attention.

"…Finals Rodeo, so they come for the Billups Stock Show and Rodeo instead. They stay here overnight on the way. Brad and Miles, they get along great now. As a matter of fact Brad still gives Miles credit for us getting hitched. We got married right here," she gestured, and looked at Brad and Mitch who were coming through the same sliding glass door that she had earlier. "Brad and I get along famously. Well, most of the time," she concluded and laughed again.

* * *

Everyone's bags were stacked neatly by the door and the couples waiting inside for the Explorer that would pick them up. Gabrielle and Brad were staying because they had things to tend to at the ranch. Bill and Alen were bickering and the others trying to avoid them, and with the welcome sound of an approaching vehicle they were headed out the door. But once outside they stayed under the rustic overhang, disappointed, because it wasn't the dark-green Explorer but a classy white Dodge pulling an aluminum gooseneck trailer. Riley couldn't believe her eyes.

Gabrielle and Brad waved and started toward the rig. Three men got out and their exchanges easily heard. Brad received handshakes and Gabrielle hugs, one lasting longer than it should, the giver tall and slender Miles Deroin.

The group started back to the house, arm-in-arm and talking and laughing. Then Miles saw Riley and faltered, hanging up the others before he quickly started moving again, this time with a big grin on his face. When he got to Riley he lifted her off the ground and she laughed with pleasure as he gave her a twirl. He set her down and his affection for her was unmistakable. He tenderly touched the scar on her cheek with the back of a finger. Then he focused on her hair and when he tugged on the ends the gleam was returning to his eye.

"I like. Spunky," he said. He threw a glance at Gabrielle. "Sorry, Gabby, but you've got competition now."

Riley blushed. Miles turned to Mitch, who did not look happy, and offered a hand.

"How you been?" Miles asked.

"I guess you guys know each other," Gabrielle said as Mitch and Miles shook hands.

"Sure do," Miles said, looking back to Riley. "I'da made a serious play for this gal if it hadn't been for family."

"What's the problem, Miles?" joked one of the men he had arrived with. "You got a wife and kids tucked away we don't know about?"

Everyone laughed.

"Don't suppose I would have gotten anywhere with her though," Miles said looking from Riley to Mitch and then to Gabrielle. "She's too much like you—has values and morals and cares about feelings." He faked a shiver.

Brad and the others laughed again. Mitch smiled civilly. The Explorer that was to take them to the airport was coming up the drive. Mitch took Riley by the arm.

"Have you talked to Jay lately?" Miles asked Riley.

She stood where she was and felt Mitch's eyes on her. She shook her head while thinking about the recent phone conversation with Marta.

"No, I haven't," she said.

"Any plans to get your horse and rig?"

"No, nothing yet. I've been dragging my feet."

"I've got to come to the big city in about three weeks," Miles told her. "I already mentioned it to Jay. We could bring your rig then and Jay'd have a ride back home."

Riley exchanged looks with Mitch. "That sounds good," she said.

Mitch produced a business card from his wallet. Handing it to Miles he said, "Give me a call a day or two before you come and we will meet you somewhere."

Riley nodded. The others beckoned, ready to leave.

"I'll give you a call soon enough then," Miles said and hugged Riley before Mitch had a chance to intervene. "I've missed you," he whispered. "We all have." He let go and Mitch stepped in to guide her away.

Riley had trouble turning her head from Miles, and for the first time consideration for Mitch's feelings didn't enter her mind.

CHAPTER 41

Jay and Miles were to deliver Dobbie the first Saturday in February, a day that started blustery with the threat of sleeting rain. Mitch said they would postpone but Riley knew they would be there, and was so sure of it that she hadn't bothered to take off her coat. They were waiting in Benjie's loft apartment in the barn and the atmosphere strained, not just because of the impending meeting. Benjie and Mitch had never hit it off and Benjie had confided that Mitch was jealous of anyone who received her attention.

Riley was standing at a window where she could see the driveway. She gazed at her old garage apartment and the tenant's Camaro parked there. Benjie said the young man was a pleasant fellow and that there were two more nice cars parked in the garage. There was only a skiff of snow in the corners of the arena, a far cry from the winter she had experienced the year before. Then she caught sight of Goliath and her trailer. She felt the familiar knot in her belly with the thought of Jay behind the wheel, as well as the crushing weight of what would never be. And then there was Miles's white Dodge. She left the window and put her gloves on, hiding the engagement ring.

Little ice crystals pelted Riley, Mitch and Benjie as they walked across the gravel. Riley saw Jay looking at her but he looked away before he put the truck in park. Then he was getting out of the old truck. Her knees went weak and her heart jumped to her throat. She forgot what she was planning to say. A simple hello seemed awkward and wouldn't open the door for anything other than a return hello. "How's the old thing running?" she heard herself say.

Jay nodded to Benjie but he didn't acknowledge Mitch. "Good, actually," he replied on his way to the trailer. "I gave it a little tune-up."

The trio fell in behind him and Riley said the first thing that came to mind. "Were you able to boost a few extra miles to the gallon out of it?" It came out lighthearted.

"No. It's still a thirsty beast," he said in a tone of practicality and with a touch of humor for her effort.

Then Miles was popping around the back of the trailer. "Hi girlfriend!" he said and gave her a hug just like he had in Arizona. She took delight in his familiar scent of cologne and tobacco. When he set her on the ground he teased, "You're gonna call me if you're ever not happy, right?"

She laughed, then held the door of the trailer open for Jay who was backing Dobbie out. Miles nodded a greeting to Mitch and Benjie and then Benjie asked Jay how the roads were.

"Recognize the place?" Riley asked Dobbie after he was out of the trailer. The sorrel gelding's head was up, taking in his surroundings, and she stroked the thick winter hair on his neck.

Jay finished telling Benjie what he wanted to know and then asked Riley where she wanted Dobbie.

"Over here," she said, starting for the pasture gate and looking over her shoulder.

Benjie, now telling Jay what he had done with the signs he had gotten from his shop so long ago, fell in step beside Jay with Dobbie.

Mitch debated joining them but was placated because Benjie was chaperoning, and the last time he had been near a horse he had to throw away a pair of perfectly good Nikes. With the thought he took a few steps to put more space between him and the back of the trailer.

"You don't live here, do you?" Miles asked.

"No," Mitch said, wishing he could reply they had a fancy house in the suburbs. He wasn't going to tell Miles they lived in an apartment, even if it was an affluent one, so he said nothing. He hunched his back against the cold.

"Is this where Riley lived before…"

"Before us? Yes, she lived over the garage."

Miles turned to look where Mitch pointed. When he turned back he caught Mitch looking at him. "What?" he asked in typical Miles fashion.

"Just how do you and Tapperd know each other?" Mitch unintentionally blurted. He was cold and wanted this over with. "You two are about as opposite as night and day," he said with second thoughts that it wouldn't help matters to offend him.

"We're half-brothers," Miles said and then spit tobacco off to the side. He grinned at the silence. "Bet you'da never guessed. If it helps you're not the first."

Mitch was having difficulty not letting his annoyance show. "Well, it's rather obvious that you and Marta are related, but Tapperd too?" he pressed. Maybe Miles was teasing. Or maybe the whole lot of them out there were related in some way, that wouldn't surprise him any.

"Well now, I don't have any cause to lie to you, do I? You can ask him yourself when he comes back if you want."

"Oh no," Mitch replied a little too hastily.

They watched Dobbie snort and shy after passing through the gate. Benjie was standing in the way and Jay let the gelding free so he wouldn't step on Benjie. Dobbie ran, bucking and playing, for the far end of the pasture, the lead rope dragging. Riley started to laugh and then she and Jay began the walk to catch him. Mitch frowned.

"Looks like we've got time, so I'll fill you in," said Miles. "Course I don't suppose you need me to detail the biologics and all." He grinned again.

Mitch refrained from giving Miles the satisfaction of responding. Instead he lifted the collar of his coat before thrusting his hands deep into his pockets.

"Jay, Marta and I have the same dad, Oliver Tapperd. Dad's an ornery cuss, kinda like me I guess you could say, and it got him into trouble a time or two. Dad and Emma—that's Jay's mom—were on the outs for a time when Jay was about five or six, maybe seven, and that's where Marta and I come in. I don't think Emma ever knew about Rene, our mom. Hell, Dad didn't even know about us—we're twins if you didn't know—until after Emma died. He came down home, sniffin' around looking for Mom, and boy, was he in for a surprise. Well Mom—you probably gather by now she was a pretty stubborn gal, probably that French Canadian in her—at first she didn't want to have nothing to do with Dad. She told him the three of us had been getting along just fine without him, but he turned on the charm and won her over. That's when we moved in with Dad and Jay at the old farm place. Jay still keeps horses there," informed Miles.

Mitch watched Jay and Riley catch the horse and thought back to the day after the fire when they had stopped to check on the horses. Then they were taking the halter off and starting the walk back. Benjie was waiting at the gate, stamping his feet against the cold.

"Jay was a quiet kid," Miles continued, "and took to having us around like a duck to water, especially Marta. And she looked up to him like nobody's business. Mom was happy living with Dad and all us kids, but she would never marry him, and she never let him change our names either. I think she was afraid he would lose interest if he got all he wanted and would start wandering again. But he was crazy over her and treated her like she was something special, even as a kid I saw that." He shrugged. "I can see that Marta reminds him a lot of Mom. The only time I ever saw the old man cry was once, only once, when Mom died."

Now Jay was holding the gate for Riley and she hung the halter on a post as she came through. Then she was laughing at something that Jay said. Mitch took in a deep breath, watching them and dealing with the facts he had just learned. He wondered how he could have been so blind—Riley hadn't picked him over Jay, she had assumed all along that Jay's half-sister was his girlfriend. Riley was simple and naive enough he could understand how it happened. He had to admit he had assumed the same thing, but, he justified, he hadn't lived among them for a year and a half. How could she have been so…so dumb? If they knew… He was already humiliated beyond words.

"You freezin' to death or did I talk you into a stupor?" Miles asked. "You're awful white except for those rosy cheeks."

The others were within hearing range and Mitch wanted to change the subject, and quickly. "So you two headed back home or going on into the city? Going to see the sights, perhaps?" he asked.

Miles shook his head. "I got business here in town."

"That's right, how could I have forgotten?" Mitch replied. "How were the roads getting here?"

Miles' brow wrinkled and he did not answer.

When Benjie, Jay and Riley came to a stop they looked at pale-faced Mitch. Jay switched his look to Miles and Riley's eyes went to Miles, too, then to Jay and then back to Miles. Miles shrugged with innocence.

"I'm beatin' feet to the loft," Benjie said. "It's too cold out here. Nice to see you again, Jay."

Jay told him good-bye and watched him start for the big barn.

"He has a studio loft apartment in the barn," Riley explained. "I used to live over there, above the garage." She pointed and then snuck a glimpse at Mitch. His shoulders were hunched against the cold and he was looking at the ground. The icy snow was accumulating on the collar of his coat and Jay's too, and on the bill of Jay's cap and Miles's black cowboy hat. She reached into her pocket and brought out a few bills. "Gas money, and for taking care of Dobbie the past few months, and the tune up," she said to Jay.

He gave her a look before going to the back of the trailer where he closed the door. She had already known he wouldn't accept it, but had to offer. She and Miles walked to where he was.

"The keys are in it," he said to her and then he shot Miles a look that implied they should be going. "Your things are on the front seat."

She didn't comprehend what he said because Miles was giving her a big hug. He planted a kiss on the scar on her cheek, told her to keep in touch and then was heading to his truck. It was just her and Jay. She avoided looking in his eyes and waited to see what he would say, or do, but evidently he was waiting for the same thing from her. She extended her right hand. He took it and then pulled her against him for a hug. It was polite and probably intended to be brief, but lasted longer than she expected. She was just beginning to get over her surprise and appreciate being there when he abruptly let go. Then he was heading for Miles's truck.

Miles honked as he drove away. Riley waved and watched them go down the drive, turn onto the road and was still standing there even after they were out of sight. When she turned to Goliath she grasped what Jay said—he was talking about the few possessions she had rescued from the house. She hurried to the door and there on the passenger side was the clothes basket and its contents. She hopped in, looking at it like it was treasure, and pulled it closer. It was obvious the basket and things in it had been cleaned and organized by Jay, or perhaps Marta. There was only the faintest hint of smoke from the fire and everything was tidy and organized.

The camera on top would contain pictures of the house after she finished painting it, the day Wooly died. Under the camera was the photo of her and Jay with Miles in the background, and the bandana necklace that Jay had bought her. She smiled sadly and fingered them. What she wouldn't give to have that day back. After a minute she kept looking—insignificant knick-knacks, framed pictures including the sketch of her and Mitch, books, her laptop and the clothes she had worn the night of the fire, washed and folded. She put everything back with the photo of her and Jay and the bandana on top, slid the basket over and settled behind the steering wheel. She took in a deep purging breath. It felt good to be there, even if it was just old Goliath. She started the truck and then remembered Mitch.

He was waiting in his car. His window went down as she approached.

"I'm sorry," she said. "There were some things in the truck that I got out of the house before the fire."

"Are you ready?"

"I have to park the truck and trailer—five more minutes."

She hurried back and parked the rig where the landlord had instructed earlier. She was out of view of Mitch and couldn't resist checking the primitive living area in the front of the trailer. As soon as she was inside she felt homesick. Wooly's dishes and her tennis shoes were side-by-side on the floor, and her cowboy hat and yellow slicker shared a hook on the wall. Draped across the back of the chair at the small table was a blue plaid shirt of Jay's—he had loaned it to her once when it was chilly. She touched a hole from a welding burn near the collar.

Inside the car Mitch shivered, but it wasn't from the cold. He had given in to the consuming feeling that he was nothing more than a charity case, ignoring the fact that pride was directing his emotions.

CHAPTER 42

Valentine's Day came and went with no mention of the romantic holiday. Whatever Miles had said to Mitch that day it irritated him badly, but he would not talk about it, no matter how Riley tried to approach the subject. When Mitch continued to remain withdrawn and refused to discuss it, she followed her heart and moved Dobbie to a stable with an indoor arena. The first time she rode, as she knew would be the case, there was no looking back. She renewed her rodeo memberships, made the first payments to several futurities that Dobbie was eligible for and test drove a new truck.

She was standing at the picture window in Mitch's apartment, watching it snow. It wasn't dark yet and she wondered how a view so spectacular at night could be so disappointing during the day. She heard the phone ring, and then Mitch was standing behind her. He said the call was for her, it was the Whispering Pines nursing home. Chloe had suffered a stroke and wasn't expected to make it through the night.

Riley was not ready for what she saw when she entered Chloe's room. The friend she hadn't seen for five months was extremely thin and pale and the distortion on her gaunt face from the stroke was apparent despite the oxygen mask. Riley thought she might not be alive except for the slow, methodical rise and fall of the cotton blanket covering her chest. She gently took Chloe's hand in her own. The old woman's eyelids fluttered but that was the only movement she made.

Riley continued to stand over Chloe for the longest time, numb with regret. When she finally looked away she saw the old trophy saddle had been squeezed against the wall and was host to blankets and a hospital gown. It tugged at her heart. She took the things off the saddle and put them in the wheelchair. She removed her coat and draped it over the wheelchair too, put her purse on the corner of the chest of drawers and caringly rearranged the framed photos there. She had seen the pictures numerous times before, but under Chloe's faded silk scarf was a photo album. In all her visits Chloe had never shared this part of herself. Riley picked up the album, situated a chair close to the bed and sat down.

The mere two dozen or so yellowed, fragile pages summarized Chloe's life. All the photos were shades of black and dirty whites. Chloe with brown hair in braids over her shoulders smiled brightly on her sixth birthday, evident by the number of candles on the humble cake. Pictures of her riding horses with her father indicated the two had been close. Corbin, her husband, looked like a good man. On the day of their wedding he had a pleasant but nervous look about him and Chloe was clutching a small bouquet of wildflowers. Her boots could be seen below the lacy hem of the otherwise simple dress. There was a newspaper article about her and Corbin's horses and a rodeo program with Chloe's name listed as one of the barrel racers. Pasted to a page all by itself were two clippings, the first announcing a baby girl, Penny, born to Corbin and Chloe, and a second for the burial notice of the infant. A small sound escaped Riley and with a heavy heart she looked at the frail woman in bed.

Riley fell asleep in the chair with the album in her lap. When the nurse unintentionally woke her she immediately got to her feet. It was almost five o'clock. She did not see any change in Chloe but the oxygen mask had been removed. The nurse, who was sympathetic but businesslike, went about her duties without saying a word except when ambiguously answering Riley's questions.

After the nurse left Riley took Chloe's limp hand in her own. She told Chloe how much she cherished their friendship and that she had finally come to understand what she had been trying to tell her the day after the fire. With a trembling voice she apologized for not visiting for so long, and as the words came out felt a frail squeeze from Chloe's hand. Then her eyes came open. At first the eyes were glazed and lifeless, but they found Riley's. There was an attempt at a smile and Chloe was trying to move her non-working mouth, and in that brief instant Riley knew for sure that Chloe was aware of her presence. Chloe closed her eyes again but continued to keep her fingers around Riley's hand. Then the distortion from the stroke lessened and the soft blanket over her chest labored up one last time. A peaceful look came over Chloe, and the grasp of her hand became nonexistent.

It was some time later that Riley retrieved the photo album from the chair. She picked up her purse and Chloe's scarf from the chest of drawers and put the album in their place. The possession of the silk scarf was comforting and instead of laying it on the album like she had found it, kept it in her hand.

She walked the long, silent hall then rounded the corner and stopped at the nurses' station. There was no one there, only car keys and a Styrofoam cup with a lid. She considered it just as well—she didn't trust herself to talk.

The cold air rudely forced her awake when she went out the front door. It was snowing and the limbs of the pines sagged with the weight. Her footprints were the only ones in the snow and her car was covered. She started the car to let it warm up and while scraping the windshield reflected. Chloe was gone, her life was over. It didn't matter how long a person was given to walk the earth, it was never long enough to accomplish all the things they wanted. Riley found she had stopped scraping, deep in thought, the snow floating down on the windshield.

When she drove by Ernie's house a light came on but she was looking in the direction of Jay's. She was already driving slow and when she saw that his lights were on her foot came off the gas. But then, behind his flatbed and his work truck, by the overhead door of the shop was the little white Saturn. She took in a jagged breath and kept the car moving until she stopped at the sign at Flat View Road.

The road had been plowed but there was an inch of new white fluff on the ground. She didn't see the countryside or even the road but instead was focused far ahead, not even noticing the wipers that intermittently crossed the windshield. Within a few minutes she was gazing at the snow-covered pasture where Jay and the fire trucks had been the night of the fire. Beyond that there was still nothing, only snow and silhouettes in black and dirty whites like the old photos in Chloe's album. Obviously she knew the house and barn were not going to be there but actually seeing it for herself was making her wish she hadn't come this way after all.

She stopped in the road by the stump of mailbox post. Spellbound, she got out and stood with one hand on the open car door and the other deep in the pocket of her coat. The spruce tree was nothing more than a blackened scarecrow topped with snow. The white mound near it was unmistakably Wooly's grave and what was left of the house's burned framing members were jutting from the cellar with their ugly black exposed—not even the pristine snow could hide that. The well house was gone and so was the light pole, but some of the steel pipe arena fence was still standing. There wasn't much left of the barn, the old boards having been nothing more than kindling to the blistering fire. The shells of her pickup and car were covered with snow and the tractor didn't look like a tractor at all. Snowflakes drifted down and there was nothing but silence. So many memories came flooding back…Wooly and the kittens, remodeling with Ernie and Benjie, starting the colts with Jay, the Thanksgiving get-together, love and laughter of good friends. A big lump formed in her throat. Not only was Chloe gone, but so were the things—and people—that had become the backbone of her existence. Angrily she dragged a coat sleeve across her teary face, and was taken by surprise with the soft touch of Chloe's silk scarf in her hand. It was as if Chloe was still with her, still trying to help her make sense of it all. She held the scarf against her cheek, and allowed herself to cry.

CHAPTER 43

Riley set her purse on the table by the door and draped her coat over the back of a chair. Mitch was sitting at the table in his trendy little kitchen. Next to his steaming cup of coffee was a bottle of Jim Beam, half-full. He was wearing the same clothes from the day before and he hadn't shaved. When she walked past him on her way to the refrigerator he put a hand on her arm. She stopped but didn't look at him.

"How are you? How is she?" he asked.

"I'm okay," was all she said. She had had her cry and now there was something she had to do. She finished the walk, reached for the water in the refrigerator, unscrewed the cap and took a long drink. Then she turned to face him. "There's no easy way to say this… We both know we're not meant for each other." She thought he didn't look surprised but it was easy to see he wasn't happy about it. "I'll be out in a few days."

Several more tension-filled seconds passed, then, "You might as well get out," he said. "You were never here anyway. You were never here when I needed you."

Her mouth gaped but she regained her poise.

"You were always out there with those damn horses, apparently more important than me, than us. And those cowboys! Cowboys everywhere," he said scornfully. "Have you been sleeping around? Is *that* where you were last night?"

She thought about Chloe and his accusation infuriated her. But before she could say anything he was grabbing his keys from the basket and slamming the door behind him.

Forty-five minutes later Mitch returned to the parking lot, uneasy when he did not see Riley's car. He made his way to the apartment, guilty feelings giving way to dread, his rehearsed apology forgotten. He unlocked the door and set his keys down, and that's when he saw her diamond ring and cell phone lying in the basket.

* * *

Since the nursing home no longer had a way to contact her, Riley called them. They asked that she handle the funeral arrangements because Chloe had no family, and they informed her that the ladies of the Baptist church where Chloe attended wanted to serve a lunch. They also told her that Chloe's lawyer needed to talk to her. When she talked to the lawyer she learned that Chloe had left everything to her. Riley ultimately gave a substantial donation to the church.

The limbs of the pines, heavy with snow, swayed in the cold winter breeze during the graveside service in the small cemetery a few miles outside of Whispering Pines. There were few in attendance, including Ernie, Muley Jones and his wife and Peggy Henderson. Riley had not seen Peggy since before the fire and as the service concluded their eyes met with a mutual look of understanding. Peggy began to move in Riley's direction but at that inopportune time Marta arrived. Marta rushed to Riley and apologized for being late before excitedly showing her the engagement ring she had received. Marta, looking quite good, was giddy, saying Jay had told her it was about time, and she would fill Riley in at the luncheon. Riley watched Marta hurry back to her car as quickly as she had arrived and then she watched Marta and the others leave. Although she knew she would disappoint the church ladies by not being at the luncheon, after everyone left she got in her car and began the drive back to Owen.

* * *

The Arizona landscape was as beautiful as Riley remembered. Her new silver Ford was a joy to be in and it towed her trailer effortlessly. The open road helped clear her mind and brought back the feeling of freedom and endless possibilities. Her cell phone rang and she assumed it would be Gabrielle—only she and Benjie had her new number.

It was indeed Gabrielle, asking when she would be arriving. Riley was spending the rest of the winter at the ranch. After the conversation was over Riley closed the phone and slid it on the dash, her hand brushing against the white bandana necklace with a small sunflower and chunk of turquoise hanging from the mirror.

CHAPTER 44

It was almost Memorial Day before Riley made it back to the Midwest. Dobbie was entered in a chain of barrel racing futurities and she used the opportunity of being in the vicinity of Whispering Pines to leave flowers on Chloe's grave. She had not decided what to do about the Colby place and had no intentions of stopping there, or any other place in Whispering Pines for that matter.

The weather was near perfect when she arrived at the small cemetery. She laid several clusters of fake sunflowers on the wheel well of her new trailer that was equipped with full living quarters and opened the drop-down window for Dobbie. The sorrel gelding, having become accustomed to life on the road, casually stuck his head out to have a look around.

The grass was plush as carpet while she strolled in the direction that she believed Chloe's grave was. She ducked to avoid a low-hanging branch and thought how different the cemetery looked than what she remembered. She entertained the possibility it was because Chloe had been buried in the cold of winter, but knew in her heart it was the fact that she was looking at it through different eyes.

The setting was serene and she read the names on headstones as she walked. Most stones were very old and she pondered what the deceased lives' had been like, then she came to a halt when she saw the inscription MOLLY TAPPERD 1950–1973. The image of the girl with Jay in the photo she had discovered the night of the fire came to mind and prickly goosebumps covered her arms.

After a time she pulled several sunflowers from the bunch and drove their artificial stems into the ground near the marker. She stood there a minute longer, thinking about the gravestone, the photo, and the stack of buckles on Jay's dresser, and wondered what else there was about him that she didn't know.

* * *

Three weeks later she was in Oklahoma.

"Don't forget to stick around for the professional rodeo and dance later tonight, folks," the announcer said while the tractors parked after working the ground. "This morning's futurity barrel race is just one of the many events going on this weekend here in Oklahoma City."

Riley tugged on her cowboy hat. Her short hair made it feel like her hat wasn't fitting like it used to when she had a ponytail. She gathered the reins in her hands and moved Dobbie toward the alley.

"Only seven more to go and up next is Riley Montgomery on Double Your Bid. The arena is ready and the clock is clear," he added.

Dobbie came close to the alley but then ducked off to the side. Riley spun him around. He had been showing signs of stress and she knew after this run she would have to give him some well-deserved time off. She straightened him out and jockeyed with her seat, legs and voice, but he sidestepped and shook his head in defiance at her persistence. He struck out with a front foot, jerking her forward, and then he bolted, running down the alley. Muscle memory kicked in and she gathered her wits while encouraging him to run.

He reached the first barrel in record time then in reply to her cue checked his momentum abruptly and wrapped the barrel wickedly tight. He shot across the arena like a ball from a cannon to the second barrel but was bearing down too close as he approached it. Riley snatched the rein against his neck and used her inside foot—he moved over and began the turn but Riley's knee bumped the barrel. It teetered but on impulse she uncharacteristically reached down to steady it as he went around and kept it from going over.

The arena was narrow but long, giving more distance to the third barrel. Riley urged him to hustle and didn't *think* so much as concentrate on what she knew needed to be done. As the barrel drew near she sat deep in the saddle, lifted her hand and checked Dobbie to turn. He completed a snappy, flawless turn and then dashed for home as if wanting to show her just how fast he could run.

They crossed the timer and she started to pull him up. He slowed but shook his head, still wanting to go. She heard the announcer declare her time as being the fastest of the morning and a gratified smile appeared on her face. It had been a wild ride but would be one of the memorable ones.

* * *

Later that evening, the rodeo announcer and clown were going through their routine to fill the lack of action before the professional women's barrel race. Riley was at the arena fence thinking ahead to the next year, knowing that Dobbie could be ready to compete professionally. A pickup with the barrels came through the gate and headed in her direction. When it slowed a man pushed the first barrel out. Her eyes followed the pickup on its way to the end of the arena where she was pleasantly distracted. There, outside the fence, was Trace and Chigger. She was hoping Miles and Jay might be with them but there was no sign of them.

Trace saw Riley coming their way. "What brings you here?" he asked after they embraced.

"I rode this morning. Just hanging around tonight," she replied in high spirits.

He briefly fixed on the scar on her cheek and then a man with blonde hair who was as big as Jay was extending a hand to her.

"Ken Walken," he said, introducing himself. "I've heard a lot about you."

"Well, hello, Ken," she said, not sure how he fit into this, but he looked like a nice fellow and he obviously knew who she was. Then she asked about Emelee to which Chigger replied the women were around…somewhere.

Trace looked past her and grinned. She turned to see Miles coming from an aisle between bleachers. He was wearing the usual black cowboy hat and long-sleeved cotton shirt, this one a soft pink. She was impressed by his choice of color and doubted he knew how good he looked in it. He glanced from the program in his hand to the arena as a barrel racer ran in and then Riley watched his head turn again, and he looked right at her. He let out a whoop. When he reached her he lifted her off the ground and twirled her as if they were on the dance floor, just like he always did, and she breathed in his familiar pleasing scent.

"Nice shirt," she told him when he set her down.

"Breast cancer pink of course," he said proudly.

She smiled, proud of him as well, and assumed Marta had kicked the disease by his attitude.

"Are you here alone?" he asked.

"Yes," she said with emphasis. "I've been on the road the past few weeks and competed in the futurity this morning."

"How'd you do?"

"Good," she said with a little laugh of happiness. "I think I have a winner on my hands."

"You're the winner," he told her.

She thanked him for the compliment while looking in Trace's direction because Peggy Henderson, Emelee and Marta were joining him. When she saw Marta she instinctively looked for Jay, but there was still no sign of him. Trace put his arm around Peggy, which made Riley smile. Miles started talking again as she watched Marta walk to Ken—they interlocked arms and kissed. Riley frowned, confused.

"You haven't talked to Jay?" Miles was asking. "By damn, I always thought you two'd get together."

At the mention of Jay's name she turned to him, her face blank and eyes troubled.

"You do know the only reason I never went after you was because of him," he went on, sounding serious which unnerved her more.

"What?" she stammered. "Jay?" She looked at the others and then shook her head. "But, but, him and Marta..."

Miles's shoulders went back and he tilted his head. "What do you mean, 'him and Marta'? Don't tell me that you didn't know that Jay is our half-brother."

The color drained from Riley's face. She couldn't believe what he said...but it made so much sense. All this time she had let Jay—and herself—believe she wasn't interested in him because she thought... "I've got to go," she said brokenly, and began to turn away.

"Just where do you think you're going?" he asked reaching for her. He held her by the arm but she continued to try to leave. Conceding, he moved with her, guiding her toward an exit. "Where's your horse and rig?" he asked with a sigh.

CHAPTER 45

Miles began the eight hour drive to Whispering Pines, glad that he hadn't been drinking. He glanced at Riley, who was staring straight ahead. She had directed him to her horse's stall and by then appeared composed but remained preoccupied.

After he dealt with the heavy traffic leaving the city he made a quick call to Trace to tell him where they were. Now settling into the drive, he replayed the night of the county fair in his mind, first smiling unconsciously at the recollection of setting up Jay and Riley so they would dance together, and then he thought about the discussion of explaining Marta and himself to Riley. He could have sworn he had included the fact that Jay was their older half-brother, but he did remember being distracted when Mitch pulled up in that fancy sports car. Damn lawyer anyway. But he knew he couldn't blame the mistake on anyone but himself—he had royally botched up this time. He hoped Jay would see the humor in it, but had his doubts. And then Riley spoke up over the radio in a faltering voice, asking who Molly was.

When Miles pulled onto the gravel in front of Jay's shop Riley jumped out before he came to a stop. She ran to the door and Miles watched, thinking when she looked dismayed that of course it was locked—it wasn't even five o'clock in the morning. Then she was jogging to the house. The flatbed was gone so he assumed Jay was gone too.

Riley miserably walked back to Miles, who was standing by the truck. She stopped in front of him just before a shooting star lit up the sky. It was too big for either of them not to notice.

"Where could he be?" she moaned after it was gone.

"Who knows," he said, trying to downplay Jay not being there. "Maybe he went to a seminar or something."

She looked at him skeptically and then her eyes darkened.

"Now don't be going off halfcocked," he lectured. "He's around here somewhere. You know Jay. Take it easy."

She took in a deep breath.

"What do you want to do with your horse?" he asked, wanting both of them to have something to do.

Riley focused on him and considered what he asked. "I'll take him to the Colby place. My place," she elucidated. "I can park there."

"Now you're talking. Want me to drive?"

The beam of the headlights revealed the debris from the fire and the sorry condition of the farm added to Riley's stress. She should have driven instead of letting Miles—she had had too much time to think the way it was. It had never occurred to her that Jay wouldn't be at his shop or house when they got there, and her fear was growing by leaps and bounds that he had met someone. What other explanation could there be? Miles parked and got out and she distractedly left the truck too. He backed Dobbie out of the trailer and she held the door, just as she had done for Jay in Owen. She watched Miles, even while he tied the horse, hung the hay bag and put water in a bucket from the storage tank on the trailer. For the first time the similarities between him and Jay made sense—their walk, their actions, their tall stature. And the fact they were brothers certainly explained their conduct with each other. He saw her looking at him and smiled. She began to pucker.

"Aw, damn it," he said. At first he did nothing but then he approached her while opening his arms.

"No!" she said raising a hand to stop him. "I'm *not* going to cry." She raised her eyes to the sky, looking at nothing, and shook her head negatively. "How could I have been so ignorant? Things could have been so different. Jay's going to think I'm too stupid to want to have anything to do with me. What if…what if…" She looked at him pitifully and used the back of her hand on her runny nose.

He pulled his tucked-in shirt from the front of his jeans and offered her the tail.

"Just in case," he said.

She laughed brokenly and affectionately grabbed a handful of shirt below his Adam's apple. Then she saw how tired he was.

"You look like hell," she said while thinking of Jay and the times he had said it to her.

Miles scoffed. "You sure know how to make a man feel wanted."

"You need some sleep, and I need to get my act together," she told him. She tied the bucket of water on the wheel well for Dobbie, finishing what Miles started, and then steered him to the trailer door. Inside, she picked up the plaid shirt of Jay's, the same one that had been in her old trailer, off the couch and told him to have a seat. The shirt was laid on the edge of the mattress in the gooseneck and she went to the counter. Miles looked around as he sat down. He took off his cowboy hat and set it on the small table. It took up half the tabletop. Riley held a glass bowl under the tap, then placed it in the microwave and reached in a cupboard for a jar of instant coffee.

"Nice trailer," Miles said.

"Thanks. Go ahead and take your hat off—" she was saying as she turned to him. "And boots," she added with a smile. "Make yourself comfortable. Can I make you some breakfast?"

"No," he replied. "Sleep sounds like the ticket."

Still looking at him, she leaned on the counter with a hand on the edge. "Thanks for driving me here. What're you going to do with your rig?"

He shook his head. "None of us took horses. We were just having a little fun."

She frowned.

"I wasn't having that good of a time anyway," he said with a wink and weary grin.

She bent down-to pull off one of his boots. He sat up and resisted. He tipped his head and they looked at each other. She began tugging again and he allowed her to remove the boot, and then the other. She placed his boots off to the side while he continued to watch her. The she went back to the microwave and removed the hot water.

"Black?" she asked over her shoulder.

"Yeah," he said.

She offered him a cup. He accepted it and leaned back, resting his head on the wall. He closed his eyes. She sipped her coffee and looked out the window at Dobbie, who was contentedly eating hay. It was getting close to dawn. Miles sat up and placed his coffee, untouched, on the table.

"Can I trouble you for a pillow?" he asked.

She took the short walk to the bed in the gooseneck, reached across it for a pillow and then, obliging his gesture, tucked it behind him.

"Ahhhhhh," he exaggerated while pushing against the wall and stretching his legs. He patted the seat of the small couch beside him.

Riley hesitated but had no reason to think he would try anything. He never had in the past, and now she knew why. She sat her coffee on the table near his and turned off the light. As she settled beside him he raised his arm. She slid closer and leaned back against him.

"Sweet dreams, future sister-in-law," he said and kissed the back of her head.

She twisted to look at him. Although his eyes were closed he grinned. She smiled with hope and settled against him again, thinking that if he was confident that Jay wasn't in a spot of trouble or off with someone else, then she should be too. But easier said than done.

Riley couldn't sit still longer than twenty minutes. She had slept off and on during the trip and was too keyed up to sleep now. She gently lifted Miles's arm off and moved away. He stirred but did not wake. She went outside and then to her truck for her purse and cell phone. She called Jay's number at the shop while going through her purse for the business card he had given her and then called that number, getting no answer from either. She wondered if he wasn't answering his cell or if the reception was bad, and then fought the alarming possibility that he was ignoring her call before she realized he wouldn't know what her number was.

She checked on Dobbie then looked around, again becoming angry with herself for not having had the place cleaned up. Grass was trying to grow but weeds were taking over, especially around scattered debris and the remains of the house and barn. She walked across what used to be the arena to the section of fence still standing and looked past what used to be the timber. All she wanted to do was look for Jay, but she didn't want to wake Miles.

She was standing near Wooly's grave, about an hour later, when Miles came out of the trailer. He was wearing Jay's plaid shirt and had his pink one draped over an arm. His cowboy hat was in one hand and he was tousling his black hair with the other. He looked her up and down and grinned.

"Ain't we a pair," he said and put his hat on.

She smiled, but it was an edgy one.

He lifted the pink shirt. "I spilled coffee on it. I don't mind wearing day old, but can't tolerate wet. Hope you don't mind."

She shook her head.

"I'll get this other shirt back to you, and I cleaned up the mess. It didn't get on the floor or the couch." He paused. "C'mon. Let's get your trailer unhooked and go to town," he said positively. "Maybe Jay's at the shop."

But Jay wasn't at his shop, or his house, and it didn't look like he had been at either since they had been there earlier that morning.

"I've got to get something to eat," said Miles. "Let me buy your breakfast. You've got to eat too, you know."

The thought of food did not appeal to her in the least.

"We'll ask around and see if we can find him," he added.

"I'll check Ernie's!" she said, chiding herself for not thinking of it before. But Ernie wasn't home and his truck was gone. Further disappointed, she made her way back to Miles.

At Wanda's Cafe Riley asked Marie if she might know where Jay was. Marie just shook her head, looking like she wanted to ask questions, but left without a word after they placed their order. Miles tried to lighten her apprehension and was partially successful by the time they left the restaurant.

"I've got to have a shower," Miles said lifting an arm and feigning a whiff. "I'll do some checking, make some calls. Marta might know something. Do you want to go with me to Jay's?"

"No," she said resignedly. "I can clean up at the trailer. If you'll take me back to the Colby place I'll stay out of your hair for a while."

"You'd never be a pest to me," he said and put an arm around her.

At the Colby place he let her out with the agreement he would be back after noon, or sooner if he found out something. She stood at the truck with her hand on the door.

"Are you sure you're going to be all right?" he asked.

She gave him a weak smile. "Yes. I'm okay. I'll wait it out… I have to."

"Jay's okay. Nothing has happened. Marta or I would know if something had."

She thought what he said made sense. "Thank you. Now go on and get," she said and made a face, "before I start bawling or something."

"Say no more," he said with a grin and put the truck in gear.

She gave Dobbie more water and hay and then took a shower. She gazed out the window at the bluff and further to Jay's pasture, and then watched Dobbie, bored, play in his water. She grabbed her cowboy hat off the hook on the wall, thinking a ride was a good idea.

Miles let himhimself in Jay's house with the hidden key. He drappeded his pink shirt over the back of the couch that was just a few feet from the door and kicked off his boots while unbuttoning Jay's plaid shirt. He had purposely brought the stained pink shirt with intentions of getting it in the wash as soon as possible, but now all he could think about was getting in the shower. He took the plaid shirt off and left it on the end of the couch as he walked past.

After cleaning up he had no choice but to put the same underwear on knowing that none of Jay's would fit, but he did take a long-sleeved shirt from the closet. On his way to the living room he called Marta. The plaid shirt had fallen off the couch but he did not pick it up, sidetracked because Marta answered. She told him that she didn't know where Jay was and asked Miles why he was looking for him. He got an earful after recounting the preceding twelve hours.

CHAPTER 46

Jay leaned over the cooler inside the back of his horse trailer and pulled a bottle of water from the melting ice. He removed the cap and took a drink while eyeing the view from his position on top of the bluff. Some of his horses grazed the pasture below and in the distance was a pickup on the road to Whispering Pines, kicking up dust. Smoky, the name bestowed on the black-and-white dog that had shown up after the fire, watched Jay and wagged his stub of a tail eagerly. The dog was a good one and it had surprised Jay when no one claimed it after the fire. Jay bent again, this time to separate a piece of raw bacon from the rest in a baggie. He tossed the piece to the dog, then closed the lid on the cooler and latched the trailer door.

Potsy, one of three horses in the corral in the trees behind him, was alert and fixed on something far away, probably the pickup on the road Jay presumed while he and Smoky walked to the campsite. The other two horses, brought along to pull logs he was cutting in the timber, stood lazily head to tail, swishing flies off each other. Potsy was in the corral with them only because of his curiosity—he was originally part of the herd down the hill but had come to investigate. Jay sat in his canvas chair and stretched before putting his hands behind his head and leaning back, looking to the sky. He remembered the falling star the night before and unintentionally guffawed that he had made a wish like he were a kid.

He finished off the water and pitched the plastic bottle to the campfire that was nothing but ashes. Then he left his chair enough to reach the cell phone lying on the cot, sat back again and flipped the phone open. Nothing. For some reason he kept thinking it was ringing, but whenever he checked there was no sign of any missed calls. He needed to make a quick trip to the shop anyway to replace the chain on the saw and he would check the shop phone then. He was hoping he could get in town and back out again without anyone seeing him—the last thing he wanted was for someone to catch him and expect him to work on something. He tossed the phone back on the cot where it slid under a classic car magazine, got up and told Smoky to stay.

Rounding the corner at his shop he saw the silver pickup parked near the house, making him curse under his breath. But he didn't drive around the block, as was his first instinct. He couldn't take his eyes off the new truck, and when he saw the license plate knew that the truck had been registered in Owen. He pulled in beside it and got out, walking without thinking, drawn to it, and then he saw the white bandana necklace with a piece of turquoise and tiny sunflower hanging from the rearview mirror.

But Riley was nowhere in sight. He didn't know what to do. Maybe he had left the shop unlocked, he speculated with doubt, and with long strides covered the ground to the shop. It was locked, just as he left it. He considered the house but he had never given her a key or told her where the spare was. Maybe she was at Ernie's, but he didn't find Ernie home and there was still no Riley. He went back to her truck. He opened the door but the keys weren't in it—he was going to pull them so she couldn't leave. He looked at the bandana hanging from the mirror as if needing reassurance. He could smell the newness of the interior and some of her things were there. There was another scent too, something familiar... *Miles*. He slammed the door.

The things he saw when he crossed the threshold of his house were the pink shirt on the back of the couch and the plaid shirt and pair of cowboy boots on the floor. He recognized the shirt as the one he had given Riley on a chilly day, and knew it had been in her horse trailer when it was returned to her. Then he heard a noise coming from the bedroom, and then the door was coming open. There was Miles, wearing only underwear and one of his shirts. Miles looked at Jay, visibly surprised. He tried to smile but guilt covered his face, knowing what he had to say.

"Where is she?" Jay asked gruffly.

Miles had seen that look before and knew it wasn't good, causing his guilty demeanor to worsen. "Now take it easy, Jay," he said diplomatically.

Jay drew back and punched Miles in the face, knocking him against the wall. Miles yowled and floundered to regain his balance, shoving auto repair books into a clay pot full of loose change on the buffet. Then he lifted a hand to his jaw.

"Whad'ya do that for?" he asked, not taking his eyes off Jay. He moved his jaw back and forth and probed it with his fingers. "I been up all night with your girl and this is the thanks I get." His eyes got big after the words were out as if realizing they were a poor choice.

Jay had already moved past him to the bedroom, not sure what to expect. He in fact did not think that Miles would go that far and had acted without thinking. The unmade bed looked like it always did and he checked the bathroom. No Riley.

"Quit messing with me and tell me where she is," Jay demanded, his brow furrowed and posture menacing.

"I *was* trying to tell you," Miles said defensively, holding up a hand. "Gimme a break. The worst has been done. You're headed for nothing but rainbows an' daisies from here on out."

"Where is she? I mean it, Miles."

"She's at her place. She isn't going anywhere. I have her truck," Miles said, still watching Jay closely.

"Yeah, so I noticed. Just how did that happen?"

"Well, it's kinda funny actually," he said optimistically but moving so the couch was between them.

Jay stood where he was while he listened. By the time Miles finished, he wasn't all that surprised. It only made him want Riley more when he understood that she had so much consideration for others that she was willing to sacrifice her own happiness for theirs. He walked to the door and opened it, feeling truly happy, something he hadn't for a long time. He looked at Miles with a big grin.

"Your face is bleeding by the way, pretty boy," he said, pointing. Then he went out the door, still grinning.

Miles touched his cheek and winced then looked at his fingertips that were tainted with blood. Then he smiled. Jay hadn't called him pretty boy since Molly died.

"It's about time," he muttered.

* * *

Dobbie gawked and shied at one thing after another on the winding trail that climbed the bluff. Normally Riley would be amused by his antics but today was too preoccupied, her mind a jumble of questions and growing doubt. She was a bundle of nerves and had no idea how she would begin explaining... if she even got the chance. The nagging thought that Jay had met someone—and was with her now—weighed heavily on her. Dobbie came to a stop with barbwire in front of him, and Riley realized she had ridden the gelding to the gate between Raney's pasture and Jay's. The ride had started on the road with the hope she would run into Jay, but knew the chances of that were pretty slim. After going through the gate and closing it again, Dobbie kept up his unrelenting joy with life as they progressed through the timber, and Riley slipped back into deep thought.

When the trail leveled at a bend on the edge of the bluff the vast landscape was an appreciated distraction and Riley reined Dobbie to a stop. The gravel road looked like a flat white ribbon and she recognized the pipe gate to the pasture where she and Jay had looked at his young horses almost two years prior. After a few minutes she nudged Dobbie with her heels and he was on the move again, entering the dense trees, but a short time later abruptly he stopped once more, at attention. About a hundred yards ahead was a campsite—Jay's campsite. Beyond the fire ring, cot and chair she recognized his gooseneck trailer and Potsy was one of the horses in the corral in the trees. The horses were looking at them and a black-and-white dog was standing near the cot, also watching her. Jay's flatbed truck was gone, or maybe it was parked on the other side of the trailer, but she doubted it. Her eyes went to the cot again—one cot and one chair. She inhaled deeply, very much relieved but still edgy.

She dismounted, conscious of Dobbie, alert, beside her, and Smoky ahead. She spoke to the dog and he sat on his haunches while continuing to watch. She led Dobbie to a small enclosure attached to the corral. He was well-behaved for the most part as she unsaddled and Smoky did not move. She slipped the bridle off Dobbie and he went to the fence where the other horses had already gathered. Dobbie and Potsy snorted and squealed across the fence at each other as she fashioned the logs to close the opening. She carried her tack to the trailer, walking past the campsite, and Smoky followed.

When she left the trailer with a bucket Smoky trailed her, a few steps off to the side. She went to the primitive well in the timber by the corral. There was a substantial stack of logs, a small mound of firewood, Jay's chain saws and tools, and a portable shower hung from a tree with wet wooden pallets underneath. The horses were still interested in each other except for Potsy who came to the log fence. She took a minute to pet him.

She carried the pail of water around the sturdy corral, Smoky trotting ahead. Before she reached Dobbie's pen Smoky froze to look at something below the bluff and she proceeded to situate the bucket inside the pen. Smoky was still looking at the road when she finished and she looked to see what had his attention. Her heart raced when she saw it was Jay's flatbed, slowing to stop at the gate.

She watched him open the gate, jump back in the truck and drive some distance before braking and then the truck was in reverse, stirring up dust, Jay having forgotten to shut the gate after driving through. Then he was coming across the pasture in a hurry, up the steep hill of the bluff and then he stopped on the other side of the gooseneck. Riley heard him get something out of the front of the trailer and then there he was, headed to the corral with a halter in his hand. He glanced to either side while saying "Smoky?" and then he did a double-take at Riley. He stopped, his eyes fixed on her.

"Hi," she said, rallying a smile.

He smiled broadly, dropped the halter and quickly covered the ground between them. He took her hat off and tossed it at the cot.

"You're here to stay," he said and gently cradled her face between his large hands.

She didn't know if what he said was a question or a statement but found herself nodding. Then Jay was leaning into her and she tipped her face to meet his. He began to kiss her passionately and she raised her arms to encircle his neck. As she did so he lowered his arms and wrapped them around her middle, pulling her against him and lifting her as he had done the night after the fire. As if his kiss wasn't enough to stir her emotions, she was intensely aware of his body pressing against hers. She wrapped her legs around his waist.

When she thought she could no longer breathe, he began to kiss her neck and throat. Then he looked into her eyes before kissing her on the mouth again—this time his kiss was soft and sensual. When he stopped he rested his head on her shoulder with his face in her neck and sighed with contentment.

She loosened her legs from around him and let her feet touch the ground. He smiled again, looking satisfied and she smiled back, apprehensive, feeling like she had some explaining to do. The kiss and way he accepted her was more than encouraging but scared her as well. She was more afraid than ever of losing him.

Her mouth opened but no words came out. Almost reluctantly Jay escorted her to the chair where she sat down, wringing her hands in her lap and nervously watching him. He pushed the magazine and cell phone out of his way and sat on the cot. He rested his palms on his knees and gave her all his attention. Although he was straight faced there was no doubting that he was happy. She couldn't help but smile because of his attitude. Then she turned serious and took a deep breath.

"I ran into Miles at the rodeo in Oklahoma City last night, and that's when I found out… I mean, well, I thought…" She blushed. "I've thought all this time that Marta was your girlfriend." She watched for a response, but his expression didn't change. "I never really questioned why Miles didn't help more with Marta when she was sick, uh, well because I assumed, well, I guess you know." She swallowed. "After the fire, at the hospital, you don't know how much it tore me up when I stood at the window and watched you walk away, and then Marta pulled up." She saw sympathy on his face but before he could say anything she laughed at herself. "Even at Chloe's funeral, Marta showed up late, flashing that diamond ring, and I thought it was from you." She shook her head and a cynical smile appeared. "All those times we were together… We really should have talked more." Her eyes softened. "I'm so sorry about Molly. I saw her gravestone. Miles told me what happened."

His eyes revealed sadness but then it was gone. "I saw the sunflowers you left." Her jaw dropped and he nodded. "You must have been at the cemetery a few days before I was."

She smiled, knowing that he appreciated the simple gesture. "I have so much respect for you, and I've been in love with you for a long time. It was after Dually was put down when I faced the fact, but that only made things worse." She paused. "I feel like an idiot. I can't believe I let myself believe something that wasn't true for so long. I wish I would have done things differently." He remained silent and just looked at her. She considered that his composure as she had talked was nothing out of the ordinary but she was a little amazed that he didn't seem more surprised by her showing up from out of nowhere. And it struck her odd that he hadn't asked a single question. "You need to say *something*," she pressed, bewildered.

He grinned mischievously. "I guess I should tell you that I ran into Miles at the house… Half an hour ago," he confessed.

She thought about what he said, coming to understand that all the time she had been talking, he already knew.

"You turd!" she said.

She smiled wickedly and sprang from the chair. He saw her coming and braced for the impact while raising his arms to receive her. She tackled him and he went backward off the cot with her in his arms. He smiled at her on top of him. With one arm she pushed herself up and he loosened his hold. She looked into his eyes, his face inches from hers.

"I think we've talked enough," she said.

He had to agree.

CPSIA information can be obtained at www.ICGtesting.com
Printed in the USA
LVOW07s0341220415

435512LV00001B/2/P